VISIONS
—of—
DESTINY

EDWARD R. LIPINSKI

Copyright © 2024 Edward R. Lipinski.

All rights reserved. No part of this book may be reproduced, stored, or transmitted by any means—whether auditory, graphic, mechanical, or electronic—without written permission of both publisher and author, except in the case of brief excerpts used in critical articles and reviews. Unauthorized reproduction of any part of this work is illegal and is punishable by law.

ISBN: 979-8-89419-316-8 (sc)
ISBN: 979-8-89419-317-5 (hc)
ISBN: 979-8-89419-318-2 (e)

Because of the dynamic nature of the Internet, any web addresses or links contained in this book may have changed since publication and may no longer be valid. The views expressed in this work are solely those of the author and do not necessarily reflect the views of the publisher, and the publisher hereby disclaims any responsibility for them.

One Galleria Blvd., Suite 1900, Metairie, LA 70001
(504) 702-6708

CHAPTER 1

At six years old, Henry Gainsvort was an average, seemingly ordinary boy, who lived in a typical middle-class neighborhood and he was not unlike the other boys on the block.

Henry wasn't very tall, but he wasn't short either, but somewhere in between, he was a typical height for a normal six-year old boy. He had a pleasant boyish face with freckles on both cheeks and a nose and mouth in between that were the right size and shape for his average boyish face. His head was crowned with a mop of sandy brown hair cut short in a traditional style. He had a pleasant voice that was not too high in pitch or low in register, nor too loud nor soft but somewhere in between.

He had one distinguishing feature—well two actually—he had two large, bright, hazel-colored eyes framed with long, soft, brown eye lashes and he had a way of looking at you with those clear bright eyes so that when he fixed his gaze on you, you were immediately taken with his quiet, steady unblinking stare. There was something about the look in those eyes that unnerved you and made you want to look away, yet, at the same time there was also something compelling in his gaze that held your attention so you really couldn't drop your eyes.

When he looked at you, it was as if some invisible force clamped on you and held you against your will and made you stand there and look back at him. And for that moment as he engaged your attention, you wondered if you were being challenged to a staring match. And just when you resolved that you were going to accept the challenge and out stare him, that's when he abruptly dropped his eyes and looked elsewhere, leaving you to wonder what that was all about. What did he see in you? What was he looking at? If you asked him, he simply said, "nothing, nothing", and he went back to being an ordinary boy again, but you still had to wonder if he saw something in you that you weren't quite aware of.

When Henry spoke to you, there was an earnest, sincere quality in his speech—even at the tender age of six. People noticed that whenever he spoke, it sounded as if he had something important to say, even if he didn't really. So, when Henry spoke, people stopped whatever they were doing and listened to him. They paused to listen to little Henry because they were generally captivated by the intensity of his big hazel eyes and the serious tone of his voice. And even if they discovered that he didn't have anything really important to say, they continued to politely listen not so much because they were interested, but because his earnest manner and captivating eyes seemed to warrant their attention and somehow, they couldn't bring themselves to look away until he finished saying whatever was on his mind.

Henry was the son of Edna and Charlie Gainsvort; he was their only child. They lived in the Greenville section of Jersey City. Charlie worked in Ryerson's Steel Mill. The mill was close to their house and he could walk to and from work each evening—Charlie worked the night shift because the pay was better than day work.

The steel mill wasn't a big operation, not like those behemoth plants in the Midwest with miles of freight cars that carry iron ore to a battery of humongous blast furnaces that are fired up night and day to produce tons of steel. No, at the Ryerson plant they didn't make steel; instead they took stock; sheet stock, bar stock, round stock, and square stock and cut it to shape and size for fabrication elsewhere.

At Ryerson's, Charlie operated a burner machine. The machine had eight acetylene-burners mounted on a suspended rack and these burners pointed straight down at a work platform. The way the machine worked was like this: a couple of guys wheeled a large sheet of steel onto the cutting platform. Then Charlie fired up the burners and lowered them to a few inches above the steel sheet.

He set the electric eye in an adjacent computer to follow a pattern. The computer eye traced the pattern and at the same time guided the burner rack which then would cut eight individual pieces from the sheet into the same shape as the pattern. Charlie did that every night. Lord knows how many pieces of steel Charlie cut in his tenure at Ryerson's but there must have been at least a billion of them.

While Charlie was working at the plant, Edna stayed home and did the house work and took care of little Henry. In the evenings, she would watch him play, then give him a bath, help him brush his teeth, change him into his pajamas, make sure he said his prayers and tuck him into bed. That was their nightly routine. When Henry advanced in school and brought schoolwork to do at home, she would see that he did it every night. All that was during the first part of Henry's tender life, when he was still young, innocent, and apparently normal.

At that time, Charlie and Edna had no aspirations for their young son although Charlie secretly hoped that maybe, in time, Henry might grow up to be a strong athlete, if not a pro, then at least a star when he was in school. When he was old enough, Henry joined the little league—mostly because of Charlie's urging—and he played second base. As a young ballplayer, Henry wasn't a star, but he could field the ball as well as the other kids on the team. He wasn't a slugger, but his batting average was acceptable and he managed to get a hit now and again and even score a few runs. In general, his performance on the team was not spectacular but …well …average.

Edna kind of hoped that Henry would learn to play a musical instrument. So they got him an accordion and she took him once a week to the Delmare accordion school on Journal Square for lessons; and even though Henry took his lessons regularly and dutifully practiced, it soon became apparent that young Henry did not possess any talent for music and after a year Edna abandoned her dream of turning Henry into a competent amateur musician and the lessons were terminated and the accordion was left in its case in the bottom of the hall closet.

In school, Henry got passing grades but never made the honor roll. He did reasonably well in all his subjects but never had a *best* subject, one that he excelled in. In fact, Henry didn't show a flair for much of anything either in school or outside.

So early in Henry's life, Charlie and Edna Gainsvort accepted the fact that their son would never be anything more than average. But that was all right with them. After all, what's the matter with being average? There are a lot of worst things in life for a young boy than being average; and at least Henry wasn't a nerd and he wasn't weird. No, thank God for that; Henry wasn't weird. Well at least he wasn't weird during the first few years of his life. And he wasn't weird when he was eight, or nine, or ten. But just before Henry turned eleven, something strange happened and it caused Edna and Charlie to wonder if little Henry was really as normal as he seemed to be. It occurred when Edna was out for a walk with Henry and it happened like this.

It was an ordinary Spring afternoon. The sun was shining, the sky was a deep blue punctuated with only a few wispy, white clouds. The temperature was mild. All-in-all, it was a beautiful day for a walk and that is what Edna and Henry were doing. Edna had just paid a visit to her mother on Danforth Avenue and she had taken Henry with her. Now they were walking down Stevens Avenue on the way back to the Gainsvort home.

There wasn't much traffic on that street. One car had just passed by and another car, a red sedan, was still some distance off but was coming up the street at a slow pace.

Henry looked at the red car approaching and he said, quite casually and matter-of-factly, "That red car is going to crash. It's going to hit the big tree."

Edna looked down at Henry. This was a surprising statement for the boy to make—just out of the clear blue like that. She looked at the red car coming toward them. It wasn't going very fast. There weren't any other cars in sight. Visibility was clear, and the pavement was bone dry. What could possibly happen to make the car crash? It was really absurd to think that the car would crash. No way could it happen.

Edna was about to challenge Henry on that statement and ask him why he said it, but just as she was about to say something, the car got closer and a surprising thing did happen. A big shaggy, yellow-brown dog suddenly appeared, seemingly from nowhere. It just came running out from one of the alleys without warning and darted across the street right in front of the oncoming red car. The driver of the car instinctively hit the brakes and turned the steering wheel to avoid hitting the mutt. Well he did miss hitting the beast who continued across the street apparently unaware that it had just narrowly missed having its guts splattered all over the asphalt. And just as little Henry predicted the red car did hit the big tree.

The driver of the crashed vehicle got out of his car and shouted curses at the happy-go-lucky dog who went on his merry way as if nothing had happened. It wasn't a serious accident, just a fender-bender;

but it happened just as Henry said it would and that startled Edna. For a long while she stood there, almost stupefied, looking at the car, the tree, and the angry driver and all the time wondering how Henry could possibly have known that it was going to happen just like it did. There was no way he could possibly have foreseen the event, yet that is exactly what he did do.

Edna stood there for the longest time looking at the scene and then back to Henry, who stood there beside her waiting patiently for his mother to continue their walk together. Eventually Edna recovered her senses and continued walking down Stevens Avenue to their home. They walked in silence but the recent occurrence of that sudden, unexpected accident kept churning in Edna's mind. Henry, on the other hand, just walked along beside his mother as if nothing out of the ordinary had happened.

Finally, Edna asked her son, "Henry, how did you know that was going to happen?"

"That what was going to happen?"

"That car crash back there. With the red car. You said it would hit the tree and it did. How did you know it would do that?'

"I donno know. I guess I just saw it."

"You just saw it. How do you mean, 'you just saw it.'?"

"I don't know it was just like a picture that appeared and I saw it."

"You mean like you just saw the picture of what was going to happen in your mind and then it happened?"

"Yeah, I guess that's what I mean."

Edna didn't know what to say to that. After all, how do you ask a ten-year old boy how he sees anything in his mind? And when you think about it, how does anyone see anything in their mind? She thought about her experiences when sometimes she saw things in her mind—or at least she thought she did—but she couldn't describe what it was like. So how could a young boy of ten, going on eleven, describe the kind of mental pictures that he had in his brain?

They turned the corner onto Sterling Avenue and Edna asked, "Henry, did that ever happen before?"

"Did what, ever happen before?"

"I mean where you saw that something was going to happen and then it happened. Where the thing you saw just happened, just like in the picture you had in your mind."

"I guess so. Sometimes."

"Sometimes?"

"Yeah."

Edna wanted to ask more, to probe deeper into this strange quirk that Henry had so unexpectedly displayed but she didn't know how. Henry seemed totally oblivious to the fact that he had just predicted an event before it happened. She really wanted to know if her young son actually had the ability to see into the future but at the same time, she didn't know what other questions she could ask or how to approach the subject, so they walked the rest of the way together in silence.

She didn't talk about it anymore with Henry, but she kept thinking about it for the rest of the day. Maybe the accident was just a coincidence; but on the other hand, she couldn't shake the fact that he had predicted it exactly the way it happened. He said he saw the picture in his mind. That thought registered with Edna and she couldn't get it out of her mind. The more she thought about it, the more she felt that she had to talk about it with someone. Her husband Charlie was the obvious candidate.

Henry was outside playing with his friends so Charlie and Edna were alone in the house. Edna walked into the living room where Charlie was reading the newspaper. In about a half hour he would get up and get ready to go to work in the steel plant, but before he went to work, he always liked to read the sports section in the daily paper to see how the teams were doing. He liked to read in silence and he didn't like to be disturbed.

Edna knew that about Charlie; she knew that he didn't like to be disturbed when he was reading the sports pages, and she almost never disturbed him—unless it was very important. Now, she considered this important—after all it concerned their only son—so she walked into the living room and sat down in a chair directly opposite the couch that Charlie was sitting on.

When she entered and sat down, she had expected that her entrance and presence would be enough to make Charlie voluntarily put down his paper and give her his complete attention, but no, that didn't happen. Charlie continued to sit there holding the open paper between his two hands up in front of his face. Edna waited but Charlie was too engrossed in the coverage of the latest Yankee game to pay any attention to her.

Finally, she spoke, "Charlie, there is something that we have to talk about."

Still hidden behind the newspaper, Charlie spoke. "What? What is it that we have to talk about? Can't it wait until tomorrow?"

He continued to shield himself behind the paper obviously determined to read the account of the previous night's game and he resented having to relinquish his perusal of the sports pages just to talk to Edna. He hoped that with his three brief questions he would effectively silence her and cause her to have second thoughts about trying to interrupt his reading. Maybe she would take his not-so-subtle hint and table her discussion until the next day—as long as she didn't bring it up at breakfast because he didn't ever like to talk about anything during breakfast.

Edna, however, was not to be put off. She wanted to talk about Henry and she was determined to do so.

"No," she said, "this is important. It's about Henry and it's something we should talk about now. It's possible that there may be a problem with Henry."

What kind of problem could little Henry possibly have? After all he was the most normal, average kid in the world. Suddenly Charlie thought the worst. Maybe Henry started smoking cigarettes on the sly. Or maybe Edna had discovered drugs in his bedroom. Charlie lowered the paper a little and looked over the top edge at his wife.

"What? What is so important about Henry that we have to discuss it now?"

Edna couldn't see his whole face, but she could see Charlie's eyes and she saw that he was not happy about this interruption, but at the same time, he was curious. She knew that she had captured at least part of his attention.

"Henry did something strange today."

"What? What did Henry do that was so strange?" asked Charlie, growing ever more suspicious.

He lowered his paper so his whole face was visible, and he looked at her and eyed her skeptically wondering at the same time what an ordinary ten-year old boy could do that could be strange. The only thing that Charlie could think of was that Henry suddenly and unexpectedly started to show some abnormal homosexual tendencies. That would be strange indeed, considering that Henry had not yet entered puberty; but who knows when the gay seed starts to sprout. And if it was sprouting in Henry then they'd have to take steps to nip that in the bud. Charlie certainly didn't want any son of his growing up to be gay. But Charlie didn't have to worry. Henry would never be gay, but at the same time, the boy was developing an uncanny ability to glimpse into the future, and these visions would set him apart from everybody else.

Charlie lowered the paper to his lap and looked hard at Edna giving her his complete and undivided attention, wondering what was coming next and what she was about to tell him. He sat there and waited for her to continue. She then related the incident that happened earlier in the day as she and Henry were walking down Stevens Avenue. She told the whole incident being careful to capture every nuance of the event so she could emphasize how uncanny the entire experience was. When she finished she sat there in silence waiting for Charlie's reaction.

It took a minute for the story to completely register with him, but when it did, Charlie snorted in obvious disgust. This wasn't at all like anything he imagined. When Edna said that Henry did something strange, he expected something really big, something really …well… strange. But this was nothing, just a little fluke. It was certainly nothing to get worked up about. Certainly nothing to interrupt the sports pages for.

"Ah come on Edna! I thought that you were gonna tell me something big; but this is nothing. It's just a chance occurrence. A coincidence. The boy just took a lucky guess and it turned out the way he said. It's nothing to get worked up about. It's a once-in-a-lifetime thing. It'll never happen again."

"You really think so?" asked Edna.

"Sure," said Charlie. "Forget about it. Henry's just a normal kid and this was just a little quirk. A minor incident. Relax, it's over and done with. It'll never happen again."

With that said, Charlie picked up the paper and buried himself once more in the world of sports. As far as he was concerned the incident was effectively closed and he erased it from his conscience. Edna wasn't so easily reassured, but she saw that Charlie was again enclosed in his newspaper cocoon and she was shut off from his attention and that there was nothing more to say.

Edna got up and went into the kitchen and made a sandwich that she packed into the lunch box that Charlie would take with him to work that night. Charlie had effectively dismissed Henry's prediction as being inconsequential and so the case was closed—at least as far as he was concerned; but Edna wasn't so easily appeased. Somewhere in the dark recesses of her mind there remained lingering doubts about the whole incident and she had to wonder how normal her son really was.

CHAPTER

Charlie's explanation of Henry's uncanny prediction seemed logical enough at the time, and since there were no further premonitions or portents from Henry, everything more or less settled into place and life at the Gainsvort home went back to its usual, normal routine. Even Edna was able to suppress her quandaries and after a while, she eventually put the matter out of her mind. She had convinced herself that Charlie was probably right: that the whole incident of the car crash was just a once-in-a-lifetime event and nothing like it would happen again, so it wasn't worth bothering about.

That's the way things went for the next couple of months, but then something happened that caused the same uneasiness to resurface in Edna's mind. This time it involved Charlie and it caused him to pause and wonder about the very same thing that had plagued Edna's thoughts. After this incident, even he couldn't dismiss Henry's behavior so lightly, because, try as he might, he couldn't come up with a rationalization to explain the situation. It happened like this.

One afternoon, Charlie was sitting on the couch in the living room watching the Yankee-Red Sox game. He had a can of beer in his right hand and a bag of potato chips on his lap. Henry was not far away, sitting on the floor, also watching the game.

It was the fourth inning and the score was two to zip with Boston on top. The Boston team was in the field and the Yanks were at bat. The bases were loaded and it looked like a chance for the Yankees to get on the scoreboard and if they got lucky, maybe even tie the score. The only problem was that the Boston pitcher had found a way to shut down the Yankee bats and he struck out two successive batters in a row. It seemed like he had found his stride and was now throwing hot stuff. It was at that time that the Yankee shortstop, Danny Jackson, came to the plate.

"Oh hell!" said Charlie. "This is where the Yanks blow their chance to score. Jackson's gonna strike out."

"No Dad," said Henry, "you're wrong. Jackson's gonna hit a home run."

"Sorry son, but that's next to impossible. Jackson struck out his first time at bat and he hasn't had a hit in seven games. He's in a slump. No way is he gonna hit this pitcher."

It seemed like Charlie was right. The first pitch was a fastball that came right across the plate and caught the batter looking. The second pitcher was a slider and went right under the batter's swing. Now it was only one pitch that separated the batter from the final out which would end the inning and leave three Yankee runners stranded on the bases.

Charlie and Henry watched the players on the small screen. The pitcher reared back for his wind-up. He raised his front leg high up, then stepped forward. At the same time his right arm came over his shoulder and straight down. His fingers released the ball and sent it driving toward the plate at ninety-one miles an hour. Jackson was expecting a fast ball and that's exactly what he got. He had started his swing a split second before the pitcher released the ball. His bat came right around and met the horsehide sphere just as it came across the plate; when the two connected there was a resounding crack and the ball shot back over the infield like a rocket, and flew far out across the outfield fence. It was a home run. Jackson hit a home run just as Henry said he would.

As Jackson ran around the bases, Henry let out a cheer. Charlie looked at him. The boy had predicted a home run and that's exactly what happened. Still, Charlie chalked it up to being just a lucky guess. After all, anyone can say *home run* anytime a batter comes to the plate. Sometimes the batter connects and sometimes he doesn't. When he does, the call happens and it seems like a mystical prediction, but actually it's just a lucky break, a coincidence. That's all. There's nothing more to it than that. So, Charlie dismissed Henry's statement as being a timely remark that just worked out, and he settled back with his can of beer and bag of potato chips to watch the rest of the game.

Well, the rest of the game was more or less quiet; both pitchers used their best stuff to blank out the opposing bats so there were no more hits. That changed in the seventh inning when Boston managed to narrow the Yankee lead by coming up with a run. New York was still on top and in the bottom of the eighth it was still four to three in favor of the Yankees.

Soon, it was the bottom of the ninth and Boston was at bat. It was the last chance for them to win—or at least tie—the game. After a shaky start, they managed to get a runner on second base in scoring position. There were two outs when the next Boston batter came up to the plate. Now if this man could get a hit he might just drive in the run to tie the game. If he got hot and managed to come up with a home run then Boston would win.

What followed next was a classic duel between the pitcher and batter. The pitcher threw a wily combination of strikes and change-ups but was unable to strike out the batter. The batter swung his bat but was unable to connect with the ball. After a few minutes, the count was at three balls and two strikes. The next pitch would decide the entire game. As the batter stood ready in the box, and the pitcher exchanged signs with the catcher, Charlie said out loud, "I bet he gets a hit and ties the game."

Henry never took his eyes off the screen. He just said, kind of over his shoulder, "No, he's going to hit a high pop-up into foul territory down the first-base line. The first baseman's gonna catch it to end the game."

Charlie eyed Henry but could only see the back of the boy's head because Henry was facing the TV. What struck Charlie about his son's statement was the manner in which the boy said it. It didn't sound like he was guessing. It was more like a pronouncement, like he knew it was going to happen. That, of course, was impossible because how could a ten-year old boy know what was going to happen before it actually happened; but still the manner in which Henry made that statement caused Charlie to wonder about what was going on in the boy's head. He looked back at the television to see what would actually happen.

The pitcher was on the mound. He went into his wind-up, then stepped forward and fired the ball. The batter swung and managed to get a piece of the ball, but it wasn't a solid hit. The bat was a little low and the ball ricocheted off the top of the bat and popped up high, out above foul territory down the first-base line. A few of the infielders ran for it, but it was the first baseman who got under the high ball. He waved and called the other players off. Charlie watched as the first baseman stood there with his shades down looking up at the bright sky. When the ball fell, he snagged it making the final out. The game was over and it was a Yankee win.

Charlie looked from the screen to Henry. The final out happened just as he said it would; but the thing that hit Charlie was in the details. It wasn't just a pop up; it was a pop up in foul territory, and in foul territory down the first-base line. And it wasn't just any player who caught the ball, it was the first baseman. That's exactly what Henry said would happen. He said it would happen exactly like that and it did happen exactly the way he said it would.

This was strange indeed, and Charlie had to admit to himself that it was more than just a lucky guess or a coincidence. It was almost as if Henry knew it was going to happen, as if he saw it was going to happen just like it did. The game was officially over and the announcers were doing the final play-by-play wrap up, but Charlie was only half attentive. He kept going over that final out and Henry's prediction, and he wondered to himself if his son really had made some sort of lucky guess; but somehow it didn't seem like a guess. And if it wasn't a guess then how did young Henry know? How did he know what was going to happen before it did?

With the game over and all the sports talk done, Charlie got up and turned off the set. Henry went outside to play. Charlie walked into the kitchen for another beer. Edna was making a meatloaf for supper. She was busy mixing the meat with the chopped onion, bread crumbs and beaten egg. When Charlie walked into the kitchen she didn't look up but asked, "Game over?"

"Yeah, the Yanks won four to three. It was good game." He paused while he took a sip of beer. "You know Henry just did the damnest thing."

Edna stopped kneading the meatloaf and looked up.

"What? What did Henry do?"

Charlie hesitated for a moment, taking the time to frame his thoughts. He wanted to describe Henry's recent behavior and his uncanny prediction in the most objective way possible. He didn't want to make it sound like he thought that maybe Henry might be possessed with some sort of secret, mysterious power. When he was sure he had everything set in his mind, when he had the sequence of events just right, he described to his wife what had just occurred.

Edna wiped her hands on her apron and then stood perfectly still as she listened to Charlie. She just stood there looking at him, listening without comment while he recounted the whole episode. He narrated the whole thing: the home run prediction and Henry's foretelling of the pop-up and final out.

Edna didn't say anything, but as she looked at her husband while he was talking about their son, Henry. She saw the expression on his face and she knew the puzzlement and doubts that were running through his mind. She could see that these were reflections of her own feelings back when Henry predicted the car accident on Stevens Avenue.

When he had finished, he added one comment: "Gee Edna! I couldn't believe it. He called that final out exactly, before it happened. It was ..."

Charlie paused, not sure of the word to use.

"Strange?" suggested Edna.

"Yeah!" he said quietly and took another sip of his beer. For the next few minutes neither of them said anything more. They just stood there, Charlie at the refrigerator sipping his beer and Edna looking down at her meatloaf in the bowl on the table.

She had thought about all this before, after the car incident. At that time, she had thought it was very strange, but when she told her husband, he shrugged it off and dismissed her uncertainties with a casual, almost flippant, explanation. So, she put the incident and her subsequent questions out of her mind assuming that her suspicions about young Henry were just the workings of her overactive imagination and she buried those thoughts in the periphery of her conscious mind and she let the incident drift into the subliminal past.

Now the same kind of thing happened again, but this time Charlie was the witness. And now he was voicing the same concerns that she had expressed earlier. As Edna stood there, looking down at her raw meatloaf, she had to wonder to herself if there was something more to Henry than either of them had ever suspected. Finally, she looked up at him and spoke.

"What do you think Charlie? Do you think that Henry really can ..." Edna hesitated, unsure what to say. The expression she wanted to use was *predict the future*, but she hesitated to employ that turn of phrase because it sounded like something psychic, something supernatural, something even abnormal; and she could not bring herself to believe that her little boy could possess a weird power like that. She had always thought of him as being a typical, average, normal little boy and she couldn't bring herself to think of him in any other way.

So now she was torn between wanting to say what she felt and at the same time not wanting to say anything that would cloak her son in some mantle of arcane, paranormal powers. She wanted her little Henry to be a normal, average kid and she was afraid to say anything that might alter that image.

While she was debating with herself as to how to best express her meaning and maybe hint at it without really saying it, she saw Charlie standing there waiting for her to finish her sentence. She hoped that maybe she wouldn't have to finish, that maybe her meaning was evident and that Charlie would intuitively pick up on her train of thought; but apparently not, so she blurted it out.

"Do you think Henry can really predict the future?"

Charlie's response was immediate and forceful. "No of course not!"

"Well then, how did he do it?"

That was the question that Charlie had no answer for. Before this, he had said that it was a once-in-a lifetime thing, that it would never happen again; but then today it did happen again and that squelched his explanation. Now his *fluke-guess* theory didn't hold water. So, he was left with nothing to say, no rational that would explain away the situation.

"I don't know Edna. I still think that it's probably nothing. For now, all we can do is wait and see. Let's just cool our jets and wait to see if Henry does it again. In the meantime, let's just put it out of our minds."

Edna nodded and a silent agreement was forged between the two of them; neither would say anything more unless Henry had another vision and did it again. So, they went about their business as usual, acting as if nothing had really happened. Still at random moments—although neither of them exchanged thoughts–both Charlie and Edna had to wonder to themselves if it would happen again, if Henry would have another vision sometime later on, down the road. And there were times, as the days passed when Charlie and Edna, independently of each other, would look at little Henry and wonder what he was thinking, what he was seeing and if he was really as normal as he appeared to be.

CHAPTER 3

So far it was only Charlie and Edna who suspected that maybe young Henry wasn't as average and normal as he appeared to be. And even though they wondered if maybe there might be something different about him; at least they were the only ones who held those doubts. For them, Henry's uncanny ability—if that's what it was—was not a proven fact; it was just a feeling that they had based on two isolated incidents. After all, he only made a couple of predictions here and there, and they couldn't really be sure if he actually predicted the future or just made some lucky guesses. Both Edna and Charlie had their suspicions and doubts, but they didn't talk much about them. They really didn't know what to say about any of this and for them there was a subtle comfort in maintaining silence.

And even though they both had their inner doubts about Henry's normality, they drew a kind of solace from the knowledge that Henry's behavior was a family secret and that no one else suspected that he had the weird capability of seeing things before they happened. Up till now this was just between the three of them, and as long as they were the only ones who knew about it, where was the harm? Let the boy have his visions and as long as they remained in the family circle unknown to anyone else, then all would remain okay. Everything would be all right as long as the world went on thinking that Henry was a typical, average kid.

But it couldn't last. They didn't realize it at the time, but sooner or later, Henry's strange ability—if it continued to reveal itself—was bound to surface in other places and come to the attention of other people. Well, Henry's ability did surface again and this time, someone outside the family witnessed it. This is how it happened.

Henry was eleven years old, going on twelve, and he was in the seventh grade. His teacher was Miss Mabel Hornung. Now Mabel Hornung had a tough face and a stern manner. It seemed that nature had run out of good, happy parts when it made her face and so she was destined to go through life with a harsh, unyielding sour puss. It was rumored that her face was so hard and her sharp eyes so intense that she could stop a clock with one stare.

Whenever she looked at one of her students with her rigid countenance and piercing eyes, the kid immediately thought the worst, like maybe he had done something wrong and was suddenly found out—although he couldn't think of what his transgression could possibly be, but he assumed that Miss Hornung knew something even if he didn't and that something was probably bad. So, even if the kids in her class didn't actually fear Mabel Hornung, at least they had a healthy respect for her and always tried to be polite and obedient rather than risk getting on her bad side.

Actually, Mabel Hornung wasn't at all mean or hard or critical, and she really didn't have a bad side—she just looked that way. The fact was, that underneath that cold exterior, Mabel Hornung was a kindly, good-spirited woman who had a pleasant disposition but had never learned how to smile.

During the first semester of the seventh grade, Henry sat quietly in her class and behaved just like the other students, no better and no worse. To Mabel Hornung he was just an average, well-behaved boy who never stood out, never caused any trouble, nor, by the same token, showed any signs of exceptional aptitude or brilliance; so, she never gave him any special attention. And that was all right with Henry. He didn't want to be noticed. So, he just sat at his desk every day without saying anything—unless called upon—and not doing anything to draw attention to himself.

He was content to let the other kids in the class shine and it was all right with him just being just average Henry. Let the other kids stand out. Bobby Cosarelli was the tallest kid in the class and the best athlete. Gail Jackson was the brightest one, who always knew all the answers and got the best grades. Carol Sawyer was the chubby, freckle-faced kid and Frank Lapone was the class clown.

But Henry? Well, he was none of those things; he was just an average kid named Henry Gainsvort. Average height, average looks, average intelligence, average grades; that was Henry and that was the way Miss Hornung saw and thought about him all during the first semester and into the second. But then sometime into the second semester, Henry did something that seemed strange and rather remarkable and it caused Miss Hornung to suddenly see Henry in an entirely new light.

Sometime in the middle of the semester, the seventh-grade class was scheduled to put on a presentation in the auditorium for the school assembly. All the grades were required to do presentations periodically and this time it fell to Miss Hornung's class to come up with something for the assembly program at the end of April.

By now the weather turned mild. Winter was over and the signs of nature's rebirth were appearing; so Miss Hornung decided upon a Spring theme for the presentation. She found an appropriate choral arrangement in one of her monthly teacher magazines. The whole thing seemed easy enough to do because it was mostly recitation work. No costumes were required and there was no elaborate staging.

Some of the kids had a flair for performing so she gave them solo parts where they would recite poems about the coming of spring, the greening of trees, and the songs the birds sing when the flowers come out. Miss Hornung also decided to feature the talents of a few of her other students who were taking private performing-arts lessons outside of school. Marilyn Bliss took piano lessons, so Miss Hornung let her play *Joy to The Springtime* as part of the presentation. Tanya Starr and Elaine Splatz were taking dance lessons, so Miss Hornung put tissue paper wings on them—the only costumes in the whole presentation—and let them do a dance number that she entitled *Dance of The Fireflies*.

The rest of the kids who lacked special talents or stage presence—Henry among them—were grouped in the background where they recited rhymey-dimey verses about the joys and glory of spring.

Miss Hornung rehearsed her class three times a week during class hours. Most of the time, the rehearsals were conducted in the back of the classroom, but once a week she took the class into the auditorium where they could practice on the stage. Miss Hornung sat in the first row of the house and coached the class through the presentation. As she watched her kids perform and recite, she realized that although they sounded good the whole presentation needed more color, something to catch the eye and interest the audience.

So, during the class art sessions, she had the students make pictures of flowers. These she mounted on cardboard and attached to sticks. Some of the students would hold these imitation flowers out of sight at the start of the presentation then push them into view to make it look like spring was blooming on the stage. She also had the kids make a large banner that read *Springtime*. It was so wide that it needed two students to hold it up. She gave the job to Richard Pearsall on one end and Barry Dwarkin on the other.

Two weeks before the presentation, everything was falling into place. It seemed that everyone in the class knew their parts and Miss Hornung was happy with the way the whole act was going. There wasn't a thing to worry about and she was confident that the whole thing would go off without mishap—until Henry came up to her. It happened when the class was going downstairs for physical education. The kids were leaving the classroom and Henry was the last one out, but just as he was about to walk out the door, he abruptly turned and faced Miss Hornung.

"Miss Hornung?"

"Yes, Henry. What is it?"

"Miss Hornung, I don't think you should have Richard Pearsall carry the spring-time banner in the assembly presentation."

She thought this was a strange comment coming from a boy who never said or did anything out of the ordinary, and she wondered to herself why Henry had suddenly come forth with this strange suggestion. Was he saying this because perhaps he secretly had it in for Richard? Or maybe he coveted Richard's part and wanted it for himself? This was certainly an odd gesture because Henry Gainsvort had never before displayed any animosity toward any of his classmates nor had he shown any desire to take the initiative in anything nor the aspiration to stand out from the group at any time. What motivated him to suddenly come forward and say this? She gave him her sternest look and eyed him suspiciously.

"Why do you say that Henry? Why shouldn't Richard carry the sign?"

"Because Miss Hornung, Richard won't be here for the assembly."

"Why not? Where is Richard going to be?"

"He'll be in the hospital. He's going to have his appendix removed."

Now this was stranger still. Why on earth would Henry say such a thing? How could he possibly know something like that?

"How do you know that Henry? Did Richard tell you that he was going to the hospital?"

"No ma'am, he didn't say anything to me. He doesn't know that it's going to happen."

Miss Hornung was truly stunned. Henry had just said that in a very matter-of-fact manner, but there was no way he could possibly know a thing like that. She tried hard not to let her surprise show through her stern exterior. In fact, she mustered up her most piercing gaze, narrowed her eyes and focused them on the young boy standing before her.

She was sure that he could not withstand the relentless intensity of her scrutiny and that whatever his ulterior motives they would come to the surface when subjected to her powerful visual rays. She was supremely confident that Henry would relent under her intense glare and confess all; but Henry continued to stand there, unflustered, unmoved, just looking at her with those two, big, innocent hazel eyes of his. As Mabel Hornung looked at his ingenuous face, she came to believe that Henry was truly innocent. She felt that he was telling her this because he really believed that what he said was actually going to happen.

Of course, there was no way that an average eleven-year old boy could possibly know something like this could happen because there weren't any clues to warrant such an assertion. That's what made this whole declaration so odd. Richard Pearsall seemed to be in the pink of health and there was no reason to believe otherwise. After assessing the situation, Miss Hornung concluded that all this was probably some good-intentioned gesture on Henry's part, conjured up in his young, boyish head but lacking in foundation. This was probably an innocent assertion based on the figment of his overactive imagination perhaps sparked from reading too many comic books.

Her face softened from hard granite to softer marble and she said, "Well, don't you worry about Richard. He's a healthy boy and I'm sure he will be just fine."

Henry simply nodded, then turned and walked out to catch up with the rest of his classmates, leaving Mabel Hornung to look after him and wonder if Henry Gainsvort really knew something that she didn't.

When the kids returned from physical education and were walking back to their desks, Richard Pearsall passed in front of Miss Hornung's desk. Miss Hornung seized the opportunity to ask Richard a question.

"How did gym class go Richard?"

"It went well, Miss Hornung. We played kickball. I scored a home run."

"That's good Richard. So, you're feeling all right then?"

"Yes Miss Hornung, I feel fine. Really good."

"That's good Richard. You can go to your desk now."

Satisfied that all was well, Miss Hornung looked away from Richard and glanced over to Henry Gainsvort who apparently had missed the whole exchange because he was busy pulling a book from his desk.

For the next days leading up to the assembly presentation, Miss Hornung started each day by casually inquiring about the state of her students' health. On one day, she would ask how Johnny or how Susan was feeling. On the next, she might inquire about Geraldine or Joseph. Each day it seemed that she asked different kids about how they were feeling. But this was just a subterfuge, a guise, because every day she also asked Richard how he was feeling. She was surreptitiously monitoring his condition just to see if there might be any grounds for

Henry's forewarning. But, at the same time, she didn't want the rest of her class to know it was only Richard that she was concerned about.

But each day whenever she asked, Richard said that he was fine, and Miss Mabel Hornung became convinced that whatever the reasons for Henry's strange premonition they were groundless and she set her mind at ease about Richard Pearsall's health. He was a healthy eleven-year old boy and there wasn't a thing to worry about and she could count on him to carry the banner in the presentation.

Then on the day before the presentation, Miss Hornung received a phone call; it was from Mrs. Pearsall. She called to say that she was sorry, but her son Richard would not be in school for the next few days. It seems that he was taken to the hospital the previous evening where he was operated on for appendicitis. Mrs. Pearsall added that the whole thing was so sudden and unexpected. Richard was feeling fine during the day, but in the evening, he started to complain about stomach pains. Finally, they took him to the emergency room where the doctors diagnosed him and declared that he needed an emergency appendectomy.

Miss Hornung was dumbfounded. Henry said it would happen and it did, just the way he said it would. Yet, there was no way he could have known Richard would be sick. No way. And yet, he did. Miss Hornung let Johnny Annito carry the spring banner and the whole presentation went off smoothly. Still, as Miss Hornung sat in the first row of the assembly, watching the kids in her class do their recitations, her eyes kept coming back to the face of Henry Gainsvort. It was an average boyish face, with an innocent, unassuming expression much like the faces of the other students; but as she studied the young boy she wondered if there was something deeper behind those two big hazel eyes—if there was something about him that made him different from the rest of the kids on the stage.

In her mind she realized that Henry had done something that bordered on the supernatural. Maybe this was just a one-time occurrence and then again, maybe not. As Miss Hornung looked at him up there on the stage with the others, reciting the silly little verses, she thought to herself that maybe someone should look into the matter. Maybe someone should examine that little boy to see if he was really as normal as he seemed. So, she sent a note home to Edna Gainsvort asking if she could come to the school so they could have a little chat.

Now when Edna Gainsvort read the note that Henry brought home from his teacher she feared the worst. Was Henry in some sort of trouble? Was he failing in school? What had her little boy done to arouse the concern of his teacher? Edna called the school and made an appointment to see Miss Hornung the following Wednesday.

On that Wednesday, Edna put on her blue dress and black dress-up shoes and Sunday hat and went to the school to meet with Henry's teacher. They met in the class room. All the students were downstairs for gym class so the two women sat alone together.

Edna had only met Mabel Hornung once before and that was during a parent-teacher night, where there were a lot of other people around so she never really got a chance to see Miss Hornung up close. This time sitting face-to-face with the teacher, Edna had the opportunity to see the hard, chiseled features of the woman who was Henry's teacher and inwardly she shuttered, fearing that she was about to hear the worst possible news about her little Henry. Perhaps Henry was about to fail all his subjects or maybe he was an incorrigible delinquent.

The minute she sat down she blurted out her fears.

"Is there some problem with Henry's school work? I hope not. I make sure that he does his homework every night and each day when he comes home, I ask him about school. He always tells me that everything is okay and I believe him. Is he behaving himself? He'd better be or else his father will have something to say to him. If there's something wrong—"

Edna Gainsvort was so anxious that she just gushed all that out in one continuous stream barely pausing for a breath when Miss Hornung interrupted her. The teacher could see the track that Edna's mind was running along and she immediately moved to reassure the woman. She put on her warmest smile, which amounted to little more than a faint line between her lips in the shape of a vague crescent, and she tried to soften her stony features. Even so, her face wasn't a beacon of warmth, but she spoke in a soft and tender voice that did, indeed, comfort Edna. Miss Hornung explained that there was really nothing wrong with Henry; he was a well-behaved, normal boy and he was doing well enough with his studies. It's just that he had this one quirk.

At that point Miss Hornung described the incident where Henry predicted Richard Pearsall's emergency appendectomy. When she finished she looked back at Edna Gainsvort half expecting the woman to maybe laugh or shrug off the episode as being inconsequential and of no substance. Miss Hornung was used to having parents trivialize the quirks of their offspring, but to her surprise Edna Gainsvort didn't do that.

Edna Gainsvort was strangely silent, but Mabel Hornung could see that the woman was thinking seriously about something. She could see the doubt in Edna's eyes and knew that the woman was mentally wrestling with herself about something—something she wanted to share and yet was hesitant about.

Finally, for whatever reason, Edna opened up. She told of the two incidents where Henry had foretold of events before they happened. She explained how both she and her husband tried to dismiss these occurrences as being minor things with little or no meaning; but now with Mabel Hornung's revelation, Edna was suddenly convinced that there was something truly extraordinary at play here.

Miss Hornung could see that Edna was really troubled by this strange aspect of Henry's behavior and she tried offer some sort of comfort. She said that maybe it was something to be concerned about but then again, maybe not. It could be something that really didn't amount to anything. The best way to get to the bottom of this and really know if Henry had a problem, explained Miss Hornung, was to take the boy to a specialist, a child psychologist, for an evaluation.

"Do you know of anyone?" asked Edna.

"Well, I don't know any child psychologists myself, but I am sure that if I talk to the school psychologist she will be able to recommend a qualified specialist."

"Well," said Edna hesitantly, "I wouldn't want word of Henry's condition to get around. I mean people all think of Henry as a normal boy and—"

"He is a normal boy," said Miss Hornung cutting off Edna's thought. "And his condition is probably nothing to be concerned about. And don't worry about word getting around. I won't mention Henry's name at all. Not even to the school psychologist. I'll just say that I have a student who might need an evaluation and some personal counseling. No one need know who it is I'm talking about or even what the situation is."

"Well okay," said Edna. "If you think that it will help and we can keep the whole thing quiet…" She let her voice trail off, not knowing what more to say. She had some inner doubts about taking Henry to a psychologist because if people found out, they might think her son was crazy or something; but at the same time, it might be comforting to discuss Henry's case with someone qualified. Someone objective, who really understood children, and who could give an unbiased professional opinion.

"You don't have to worry, Mrs. Gainsvort. No one will know that you are taking Henry to see a psychologist. Besides, I'll just get you a referral. Once you have the doctor's name you and your husband can decide where to go from there."

Edna nodded. That sounded good to her. Once she had a doctor's name, she and Charlie could talk it over and decide if taking Henry to a psychologist was a good idea or not. So, she agreed. Miss Hornung said that she would get back to her as soon as she had a doctor's name.

With that, the meeting was over. Both women stood up and tried to smile at each other. Their smiles were weak, partly because Miss Hornung had never mastered the art of the smile and partly because Edna still had her doubts about her son and was apprehensive about what was happening to him. They shook hands and Edna turned and walked out of the class room.

Mabel Hornung sat alone at her desk for a few minutes after Edna left. Then she got up and went to the window where she could look down and see Edna Gainsvort leaving the school building, going down the steps and into the courtyard. Mabel continued to watch the Gainsvort woman as she walked along the sidewalk on her way home.

She thought back to that time when Henry approached her and predicted Richard's impending illness. She recalled her subsequent surprise and shock when Henry's prediction did come true, exactly as he said it would. At the time she thought that it was a little eerie but later she told herself that maybe it was nothing. After all, Henry seemed normal enough in every other way. But after talking to Edna Gainsvort her doubts had only increased. Their conversation revealed that this strange quirk of precognitive behavior on Henry's part was not an isolated incident; that there were precedents. She could also see that the boy's mysterious ability deeply concerned his mother.

Well not to worry, a good child psychologist will be able to sort through the matter and get everything set right in no time. Yet, as Miss Hornung thought about it, she wondered what the psychologist would think when he confronted the young Henry Gainsvort.

CHAPTER 4

A few days after their meeting, Mabel Hornung called Edna Gainsvort with the name of a child psychologist, Doctor Wolfgang Holtz. When Charlie came home that night after working his usual night shift, it was after midnight. Henry was sound asleep in his bed and Edna was in her bed. Usually she was asleep in bed when Charlie got home, but this time she was still awake. She had intentionally kept herself awake so that she could talk to her husband about bringing their son to a psychologist. When Charlie undressed and climbed into bed, she broached the subject.

She quietly told him of her visit to the school to see Henry's teacher and of Miss Hornung's tale of Henry's recent prediction and of her suggestion to bring their son to a child psychologist. Charlie just lay in bed, in the dark, beside his wife and listened carefully and without comment until she finished. Even then he was silent and he didn't say anything for the longest time. In fact, Edna thought that maybe he had fallen asleep; but no, he was awake and thinking over all she had said. Finally, he spoke.

He expressed his reservations about his son seeing a head-shrinker. After all, if word got out that little Henry, his son, was seeing a psychologist then people might think the boy was crazy and by reason of association, think that maybe he inherited his mental malady from his old man. That would be a hell of a thing to try and live down.

Edna, however, assured him that the whole thing would be very confidential and that no one would know anything about it. With some reluctance, Charlie agreed. At the same time, he thought to himself that maybe, after all, it really was a good idea; because maybe, in this way, they could get to the bottom of these strange incidents in Henry's behavior and then find out what was really inside the boy. The next day Edna called doctor Holtz's office.

Now the name, Wolfgang Holtz, might seem Germanic in the extreme and upon hearing it, one might think that Doctor Holtz was a medical man of the old Prussian tradition, schooled at Heidelberg University and have an office with pictures of Otto Von Bismarck, Friedrich Nietzsche and Paul Von Hindenburg hanging on the walls. But no, Wolfgang Holtz was born and raised in the Bronx, went to City College for his undergraduate studies and Columbia for his graduate work. In spite of his name, Doctor Wolfgang Holtz was as American as any McDonald's fast food restaurant. He had a modest office on the Boulevard in Jersey City and the only pictures he had in his office were of George Washington and an autographed photograph of singer Frankie Valli.

Edna Gainsvort called Doctor Holtz's office to ask if she could bring her young son in for an examination. She talked directly to the doctor who agreed to see young Henry Gainsvort the beginning of the next week. He declined, however, to discuss the boy's case over the phone, saying that he preferred to reserve judgment and wait to make his initial diagnosis until personally meeting with the patient and his parent. They discussed his fee and scheduled an appointment for Monday evening.

When he hung up the phone, Doctor Holtz was not duly concerned about the boy's condition. After over twenty years of practice, he was confident that he had seen every kind of patient and handled all possible psychological conditions. For him, seeing a new patient was simply a matter of talking, getting to know the patient, listening to the problem, then cataloging the diagnosis and applying one of his tried-and-true treatments. Whatever problem this Gainsvort boy had, Doctor Holtz was sure it was one that he had seen and treated many times before, and he was confident that he could straighten out the boy and put everything right in short order.

When Edna and Henry came in for their first visit on the appointed day at the scheduled time, Doctor Holtz met them in his waiting room. He looked at them both and decided that Edna was a typical, middle-aged housewife with a typical young son. He looked at the boy and felt instinctively that there was probably nothing seriously the matter with the kid and judged off the top of his head that he could probably affect a complete adjustment in three visits at the most. He shook hands with them both then had Henry sit in the waiting room while he brought Edna into his office. Once they were comfortably seated with the door shut, he asked her to tell him about the problem.

Edna sat in a chair facing Doctor Holtz. She immediately recounted the history of Henry's premonitions, starting with the car-crash accident, going through the baseball-game incident and culminating with Henry's prediction before his seventh-grade teacher.

Doctor Holtz sat there and took notes on a yellow pad, but he didn't say much; he listened without comment, asking only an occasional question now and then for clarification. As he was listening, he thought to himself that there was really no problem here. He was a staunch empiricist who only believed in the data gleaned from his five senses. He didn't believe in God because there was no empirical evidence for such a being, and he didn't believe that anyone could see into the future because the future was really a hypothetical concept that really didn't exist until we were in it. Whatever peculiar behavior the boy displayed could be easily explained rationally once the facts were established, clinically examined, and objectively analyzed.

True, the boy had shown remarkable insights into forthcoming events, but that's all they were, insights. Holtz was sure that Henry really couldn't predict the future nor could the boy have any real way of seeing into what was coming before it actually happened. It only seemed that the young boy possessed this uncanny ability because he had made some lucky guesses here and there. That, and coincidence, made it seem like he could predict the future; but Doctor Holtz knew that precognition, like all fortune telling, was superstition and he was confident that he could quickly debunk this myth surrounding the young Gainsvort boy.

As he sat there and listened to Edna, he was absolutely certain that this case would be a piece of cake, but at the same time he knew that he had to go through the motions of treatment so it wouldn't appear as if he was simply dismissing the boy out of hand. He could see that the boy's mother was concerned about her little Henry and he knew that he would have to say something to reassure her. He would, of course, have to talk to the boy. So, when Edna finished, he asked her to change places with Henry.

Henry came into the office and Doctor Holtz had him take up a seat in the big wing chair facing him, then they began a dialogue. The boy didn't seem at all nervous or ill at ease. He sat there, calmly, silently waiting for the doctor to begin. In an effort to break the ice and establish a comfortable rapport, Doctor Holtz began the conversation with talk about sports and school and anything he could think of that would interest a young, average, typical boy of eleven-years old. All this was just an attempt to try and bond with the young man and get him to open up and talk freely. These were just the preliminaries before Holtz got to the real issue at hand.

As they talked, Holtz carefully observed the young boy seated before him. Henry seemed at ease, relaxed, slightly shy, and at first, a little reticent to talk. He just sat still with his hands resting on the arms of the chair, looking back with his big hazel eyes at the doctor on the other side of the desk. He responded to questions but didn't add much of his own thought. Well, this was a normal trait of most young kids, so Doctor Holtz was not unduly concerned. In fact, as he talked to, and observed Henry, he came to the conclusion that the boy sitting opposite him was an average, perfectly normal boy without any real problem. All this talk of visions of the future was probably just a misunderstanding and mostly likely had a logical explanation.

When he felt that they were comfortable together, Doctor Holtz started to ask questions that were more to the point.

"Tell me Henry," he started, "do you know why you are here?"

Henry just shrugged. "I don't know. Mom just said that you are a man that I should talk to."

Doctor Holtz nodded. That was a simple enough answer. Now the doctor asked the big question: "So Henry, your mother tells me that sometimes you see things. You see events before they happen, and then later they happen just as you saw them. Is that right?"

"Yes, I guess so."

"And how do these pictures come to you? Do you look at something and wonder what is going to happen? Do you try to see things?"

"No, they just come to me. I don't try to make them happen."

"I see. Now tell me, have you had any of these visions recently?"

"No. The last one was in school, a few weeks ago."

Doctor Holtz looked at his notes. "Yes, that was when you saw that your class mate, Richard, was going into the hospital to have his appendix removed."

Henry nodded.

"And what exactly did you see?"

"I saw Richard Pearsall lying on a table with the doctor leaning over him poking a finger at his stomach."

"How did you know it was a doctor?"

"Because he wore a long white coat and had the thing that doctors wear around their neck. The thing they use to listen to your heart beat."

"The stethoscope," suggested Holtz. "Could you describe more of the picture that you saw?"

The boy related his vision, and described the examining room, the examining doctor, and Richard in vivid detail. Holtz listened with interest and at the same time he looked at the boy's face. The face was calm and had an expression of innocence about it. His bright, hazel eyes started straight ahead into the space before him as if he were seeing the same vision with the room and Richard and the doctor all over again.

When Henry finished, he sat there and waited for Doctor Holtz's next question; but the doctor was silent. He was still thinking about all Henry had just said, about that vision that he had. Doctor Holtz was impressed. Henry had just created a verbal picture in vivid and exacting detail. It was almost as if Henry were in the room watching the examination, seeing and hearing everything. Doctor Holtz had to admit to himself that Henry's vision did have an uncanny and mysterious overtone to it, but still, he knew that when all is said and done, there was a scientific explanation for everything and Henry's case would be no different from any other of the many cases that he had successfully treated. Possibly the boy had unintentionally conjured up the vision based on a recent television show that he had seen.

Based on this initial interview, Doctor Holtz concluded that Henry had a vivid imagination and his visions were simply a product of that imagination. The boy had the extraordinary ability to imagine scenes and create lucid pictures in his mind. These scenes just happened to work out and coincide with future events. Doctor Holtz was sure that, in the final analysis, young Henry's visions were nothing more than coincidence.

The incidents were curious to be sure; Holtz had to admit that to himself, but still there was no reason to think that they were anything other than spontaneous, imaginative stories that just happened to relate to real events now and then. Just lucky guesses. But then there was the nagging fact that Henry had three visions in a row, and they just happened to work out exactly as he predicted. That was stretching the coincidence hypothesis a bit, but still, it was not beyond the realm of plausibility.

Doctor Holtz looked at his watch. The hour was up. He rose from his chair and led Henry to the waiting room where the anxious Edna was sitting. Doctor Holtz could see the look of concern on her face. Now what would he tell her?

He began in his most reassuring professional manner: "Well Mrs. Gainsvort, after talking with Henry here, I'm convinced that there's nothing seriously the matter with your son; but I think that maybe we need another session together. Maybe two more. But after that I am sure that we can come up with a satisfactory explanation for everything. In the meantime, I shouldn't worry about Henry. In my opinion he's a very healthy and very normal boy."

Edna was a little relieved. The good doctor seemed so confident and so sure about her son, that she began to set her mind at rest concerning Henry's recent behavior. She felt that she was in the good hands of a competent professional who would set everything right. She reached in her purse and pulled out the check that she had already written to cover the fee for this session. Then, she and Henry went home. Doctor Holtz returned to his office and looked at his appointment book to see what patient was coming next. From then on, he didn't think about little Henry Gainsvort until the boy arrived with his mother the following week.

The second visit went more or less like the first one with Doctor Holtz and Henry talking over the general topics, sports, television, movies then going over the three incidents where Henry had his visions. By the end of the second session, Holtz was convinced that Henry's visions were nothing more than the product of his vivid imagination and he felt that he could wrap the case up at that point. Still, he decided that he should have one more get together with Henry just to be certain of his diagnosis.

He wanted this additional session because he hoped that in the meantime Henry would have another vision. If the boy did, then he could apply his explanation, test his hypothesis, and satisfy himself that the boy was really as normal as he seemed, truly without precognitive abilities, and that there was no cause for concern. He scheduled one more meeting with Henry Gainsvort.

The following week Edna Gainsvort brought in her young son at the appointed time for the third session. She sat down in the waiting room while Henry went into the office to talk with Doctor Holtz. The two sat down in their respective positions and commenced with the usual dialogue. At first, it seemed like everything was going exactly as with the previous sessions. But then halfway through the hour, events took a strange turn and suddenly everything changed. Henry revealed something that completely unnerved the good doctor and deflated his confidence quicker than a leaking balloon. This is how it happened.

The doctor casually asked Henry a question. "So, tell me Henry, have you had any visions lately? Anything you want to talk about. Anything that will tell us what will happen in the future?"

"Yes, Doctor Holtz, I saw something yesterday."

Ah! This is what the doctor was hoping for, another, fresher, vision. One that he would be in on from the beginning, where the event was yet to happen. This would be a vision that he could dissect and examine in minute detail. Then he could pick up on any significant details, analyze them, and show that the prediction was just a coincidence and thus debunk the myth of Henry's fortune-telling abilities.

So, Holtz launched into his interrogation. "Now, why don't you tell me about this latest vision"

"It was about you. I saw a picture of you."

This was a little unexpected, but Holtz tried not to show his surprise. Instead he maintained his amicable, professional demeanor.

"Oh, and what did your picture tell you about me."

"I saw where and how you are going to die."

Doctor Holtz's good-natured, avuncular, breezy manner suddenly fell apart and he sat there stunned. Here was something totally expected, something he was not prepared for; something that was beyond his many years of experience. He sat up and leaned forward across his desk and focused on Henry. He looked hard into Henry's face and eyes and tried to determine if the boy was serious or not.

Did the boy really believe what he had just said or was just being tantalizingly malicious? Was he playing some sort of game, trying to be a smarty-pants, or a wise ass? Was he deliberately trying to throw the psychologist off his guard and upset his professional equilibrium? Doctor Holtz looked into those two, big, clear, hazel eyes and at the young, gentle face, and after studying them for a bit, he thought to himself that there was no malice or mischievousness there. Instead,

Holtz saw an innocent sincerity in that young face and he could not believe that the boy meant any harm to anyone. The boy had simply said something that he truly believed he saw.

Holtz leaned back in his chair totally unsure of how to proceed from that point.

"You say that you know how I am to die?"

"Yes, I know when too."

Holtz was dumbfounded. He couldn't believe what he was hearing. "You're saying that you've had a vision of my death and you know when and where it will happen?"

"Yes. Do you want me to tell you?"

So, there it was. The boy had another vision of the future. This time it was a vision of Holtz's demise. This was something that Doctor Holtz was not prepared for, but still, as he thought about it, it should be something that he could easily deflate. After all, all he had to do was say, "Yes! Tell me where and how I am to die. Tell me when also. Then I'll outlive that time and show you that there is nothing to your predictions and that your visions have no substance. Tell me the time of my death and I will live beyond it and show that not you, nor anyone, has the power to see into the future."

And that would be the end of the matter. It would be so simple to accept the challenge and confront the boy's vision. All he had to do was live beyond the prediction and thus he would disprove it. Yet somehow, at that moment, Doctor Holtz hesitated. Inwardly he felt that this might not be such a comfortable path to take. For the first time in his professional career, Doctor Holtz found that there was a crack in his rock-solid foundation of empirical reasoning. It was as if this mere boy had found a way to breach the solid wall of the good doctor's impenetrable fortress of scientific logic, professional experience and supreme self-confidence.

He was a man of science, and as such, his intellect told him that no one could see into to the future—certainly not an eleven-year old boy—but something else, a vague impulse, deep within his soul, some nebulous atavistic feeling that up till now he never realized was there, told him not to be so sure of himself and that it was not wise tread into this unknown territory.

And as Holtz looked into Henry's eyes trying to decide if the boy really possessed the ability to see into tomorrow, his brain started to think all manner of things: "What would it be like to know the exact time of your death? Every day would be a countdown to the inevitable; and suddenly you would be confronted with the fact that this was your last Monday on earth and that next week you would be part of eternity—if, in fact, there really was an eternity. What would it be like to know that you had exactly one or two weeks to live or just one more day on the face of the earth?

"What would you do? Would you chuck everything you've worked for and go out and spend the last weeks of your life seeking pleasure, indulging in reverie and hedonism? And if you did, what would happen if the prediction turned out to be wrong? What then? You would find that you spent those two weeks of your life making a damn fool of yourself all because some eleven-year old boy told you that you were going to die.

"No! Better not to have that knowledge. Better to go through life not knowing when it will come to an end. Better to live each day, taking every day as it comes, than to throw caution to the winds and indulge in reckless abandon just because the end is in sight. Better to enjoy your moments as they come instead of living in fear and dread, marking each hour and constantly looking at the calendar and the clock waiting for that dreaded last minute, all the time wondering if the prediction will come true."

So, Holtz looked back at Henry who was still sitting quietly and calmly in his chair waiting for the doctor to reply.

Doctor Holtz leaned forward. "No, Henry. I don't want to know about your latest vision." The boy simply nodded.

Then Holtz looked down at his watch and saw that mercifully their session was just about up.

"Well Henry, that concludes our time today. Why don't you go out into the waiting room and ask your mother to come in. You sit out there while I talk to her, okay?"

Henry nodded and got up and went to the waiting room as the doctor requested. While he was waiting for Edna Gainsvort to come into his office, Doctor Holtz thought to himself that this would have to be their last session together. He could not ever see Henry Gainsvort again. If they continued meeting, Henry might at some time inadvertently reveal the content of his latest vision and Holtz did not want to chance learning about his own end. He knew that he simply could not bring himself to confront that kind of knowledge.

Maybe as a man of medicine he should pursue the matter further if only as a matter of scientific inquiry. Another session would be a deeper investigation to see if someone really did have the power of precognition. Yes, maybe as a man of science he should do that, but as a mortal man, he knew that he could not take that step. Better to let it end here and now so he could go back to blissful ignorance and continue his peaceful life without sharing the dark knowledge that the boy might, or might not, possess. Better not to know if that boy really did possess the uncanny ability to see into the future than to know that he really did see death on the horizon. Better not to tread in the realm of the unknown and live in the dread of things to come.

But now he had to tell Edna Gainsvort something. She entered the office and sat down in the chair. She said nothing but waited for him to begin. He stood against the edge of his desk. He could see the poor woman was waiting for some comment, some sort of opinion as to Henry's condition. He had to say something; but what? What could he say to her? He didn't dare tell her that Henry had another vision, one that frightened him because he suspected that it might come true. He couldn't say anything about that, because then she'd ask what he was going to do about it, and he didn't know what on earth to do. He couldn't say that this case was beyond his abilities. No, he couldn't talk about that, but he had to say something.

Hesitantly Holtz began.

"Well Mrs. Gainsvort, your son, Henry, and I have had a long chat—several in fact—and after talking with him, I am convinced that he is a normal eleven-year old kid. He doesn't really see into the future."

"Well then how—"

Doctor Holtz held up his right hand to silence the question she was about to ask. He didn't want any interruptions now, not when he was trying to fabricate some sort of explanation for the boy's behavior. He wanted to be left to continue his train of thought so he could put together some explanation that sounded plausible and like the reasoning of a professional mind. Any questions now might upset his equilibrium forcing him to address topics that he really didn't understand or come up with answers that he didn't have.

He continued. "What Henry does have is remarkable perception. He has the ability to see details and nuances that the rest of us miss. For instance, take that incident of the dog and the car and the tree. Now Henry told me that he saw the dog running around, playing in the alley. The dog looked excited and it occurred to him that it was getting ready to run. He also saw the car coming up the street and he simply put two and two together. When it happened like he said, it looked like a vision of the future but he was just putting a few of the things that he saw together. That's all. Nothing more."

Edna nodded, slowly and somewhat doubtfully.

"What about the Pearsall boy? Henry's classmate who had the emergency appendectomy? How did Henry know that was going to happen?"

Damn! though Holtz to himself. *She would have to ask about that one.* He was hoping that he could sidestep that incident because he didn't have a rationale for it; but now he was forced to think of something.

"Well, that is a little more difficult to understand, but there is an explanation for it. Let me see if I can explain it to you. Sometimes people who are ill—well just on the verge of an illness—will, from all outward appearances, look and act perfectly normal but will, nevertheless, sometimes show some subtle signs of that illness. Now, as I said, these signs are so subtle that they go by most of us, but a few people are perceptive enough to notice. That's why some doctors can become expert diagnosticians, because they see these little tell-tale signs that go unnoticed by everyone else. The Pearsall boy probably was showing something like that and Henry picked up on it. Henry just happened to see what others around him failed to notice."

"But how did he know it would be appendicitis?"

Double damn! thought Holtz to himself. *Why can't the woman just accept my explanation without asking questions. Why does she have to know all the details?*

"Well," began the Doctor, "that's not really so difficult to explain." Actually, it was, and Holtz found that his mind was working furiously—although he was struggling to keep his outward, calm demeanor—to come up with an explanation off the top of his head. *What could he say that would sound even faintly reasonable?*

"Young people Henry's age don't, as a rule, know of many illnesses that can come on suddenly—at least not in people their own age. And too, Henry might have seen or heard something about appendicitis on the television or in some recent conversation. When he suspected the

Pearsall boy was going to be ill, appendicitis was probably the only condition that came to mind."

Doctor Holtz was making up this fabric of lies on the spur of the moment, but. it was the best he could do under the circumstances. He went on, adding whatever bits and pieces of knowledge that he could come up with to make it all sound plausible—at least he hoped that it sounded plausible. When he finished, he looked at Edna Gainsvort for a reaction to see if she bought into any of his smoke and mirrors. He looked back at her, but he couldn't be sure what she was thinking because for a long moment, she sat perfectly still, not saying anything and with no telltale facial expression: apparently, she was mulling over everything he had just said.

Finally, she nodded and said, "All right doctor, I suppose that is the most logical explanation for Henry's behavior."

Greatly relieved that his newly concocted explanation had passed muster, Holtz continued, "Let me give you one word of advice, and you can pass it along to Henry. For his sake, and for the sake of those others around him, whenever he has these little …ah, insights …he should keep them to himself. I mean, he shouldn't tell anyone about them. We know that he's not really predicting the future, but the way he phrases his observations …well …they sort of sound like predictions, and that has a way of unnerving people. Do understand what I'm trying to say?"

Edna Gainsvort nodded slowly. "All right doctor, if you think that's best, I'll do as you recommend. I'll tell Henry not to say anything more about it whenever he thinks that something is about to happen."

Holtz could tell that Edna Gainsvort was not totally convinced, and that she was still mulling all this over in her mind. For now, she was just accepting his explanation on the strength of his professional credentials, but that was all right with him. Maybe in time it would all smooth itself over. Maybe in time, Henry would stop having visions and return to being a normal kid, but, in the meantime, it would be best to keep a lid on everything. If Henry kept silent, then no one would ever be aware that this seemingly ordinary boy saw things before they happened. No one would suspect that anything was out of the ordinary and everyone would continue to live more or less contented and at peace totally unaware of Henry's strange ability. And if everyone was okay, then Mrs. Gainsvort would be satisfied and not bring her son back for another session.

Edna looked into her purse and produced the check that she had previously written out. It was the doctor's fee for the session that had just occurred. She reached out and handed it to him, but he didn't take it. Instead he waved it away and said, "No Mrs. Gainsvort, you keep that money."

She looked back at him in surprise.

"No Mrs. Gainsvort, you keep that money because this last session was just a friendly chat between me and Henry. We just covered old ground so that I could be sure that there was nothing really the matter with him. I didn't actually do much in this session, so I won't take your money."

Well that last part wasn't true. In fact, Doctor Holtz had done something, he had just lied to Edna Gainsvort. He had just told her that her son was normal and there wasn't anything different about him. He had told the good woman that there was nothing peculiar or unusual about her son, but deep down he didn't really believe that.

Somewhere in the back of his mind, deep within his inner subconscious, during that last session with Henry, he had come to believe that young Henry Gainsvort really did have visions of destiny; that at times, the young boy could, in fact, glimpse into the future. Yet, somehow, he couldn't bring himself to admit this, not to her, not even to himself, because it went against all he had been trained to believe.

His was a logical world solidly based on empirical evidence and there was no room in it for precognition.

He had told the woman that her son was a typical normal boy because he had to say something—he had to end it all. And he told her that this last session was just a casual get-together because he had to offer some explanation as to why he wouldn't accept his fee for the final session. The real reason that he waived away the check, however, was because he knew that if he took that check he would be accepting Edna Gainsvort's money for services he did not provide and he could not, in good conscience, bring himself to do that. After all, he had just lied to her by telling her the boy was normal. He only said that to get rid of her, so she would not return with her son and his strange visions. Bad enough that he had just told her a lie about her son but it would be even worse to profit from his deception.

Edna thanked the doctor and put her check back in her purse. Then she got up and went to the waiting room where Henry was sitting. Doctor Holtz accompanied them to the door and watched them as they exited and walked down the hall to the elevator.

As he watched them standing there in the hall before the elevator doors, he wondered to himself if Henry would continue to have those eerie visions, if the boy would sometime see again into the future. Doctor Holtz also wondered if Henry really did see a vision of his death, and if so, when and where did the boy see it happening? For one moment as he looked at the two figures standing there before the elevator door, he had the impulse to call them back.

Maybe he should ask Henry to tell him about that recent vision. He could ask Henry to tell him how he was going to die. When it was going to happen. Maybe he could even avoid it. But just as Holtz was about to call out to them, to summon them back, the bell rang and the elevator doors opened. Edna and Henry got into the car, the doors closed, and they disappeared.

So be it! Thought Holtz to himself. *Maybe it's better this way. Maybe there are some things that it's better not to know.*

He turned and went back into his office. He sat at his desk and tried to erase the image of Henry Gainsvort from his mind. But he couldn't do it. The picture of the young boy with his innocent face and big, clear hazel eyes came back to him; and as he thought about Henry and his prediction of death, he assumed that the boy's recent vision was something he would never know about. Well, that's what he assumed at that time, the moment right after Edna Gainsvort departed with her young son.

Maybe later, however, he would have come to a different understanding because, in a way, he might have inadvertently found out about the boy's prediction without having to ask. Ten days later Doctor Holtz collapsed on the street just outside his office. An ambulance came and it took him to the hospital, but the good doctor died of a massive heart attack before they could get him to the emergency room. But while the doctor was lying on the gurney, taking that last ride in the ambulance, did he think back to Henry Gainsvort? Did he think to himself that maybe this was Henry's prediction coming true? That is something that we'll never know.

CHAPTER 5

Well, Edna Gainsvort followed the doctor's orders and told her son never to talk about his visions. The young boy dutifully complied and all through grammar school and into high school he was silent and everything seemed to be perfectly normal again. Neither Edna nor Charlie mentioned the subject. It was as if the young boy's visions were a forgotten issue, something that would remain buried in the past. With that, their young son was back to being a typical, average boy like any other kid in the neighborhood.

Still, there were times when Edna looked at Henry doing his homework, playing in the yard, getting ready for school, or doing any one of a thousand things, and she wondered if he had any more of those strange visions. Did he, she wondered, still have those strange glimpses in to the future, but was not talking about them? Were they still part of his life? Or was that just some sort of phase that he went through and had now outgrown?

So many times, she wanted to ask him those questions, but always she stopped herself. She couldn't ask him because she had told him not to talk about those visions and she realized that she was bound by the same rules. So, she kept her peace. She didn't ask, but nevertheless, inside, she had to wonder to herself.

Well, the fact was that young Henry Gainsvort was still having visions. Oh, not every day, but occasionally, now and then. Sometimes months would pass without him seeing anything, but then suddenly, without warning, he would suddenly see an incident that was about to happen. Being a good, obedient boy, however, Henry obeyed his mother's orders and kept these visions to himself.

So, no one ever knew that Henry Gainsvort had these glimpses into the future and was seeing things that others around him couldn't see. It was that way in grammar school and during the first three years of high school, but in his senior year, there was a change. Henry was only months away from graduation at Snyder High School in Jersey City. It was then that he had another vision and this time he forgot about his mother's instruction and without realizing it, he told about what he saw. This is how it happened.

One fine day, Henry was sitting in his afternoon English class with the other students. The teacher was Mr. McKinney and the students were discussing their required reading, *The Crucible,* by playwright Arthur Miller. The play is ostensibly about the Salem witchcraft trials that took place in colonial America; but there is a subtext to the play.

Miller wrote *The Crucible* during the turbulent time when Congress was holding investigations looking into suspected subversive communist activities in the government and in American society at large. At that time, it seemed like everyone was under suspicion of being a communist and no one was safe from the scrutiny of the government. Miller, as well as many others, thought that the Congressional investigations had gone too far and likened them to the witch hunts of seventeenth-century colonial times. So, the play has a message on two levels and these were the issues that the students talked about in Mr. McKinney's English class.

The discussion wasn't particularly spirited because both topics, the Salem witchcraft trials and the Congressional investigations, were so far in the past that the students didn't find them relevant to their current lives. The only reason that anyone voiced an opinion or observation was because he or she knew that Mr. McKinney graded on class participation as well as test scores. So, sooner or later, each student made some sort of comment just to be sure of getting a passing grade from Mr. McKinney. Even Henry managed to say something now and again, although his comments were trite because he didn't have much enthusiasm for the play.

Each class discussion seemed to drag on for what seemed like an eternity. There was always an audible sound of relief when the bell sounded and class was over. After the class came the lunch period. Henry usually walked with Billy Hirsch, Tom Harney, Judy Shaw, and Lynn Brettner to the fourth-floor cafeteria. They went through the line and got their food, then sat down at a table together. They munched and chatted and joked and giggled in typical, teenage, high-school fashion.

On Wednesday they followed this routine and they were sitting in the cafeteria eating and chatting when Judy casually asked, "You guys going to the basketball game Friday night?"

Well, this was kind of a rhetorical question, because it looked like this was Snyder's big year on the basketball court and it was almost a foregone conclusion that anyone with any school spirit—and this year everyone in the school was loaded to the gills with school spirit—was going to the game. The athletic department had put together the best basketball team that the school had ever seen. It was doing so well that it was almost required viewing for all the students to attend every game; either that or risk being ostracized by the student body for lacking school spirit and being a turncoat. The Friday night game was an important one because if Snyder won, they would be on their way to the state finals.

So, in answer to Judy's question, everyone at the table either nodded or made some sort of a perfunctory affirmation and it was agreed that the five of them were going to the big game. They decided on a rendezvous time and made plans for a meeting place. They also decided that after the game—after Snyder won—they would all go out to celebrate together at the local pizza joint.

Friday night came around and Henry met up with Billy, Tom, Judy and Lynn. Together they went to the gymnasium. As might be expected, the place was packed. They had arrived early so they were able to get seats not too far up from center court where they had a good view of the action.

Now this was an important game because Snyder was facing its arch rival, St. Peter's Prep. St. Peter's was a Catholic boys' school that had a reputation for putting together the best basketball, football, and baseball teams in the city. This year they had a good basketball team, but it wasn't as good as the Snyder team.

That's because Snyder had two top stars, two players who were destined to make all-state, Mitchell Rooney and Pete DeVry. These guys worked magic on the court, dribbling and passing the ball with flawless precision and shooting baskets with unerring accuracy. When they played together it was like watching genius in motion; they were unstoppable.

St. Peter's had faced the Snyder team, with Rooney and DeVry, at the start of the season and they lost. They had come into that game as the favorites, but Snyder flattened them like a steamroller. Now they were returning for a replay and they were coming back with a vengeance. They were determined to win this game. But the Snyder team wasn't worried. They were confident of victory because they had Rooney and DeVry, and with this dynamic duo, victory was in the bag.

So, there was tension and excitement in the atmosphere as the spectators filled the gymnasium. Soon everyone was inside and they settled down in anticipation of a game that everyone knew was going to be exciting. The game started with the usual toss-up and almost immediately the play became fast and furious. The St. Peter's team played a competitive game with each player doing his best, performing with grim determination; but it was all to no avail. Rooney and DeVry were at their sharpest and by the half-way point Snyder was well ahead by over twenty points.

Needless to say, the Snyder fans were ecstatic. It looked like their team was well on its way to the state finals. As the game continued, Billy, Tom, Judy and Lynn were jumping up and down and cheering for their team at the top of their lungs, but Henry just sat there. In the midst of all the reverie and shouting and physicality, Henry was strangely quiet and still. The truth was that Henry was having another of his visions. As the game was progressing and Snyder was rolling along to what looked like certain victory, Henry was seeing disaster in the making.

He sat there and he saw what no one else could; he saw that soon there would be a mad scramble for a fumbled ball. In the midst of the court commotion, Rooney would stumble, fall and sprain his ankle. That injury would put him out of the game and Snyder would go down to defeat.

Henry was sitting between Tom and Judy while he watched the game being played in another dimension. He said nothing because this sudden, unexpected vision disturbed and depressed him. Tom looked to his right and saw Henry sitting there almost like a statue, mute and staring into space.

"Hey Hen, whatsa matter? You lost your school spirit? You feeling okay? You're not sick or something?"

Judy heard this, and so did Lynn. They both looked to see if Henry had suddenly taken sick. Henry looked up at them and tried to reassure them that he wasn't ill.

"No, not really. I just …well, I saw something that bothered me."

Tom looked around trying to find whatever it was that Henry had just glimpsed. But there was nothing except a basketball game and screaming fans.

"What? What did you see? Where?"

"Snyder's gonna lose this game."

"What are you talking about? We're ahead by twenty points and our team is red hot. Prep can't touch us."

Henry shook his head. "No, there's gonna be a scuffle. Rooney's gonna get hurt. It'll put him out of the game. Without him, the team won't function. We're gonna lose."

Tom looked back at Henry and he wondered what had suddenly happened to bring this saturnine cloud of gloom unexpectedly upon his friend.

"Ah, come on Henry. Lighten up. Don't be such a worry wart. Nothing's gonna happen. The team is red hot and nothing can stop—"

Tom never finished that sentence because at that very moment, on the court, one of the players attempted to pass the ball to his teammate, but it was deflected in mid-air. The ball bounced out of control and a few of the boys tried to grab it before it hit foul territory. A mad scramble for the wayward sphere followed, and in the struggle, one player tripped over another and fell to the floor. He was followed by another and another and soon there was a pile of arms and legs and torsos all thrown together in one human heap. Somewhere near the bottom of that mass was Mitchell Rooney.

The ref blew his whistle to stop the action and restore order. The struggle ceased, and one by one, each player got to his feet and stood aside. Everyone got up, except one, Mitchell Rooney. Rooney lay in the middle of the court clutching his ankle, his face twisted in pain. The coach immediately came over, helped him to his feet. Rooney was out of the game.

And sure enough, with Rooney gone, DeVry had suddenly become ineffective as a player. It was as if he had suddenly lost his right arm and couldn't function properly. With its Achilles heel exposed, the Snyder team became impotent and within minutes their commanding lead had evaporated. Now they were no longer playing to win, but simply to avoid ending the game in a humiliating defeat.

The last fifteen minutes of the game were agony for the Snyder team and only slightly less unbearable for their fans. But at last, mercifully, it was over with Snyder the losing team. And it had all happened just as Henry predicted.

As the five got up and started to leave, Tom looked at Henry and said, "Damn it, Henry, why couldn't you have kept your big mouth shut?"

Henry looked back at him in surprise. "Me, what did I do? I was sitting here with you guys. I didn't do anything."

"You said that Mitch would fall and hurt his ankle and it happened. Just like you said it would. You jinxed the team."

"No, I didn't. I just said what I thought was going to happen. That didn't make it come true. I wasn't a jinx. You can't really believe that."

Henry looked to Tom and Judy and Lynn for support, but he saw the look on their faces and the glare in their eyes. He could see that they too believed that he was a jinx, that he had caused the downfall of the mighty Snyder basketball team. Henry was at a loss for words. How could he explain that sometimes he saw things that others didn't? That he had no control over what he saw. The visions were what they were and there was no way for him to change the channel if he didn't like them.

"Sometimes I see things before they happen. And then they happen just like I saw."

"Well if that's true, then what's gonna happen tomorrow?" asked Tom.

"I don't know. I haven't seen anything about tomorrow."

"How come you never saw anything before tonight?" asked Lynn.

"Well I did ...sometimes ...a lot of times ...it's just that my mother told me never to talk about the things I see."

"Yeah right!" snorted Judy sarcastically.

When he looked from Billy to Tom to Judy to Lynn. Henry saw that they didn't believe him. He knew that they couldn't possibly understand what if was like to see into the future, to have visions of destiny. How could they know what it was like for him, and how could he possibly defend himself?

They walked out of the gymnasium and outside they parted company. Henry went home alone feeling sad and lonely, not joining his friends for pizza, knowing that they blamed him for the lost game.

Henry hoped that after the weekend all would be forgotten and he would be among friends again, but it was not to be. By Monday afternoon, word of Henry's prediction spread through the school like wild fire and before long, every student believed that Henry Gainsvort had jinxed the basketball team. Soon they all came to look upon him as some sort of a pariah and wherever he went, all the students eyed him with suspicion. They avoided him whenever possible and called him a modern-day witch behind his back.

During the next weeks, Henry found himself to be a solitary figure, alone in the big school without any friends. To Henry it felt as if he were living in *The Crucible* and the message that Miller had tried to deliver when he wrote his play assumed a new relevance for Henry Gainsvort.

Those last few months in high school were miserable for Henry Gainsvort. All the students believed that he was a jinx and a weirdo, the warlock of the community, and they went out of their way to avoid him. He went from being an average, typical, popular high school kid to becoming the malignant leper of the student body.

In addition to being isolated, ostracized and alone, Henry had to come to grips with another realization. He had had other visions in the past but when he had revealed them, nothing much had happened. The events came to pass as he predicted, and he saw that people around him looked at him with a mixture of curiosity and skepticism; but in a few days, that faded and it seemed that his situation more or less returned to normal.

But not this time. This time it was different. This was the first time that one of his visions had come back to harm and torment him. Now he understood the wisdom behind his mother's instruction to keep quiet and say nothing, and he resolved that in the future, if he ever had another vision, he would keep it to himself.

At the same time, he had another thought: as he recalled his vision at the basketball game, he began to wonder to himself if the events he saw happened because he saw them happening or because he said they were going to happen. In other words, did talking about his visions actually make them come true? Maybe Tom was right when he said that if Henry had just kept his mouth shut, Rooney wouldn't have gotten hurt.

Henry tried hard to think back to all of his other visions and he tried to remember if they all came true just as he saw them, or if it was only the ones that he talked about came true, but they happened so long ago that he couldn't remember exactly how the events materialized. It seemed that they came to pass whether he said anything or not, but as he thought about it, he really wasn't sure because he didn't remember all of the details. So, he had no way of knowing how the future really came about. Was it already there for him to glimpse at in his visions, or did his visions and talking about the future make it come into reality? The more Henry thought about it, the more he wondered if he would ever know the answer to that riddle.

CHAPTER

Henry finally graduated from Snyder High School and for him it was an immense relief to get away from the school and from all his classmates who had branded him as a later-day witch. With high school behind him, Henry looked forward to getting on to college. He enrolled in Farleigh Dickinson University and took a major in accounting. Mercifully all of his former high-school classmates went to other colleges so his reputation as the "Witch of Snyder" did not follow him to college.

For Henry, college was like a new beginning, a fresh start. At Fairleigh Dickinson, no one knew of Henry's strange visions and he was determined to keep that knowledge a deep, dark secret. His vision during the big high school basketball game caused him a lot of trouble and he wasn't going to let anything like that happen to him again. He knew that he couldn't stop his visions from coming on, but he believed that as long as he never said anything about them, then he could at least keep them under wraps and retain his image as a normal, typical college student.

The Farleigh Dickinson Florham campus was in Morris, New Jersey. Henry continued to live at home and he commuted to the school each day. He went to his classes and studied his subjects. The result was that he became a typical college student getting average grades and advancing from one course to the next without distinction, and always maintaining a low profile. And, of course, this suited Henry because he dreaded standing out in a crowd or being the center of attention. For Henry obscurity was a blessing. After being branded as a witch and ostracized during his senior year in high school, Henry was able to meld into the academic woodwork and retreat into anonymity by assuming the image of an average college student.

All went well for the first three years of his matriculation. He continued to have his visions now and again, but they were look-sees into relatively minor events and he was able to keep them to himself so nobody knew or even suspected that he had this creepy ability to sometimes see into the future. In fact, during those three years the intervals between his visions lengthened and Henry was beginning to think that his precognitive abilities were fading and that eventually they would atrophy into non-existence.

That was something he wished for because he looked upon his visions as a real detriment to normality. However, there seemed to be nothing he could do to prevent them, so in the meantime, all he could do was keep silent about the little things he saw and hope that they would never intrude into his daily life.

For those first three years of college he managed to keep his visions a closely-guarded personal secret, and so as far as the other college students knew, Henry Gainsvort was just like anyone else, a typical, average, college kid without any special abilities or attributes and pleasant enough to be around and chat with.

Henry liked it that way and he hoped that his image as a relative nobody would remain intact forever. Unfortunately, the problem with a special and unusual talent is that it has a way of surfacing unexpectedly and attracting attention at awkward moments. Henry's talent was particularly unusual and, as such, it was bound to come out sooner. Sure enough, it did surface. In his senior year Henry had another vision, one that others found out about. It happened like this.

As he was walking past the library on the way to one of his business classes, he glanced through the library windows into the reading room. It was a quiet scene with students sitting at tables reading and writing. Suddenly, Henry saw the ceiling buckle and collapse then come crashing down. The ceiling was constructed of large acoustical tiles suspended in a light-weight metal grid that hung from wires attached to hooks in the superstructure. The collapse occurred because one of the sprinkler pipes above the tiles sprung a leak and doused the tiles with water. The grid could no longer hold the extra weight of the water-laden tiles and the whole mess suddenly, and without warning, dropped down onto the students below.

No one was seriously hurt, but the whole crash made a loud stir and created quite a mess and for a time the pipe continued to spray water and the tiles continued to fall. Finally, someone managed to cut off the main shutoff valve and stop the water from gushing out. By then, however, a lot of damage had been done and the reading room was a disaster area.

Henry stood there, transfixed, watching the whole incident in his mind's eye. No one else could see it because it wasn't really happening at that moment; it was a vision of a future event. For Henry it was very real; he was seeing it as if it was actually happening at that very moment that he was standing there looking through the windows. He was having his vision of an event that was yet to come, but for him it was a very vivid and very real event. He stood there transfixed until finally the vision stopped, the image faded, and he found himself back in the present moment.

He looked around and saw that no one had noticed him standing there motionless, rooted to the spot, staring through the library window, mesmerized by an event that only he could see. When it was over, he breathed a silent sigh of relief because he realized that he had just had a vision and no one else was aware of it. This was another vision that he wanted to keep to himself.

He turned and went on to his class, but even though he had turned away from the library and it was no longer in his view, the image of the disaster stayed with him somewhere in the back of his brain and as he walked along the path, entered the hall, and climbed the stairs on the way to his class, the whole incident continued to pop up and replay in the corners of his mind. Try as hard as he might, he just couldn't shake the vision of that dreadful happening.

In class Henry tried to concentrate as his professor droned on about some sort of problems facing modern companies when they try to market their products, but the scene with the broken pipe and the falling, water-logged tiles kept coming back to him.

Now in the past, most of Henry's visions came and went quickly and he was able to go back to his routine more or less without much interruption. In rare instances, a vision sometimes persisted and came back at odd moments to haunt his conscience. When that happened, it was harder, much harder, to go on with his normal existence but eventually with time, the vision faded and Henry was able to get back to his life. The falling ceiling in the library was just such a lingering vision. He couldn't shake it; he just had to let it play itself out.

Still, Henry wasn't unduly concerned. He was sure that in time, perhaps in a few days or more, the image would eventually stop replaying in his mind. He also knew that it would certainly come to an end when the event he witnessed actually did come to pass.

So, Henry was content to go about his school routine and maintain his silence while this inner vision just ran its course; and yet, there was a nagging little mental glitch that stuck in his conscience. The library ceiling hadn't fallen yet, but it would happen soon—although he had no idea exactly when it would actually occur. Most likely within the next two weeks. Now as the moving pictures of the falling ceiling replayed in his mind, he thought to himself that maybe he should tell somebody about it. Maybe he should warn someone in the library. Maybe he could avert a disaster before it happened. That thought bugged him and he debated with himself whether he should say something to somebody about the calamity that was going to happen; on the other hand, maybe he should just keep silent.

After tossing that about in his mind, he finally decided not to say anything. *Why sound the alarm?* How could he possibly explain to anyone that he knew that the ceiling would come down? After all he didn't know when it was going to happen and if it didn't happen in a day or two then people would assume that he was just hallucinating and they would laugh at him; and once again he would appear to be a crackpot with an overactive imagination. An alarmist weirdo.

He had faced that situation before. When he told people about something that was going to happen nobody believed him—until it actually happened. And then they looked at him like he was some kind of freak who came out of the dark regions beyond normality and after that they avoided him. *So why go through that now? Why risk alienation and condemnation when everything was going so well?* Besides, in this, his latest vision, nobody got hurt. Maybe a few people got a little mussed up and a little wet; but nobody was seriously hurt. *So why raise a fuss?*

Thus, Henry had managed to rationalize his motivation for keeping his silence. At first, his conscience bothered him a little, but then a week passed and the ceiling was still hanging in place and the sprinkler pipe was still solid, so Henry was able to put the polemic out of his mind. He figured that the whole thing would just pass over like a gloomy cloud. But alas! It was not to be. This is what happened.

Sometime in the beginning of the second week after his fateful vision, Henry was walking with his chum Andrew. They had just come out of class together and were walking across the campus.

Andrew said, "Say Hen, why don't we take some time and study for the English Lit test that's coming on Thursday?"

"Okay, sounds good to me. Where shall we go?"

"How about the library?"

The brief mention of the word *library* was enough to send a chill up Henry's spine. Suddenly the picture of the soggy ceiling tiles and the spraying water shot back into his conscious mind. It was a brief replay of the vision that he had had the previous week. Since that vision, he avoided going into the library. That disaster hadn't happened yet. The ceiling was still up there, still in place; but Henry knew that it would fall sometime soon and he didn't want to be there when it happened.

"No, I don't want to go to the library."

"Why not? What's the matter with the library?"

"Well ..." said Henry tentatively stalling as he tried to come up with a reason for steering clear of the library. That wasn't easy because the library was an ideal place to study; quiet—well-lit, and roomy—so how could he avoid going there? "Why don't we go to the student center instead?"

"The student center's too noisy. The library's better."

"Yeah, but we'll want to talk and quiz each other. You can't talk in the library."

"Sure, we can. We can go to the reading room and take a couple of chairs in the corner. We'll talk quietly. We won't bother anyone and it'll be all right."

So, there it was: Andrew not only wanted to go to the library he wanted to sit in the reading room. That was the spot where the calamity was going to happen. Henry knew he didn't want to go there. He knew that if he went there, he would spend the whole time looking up at the ceiling, wondering when the overhead pipe would break, when the water would saturate the tiles and when the whole mess would come crashing down. It was going to happen. Henry knew that and he didn't want to be there when it did; but how could he not go? What could he say to Andrew? What could he say without telling about his visions? Andrew was waiting for Henry to explain himself; meanwhile they were walking toward the library.

Henry stopped walking. "Look Andrew, I just don't want to go to the library."

"Henry!" said an exasperated Andrew. "For Pete's, sake why not?"

Henry felt pressured. He had to come up with something, some sort of reason but he couldn't think of anything. His brain didn't work that fast.

"Well...I'm just afraid that something might happen there."

"Henry, it's the library. What the hell can happen in a library?"

"Well...something."

"What?"

Up against the force of Andrew's relentless determination to get an explanation, Henry blurted out, "I'm afraid the ceiling will fall down."

Andrew stood stone-still for a minute and looked at Henry in complete astonishment. He wasn't sure if he heard that last statement correctly. *Did Henry actually say that he was afraid the ceiling will fall down. Is that what he said?* He looked at Henry's face, into Henry's clear hazel eyes. *Was this guy pulling his leg or what?* Andrew couldn't be sure, because Henry seemed sincere.

"What did you say?"

Henry repeated his statement. Andrew just looked at him for the longest time, trying to decide if Henry was really serious or not. Finally, he said, "All right Henry, if you're going to be a nutcase about this then let's go to the student center to study."

With that, Andrew turned and headed to the student center. The two walked the rest of the way in silence. Henry could tell that Andrew was puzzled and a little annoyed by his insistence on avoiding the library, and Henry was dismayed and even a little upset with himself because he couldn't come up with a plausible reason for not going to the library.

He was also irritated that he had blurted out his latest vision, but at least it worked. Andrew had reluctantly agreed to humor Henry's strange request and so, unbeknownst to Andrew, they were avoiding a potential danger in the library.

They two got to the student center and settled in at an empty table to study Keats and Byron and Shelley. After about a half hour of quizzing each other on *Don Juan* and *La Belle Dame Sans Merci*, they had managed to put the incident about the library completely out of their minds and were focused on English literature.

They were now discussing Shelley's *Prometheus Unbound* when George and Kathy came into the student center and approached them.

"Hey guys," said George. "What are you two doing?"

"We're studying for the upcoming English Lit exam."

"Why here? Why not go to the library where it's quieter?"

"We were going to the library but Henry didn't want to go. He was afraid the ceiling was going to fall down."

"What?" said George and he looked back at Kathy. The both of them started to laugh. They took up seats and George said to Andrew, "You gotta tell us about this."

So, Andrew told George and Kathy about how Henry refused to go and study in the library because he was afraid that the ceiling would fall down.

"Sounds like Henry has turned into Chicken Little crying that the sky is falling down," said George.

The three started to laugh at poor Henry who could only sit there and try to take it like a good sport. The three were giggling and joking with Henry just sitting there trying to stoically endure their good-natured ridicule. At that moment, their friend Paul Galloway came rushing into the cafeteria. He saw his four friends sitting together and he immediately came over to them.

"You guys won't believe what just happened."

As soon as he approached them, Andrew and George and Kathy stopped laughing. They could see that Paul was agitated about something.

"What?" asked Andrew. "What just happened?"

"The ceiling in the library just crashed down."

Andrew and George and Kathy all turned in unison and they looked at Henry. They stared at Henry without saying a word. Henry felt the intensity of their relentless, unblinking scrutiny and knew that his reputation for being a typical, average college student had just evaporated. For Henry it was *déjà vu* all over again.

CHAPTER

After the library incident, word went around campus about Henry's premonition. But this time no one thought of Henry as a witch and he wasn't ostracized for being a freak. Still, life was not the same for poor Henry Gainsvort after that vision. Most of the students thought the whole thing was a big joke and they ribbed Henry at odd moments. Some of them ragged him about being a dark prognosticator and called him the college Nostradamus. Others joked about him having a crystal ball—some of the guys made reference to his crystal balls as a sexual innuendo. Most of this was in sport and just harmless kidding, but occasionally there were a few people who were more sarcastic and made snide remarks.

They teased him by asking silly questions like: *Who's going to be the next President? When will a big meteor hit the earth? Who's gonna win the game next Saturday? When will an earthquake hit California and drop Los Angeles into the Pacific Ocean?* And, *who's going to lose their virginity at the next frat party?*

Of course, these people were just pulling his leg and no one believed for a minute that Henry could actually see into the future, but they continued to goad him just to see what kind of zany answers he might come up with.

Henry, for his part, accepted their kidding with good grace and tried to go along with their relatively harmless mockery as a good sport, but deep down he was troubled because he knew that he had become a kind of weirdo in the eyes of his fellow students. Still, he had a consolation knowing that at least he wasn't an outcast nor had he turned into the leper of the campus; in fact, in an odd sort of way, Henry had become a sort of minor celebrity.

This was a strange experience for him because as a young man he had never attracted much interest and he always found comfort in being an average nobody. Now, however, he found that for the first time in his life, he was often the center of attention and he wasn't quite sure what to make of it.

Just as Henry was getting used to the glow of the limelight, however, it faded. His amazing prediction about the tumbling tiles eventually became ancient history, the jokes about being a soothsayer lost their edge, and Henry's profile dropped back into the contours of the woodwork. He was no longer the Nostradamus of Farleigh Dickinson and he reverted to being just plain old Henry Gainsvort. He retreated into the comfort of his former shell and went back his usual, mundane, humdrum lifestyle as if nothing had changed. For Henry, life went on as before.

Well, not quite, because unbeknownst to him something had changed and without warning, somebody came into his world and suddenly, for the first time in his life, Henry Gainsvort found love. It happened like this.

Henry was sitting alone in the cafeteria drinking a cup of coffee and reading a newspaper. He had his nose buried deep in the tabloid and was totally oblivious to anything else around him. He was so engrossed that he failed to notice when a fellow student, a beautiful woman, approached him. She came right up to him as silently as a cat and positioned herself before him. She just stood there and waited for him to look up from the pages of the paper, but his face was shielded from the outside world and he was totally unaware of her presence. Finally, after a full two minutes of waiting, she spoke his name. Shaken from the seclusion of his small world, he lowered the paper and looked up. He was taken completely by surprise to see the figure of a beautiful strawberry-blonde standing right before him. He recognized immediately that this was Tiffany Blaine.

Now Tiffany Blaine was the talk of the Farleigh Dickinson campus. Not only was she drop-dead gorgeous with a perfect hour-glass figure and a beautiful face framed with a mane of glowing strawberry-blonde hair—she certainly was a looker—but she also had money. Her father, Judson T. Blaine, was some sort of real-estate tycoon and he was rumored to be worth millions.

Tiffany had a big allowance and it showed: she wore clothes in the latest style, that sported designer labels from Saks, Bergdorf's, and Bloomingdales and she drove around in a shiny red Corvette. Her jewelry, which she treated as common baubles, was nothing less than the best of Fortunoff and Cartier.

Tiffany was also known to be a bit of a snob. She rarely associated with anyone on campus. She walked around with her nose in the air and had an attitude that suggested the rest of the student body belonged to the peasant class and, as such, was beneath her. With an attitude like that, it was a wonder that she enrolled in Farleigh-Dickinson in the first place, and not some posh ivy league school where she might find students of her social class and economic standing.

Well the truth was, that she regarded college as a chore, something to do and get over with. College was a necessity for common people who had to learn a trade so they could eventually graduate, then go out and get a job and earn money; but Tiffany felt that she didn't need to go to college because she already had money, so why bother to learn a trade? *Why not just sit home and enjoy Daddy's wealth? Why bother to go to any college?*

Why indeed? Well the reason that Tiffany found herself in college instead of on the beach in the Mediterranean was that her father insisted that she go to a school of higher learning. He may have felt that way because everyone her age was expected to go to college and get an education. It is also possible that his desire to see his daughter enroll in school and get an education was really an attempt to give her some purpose in life.

Tiffany, however, felt that she had enough purpose just keeping the department and jewelry stores in business, so there was no need to clutter her life with textbooks and studies. But her father controlled the purse strings and if he wanted her to go to college then she would comply if only to keep him happy. For Tiffany Blaine then, college was just a necessary nuisance that she had to endure as a way to placate her sugar-daddy father so she could continue to collect her allowance.

So, Tiffany Blaine enrolled in Farleigh Dickinson and took a major in liberal arts. She decided on this major because she figured that it would require the least amount of effort and concentration and might possibly be less boring than the other majors. Guidance counselors warned her that this major would not automatically open the doors to future employment but Tiffany dismissed their advice because finding a job was not a goal in her life. A job would entail work and that concept was abhorrent to her.

Henry had seen and heard about Tiffany Blaine, but their paths had never crossed and he had never spoken with her. Now in their last semester at college, they found themselves together in the same art history course. Neither was much interested in art history but they enrolled in the course to fulfill their humanities requirements.

Even though they were both in the same class, they didn't speak to each other. Henry always sat in the back of the class because it was the best place to be inconspicuous and go unnoticed. Tiffany always sat in the first row in front of the class so she could have her back to the rest of the students and avoid looking at them. Thus, Tiffany and Henry moved in decidedly separate orbits that only crossed paths when the art history class met twice a week. Still, in spite of their proximity to each other, they never spoke or even exchanged greetings.

That was why Henry was so completely taken by surprise to see the lovely, pristine, and socially inaccessible, Tiffany Blaine standing before him and actually addressing him by name. Henry just looked up at her and was completely dumbfounded. For a long moment he couldn't find his voice. *Was it possible that this exquisite goddess had actually descended from the heavens and lowered herself to his level? And was she actually addressing him, the lowly and inconsequential Henry Gainsvort, possibly as an equal? Was that even remotely within the realm of possibility?*

Apparently so, because there she was, standing before him, and lo-and-behold, she actually said his name a second time. This time, Henry was able to shake off his paralysis and find his voice. He said her name and uttered a few syllables of response, but he hesitated to say more because he was unsure how a mere mortal like himself should address a goddess.

Tiffany seemed unaffected by Henry's awkwardness. Apparently, she was used to this kind of stupefaction whenever she spontaneously addressed men of the lower classes.

"Henry, do you mind if I sit down? There is something I really must talk to you about."

Now this was stranger still. Not only had she approached and talked to him, but now she wanted to sit with him and—wonder of wonders—there was something she wanted to talk to him about. Again, Henry had trouble finding his voice, but she didn't wait for his reply. Instead, she immediately took up the chair beside him, assuming perhaps, that if he had a voice he would invite her to join him.

Once seated, she looked squarely at him, and he looked back into her beautiful brown eyes and smiled weakly. Henry wasn't sure what he had done to deserve such good fortune, and he suspected that she had mistaken him for somebody else and that at any moment she would stumble upon the error of her ways then rise up and depart as quickly as she arrived. But for that moment, she was there seated beside him, and he was happy to accept his serendipitous good fortune without questioning the winds of fate.

He said nothing, but waited politely for some sort of explanation as to why Tiffany Blaine had singled him out from all the others in the cafeteria. He still thought that there was some sort of mistake here, yet at the same time, he remembered that she had addressed him by name so she had to have some idea who he was. At any rate he was not about to question her motives. After all, why look a gift horse—or in this case, a gift strawberry-blonde bombshell—in the mouth when it is as captivating as Tiffany Blaine?

"Henry, I wanted to talk to you about our art history class."

He nodded. At the same time, he looked at her flawless skin, her beautiful red lips, and her clear brown eyes and he inhaled the delicate scent of her sweet floral perfume. He was becoming intoxicated by her very presence and he began to wonder to himself if this was really happening to him or if he was somehow dreaming the whole thing up. If he was dreaming, however, he knew that he didn't ever want to wake up.

"You know, Henry, we have an exam coming up in two weeks and I wondered if you are prepared for it."

"Well," said Henry with some hesitation. The truth was that he wasn't at all prepared for the upcoming exam. He hadn't even opened his textbook and had no intention of doing so. His idea of preparation involved opening the book the night before the exam and reading furiously, trying to cram enough knowledge into his brain to carry to carry him through the exam hopefully to a passing grade. That was his usual *modus operandi* but he decided against telling her that, because he suspected that if he did, she would look upon him as a laggard, which, in fact, he was. It occurred to him that she had the impression that he was somehow knowledgeable about art history and if she found out differently she might just go away.

So, he tried to think of some sort of response which would be agreeable to her sensibilities and at the same time cast himself as a conscientious student of art history.

"Well," he said again. "I have been following along with the lectures and perusing the textbook, but I still want to go back and go over the material carefully, reviewing my notes and rereading the textbook with more intensity. That, I believe, will give me a thorough grasp of all the concepts and theories involved."

Henry realized that he was treading on thin ice here. After all, he wanted to appear knowledgeable and studious so she would remain interested in him, but at the same time, he couldn't appear too authoritative in case she decided to ask him all sorts of questions—questions that he couldn't possibly answer—about the course material.

As Henry said all this, he looked carefully at Tiffany's face for any possible reaction or nuance of expression that might tell him if he was saying the kind of things that she wanted to hear; but her face betrayed nothing and Henry was at a loss as to how to continue. He paused to see if she had any response, but she just sat there next to him and he sensed that she was waiting patiently for him to say more. So, he launched into further artifice.

"I'm planning to start my real, hard-core studying this week, possibly tonight. Then, by the time I have to take the exam, I'll be thoroughly prepared to tackle it."

As he was saying that, Henry thought to himself that perhaps he should have leveled with her and openly declared that he had never been much of a student and in the past he only studied enough to get a passing grade. It would be so much easier at that point to just come clean and confess that he hadn't paid any attention to the lectures nor taken notes nor even opened the textbook, and he didn't know Egyptian art from subway graffiti and hadn't the foggiest idea when the Renaissance began or ended—if, in fact, it did end—or who Caravaggio was, or why the Greeks decorated their vases with paintings of naked men.

He wanted to be honest about all of that, but at the same time something deep within told Henry that this was not the time for the unvarnished truth and that if he wanted to keep Tiffany sitting there beside him, he had to resort to fabrication in order to cloak himself in the mantle of scholarship. Perhaps that would keep her interested enough to stay beside him just a little longer so that he could continue to inhale her perfume, listen to her melodious voice and look at the light that bounced off her beautiful strawberry-blonde hair.

Well his subterfuge seemed to work because Tiffany didn't get up and go away. Instead she replied, "Oh Henry, that is sooo impressive. I knew that you were real, smart and studious when I first saw you in class."

Now this was a bit of a surprise because Henry had always had the impression that Tiffany Blaine had never even noticed him.

She continued: "You know that I find art history rather complicated and try as I might, I don't think I really understand what it's all about."

This also struck Henry as being rather curious; after all, art history was relatively straight forward—it certainly wasn't rocket science—and there didn't seem to be anything complicated about it; but he kept his peace and didn't say anything because he didn't want to appear argumentative. He just nodded as if he understood and agreed with what she was saying.

"Well," she continued. "Since you're such a good student and are so smart, I was wondering if maybe the two of us could study together and you could help me learn the material."

Henry looked hard into her eyes to see if she was really serious or not. She said this in the sweetest possible voice and her face looked so innocent and charming, yet Henry couldn't bring himself to believe that she really wanted to study with him. After all, in all his school years, he had never appeared as a paragon of scholastic aptitude and it was difficult to believe that anyone thought of him in that light. But now here he was sitting next to the scrumptious Tiffany Blaine and she had openly declared that she wanted to study with him, so why question this sudden blessing from heaven? Better to go along and enjoy the ride, and he replied that he would be glad to help her study.

Yet, at the same time, Henry realized that he had a serious problem: since he had never looked between the covers of his textbook, he didn't have a clue as to what art history was all about. If they started to study now, Tiffany would see that he was a fish out of the academic waters and a big faker to boot. His best tactic then, would be to stall for time, to put off the study session until he could hit the books and get his act together.

"Well Tiffany, I'd certainly like to study with you. I think that's a real good idea; but I can't do it today. I have something else that I really must do. How's about we get together later on in the week? Say Thursday afternoon?"

"But Henry," she whined in a petulant, cute-little-hurt-kitten voice, this is Monday and Thursday is such a long time away. Couldn't we get together sooner?"

Well, of course, Thursday was only three days away, but Tiffany made it sound as if those three days were a geological epoch beyond the limits of human endurance and Henry, moved by the urgency in her voice, responded: "Well how about tomorrow then? Suppose we get together tomorrow at this time?"

Her face brightened up. "Gee Henry, that would be great! Where shall we meet? The library?"

The mere mention of the word *library* was enough to make Henry shiver. He remembered his vision of the falling ceiling and even though he knew that was a one-time incident confined to the reading room, he was still wary about going into that place. "No, not the library; how about meeting here? Then we can have coffee or a snack in case we get hungry."

"Oh, Henry, that is a brilliant idea. You are so clever. You know, I think it will be so much fun studying together, and I know I'm going to learn a lot from you." She glanced down at her gold wrist watch. "Oh! It's getting late and I have to be running along, but I'll see you here tomorrow at three. Bye for now."

With that, she shot up from her chair and started walking toward the door; but about half way to the exit, she turned back to him, flashed a big smile and gave a cheery wave. Then she did an about-face and walked through the doors.

Henry watched her walk away, turn back and wave, then exit through the doors to the outside and all the time that he watched her, he wondered to himself why the gray clouds overhead so unexpectedly parted to allow this ray of golden, delightful, good fortune to shine upon him. What had he done to generate the attention and enthusiasm of the most beautiful woman on campus? He didn't know, but he wasn't about to question it.

Henry had one more class that afternoon. After it was over, he drove home, had supper, then immediately retired to his room. He knew that on the following day he would meet with Tiffany and she would expect him to know all about Egyptian sculpture and painting and architecture and he didn't want to disappoint her. So, he pulled out his art history textbook and started to feverishly read about the great works of ancient Egypt.

He plowed through the text describing the Old, Middle, and New Kingdoms of ancient Egypt and about the Armana period, in the hope that he could acquire enough expertise to appear knowledgeable for their study session the next day.

Now all this material was new and unfamiliar to Henry, and at first, he found it rather tedious going because he really had no interest in art and scant knowledge of history, but he plodded on and for the first time in his life, Henry became a master of self-discipline. He read and re-read that first chapter making a supreme effort to digest the essentials; all this because he wanted to appear like a shining knight of scholasticism before his fair lady, the beautiful Tiffany Blaine.

Henry became so engrossed in his reading that he totally lost himself in his studies. It wasn't until he looked up at the clock and saw it was past midnight that he realized how hard and concentrated his effort had been. He had been studying for over five hours without taking a break. That amazed him because he had never put in such a long study session, and never in all his young life had he worked so hard at a single task. He was stunned that he had actually been able to concentrate so hard that night. But then, he thought to himself, he never had Tiffany Blaine for inspiration before.

The next day, Henry and Tiffany were to meet in the cafeteria for their first study get-together. About an hour before their scheduled meeting, Henry found a vacant classroom in a hall adjacent to the cafeteria. He ducked into it and sat down at a nearby desk. He wanted to use this last hour to review all the stuff he had read about the previous evening so that the facts of Egyptian Art would be fresh in his mind when he met with Tiffany.

He opened his textbook and delved again into the world of Ancient Egypt and again he became so absorbed in the study of art history that he lost track of time. When he glanced up at the wall clock he saw that it was five minutes before the hour. It was almost time to meet Tiffany. It wouldn't do to keep the elegant lady waiting on their first date. He knew that he'd have to get a move on if he didn't want to be late. Quickly he gathered up his stuff and made a mad dash to the cafeteria.

Henry got to the cafeteria two minutes before three and was relieved to see that Tiffany hadn't arrived yet. He took a seat at the same table he had on the previous day and he waited.

As he sat there waiting, he thought to himself that he had done a good job studying and he felt confident in his grasp of Egyptian Art. He had only read about Ancient Egypt because that was all that was covered in the first chapter of the textbook; but suppose, just on a whim, Tiffany asked him about other periods in art history? Suppose she asked about Roman Art or about the Gothic period? What then? Then he would be sunk; his ignorance would be glaring because he hadn't had time to learn about any other kind of art. Maybe then she would see him for what he was, a scholastic charlatan. Oh well, he could only hope that their first study session would be limited to the subject matter in that first chapter and he wouldn't have to cross the bridge into the realms of opaque, uncertainty.

By ten minutes after the hour Tiffany had not arrived. Henry continued to wait. By twenty minutes after the hour Tiffany was still a no-show. Henry began to wonder if maybe he hadn't gotten his wires crossed and gotten the place or the time wrong and he cursed himself for not having the foresight to get Tiffany's cellphone number when they arranged the meeting the previous day. Well it was too late to cry over spilt milk; the only thing he could do now was wait.

And wait he did. Soon it was three-thirty and still there was no sign of Tiffany. Henry was beginning to wonder if he was being stood up; but at that very moment Tiffany rushed in. When he saw her come through the doors, Henry stood up to greet her.

She looked lovely. She was wearing Navy-blue slacks that had a silken sheen and she had on a powder-blue blouse with the collar turned up and the front open down to the third button. She wore a silver chain around her neck and a silver bracelet around one wrist and silver watch around the other, and had elegant, silver pendant earrings dangling from her ears.

As she came closer, he became more impressed with how lovely she looked and how expensive her tastes were. He was wearing loafers, chino slacks and a knit polo shirt. He felt that he must look awfully drab in comparison to her.

She saw him the minute she came into the cafeteria and immediately came over to him. Before he could say anything, she gushed out, "Oh Henry, I am sooo sorry for being this late. I imagine that you are furious with me for being sooo delinquent, and maybe you should be, but the truth is that it wasn't really my fault. Let me tell you what happened.

"The truth is I left my house way early so I wouldn't be late. Well, as I was driving over here I realized that I had just oodles of time and I thought that on the way I could stop off at my jewelry store and pick up the bracelet that I had ordered. The jewelry store was on my way—well almost; I only needed to take a small detour—and I figured I could bop in and pick it up and still toodle over here without being late."

She said all this is a rapid-fire verbal barrage and it all came out so fast and with such vigor that Henry couldn't get a tiny word in edgewise; all he could do was stand there and take it like a helpless target. When she got to the part about the bracelet, Tiffany raised her right hand and gave it a shake to show off the expensive new bracelet wrapped around her wrist.

"The jewelry store had phoned me earlier to say it was ready, and I figured how long does it take to pick up a tiny package and run my credit card through the machine? Well when I got there, sure enough they had it ready; but you'll never guess what happened when I tried it on."

She paused then to see if Henry had some sort of guess as to what happened in the jewelry store, but poor Henry was a total blank, so she continued.

"Well, when I tried it on, I found that the clasp was loose. Can you imagine that? I mean this thing cost enough and they have the nerve to stick me with a junky clasp. Well, I certainly wasn't going to take the thing with a bum clasp, so I insisted that they replace it right then and there. Needless to say, I had to wait for them to get it right. So, what I thought would be a five-minute stop took over thirty minutes. Oh! I hope you're not too angry with me Henry. I promise I won't ever let it happen again."

With that she reached up and gently stroked the side of his cheek. It seemed that she was positively purring. Of course, Henry couldn't possibly be upset with her after that and he said that no it really didn't matter and he was glad that she finally arrived. With that they sat down and opened their text books to study.

"Now Henry, I must confess that I know absolutely nothing about art history and I am depending upon you to teach me all there is to know, sooo you tell me everything and enlighten me. I want to drink from the deep fountain of your knowledge."

Henry was a little shaken. He had certainly never considered himself to be a fountain of knowledge and her unbridled confidence in his ability to explain all about art history kind of unnerved him; and inwardly he wasn't sure that he that he would be equal to her mandate—after all he had only introduced himself to the subject the previous night—but he felt that now all he could do was try. He turned to the first chapter and started to talk about the predynastic period in Ancient Egypt.

His first words were hesitant and a little unsure, but in a few minutes, he found his confidence. All the facts, data, and material that he had so assiduously studied the night before came back to him and he began to speak with more authority. He launched into the Old Kingdom and talked about the pyramids and the artworks that adorned the tomb walls. He talked about the great Sphinx and other important works of sculpture. Occasionally he glanced up from his book to look at Tiffany and see how she was taking all of his discourse.

He saw that she was looking back at him with wide-eyed attention. It seemed that she was hanging on his every word. Whatever he was doing and saying was apparently working, so with added confidence, he continued his lecture and tried to maintain the scholastic spell that he had so effectively created. He talked on about the first Intermediate Period and then the Middle Kingdom and Tiffany continued to sit there ostensibly absorbed by his every word.

Just as he was launching the New Kingdom, Tiffany glanced down at her watch and interrupted him.

"Oh Henry! This is sooo fascinating and I am learning sooo very much, but I see that it is almost four o'clock and I have to be going. Try not to be upset with me, but Daddy is having a dinner party tonight for some of his business associates and he wants me to be there. It's going to be at seven and I have oodles to do to get ready. I have to bathe and do my hair and nails and…well, you know how long it takes women to get ready."

Henry nodded, but actually he had no idea how long it took women to get ready for anything; and when he looked at Tiffany he thought that she already looked perfect so she really didn't have to do anything to change herself. But if she said she had oodles to do to get ready, then who was he to question it? He simply nodded again.

"But Henry I really did enjoy this study get-together and I learned sooo much. Maybe we can pick up where we left off tomorrow at this time. Do you think that we could do that? You're sooo smart and I really want to study with you."

"Well of course Tiffany, if you want to. I'd be happy to meet with you tomorrow."

"Oh, you're such a dear." And with that she leaned over and kissed him lightly on the cheek. Then she bolted up and darted toward the door, but once again, at the halfway point she turned and gave Henry a big smile and a cheery wave. Then she turned again and disappeared into the atmosphere like an ephemeral sprite.

Henry continued to sit there mesmerized, in total stupefaction. The study session and the abrupt parting had passed so quickly that it hadn't had time to really register in his brain. All he knew was that something wonderful had happened to him and that it was likely to happen again at the same time and place tomorrow. He sat there for a few minutes trying to let it all soak in.

Then suddenly the realization struck him that if he and Tiffany were going to study art history again, he would have to go home and hit the books again so he would be prepared to discuss the next chapter. He gathered up his textbook and notebook then headed to the parking lot to his car.

He got into the car and started his drive back home. He knew that he was in for another night of study, but that didn't bother him. If learning art history was the price he had to pay to be with the exquisite Tiffany Blaine, then he was prepared to pay it. As he drove, he thought about her: about how beautiful she was; her sparkling hair; her clear, bright eyes and the scent of her lovely delicate perfume. And as Henry thought about her, it occurred to him that he must be falling in love.

CHAPTER

Now Henry and Tiffany met for their study session the next day and the next. In fact, they continued to meet almost every day for the next three weeks. In order to prepare for their study sessions, Henry had to hit the textbook each and every night to bone up on the subject matter that they would go over during their study encounters. Thus, without actually realizing it, Henry was turning himself into a first-class scholar of art history.

Gradually they added other activities to these study meetings. They did lunch together and once they went to the movies. During all this time, Henry couldn't believe how lucky he was to have found a girl as beautiful as Tiffany Blaine. He thought to himself that he must be living in a kind of surrealistic, dream-like state; and all the time he was with Tiffany, he thought to himself that this couldn't actually be happening to him. After all, he was the lowly Henry Gainsvort, a veritable toad in the social world, and she was the rich princess. There was no way that this could be happening to him, yet, in fact it was.

Up till now, he had never thought of himself as anyone out of the ordinary—certainly not a ladies' man—but now with Tiffany's attention, Henry began to see himself in a new light. Maybe, after all, he had that certain something, a kind of hidden masculine charisma, that women admired; and for the first time in his life, Henry Gainsvort began to see himself as a little special in the world and man beyond the definition of average.

Their relationship seemed to be blossoming and while it was happening, Henry felt like he was riding the glory train to sublime ecstasy; he didn't know how he managed to get on it, but all he knew was that he was enjoying the ride of his life and he never, ever, wanted it to stop.

Henry couldn't know it at the time, but this wonderful burst of springtime love, his glory train to paradise, was about to carry him into very strange territory. This is what happened when he got there.

The semester was more than half over and Henry and Tiffany had been seeing a lot of each other. Their relationship started with Tiffany's apparent desire to learn about art history. In an effort to help her, and as an excuse to continue meeting with her, Henry had become a model student of art history. But now it seemed like their relationship was progressing to another, higher, level. They were doing more and more together. Henry was truly in love, thoroughly captivated and enchanted by the beautiful Tiffany Blaine. He assumed that she had similar feelings toward him.

One day in the middle of the week, after art history class, Henry walked Tiffany to the college parking lot where her shiny red corvette was sitting. She unlocked the car and he opened the door for her. At that moment she turned to him.

"Henry," she cooed. "Daddy is throwing a little get-together this weekend at our summer cottage in the Hamptons. Why don't you come out and spend the weekend with us? This way you could meet my father. I've told him all about you, and he's been dying to meet you."

"You told him about me?"

"Well of course!"

"What did you tell him?"

"Well, I told him how smart you are and about the things that you do."

"Things? What things?"

"Well, about...well, things. Now come on. Say you'll come out and spend the weekend with us."

Henry agreed. Of course, he wanted to spend the weekend with Tiffany. During the course of their budding relationship, Henry and Tiffany had done a number of things together but they had never been really alone. Oh, they had lunch together and they took in a movie, and then it was just the two of them; but there had always been other people around. They always got together in a public place, so they were never really alone. They never had those private moments when it was just the two of them.

But now, Henry thought to himself that maybe all that was about to change. Maybe during this weekend in the Hamptons, in the quiet secluded country, they might find a few moments where they could sneak off and spend some quiet time alone together—just the two of them with nobody else around. Maybe that way, their relationship could move toward closer intimacy.

Henry also realized that he was going to have the opportunity to meet Tiffany's father. He had heard about Mr. Blaine, the successful real-estate tycoon, but Tiffany had never actually talked about him. Well, now Henry would have to chance to meet the man. And of course, Mr. Blaine would meet Henry. Tiffany said that her father was anxious to meet him, and Henry had to wonder to himself, why? What had she told her father about him and what was Mr. Blaine expecting of him?

On Saturday morning, Henry drove out to the Blaine residence in the Hamptons. Henry had never been to the Hamptons before, but he heard that it was the playground for the rich and famous. He heard, for example, that the famous director Steven Spielberg had a place somewhere in the Hamptons, and the actor Alec Baldwin was also rumored to have a house out there too.

On route to the Blaine summer cottage, Henry drove along roads that were new and unfamiliar to him, but he was guided by the directions that Tiffany had written out for him and they proved to be accurate. It took him well over two hours to find the locale where the Blaine summer cottage was nestled, but eventually he made it. He turned off the main road and went along a few secluded back roads and finally turned up a long driveway that was lined on either side with tall trees. At the end of the driveway, Henry came to a large, expansive white house.

Henry stopped the car and looked at the edifice in amazement. The house was huge. Was this what Tiffany called their *summer cottage*? When Tiffany mentioned summer cottage, Henry had envisioned something like a modest six-room house just off the beach. But as Henry gaped at this place he saw that it was more like a country club with a sprawling mansion, auxiliary buildings and expansive surrounding grounds. It looked as big as the Farleigh Dickinson campus. Henry felt as if he had somehow landed in a foreign country. Well, in a way it was a foreign country to Henry, because now he was in the land of the wealthy gentry. This was a heady atmosphere that he had never breathed before.

He suddenly felt drab and plain and very much out of place and he wondered to himself if maybe he had made a mistake in coming here. He had the impulse to turn his car around and beat a hasty retreat back to his home where everything was humble, simple and familiar. He might have done just that but he was stopped by the sight of Tiffany who at that moment came running up to him. She saw his arrival and immediately came out of the house to greet him.

"Oh Henry, I'm sooo glad you made it. Did you have any trouble finding us?"

"No, your directions were very clear. Is this your *summer cottage*?"

"Yes, do you like it?"

"Yes, it's very...er...nice." Henry had to grope for an adjective. After all, where do you find the words to describe a mansion that seems like the Taj Mahal of the Hamptons?

"Come on, I'll show you around."

She started to lead him away, but Henry resisted.

"Wait a minute Tiffany; I shouldn't leave my car sitting there in the driveway. I should move it shouldn't I? And what about my suitcase? Shouldn't I take it inside?"

"Oh, don't worry about those things. Just leave the keys in your car. I'll have James, our chauffeur, move your car to the back and William the butler will bring your bag up to your room."

James the chauffeur! William the butler! Tiffany had servants as well as a stately mansion! The thought of all this luxury was enough to drive Henry into a state of robotic stupefaction and he might have remained rooted to the spot transfixed like a statue beside his car but Tiffany pulled him by the elbow toward the house. As he started walking with her, he glanced back; he wasn't sure he should allow the servants to touch his car or his bag lest they become infected with commonality, the blight of the peasant class, but Tiffany was already pulling him with carefree indifference, so he had no choice but to abandon his possessions to the care of the Blaine staff.

Tiffany escorted Henry around the grounds. She showed him the tennis courts with the tennis house and the pool with the pool house. The pool house was ostensibly created so people could change into their bathing suits and get fresh towels, have a drink at the bar or use the sauna or steam room before taking a tip in the huge outdoor pool. Henry and Tiffany walked inside and Henry noted that the pool house was bigger than the house that he lived in.

After seeing the pool house, they wandered about the rest of the grounds. As they walked about, Henry felt like he was visiting a national park. The Blaine property was so big and sprawling. The lawn looked like a lush green carpet and all the bushes and shrubs were manicured and trimmed with sculptural finesse. Henry was amazed that a single family could have so much money and so much luxury.

Eventually, after they had wandered about for a time, they headed back to the manor house and they entered a room which Tiffany called the sunroom. The room was crowded with about a dozen people. Some were standing about holding drinks and chatting, others were seated at nearby tables eating and talking. All were elegantly dressed, all stylishly clad in country club attire. Henry had the impression that he had suddenly stepped into a movie set for *The Great Gatsby*.

Still leading him by the elbow, Tiffany said, "Come on Henry. I see they've already started serving lunch. Don't expect a sumptuous meal. This is just simple fare that we've put out for a casual lunch."

Henry and Tiffany walked over to the end of the buffet table where the plates, napkins and utensils were stacked. With Tiffany in the lead, they made their way along the table and dished food from the gleaming silver pans onto their plates. As Henry surveyed the assortment of trays and pans before him, he recalled Tiffany's declaration that this was but simple fare. *Simple fare!* thought Henry to himself, *if this was simple then did what did Tiffany consider to be an elaborate meal?*

When they had their plates of food, Tiffany led the way to a small side table where they put down their plates. Then they walked over to the bar for drinks. Tiffany took a bottle of Perrier; Henry took the same and they started back to the table where their plates of food lay, but before they reached the table they encountered a gaunt gentleman clad in a lemon-colored silk blazer and light green slacks.

Tiffany, of course, knew him. "Mr. Sinclair!"

"Ah Tiffany. It's always so nice to see you, and as always you look beautiful!"

"Thank you, Mr. Sinclair, you're always so sweet. Mr. Sinclair, I'd like you to meet a very good friend of mine. This is Henry Gainsvort. Henry and I are both in our senior year at Farleigh Dickinson."

The man made a slight nod in Henry's direction and extended his hand.

"So, you're at the University with Tiffany. What is your course of study?"

"I'm majoring in accounting sir."

"Ah, accounting!" exclaimed Mr. Sinclair with what seemed to be the light of recognition. "So, you are preparing to enter into the competitive world of business and high finance I assume."

"Yes sir," said Henry with a slight nod. Henry said that to be agreeable but, actually up till now, he hadn't given any thought as to what he wanted to do with accounting when he graduated. Henry had only chosen accounting as his major because it was the first course listed in the school catalog and it seemed like a straight forward subject, one that he thought he could grasp with a minimum amount of effort.

"Well, that's good young man. Business and finance; those are the areas to get into because those are the fields that make up capitalism and capitalism is engine that drives the civilized world of business and commerce. And if you're going someplace, anyplace, then you want to be in the driver's seat. You agree?"

Henry nodded politely even though he had no idea what the man was talking about. Encouraged by Henry's nod of agreement, Mr. Sinclair launched into a didactic prolix about the importance of fresh, creative thinking in the competitive world of the free market in today's civilization. He droned on and on and Henry did his best to try to follow the man's discourse with attention and even feigned interest, but Mr. Sinclair used so many obscure metaphors, like monetary policy being the forge of economics, or vice versa, and marketing strategy being the transmission and drive shaft of product development that Henry wasn't sure if the man was talking about capitalism or applied mechanics.

Still, he listened with as much interest as he could possibly muster because he recognized that Mr. Sinclair was genuinely trying to offer advice and counsel to a young man who was about to go out into the business world. The only trouble was that Henry had no idea what kind of advice the man had to offer other than taking command of the wheel, revving up to high gear, and never down-shifting to neutral.

As he stood there trying his best to listen politely, Henry had the unpleasant feeling that Mr. Sinclair was just warming up to his subject and might possibly go on to talk for at least an hour or so. Indeed, he might have done just that except that Tiffany mercifully interrupted him to point out that their food was waiting at a nearby table and they had to eat it before it got cold. Mr. Sinclair nodded and they excused themselves, but when the two turned to leave, Mr. Sinclair touched Henry's elbow.

"Let me give you just one last word of advice," he said to Henry. "Subscribe to *Barron's* and read it faithfully, cover-to-cover every week. That will give you the background knowledge that you need to navigate in today's cutthroat business world."

Henry thanked Mr. Sinclair for his advice even though he had no idea what *Barron's* was—although he assumed that it was some sort of business publication. Henry and Tiffany went over to their table where they sat down and started eating. The food was very good and Henry was beginning to enjoy himself just sitting there at the table with Tiffany when a full, resonant voice boomed from behind them.

"Well Tiffany, it looks like your friend found our little hide-away in the boondocks."

Henry turned to see where this new and unexpected voice came from. A tall, slightly overweight man with thinning black hair was standing beside them. He had approached them so quietly that Henry wasn't even aware of his presence until he spoke.

"Oh, hello Daddy." Tiffany rose up from her chair to greet the man. She leaned up and kissed her father lightly on the cheek. "Daddy, this is Henry, the boy I've told you so much about."

Judson Blair cut an impressive figure. He was dressed in white slacks and a rose-colored silk sportscoat. Under the sportscoat he had on a white silk shirt and an ascot. He looked the very picture of the lord of the manor. With Tiffany's introduction, he smiled graciously and extended his hand. Henry rose from his chair and responded to Mr. Blaine's overture with a handshake and a weak smile. Blaine's handshake was firm and assured and Henry tried to match it.

"Well Henry, it is a pleasure to welcome you to our summer home. Tiffany's told me a lot about you. I certainly hope that you'll enjoy spending the weekend with us."

The older Blaine seemed genuinely pleased to meet Henry, and Henry wondered what Tiffany had said about him and what he might have to live up to.

"Well Henry, maybe after you have lunch, Tiffany will take you outside to enjoy the afternoon. You might want to play a little tennis or maybe take a dip in the pool. But later, perhaps after dinner, you and I can get together for a little chat. I'd like to talk to you about a project that I think you might find interesting. Now, however, I'll leave you to your lunch, but I'm looking forward to talking with you later."

And with that short, cryptic speech, Mr. Blaine turned and made his exit. Tiffany and Henry sat down again at their table and continued with their lunch. As they were eating, Henry thought to himself that Judson Blaine seemed like a very nice man, yet at the same time, Henry wondered to himself why the older man seemed so eager to chat with him and what sort of project did he have in mind that he thought would be interesting to a young, inexperienced, pedestrian fellow like young Henry.

They finished their lunch, then got up and Tiffany led Henry around the room to mingle with the other guests who were still milling about engaged in idle chatter. Henry tried his best to talk with the people, but it was apparent from their conversation that he was not of their class. They were all well-fixed with bulging bank accounts and a plethora of assets and even though they treated Henry with friendliness and courtesy, he felt a little out of place among them. He imagined himself to be a poor church mouse among the fat cats. He felt awkward and wished that somehow, he could crawl into a safe crevasse in the woodwork, but Tiffany was there at his side so there could be no escape. After about an hour of mingling, the afternoon fete played out and most of the people left ostensibly to pursue other interests.

Tiffany took Henry outside for a little stroll.

As they were walking aimlessly about, Tiffany asked, "Well Henry are you enjoying yourself?"

"Oh yes I am, Tiffany." Henry tried to sound enthusiastic, but in truth he had felt awkward and self-conscious from the moment that he stepped out of his car. Yet, he couldn't tell her that; after all she had been kind enough to invite him and he didn't want to hurt her feelings. *How could she understand his feelings of inferiority? How could she know what it was like to be a peasant among the upper crust?* She had been born and lived in this rich, rarified atmosphere all her life, so she couldn't possibly understand his feelings of inadequacy.

They decided to spend the rest of the afternoon at the pool. They went to the pool house and changed—the Blaines had spare bathing suits in assorted sizes for their guests—then jumped into the pool. For the next couple of hours, they had a grand time, cavorting and splashing about in the water. There were a few other guests lounging around on recliners on the pool deck, but Henry and Tiffany had the water to themselves.

When evening came around they went back to the house to change for dinner. Henry put on his blue blazer, gray slacks, with a striped tie—a common uniform for the typical college student. Then he went downstairs to join the guests who had recently arrived.

Before dinner, the guests gathered in a room beside the main dining room for cocktails. Tiffany hadn't come down yet, so Henry found himself alone among the well-heeled guests. His good conscious told him that he should mingle if only to appear well-mannered and polite, but somehow, he dreaded the thought of trying to make idle conversation with a bunch of people that he had nothing in common with. Instead he grabbed a white wine and sat in a corner by himself and waited for Tiffany to arrive.

Shortly thereafter, Tiffany entered the room and when he saw her, Henry rose from his seat. She looked lovely. She was wearing a white flowered dress with a frilly skirt and a top that left her shoulders bare. She had a string of iridescent pearls around her neck and large pearl button earrings clipped to her ears. Henry felt a rapture of delight grip his heart as he looked at her. He immediately walked up to her and took her hand. She smiled back at him. He was about to tell her how lovely she looked and how glad he was to see her, when the butler announced that dinner was being served.

All the guests then walked into the main dining room where the butler directed each person to an assigned seat. Henry had hoped that he could sit next to Tiffany during dinner, but instead he found himself positioned between two older women somewhere at the midpoint of the table. Tiffany was at the far end.

The woman on Henry's right was a large lady with plump, flushed cheeks. She was dressed in an organdy gown festooned with so many frills and ruffles that her dress seemed to have more fabric in it than a military parachute. During dinner, she talked to Henry about her hobby which was raising orchids. She told him that she had over sixteen different and distinct species that she cultivated and then she proceeded to list and describe each specie in exact detail and tell how she fertilized her precious posies with fermented African manure—which was expensive but worth it—because it made her orchids so hearty and beautiful that they garnered all sorts of awards and accolades. Then she proceeded to go through the litany of the many blue ribbons, trophies and commendations that she had collected in a multitude of international flower shows.

The woman on his left was no less monotonous. She was wearing a navy gown that was bedecked with an assortment of glass beads and baubles. She looked like she had walked through a crystal chandelier and taken half of it with her. She was emaciated and pale, with an ashen complexion. She had a thick layer of pasty makeup on her face and she looked like death warmed over. She talked to Henry about her health, which she declared was in such a precarious state that she was afraid that she might keel over at any moment. She added that her digestion was so bad that she could not eat meat because it made her constipated and that necessitated administering frequent enemas. Now, she declared, she ate only vegetables which improved her regularity but which also gave her gas.

Seated between his two tedious dinner companions Henry suffered through the five-course meal wondering if he had died and gone to social hell. After what seemed like an interminable time, dinner did eventually end and the guests left the table to congregate in another room. Henry immediately sought out Tiffany hoping at last that he and she might sneak off somewhere for some quiet time alone. Indeed, he had just approached her and was about to suggest that very idea when Mr. Blaine came up to them.

CHAPTER

"Ah Henry," he said. "Did you enjoy our modest little dinner?"

Henry lied demurely that he did although he thought to himself that the dinner was a far cry from being modest or little.

"Well, that's good. You know, I was thinking that now might be a good time for our little chat. What do you say? Are you up for it?"

What could Henry say to that? He wanted to be alone with Tiffany, but here was his host, the lord of the manor, beckoning him on to other things; how could he say no? Still he looked to Tiffany hoping that she might object and tell her daddy that she wanted to be alone with her young man.

Instead she said, "Well I see that you two men want to put your heads together to talk about business and big deals and high finance. Things a woman can't possibly understand. Well, who am I to stand in your way when important projects are on the horizon? So, I'll leave you two intellectuals alone so you can do some male bonding. I'm sure you'll have a lot to chat about."

Henry felt that his ship had just been torpedoed. Now there was nothing to do but follow Mr. Blaine into the world of big deals and business projects, and so he let Mr. Blaine lead him out of the room and away from Tiffany.

Mr. Blaine escorted Henry down the hall away from the noise of the other guests. As they were walking in the hall, Henry thought it curious that Mr. Blaine would want to have a chat with him. After all, judging by appearances alone, they didn't seem to have anything in common so what could they possibly have to chat about? The only thing that Henry knew anything about was art history and somehow, Mr. Blaine didn't like the type to be interested in the religious symbolism in Gothic architecture or the aesthetic significance of Marcel Duchamp's Dadaesque urinal.

They came to a large room at the end of the hall. The two entered it, and Mr. Blaine closed the huge double doors behind them. Now they were alone together in a room that looked like some kind of library/study. Henry looked around to assess his surroundings and as he was looking up at the ornate ceiling and the magnificent stained-glass light fixture in the center, Mr. Blaine called out to him.

"Come over here Henry; I want you to see this."

Henry dutifully walked over to a large table. On the table was some sort of model of a city. It looked like a layout for a miniature railroad except there were no trains.

"Well Henry, what do you think of this?"

Henry had no idea what he was looking at. It was a model of a city obviously. A miniature city with Lilliputian buildings and tiny trees and bushes and diminutive statues of people walking on small representations of sidewalks weaving between the buildings. *But what city was it?* Henry was sure it wasn't Manhattan, nor Jersey City, and it didn't look like Brooklyn or Queens—at least as far as Henry could tell; but then he had never seen those places from the air so how could he really know what they looked like? Thus, Henry had no idea if he was looking at a model of some real, existing city or a doll-house version of some imaginary metropolis that had no counterpart in the real world. *And why was it here? Was this Mr. Blaine's hobby, playing with miniature towns?*

"Well, what do you think Henry?"

Henry didn't know what to think, but he could see that Mr. Blaine was waiting for some sort of response so Henry said, "Oh it's very impressive sir. Yes sir, very impressive."

"Yes, I think so, and I'm glad that you think so also. Do you know what it is?"

Henry shook his head, but said nothing.

"This is a dream in the making. This is the ideal modern metropolis. What do you think of that?"

"Oh sir! It's...er...very...impressive. Yes sir, very impressive."

"Yes, my thoughts exactly. I'm glad that you share my enthusiasm."

At this point Henry had a sickly premonition in the pit of his stomach that they might spend the rest of the evening going back and forth telling each other how impressive was this thing before them—whatever it was—and that each was glad that the other was equally impressed. *How long could this game continue?* Henry asked himself. He decided to push another pawn forward.

"Sir, exactly what is this? I mean sir, that I know it's a city; but I don't seem to recognize it. I mean, sir, what city is this?" Henry didn't want to appear impertinent so he peppered his questions with the word "sir" whenever he could.

"Henry, what you see before you is Blainesville. Now what do you think?"

"Well sir, that is very impressive. Indeed, it is. But...er...where exactly is Blainesville? I don't think I've ever been there."

Henry said that softly, hoping not to appear too ignorant nor too impolite. Mr. Blaine only chuckled at Henry's remark.

"Well, of course, you haven't my boy. That's because Blainesville isn't anywhere. At least not yet. Right now, it only exists here."

With that last statement, Mr. Blaine tapped his forehead with his index finger, then he continued.

"Yes, right now, Blainesville only exists in my mind. It's in my imagination. But I intend to bring it to life. I intend to build Blainesville and put it on the map. What do you think of that, huh?"

"Well, sir, that's very...impressive."

Drat! thought Henry to himself. That was the fourth or fifth time that he used that word. He hoped that he wasn't wearing it out, but he couldn't, on the spur of the moment, think of any other word to describe the imaginary pipedream that lay before him.

And he couldn't understand why he was here, alone in this secluded room with Mr. Blaine. And why the hell Mr. Blaine was telling him all about his imaginary city, his ideal modern metropolis. Surely there were other people around who would have a greater appreciation for Mr. Blaine's grandiose schemes than Henry, the young and inexperienced college student.

"But in order to build this dream I have to have the right key. Do you know what that key is, Henry?"

Henry shook his head but said nothing lest he appear totally stupid.

"The land, Henry, my boy! Yes, the land. In order to build a city, you have to have land to build it on. Without land you cannot have a city. You follow me?"

"Yes sir, I'm following you." Indeed, Henry had grasped that much; so, he was following Mr. Blaine, but he still wondered where Mr. Blaine was going with all of this.

"Now I've got my eye on a pretty piece of real estate up north, and I can pick it up for a song. In fact, I can get that land at bargain-basement rates. What do you think of that?"

"That's very impressive sir." *Drat!* He used that word again.

"I think it's a good deal. Some of my advisors, however, think that it's *too* good a deal. They think that something may be wrong with that real estate and that the seller is trying to dump it. What do you think about that, huh?"

"Well, sir, I think that—"

"But I say that maybe they're just a bunch of worry warts. Sure, they're my advisors, but after all, I'm the boss. And I got to be the boss by having sound judgment and savvy instincts. Sometimes you've got to throw caution to the winds and follow your instincts. What do you say to that, my boy?"

"Oh, yes sir! Sometimes it's good to follow your instincts." Henry said that to be polite but at that moment his instincts told him that this was the strangest conversation that he had ever been engaged in.

"Yes indeed, my boy! When there's a good deal under your nose, you've got to seize the moment. Grab the bull by the horns! Strike while the iron is hot! You agree?"

"Well, yes sir; I think that sometimes when an opportunity is at hand you—"

"Good! I'm glad you see things my way. I was hoping that you would. Well, it was nice to have had this little chat with you; but I imagine that now you'd like to get back to the party."

Mr. Blaine put his arm around Henry's shoulders and led him out of the room. As they walked down the hall to the party room, Mr. Blaine said, "Well Henry, I want you to know that I enjoyed our little chat together. I certainly found your insights to be valuable, but I want you think more about what I told you. Sleep on it tonight and in the morning tell me what you've seen. You'll do that for me, right?"

Henry assured Mr. Blaine that he would think about all that their conversation although he really had no idea what they talked about but, of course, he didn't tell Mr. Blaine that. The two men walked back to the room where the other guests were mingling in polite conversation. Tiffany was in the center of the room and Mr. Blaine, with Henry under his wing, walked over to her.

"Well Tiffany, my beautiful princess, I've brought your knight-in-shining-armor back to you."

"Did you two men have a good time putting your heads together talking about high finance and important business deals?" asked Tiffany.

"Yes, we did my little turtle dove, and I don't mind telling you that Henry here impressed me with his insights and his shrewd business sense. Someday he's going to be a successful businessman.

"Well, I'll tell you what," said Mr. Blaine yawning. "It's getting late and I think I'll retire for the evening, so I'll leave you two. I imagine that you'll want to spend some time alone together. I'll see you in the morning. I'm looking forward to continuing our chat, Henry."

With that, Mr. Blaine made the rounds of his guests then exited and went up to his quarters.

Now Henry was back with Tiffany and he thought that his long-awaited moment to go off with Tiffany and be truly alone with her had finally arrived.

"Say Tiffany," he said. "Why don't we go for a stroll outside. It's such a beautiful night and the moon is up and we could go out and look up at the stars in the sky."

"Oh, that sounds nice Henry. It really does, but I have a splitting headache and I thought that maybe I'd go to my room and turn in early. I hope you don't mind."

Well actually, Henry did kind of mind, but what could he say? He certainly didn't want Tiffany to suffer with a splitting headache, so he just nodded and said that it was all right and that maybe a good night's sleep was just what she needed to banish the pain and get her feeling back to normal.

"Thank you," she said. "You're such an understanding dear. But don't feel as if you have to leave. I don't want to spoil your fun. Why don't you stay and have something to drink and mingle with all the guests and enjoy the rest of the evening."

Then she exited leaving Henry standing there by himself. Henry looked around. He saw the unctuous, loquacious Mr. Sinclair, the large orchid lady, and the beaded, flatulent, cadaver-woman among the guests. And Henry thought to himself that those three, and indeed all the rest of the people, were just characters in this strange carnival. He remembered the previous conversations that he had with them, and he dreaded the thought of trying to talk to any of them. Instead, he went up to the bartender and asked for a double shot of bourbon on the rocks and he took it back to his room with him.

In his room, Henry took a hefty swig of bourbon and then took off his clothes and threw them on a nearby chair.

He propped up the thick pillows against the headboard and sat back on the bed with his drink in one hand. As he sat there he looked about the room and he thought to himself that this was a strange situation to be in. True, it was a life of luxury and comfort and somehow, he had stumbled into it, but he felt that he didn't belong here. He asked himself why he was here in the first place. *What had he done to deserve a place among the rich and weird?*

Well, all this happened because Tiffany had approached him and seemed interested in him. *And what had he done to capture her attention? Was it his brilliant mastery of art history? Or was it some sort of masculine charm that he exuded, some sort of appeal that he possessed that he didn't even know he had?* Whatever it was, Tiffany seemed to find him irresistible and that pleased him, but still there was something that didn't seem quite right, although he couldn't place what it was.

And then there was Tiffany's father, Mr. Blaine. He apparently had also been impressed with Henry. *But why?* What was it about average, ordinary, humble Henry that would interest and engage a powerful tycoon like Mr. Blaine. Henry couldn't imagine. By now the bourbon had taken effect and Henry dropped off into a deep, sound sleep.

The next morning everyone gathered in the sun room for brunch. Brunch was a buffet, with pancakes, and waffles, and French toast, and eggs Benedict and sausage and fresh fruit and coffee and juice and champagne cocktails.

Henry came down and found Tiffany sitting at table sipping coffee and talking with two of the guests who had spent the night at the Blaine mansion. Henry was ambivalent about what he should do. He wanted to go over and greet Tiffany, yet at the same time he dreaded the thought of a meeting with two more stuffy characters and getting roped into an inane conversation about something that he knew nothing about.

He stood there trying to decide what he should do when Tiffany looked around and saw him standing there. She immediately rose from her chair and went over to him. After exchanging the usual good morning greetings, the two went through the buffet line and then with plates of food and silverware in hand, they found a nearby table and sat down to eat breakfast.

It was a beautiful morning. The sun was shining through the windows and Henry and Tiffany were just sitting there eating and chatting pleasantly. Henry was just beginning to relax and enjoy himself when a familiar, full, resonant voice boomed from behind them.

"Well, it's a beautiful morning, is it not? And how are you two young people doing this fine morning?"

Henry turned to see Mr. Blaine standing behind them. Once again, he had approached so quietly that Henry wasn't aware of his presence until he spoke.

"Do you mind if I join you?" Mr. Blaine asked. "I hope you don't mind if an old codger sits down and joins you two youngsters."

Tiffany chuckled. "Oh Daddy, don't be silly. Of course, you can sit with us. We'd love to have your company. Wouldn't we, Henry."

Henry dutifully nodded because he knew it was expected of him.

"Well, did you have a good night's sleep?"

"Yes Daddy, I did."

"And how about you Henry? Did you sleep well?"

"Yes sir, I did. Yes indeed, I slept very well."

"That's good! I'm glad you did. But tell me, did you see anything about what we talked about last night? You know about my dream project."

By now Mr. Blaine was leaning forward and had a look or wide-eyed anticipation on his face. Henry could see that the older man was expecting some sort of response from him, but what could he say? The truth was that last night's bourbon had hit Henry so hard that it put him into a black void of unconsciousness for the entire night. He didn't have any dreams. He didn't see anything. His sleep was just a continuous opaque veil that completely shrouded his mind until he woke up. He might have had some dreams, but if he did, he couldn't remember them.

But as he sat there and looked across the table into Mr. Blaine's face, Henry realized Mr. Blaine was expected something from him but he felt that he couldn't tell the older man that his night was a blank, totally devoid of any images. Mr. Blaine was clearly anticipating something and Henry didn't want to disappoint him. He had to come up with something, so he fabricated a white lie off the top of his head.

"Yes sir, Mr. Blaine; somehow during the course of the night I saw Blainesville. Yes, I saw it in my...well, I saw it."

"Oh, that is magnificent!" cried Blaine with enthusiasm. "So, you actually saw Blainesville coming into existence."

"Well, yes sir. Sure! Well I mean sort of...kind of like."

Now Henry only mentioned Blainesville because it was the first thing that popped into his head, and he thought it might be something that Mr. Blaine wanted to hear about. At the same time, he thought it was an innocent remark that could be easily dismissed, but apparently Mr. Blaine had found a deeper meaning in Henry's casual statement. For Henry this was just an innocent white lie, but now he saw that the older man was somehow gleaning some sort of significance and meaning from the passing reference to Blainesville in his dream. Mr. Blaine somehow found a relevance and substance that Henry had never intended. Henry suddenly felt that the conversation was about to go down the wrong path, but now it was too late to change course now and there was no retreat.

"So, Henry," continued Blaine. "You saw Blainesville. I take it that you feel that everything looks good and that I have a green light to go ahead."

Henry gulped and said timidly. "Well sir, it certainly looks that way."

"And you think that I should proceed? Throw caution to the winds, and strike while the iron is hot! He who hesitates is lost. Is that the way you see it?"

Henry suddenly had a sickening feeling in the pit of his stomach. *Why was Mr. Blaine asking these questions? What exactly did the older man want from him, and what should he say in reply?* He looked to Tiffany for some kind of support, but she only sat there with a big smile on her face. Apparently, she was satisfied with Henry's responses and totally oblivious to the strange tone of the conversation going on before her.

"Well sir, I think that you know what you're doing and I don't see why everything shouldn't turn out as you envisioned it."

Mr. Blaine's smile broadened into a wide grin. He leaned back and rubbed his hands together. He was obviously delighted with everything Henry had said.

"Well, that's good! That's splendid! Yes, indeed; I was hoping that you would see that, and I can't tell you how pleased I am with your input."

What input? Henry hadn't been aware that he had put anything into his statements but now he realized that he must have said something without intending to—although he hadn't the foggiest idea what it was that he had said. But Mr. Blaine had apparently interpreted his words and found some sort of significance that seemed to satisfy him. At this point, Henry thought that maybe he should set things right before they went any farther. He leaned forward and cleared his throat. He was about to speak when Mr. Blaine shot up from his seat.

"Well Henry, this has been a particularly enlightening conversation. I am delighted that we had this little chat and I am certainly glad for your contribution. Now if you'll both excuse me, there are some things that I really must do. Some phone calls that I must make."

With that Mr. Blaine abruptly got up and departed leaving Henry to sit there and gape after him. Henry wasn't at all sure what he had done or said to make such an impression on Mr. Blaine, but it didn't matter now; the older man was gone leaving Henry and Tiffany to sit and eat brunch together. Well, whatever it was that happened, happened and it was over and done with. There was nothing left for Henry to do but to try and put that strange conversation out of his mind and enjoy the rest of the morning.

Henry looked around and saw that many of the guests had already departed. It looked like the weekend was over for them and they were taking leave of the Blaine mansion to return home. Henry began to think that maybe now his chance to be alone with Tiffany was on the horizon. He was about to make some small talk and kind of lay the groundwork for moments that would be more personal and cozier, when Tiffany excused herself, got up from the table and walked out of the room.

Henry didn't know where she went off to, but he assumed that she had to go to the ladies' room or something like that. He wasn't unduly concerned because she left her food and drink so he was sure she would return soon. And sure enough, she did; she came back and sat down again and the two continued to eat and drink and chat while the number of guests in the room gradually diminished. Henry smiled to himself. Pretty soon everyone would be gone and he would have Tiffany all to himself.

They finished their brunch and stood up. There was only one other couple in the room, but it was obvious that they would soon be leaving. Henry figured that this was the right time to suggest that he and Tiffany wander off and do something together. Perhaps a quiet stroll through the garden or maybe a return to the pool where they could have the facilities all to themselves.

He was about to suggest that when Tiffany spoke up. "Oh, Henry, look at the time. It's already approaching one. Can you believe how the time has just flown along? You realize that you have to be driving back soon or else you'll get stuck in horrible traffic."

"Well Tiffany, I'm sure there's no hurry and I don't mind running into a little congestion on the road, after all I'd rather—"

"Oh, but Henry you have no idea how horrendous the traffic can be on the weekend. Why soon everybody will be leaving the Hamptons and heading back into Manhattan. Well, you know how small the roads are around here. You know that because you drove in on them."

Henry nodded meekly and tried to get a word of his own in, but Tiffany continued without pause.

"Well, during the summer those little roads can be a nightmare to drive, what with all the cars going back to the city and beyond. And the Long Island expressway! Well, I don't even want to think about that. In another two hours it will be bumper to bumper all the way into the city, just like one long parking lot. If you get stuck in that, why you won't get home until after midnight, and I'd hate for that to happen to you. That would be a terrible way for you to end your weekend out here."

"But Tiffany, I really don't mind. I'd like to spend some time with you and—"

"Oh, that is sooo sweet of you. Believe me, I would like to spend time with you also; but at the same time, I'd never forgive myself if I let you get snarled up in all that traffic. Besides, we can spend oodles of time together back on campus.

"Now you don't have to worry about a thing. A few minutes ago, I got up and went out and found James and William and I told James to bring your car around to the front. And your packing is already taken care of. I talked to William and had him pack your clothes and put your bag into your car. So, you see everything is arranged and all set. Now come on, I'll walk you down to your car."

She threw all those words at him like the rapid-fire barrage of a machine gun. Henry was totally overwhelmed and unable to come up with a suitable response. Before he knew it, he and Tiffany were walking down the drive way to his car. At his car, Tiffany gave him a light kiss on his cheek. She told him how sweet he was and gently shoved him into the driver's seat then stood there while he started the motor. As he started down the driveway, she gave him her usual cheery wave.

In a few minutes Henry was driving through the Hamptons, away from the Blaine summer cottage and on his way back to New Jersey.

As Henry was driving along the Long Island Expressway, he tried to collect his thoughts and go over all that had happened over the weekend. The weekend had started off slowly and quietly enough. At first, it seemed like it would be a quiet weekend in the suburbs; but at some point, events took a strange and mysterious turn. Now, as he was driving back to his home, Henry had the nagging feeling that somehow, he got involved in something back at the Blaine mansion. He was sure that something had happened, yet he had no idea what it was.

As Henry was crossing through Manhattan toward the tunnel, he mentally reviewed the weekend; the food was good, the surroundings glamorous, and Tiffany looked beautiful; yet at the same time, there was something that bugged him. Somewhere in his brain was a nebulous, vague notion but he couldn't quite grasp or bring it into focus. It had to do with Mr. Blaine's manner and the way Tiffany seemed to shuffle him about as if he were some sort of prop that was constantly being repositioned to fit the situation at hand.

He tried to go over the conversations that he had had with Mr. Blaine and he recalled the conversation that very morning at breakfast when Mr. Blaine had thanked him for his insights. *Insights?* Henry thought to himself. *What the hell had he said anyhow?* He certainly couldn't recall having dropped any insights in the course of their brief conversation. But Mr. Blaine had picked up on something.

Henry thought back to the private little session the night before in the study, alone with Mr. Blaine. Henry remembered the two of them standing there together, looking at the model of Blainesville, and it seemed that Mr. Blaine was genuinely taken with him. The nagging part was that Henry couldn't imagine what he had done to spawn such affection from the older man.

Henry thought about all of that while he was driving home. When at last, he turned into his own driveway in Jersey City, he thought to himself that now the weekend was over and that whatever had happened was now but a memory. As he got out of his car and walked to his house, he pushed the past events of the weekend into the back of his mind. Whatever had happened, happened over the weekend; but it was over now so there was no sense trying to rehash it. Better to look forward to tomorrow and the week ahead.

Well, it was out of Henry's mind for the time being, and even though he couldn't know it at the time, in a few short weeks the quirks and uncertainties that he experienced at the Blaine place would resurface and then everything would be explained and the answers to the questions that had been bothering him about Mr. Blaine would soon become crystal clear. Yes, that would happen and he would also come to see the underlying reasons for his relationship with Tiffany. Henry didn't know it at that time, but he was in for a major shock. And this is what happened.

Three weeks passed from the time of the weekend at Blaine estate in the Hamptons. During that time, Henry and Tiffany continued to see each other, but not as frequently. Tiffany often said that she was busy with something or other and they only managed to see each other once a week. This week they were scheduled for another of their study sessions. Henry had boned up on cubism and fauvism and a bunch of other artistic *isms* and was ready to resume his role as the learned tutor of art history. He was seated at their usual table waiting for Tiffany to arrive. And arrive she did. She burst into the cafeteria and came straight for Henry.

As Henry watched her approach, he noticed immediately that there was something different about her manner. The bubbly disposition, the cheery manner, the bright and sunny smile were all absent. Instead, there was a hard look to her face; her eyes were sharp and intense with a fierce glare. Her mouth was a firm, tight line. He had never seen her like this and he looked at her in disbelief, wondering what had happened to bring about this sudden, dramatic change in her expression. He rose to greet her with a smile, but before he could say a word, she unleashed an attack.

"You rat! You skunk! You pretentious bastard!"

Everyone in the cafeteria turned to see where this outburst had come from. Henry took a step back. He couldn't believe his ears or her sudden change in attitude.

"Tiffany," he blurted out. "What's wrong? What did I do?"

"You know very well what you did!"

"No, I don't."

"I told my father that you could see into the future. That's why he wanted to talk with you. That's why he told you all his plans. When daddy asked you about that land Upstate that he was going to buy, you predicted it would be a good deal. You said he should go ahead with it."

"I didn't say that. All I said was that it sounded like—"

"Yes, you did say that. And because of you he bought all that land." She paused to get a breath then she renewed her attack with even more vigor and volume. "Well, it turned out that the land is loaded with chromium. It's polluted! It's all crap! He can't build anything on it until it gets cleaned up. That will cost millions. You were supposed to be able to see into the future and warn him about that, but you didn't and because of you and your lousy predictions, my father lost a ton of money. All because of you! You're nothing but a big fake!"

After that outburst she turned and walked away without flashing a smile or throwing a cheery wave. Before she got to the door, however, she turned for one final blast.

"Now because of you, Daddy can't afford to send me to the Riviera this summer. I hope you're satisfied!"

Then she turned on her heel and walked out of the cafeteria and out of Henry's life. He was left standing there with everyone in the cafeteria staring at him, wondering what had just happened to him and what Tiffany's tirade was all about.

Henry was in a state of shock, and for a minute he just stood transfixed in place as if he had been turned to stone by Tiffany-turned-Medusa. Finally, he roused himself and looked about. Everyone in the cafeteria was looking at him and he felt acutely self-conscious and embarrassed. He hastily picked up his books and meekly made his way to the exit. That was the last time that he and Tiffany ever spoke to each other. Their relationship was over, kaput.

His breakup with Tiffany with had a profound effect on him. Henry retreated deeper into his former shell and he avoided contact with people as much as possible. He told himself that he would never, ever, get involved with a woman again. His one consolation in that whole affair, however, was that he got an A in art history; the first and only A that he ever got in college.

Later, when he thought back over the whole incident, he was struck by the irony of it. Up till now his visions had always caused him problems. Whenever he saw things, people always misunderstood. It seemed that no one understood or empathized with the things that he saw or the way he came to see them. But this time it was different; because this time, he got into trouble for not having a vision, for not being able to see into the future. This time, someone, Tiffany, wanted him to have a vision and tell what was coming; but he didn't see anything and because he didn't have a vision, she turned on him. Henry began to think that maybe he couldn't win for losing.

CHAPTER 10

After the incident with Tiffany, Henry started to do some serious thinking about his visions. He wondered if maybe it was time to seek the help of a professional counselor. Perhaps a competent therapist could help him explore his psychological make-up and find the source of his visions. Up till now, Henry had been reluctant to go to a psychologist because of his experience with Dr. Holtz. Holtz had dismissed Henry's visions as nothing more than acute perception. His mother accepted Holtz's diagnosis and told Henry never to talk about his visions. At that time Henry was only eleven years old, and he felt that he had to follow his mother's direction.

But when Henry was older and in high school, the strange visions continued to appear at odd times and he began to wonder if there was something more than acute perception involved. It was then that he began to question why he had these strange visions and where they came from.

He wondered if anyone else ever had similar experiences, or if he was the only one. If that was the case, then what strange quality did he possess that enabled him to sometimes—at odd moments—peer into the future when no one else could? Was it something in his physiological make-up that enabled him to have these strange visions? Or was there something in the atmosphere, some sort of strange waves or vibrations that only resonated in his brain? But why in his brain and not in anyone else's conscience?

There were so many times—in high school and later in college—when poor Henry longed for someone that he could confide in and talk to about the things that he saw. But there was no one. While he was in college, Henry thought about going to the psychology department and consulting with someone there. Maybe they could run some tests or do some sort of experimental work to find out the source of his visions.

But then as he tossed that alternative over in his mind, he decided against it because he was afraid that if word got out that he was being studied by the psychology department then he would really be branded as a weirdo and that would become something else to contend with. So, he never visited the university psychology department and never told anyone about his visions. Well, not until he told Andrew about the ceiling business in the library. After that incident and the unpleasant repercussions that followed, Henry became more determined than ever to keep silent about any future visions that he might have.

After he graduated from Farleigh Dickinson University, Henry again wondered if maybe he should consult with a psychologist about his problem. He told himself that if he consulted a psychologist, he could engage in a meaningful dialogue and maybe get at the cause of his strange clairvoyant malady.

Henry had just about convinced himself to find a therapist and make an appointment but then he thought about the cost of therapy session. He didn't know exactly how much money he'd have to shell out for the sessions, but in all likelihood, they would be expensive and at the moment Henry was still unemployed. Better to wait until he landed a paying position before he sought professional help.

Well, after a few months of searching, Henry did land a job as an accountant with a new, dynamic energy company, called Entrac. Now with a job and a steady income, Henry felt that he might be able to afford consultation with a psychologist who could help him explore his problem. Once again, he was ready to find someone and get started with therapy but once again, he decided to put it off. Henry thought that maybe it might be better to hold off on therapy until he had another vision. Then it would be fresh in his mind and he could describe the vision in vivid detail. So, he postponed seeking the help of a psychologist while he waited for that next vision to appear.

A month went by, then another and another without a vision. Finally, a full year passed, followed by another full year and still there were no visions. This was the longest period that Henry had ever gone without seeing something and he began to think that maybe he was free and clear from having these strange visions and that, at long last, he was normal just like everyone else. So, at this point, he felt that there was no need to seek therapy.

But just as Henry Gainsvort was convinced that he had outgrown his visions, he had another one, and this is what happened.

Henry was working at Entrac as an accountant in the payroll department. It wasn't a very exciting job, nor did he have an important position within the company. Henry didn't mind having a mundane job because at least he was able to avoid the responsibility of an important position and the pressure that comes with it and he made enough money to move into a small apartment in Manhattan.

One day while he was looking at the company payroll lists on his computer screen, he saw another completely different set of numbers before him. These were not the usual payroll figures, but figures and tabulations from the corporate books. They showed assets and liabilities and investments and outlays of the company. As the figures flashed before his eyes, Henry realized that he was looking at the entire financial structure of the company. As he looked over them, he realized that he was looking at some serious accounting problems. Something was dreadfully wrong.

Of course, Henry's screen wasn't really showing the alarming corporate accounting picture. Those figures and tabulations were a manifestation of the vision that was in Henry's mind. The monitor was still displaying the payroll spreadsheet, and anyone who happened to look at the monitor over Henry's shoulder would have seen the list of payroll outlays for the coming week. But Henry wasn't seeing that picture. He was having another vision; he was seeing the entire corporate financial picture in the future. Henry was seeing a financial disaster in the making and he was frightened by what he saw.

Henry immediately went to his supervisor, Mr. Arthur Pearlmutter, to tell him about what he had just seen. Pearlmutter was a rather pudgy, slightly unkempt man with a red face, a bald head and a short black mustache. He looked more like he should be a glockenspiel player in a Swiss oompah band rather than the manager of a corporate payroll department. But he was a kindly gentleman who ran the payroll department much like a benevolent uncle. When Henry approached him and said that he had an urgent matter to discuss, Pearlmutter led the young man into his office, shut the door and sat down to listen.

Henry explained that he saw some serious discrepancies in the corporate books and unless someone took steps to make the necessary corrections, the company was headed for disaster. Pearlmutter listened to Henry without saying a word. When Henry finally finished he asked, "What makes you think any of these problems exist? How do you know all of this Henry?"

And there it was again, that nagging question that always plagued him. *How to explain his visions without appearing to be some kind of crackpot psychic? How to explain what he knew without having to talk about precognition and visions from another dimension?* Henry was now face-to-face with the dilemma that he had confronted so many times before. Somehow, he had to come up with an explanation that would give credibility to his apprehensions without having to say anything about where they came from, without talking about the visions that appeared mysteriously into his conscious.

In the end, the best that Henry could do was say that he did some deductive reasoning based on a hunch that he had after looking at different figures and sums. As he was saying all of this, he realized that his explanation sounded lame and even dumb, and he felt foolish for trying to alert Pearlmutter to a potential financial disaster that he had no real evidence to support. Nevertheless, Henry believed that he should at least try to sound a warning and head off a disaster before it actually happened.

When Henry had finished and after he left the office to return to his desk, Arnold Pearlmutter remained seated and pondered over all that he had just heard. Henry had just come to him with warnings of a serious problem in the making, but he offered very little substantial evidence to back up his alarm. So Pearlmutter was in a quandary as to what to do. The warning sounded serious and maybe someone should look into it, yet at the same time, the warning might be based on a figment of Henry's imagination. Maybe Henry was just the boy who cried "wolf".

Pearlmutter felt that perhaps someone should look into the matter and see if some sort of action was required; but he was a kind of corporate coward. He was the kind of man who didn't like to make waves nor take the responsibility for any risky decisions. Arthur Pearlmutter liked to play it safe whenever possible. But here he was with a dilemma: someone had come to him with a serious concern about the company's financial standing but offered very little evidence to back it up. That left poor Pearlmutter in a serious predicament. *What to do about this problem?*

Arthur decided that the best course of action was to go to his immediate supervisor and dump the whole bucket in his lap and that's exactly what he did. Now that left Arthur's supervisor with the problem, and he too was a corporate coward who was afraid to disturb the company equilibrium in any way. So, rather to take any kind of personal action, he pushed the problem off on his supervisor. And that supervisor went to his boss and so on and so on up the chain of command.

Eventually, word of Henry's dire warning went up to the very top of the corporate ladder to an executive vice-president. He too, was inclined to dismiss Henry's premonition as groundless nonsense, but just to be on the safe side, he decided to take up the matter with the CFO, who had the euphonious name of Cash Cassidy. Cassidy sat behind his desk and listened as the executive vice-president unfolded the tale of a lowly payroll accountant who feared that the company was embarking on some dangerous financial waters that threatened its very existence.

After listening patiently and calmly to the executive vice-president, Cassidy thanked the man for bringing this matter to his attention but, at the same time, assured the VP that these apprehensions were groundless and the company was in good financial standing without any shady underpinnings. Cassidy remained the picture of self-assurance and confidence. The two men parted company; but the minute he was alone behind closed doors, Cassidy reached for his phone and dialed the personal extension of the CEO, Paul Jessup.

"Jess, this is Cash. You got a minute? I think there's something we should sit down and talk about. Yeah! I think we may have a problem. Okay, I'll come right over."

Cash Cassidy hung up the phone and walked down the hall to Paul Jessup's office. He walked in and took a seat in the big, soft leather chair facing Jessup's desk. When he was seated and facing the CEO, Jessup asked, "What's up?"

Cassidy leaned forward and carefully repeated all that the executive vice president had just related to him. Jessup listened to Cassidy without comment until the latter had finished speaking. He thought about all he had heard for a minute then asked, "Who is this Gainsvort guy anyhow?"

Cassidy shook his head doubtfully. "I'm not really sure. They say he's some peon who works in payroll."

"Payroll! How could some schmuck in payroll know anything about what we're doing on the corporate level? Our own accountant boys aren't even on to our dealings."

"I don't know. All I know is that he seems to have somehow stumbled onto what we're trying to do and when I heard about it, I thought I should run it by you just to see what you thought. Do you think we should just ignore it? After all this guy's a nobody. Maybe people will think he's just blowing hot air of the top of his head and they'll ignore him."

"Maybe," said Jessup doubtfully. "But it got all the way up to us didn't it? So, some people are obviously listening to him. And if he continues to talk, who knows how many more might lend an ear to his prattle."

"So, what are we going to do?"

"Well, we gotta get rid of him."

"You mean," gulped Cassidy, "you mean kill him?"

"No," said Jessup scornfully. "What do I look like, a mobster? How would I know how to kill someone?"

"Well, I thought that maybe you meant to put a contract out on him."

"Yeah right! Now where would I go to get a contract out of someone? The murder department at Walmart? Come on, get real! There's an easier way to get rid of this guy."

"How?"

"We can fire him."

"Sure, but wouldn't that cause a lot of suspicion if we just upped and fired this guy right after he blew the whistle on our dealings. It would look like we were trying to get him out of the way just to keep him from talking."

"Sure, it would—if he were the only one we fired. But we could have a group layoff of, say, thirty people."

"How are we going to justify that? After all, we just announced that the company is doing well with a rosy outlook. How can we turn around and say that we've got to fire thirty people?"

"We won't be firing them. We'll be laying them off. We'll say that due to recent expansions we want to take a step back and re-evaluate our needs and priorities. We'll add some bullshit that this is just a temporary measure for restructuring and that as soon as we organize we'll probably hire everyone back again. And after a few months, that's what we'll do; we'll bring everyone back."

"Everyone?"

"Everyone except one."

"Gainsvort?"

"Exactly, everyone except for Gainsvort."

That seemed to solve the problem and they both men leaned back in their chairs and smiled like two fat cats who had just eaten the prize canary.

VISIONS OF DESTINY

Three days later, thirty pink slips went out. Thirty people were being laid off, including Henry Gainsvort. There was also a letter of explanation stating that the layoffs were just a temporary cost-cutting measure put into place while the company re-evaluated its organizational priorities and business strategies. In due course, everyone would probably be called back. The letter sounded very official and conciliatory and was signed by the CEO, Paul Jessup.

Everyone took it at face value and believed what was written—everybody except for one person, Henry Gainsvort. Henry had correctly surmised that the lay-offs were just a scam to get him out of the way. It also made him realize that his vision of Entrac's risky financial status was far more serious than he had first imagined. It was now obvious—at least to Henry—that the very heads of the Entrac corporation were up to no good. Henry knew that the company was headed for certain disaster.

In a very short time, that is exactly what happened. Two weeks after the layoffs, the Entrac corporation had to declare bankruptcy. The paperwork empire that Paul Jessup and Cash Cassidy had constructed collapsed like a house of cards. Both men were investigated and later indicted for fraud and conspiracy. But the damage was done. The company went belly-up and all the employees suddenly found themselves unemployed.

After reading of the total collapse of Entrac, Henry understood the mistake that he had made. In his vision he had seen the precarious financial state of the company and in an effort to prevent a financial disaster he talked to his immediate supervisor about his vision. He assumed that the financial maneuvering he saw was just the machinations of some over-zealous corporate whiz-kids who were trying to make some fast money and that maybe he could turn things around by alerting a few responsible corporate officials.

At that time, he thought that the whole problem could be resolved satisfactorily once it was brought to the attention of the top brass. What he hadn't seen was that there was some serious book-cookery involved and that the two top bananas were the ones doing all the chicanery. Now he realized that he should have gone outside the company to government regulators and blown the whistle.

Well, it was over and done with. The big company, Entrac, which at one time seemed like a shining star on the corporate horizon, was now a lifeless relic with twenty-one thousand people out of work. And it happened just the way Henry saw it in his vision. Even though he tried to warn people, no one listened. The big, powerful corporate giant had fallen and died. Henry felt sad because he saw disaster in the making and was powerless to prevent it. He felt sad that so many people were now out of work because of the scheming of a couple greedy men.

CHAPTER 11

Now Henry was without a job and no steady income. He managed to squeeze out a living doing freelance accounting work, sometimes in an office and sometimes working in his apartment doing people's income taxes. He also picked up whatever temp work he could get, doing office work, or ushering in one of the theaters in Manhattan. He managed to survive without a steady source of income, but he could no longer afford to live in Manhattan, so he moved to Sunset Park in Brooklyn. Sunset Park was, and still is, an ethnic neighborhood with a mostly Hispanic population but many Afro-Americans and Asians.

Henry found a dingy apartment on Fifth Avenue directly across from a Catholic Cathedral, *Our Lady of Perpetual Hope*, the largest basilica in Brooklyn. That's what people told Henry when he moved in—that he was living directly across the street from the largest basilica in Brooklyn—this didn't make much of an impression on him because Henry didn't know what a basilica was. To him it was just a big church, and since he didn't go to church, he didn't much care one way or the other about *Our Lady of Perpetual Hope*.

Henry's apartment was on the second floor, directly above a veterinarian's office. There were two apartments above his. The top floor was occupied by an Asian family, two adults with three kids, two girls and a boy.

On the third floor there lived a strange little man. Henry didn't know much about the man, only that his name was *A. Martello*. Henry found that out by looking on the mailbox. So, he knew the man's last name, but he didn't know what the *A* stood for. He also knew that the little man smoked a lot. He knew that because whenever he saw that little man coming or going from the building, he always had a cigarette in his mouth and Henry could also hear the sound of coughing, incessant hacking, coming from the apartment above, through his ceiling at night and during the day.

Henry's apartment was large with five rooms, not counting the bathroom. But it was rather dingy without much natural light. Since there were adjacent buildings on either side of his, the only windows were in the front room, which he turned into his bedroom, and the rear rooms which were the kitchen and bathroom. He didn't have air conditioning and during the hot, humid months of July and August, he had to make do with a small fan that he carried with him whenever he moved from room to room. The heating was uneven. In the winter, the two end rooms were usually cold and the middle rooms were excessively hot and there was nothing Henry could do to equalize the extremes in temperature.

Probably the worst feature of his miserable hovel was that it was constantly visited by large, brown, ugly cockroaches. The cockroaches were big, almost two inches long, and whenever he looked about, he saw one or two sitting on the walls, furniture or ceiling or scurrying across the floor. People told him that they were really water bugs, but to Henry they looked like big cockroaches, so that's what he called them.

In an effort to keep the loathsome insects at bay, Henry laid down some roach powder around the perimeter of each room, and put out roach disks that contained a kind of bait that was supposed to end their existence by destroying their sex lives. He also stomped on them and sprayed surfaces with toxic aerosols, but nothing seemed to work. No matter how many he killed they kept coming back. At times it seemed as if he were fighting an invading army of alien insects whose numbers increased exponentially every day.

As if the roaches weren't bad enough, during the cold winter months he was also visited by small gray mice. These vile, little creatures probably came into his apartment to get out of the outside cold and also to pillage whatever food they could find in his cupboards.

Henry tried to keep the mice out of his dwelling by stuffing steel wool into any cracks and crevices that he found in the floor, in the baseboard molding and around the holes where the pipes came through the wall; but somehow, in spite of his best efforts, the critters found ways to get into his apartment anyway. So, Henry resorted to laying out glue traps in strategic locations around his place.

The traps were essentially small plastic trays that contained a blanket of thick, viscous, gooey liquid. In the center of the goo was some tantalizing bait that would attract a mouse, cause him to throw caution to the winds, and venture onto the trap to eat the morsels. When he did that, he would get stuck in the adhesive and no amount of wiggling or struggling would extricate him. The things worked like a kind of small-mammalian flypaper or a miniature version of the La Brea Tar Pits.

Henry found after placing the traps around his apartment that they did, in fact, work. The trouble was that they trapped the mouse but didn't kill it. When Henry inspected his traps in the morning he usually found a live mouse hopelessly stuck to the glue tray. When he approached the trap, the pathetic little creature would look up a Henry with its sad black eyes as if pleading for mercy. That created a problem: *what was Henry to do with the helpless little animal?*

After thinking about it for a while, Henry hit upon the solution of covering the tray and trapped mouse with a paper towel then slamming it with a heavy, cast-iron frying pan. That effectively flattened the mouse, smashed his skull and presumably put him out of his misery. Henry then disposed of the tray with the mouse carcass and the paper towel in the trash and then put the matter out of his mind—until the next time that he found a mouse in another tray then he had to do it all over again.

Each time he did this, he assumed that he was decreasing the Brooklyn mouse population; but as far as he could tell, his efforts did not affect their numbers one iota because the next week and the next, he found another wretched little creature hopelessly mired in another trap. No matter how many trapped mice he smashed and disposed of, they kept on coming. He thought that after killing the first dozen or so, word would get out among the mouse world that his apartment was a place to be avoided, but no, the mice continued to visit him and he continued to trap and smash them.

That was Henry's life, going to work during the day—sometimes at night—then after work coming back to his home, "the wild kingdom" as he came to think of it—to make a simple supper then spend some time fighting nature's invading vermin then try to enjoy the rest of the evening reading or watching television. Some nights when he wasn't working or sleeping or reading or watching television or fighting the onslaught of nature, he went for a stroll—weather permitting. He ate most of his meals in his apartment, except when he was working in an office and then he brown-bagged his lunch.

Henry didn't have a particularly exciting, or even interesting life, but he accepted it for what it was. He had come to believe that this was his lot in life and there was nothing he could do to change it. To everyone in the neighborhood or at the places he worked, Henry was a typical, average guy who went about his business without causing a stir or making waves. No one really noticed Henry Gainsvort, because he was an average, everyday guy who never stood out in a crowd and never did anything out of the ordinary.

And Henry was content to let it be that way. He really wanted to be normal like everyone else, but deep within, he knew that actually he was different from all of them. He secretly knew that he wasn't really average because he possessed the unusual and uncanny ability to see things, visions of destiny, that no one else could see and that sometimes—if he wasn't careful—he might make waves. Whenever he told anyone about the things he saw, about his glimpses into the future, it usually turned out badly for him. The people he told looked at him with skepticism, suspicion and even mistrust and gradually they drew away from him until eventually he became a man alone, without friends and without anyone to talk to.

By now Henry had come to accept that loneliness was to be the cornerstone of his existence and he knew that there was nothing that he could do to change that. Well, that's what he believed, but then things did change, suddenly, unexpectedly. They changed one day, when Henry found a friend. He found someone who understood him and who accepted him for what he was. It happened like this.

Henry had settled in his dingy Sunset Park Apartment sharing his rooms with itinerant mice and visiting roaches and only venturing out for groceries, going for an occasional stroll or commuting to a job assignment. He had just finished one of those office temp assignments and was returning to his apartment. He stopped in the hall to open his mailbox and pull out the envelopes and papers that were lodged within.

He was going through his stack of bills and junk mail when the little man from the third floor came in. Henry barely glanced up, but he made a token murmur of greeting while, at the same time, continued looking through his recent mail trying to decide what he had to keep and what he could discard.

The little man responded to Henry's murmur with an equally nondistinct murmur of his own and walked past. Then suddenly he stopped and abruptly turned around.

"Say," he said. "You're the guy in the apartment below me."

Henry looked up from his mail, surprised that this man who he had seen a number of times before had suddenly decided to stop and speak to him.

"Hey, since we're neighbors we should get to know each other don't you think? The name's Augie Martello. Put it there, pal."

With that, he flashed a broad, friendly smile, one corner of which held a smoldering cigarette, and he extended his right hand. Henry was a little surprised by this unexpected display of spontaneous neighborliness and his instantaneous elevation into Augie's "pal" status, but he made no protest—perhaps because he was taken with Augie's overt good will and sunny disposition. He pushed his mail into his left hand and extended his right and shook hands with the little man and at the same time, murmured that his name was Henry.

"Well, Henry—you don't mind me calling you by your first name, do you? I figure that neighbors should always meet and get to know one another and be on a first name basis. You know what I mean? I mean that it makes living together in the same building more civilized. Don't you think? And that's important when you live in New York City because in New York there are so many people and it's easy to get lost and forget you're a human being. You become a zombie without any kind of life. You know what I mean?"

"Well—" began Henry in a slow attempt to address the little man's barrage of questions. But Augie Martello really didn't pause long enough for any kind of response. He just rattled on with his continuous, stream-of-consciousness monologue, assuming that Henry was following in his wake and agreeing with everything he had to say.

"Say Henry, you doing anything tonight? I mean, it's Friday night. You got a hot date or anything?"

"No, I haven't got anything like that, but I thought that—"

"Well, good! So, how's about you and me going 'round the corner to Gallagher's for a couple of beers. What's say we do that, huh?"

"Well I don't know, I thought that maybe—"

"What? You got big plans for tonight?"

"No, it's not that, but I thought that—"

"So good! If you've got nothing sitting on the burners then you and I can spend some time together. I figure that's important. I mean I think that spending time is what neighbors should do now and then. You know what I mean? I mean it's a way for neighbors to get to know one another. Establish lines of communication and do some bonding. You know what I mean?"

"I think I do, but—"

"So good! Then it's settled we'll go out together for a couple of beers. Say, I'll tell you what. I'll even spring for the first round. You know why? I'll tell you why. It's because I'm celebrating, and you know what I'm celebrating? I'll tell you what I'm celebrating. I'm celebrating because the horse that I bet on came in royally today. That's right! I put twenty smackeroos on the long shot in the fifth at the big A and guess what. Yeah! That's right! The nag came in first over the finish line. It paid twelve to one. Don't mind telling you that I made a pretty nice chunk of change on that nag. You might even say that I made out big time. How about that for good luck? That's really something ain't it? So, what's say the two of us go out for a couple of cold brewskis together? Huh? Come on. Let's live a little!"

Henry was still a little hesitant because all this was happening so fast and he couldn't think quickly enough to keep up with this little man's running monologue. After all, he had just met this strange little man and now, suddenly, they were planning a night out. It had been so long since Henry had a night out—not since his college days—that Henry wasn't sure if he remembered how to socialize with another human being. Besides that, Henry was so used to his routine of coming home—fixing his supper then assaulting the bugs and mice in his wild kingdom—that he wasn't sure that he knew how to do anything else. Now, suddenly, on the spur of the moment he had decide whether he should abruptly break his routine and go out for a beer.

Augie sensed Henry's hesitation but was not to be put off.

"Whatsa matter? You don't drink? You don't like beer maybe? Or maybe it's me. Maybe you don't like me?"

"No," said Henry quickly. "You seem like a really nice guy, and I do drink, and I like beer well enough, but—"

"So, then there's no problem and it's settled. Come on then. Whatta we waiting for?"

With that Augie grabbed Henry by the elbow and started to pull him toward the front door.

"Wait a minute!" cried Henry. "I have my mail. I've got to put it in my apartment."

Augie glanced down at the envelopes in Henry's hand.

"You got any money in that stack?"

"No, no money. It's probably just junk mail and maybe some bills."

"So, leave them on the floor there, under the mailboxes. Nobody'll take them. Who wants junk mail? And who cares if they take your bills? Maybe they'll pay them for you. You know what I mean? Go ahead, leave them there. Trust me! Nobody'll take them."

The little man laughed and pulled Henry through the hall and out the front door. Henry barely had time to drop his mail on the floor.

Outside, Henry accepted the inevitable and went with the diminutive Augie Martello because he realized that packed within that pint-sized figure of a little man was a mountain of determination and there was no fighting it.

But as they walked, Henry lost all hesitation and doubts and fell into step with Augie's brisk pace. In his own little exuberant way, Augie Martello was very likable and very persuasive, and Henry found that as they walked down the street together, he was actually looking forward to going the beer joint called Gallagher's Bar & Grill. After all, maybe it was time that he *lived a little*.

They walked two blocks then crossed the street to Gallagher's Bar & Grill. Henry had passed this neighborhood haunt many times. Always there was the sound of talking and shouting and laughing as if the place was perpetually packed and everyone was always having a good time. So many times, he wanted to stop and go inside, just to have a peek and see what was going on and maybe partake in some of the merriment, but each time he hesitated.

No matter how much he wanted to go in, Henry always stopped at the front door because something inside of him made him pause. Maybe he was afraid that he wouldn't fit in and if he ever did go inside, he would feel awkward and out of place. Or maybe he suspected that he had been alone for so long that he had forgotten how to be among people and laugh and socialize. Whatever the reason, he never went through the front door but instead always passed by figuring that maybe the next time he would go in. But there never was a *next time* and he never did go in. He continued to walk past Gallagher's, always wondering what it must be like inside that noisy neighborhood hangout but each time he walked by without ever knowing.

Now with Augie in the lead, he was actually going inside and now, at last, he would see the mysterious magic that Gallagher's had to offer.

CHAPTER 12

Augie pushed his way through the front door with an air of authority. The minute they got inside, it was as if Augie's personality expanded to fill the room; everybody knew that he had arrived. The men clustered at the bar all turned and greeted his entrance. Some called out his name, others raised their glasses in a salutatory gesture or gave a friendly nod or wave in his direction. Whatever the gesture, whatever the sign, everybody acknowledged that Augie Martello, every man's good buddy, was among them.

Henry saw instantly that everybody in the room knew and liked Augie Martello, and he felt a measure of pride to be Augie's companion. True, their friendship was only minutes old, but nobody in the place knew that and Henry was content to let everyone think that Augie and he were true friends of long standing.

With Henry in tow, Augie went up to the pack of guys standing at the bar.

"Hey Barney!" said Augie to some overweight, round-faced guy who was dressed in a red tee-shirt and overalls that were covered in white dust. "Where ya been? Long time, no see. Whatsa matter, you been on the wagon?"

"No," confessed Barney. "I was working far out in Queens for the past month. There was a lot of overtime and I didn't get out until late, so I didn't get to come here much. But now that job's finished and I'm working closer to home."

"Yeah? Whereabouts?"

"I'm doing a remodeling job on Seventh Avenue not too far from here."

"Hey, that's great!" exclaimed Augie enthusiastically. "So now you can drop into this joint for a brewski after work and you won't be such a stranger. Say Barney, I want you to meet a friend of mine, Henry Gainsvort. Henry, this is Barney Kruperman."

Barney extended his big, ham-like hand, and said, "Nice to meet you. You known Augie very long?"

"Well..." began Henry somewhat reluctantly. He wasn't sure how to say that the extent of his friendship with Augie could only be measured in minutes. Before he had a chance to frame his reply however, Augie cut in.

"Are you kidding? Henry and I go back to the dark ages."

Henry had to smile to himself. He had only met Augie a few minutes ago, but already they were bosom buddies from the good old days—at least in Augie's mind. Augie grabbed Henry by the elbow and pulled him around to meet the others at the bar.

There must have been at least thirty guys at the bar and Augie knew every one of them. He knew their names, where they lived and what they did for a living. And they all knew and liked Augie. As Henry watched Augie mingling and chatting with the guys, he thought to himself that Augie was such a good-natured, friendly person that it was really impossible not to like him. Henry thought to himself that this was the first time in his life that he had ever met a guy as outgoing as Augie Martello.

Augie walked up and glad-handed each man and exchanged warm salutations then Augie introduced Henry as his long-time, good friend and neighbor. In response, everyone greeted Henry enthusiastically and automatically accepted him as if he was a tried-and-true buddy and member of the pack. Henry found that he was suddenly and instantly everybody's pal just because he was Augie Martello's friend. It seemed to be a fact of life, the law of the land, that any friend of Augie's was automatically a friend to everyone in Gallagher's.

As they walked around and mingled, Henry saw that he was in the midst of a bunch of close-knit guys, a clan of blue-collar workers who shared the common link of manliness and that he, Henry Gainsvort, had suddenly become one of them. For the first time, in a very long time, Henry felt like he was a card-carrying member of society and no longer the lone wolf looking at the pack from a distance.

They talked and mingled with the crowd for the better part of an hour, then Augie said, "Come on Henry, let's go in the back room and grab some chow. I'm getting hungry."

They left the bar room and walked through a large, open doorway into the back room. Augie crossed the room and headed to a booth in the far corner. He assumed that Henry was following him; but Henry didn't follow immediately. He entered the room, and stopped just past the door way. He stood there looking around and taking in the features of the room.

Up till now he hadn't had much of an opportunity to look around and see much of Gallagher's because he had been so busy mingling with all of Augie's friends. He had only caught glimpses of the surroundings between greetings and comments and jokes, but now he took a moment to pause and examine the walls, floor and ceiling.

The back room was similar to the bar in that it was paneled in the same dark wood. Judging by the thick, black, patina of aged vanish and grime on the molding, Henry guessed that the place had been built somewhere around the turn of the last century. The floor was tiled in small white, porcelain hexagons that were in vogue at the early years of the century but had long since gone out of fashion. In the center of the room were a few tables with chairs. Each table had a red-and-white checked table cloth. In the center of each table was a stainless-steel napkin dispenser, a bottle of ketchup, and salt and pepper shakers.

The walls were a mosaic of framed photographs, many yellow with age, mostly of sports events, though there were a few political scenes also. Among the many pictures, Henry was able to pick out a photo of Lindbergh, and FDR, and Joe DiMaggio, and Joe Louis, and the famous picture of the Hindenburg explosion at Lakehurst. There didn't seem to be any recent pictures at all—at least not of any events or figures of the last twenty-five years.

There were a few framed newspapers also; one with the headlines that announced the surrender of the Nazis near the end of World War II, another that publicized the stock market crash of 1929, and another chronicling the death of the famous silent-film star, Rudolf Valentino. Judging by the subject matter of the photos, the tiles on the floor, the antiquated tin ceiling and the old wooden wall paneling, Henry estimated that this place had stood for decades, maybe even a century without change or remodeling.

For a few long minutes, Henry continued to stand there, looking about and absorbing the nuances of the decor. As he looked, he thought to himself, *So, this is Gallagher's!* Standing there in the middle of that antediluvian, old room, enclosed in antiquated woodwork, with an archaic floor, and old-fashioned tin ceiling, and hundreds of photographic relics, Henry was overcome with odd feeling that he had stepped back in time where the modern world of cellphones, the internet and CD players did not exist. This was a strange and peculiar feeling for him, because although he had looked into the future so many times, he now found himself standing in a portal to the past.

Henry's thoughts and impressions were interrupted by Augie's voice.

"Hey kid! I'm over here."

Henry looked up and saw that Augie was sitting in a booth in the far corner of the room. Henry walked over to join him. He sat down in the booth and faced Augie.

Augie looked at him with a warm smile. "You looked like you were lost in another world. Whatsa matter, you never been in here before?"

Henry shook his head. "No, I've passed by it a number of times, going to and from my place, but I never came in."

"Never? Not once?" asked Augie in genuine amazement.

Henry shook his head.

"Well then, since this is your first time, you should make a wish."

"A wish? Why?"

"It's something you do whenever you come to a new place that you've never been in before. You're in a new place; it's like a new adventure. Sort of like a new start. So, you get to make a wish for good luck. Go ahead, make a wish."

"What should I wish for?"

"I don't know. It's your wish, you gotta make it."

Henry nodded and then considered what he should wish for. He thought for a couple of minutes. Then he had it. He closed his eyes and thought to himself, *I wish that all good things would come my way from now on.* Then he opened his eyes.

All this time Augie had been watching him, just looking on without saying a word. When Henry opened his eyes, he asked, "You made your wish?"

Henry nodded. "Yeah, do you want to hear it?"

"No man, you can't tell your wish! It's yours and you gotta keep it to yourself. If you tell anyone, then it won't come out."

Henry smiled. It amused him that Augie seemed to know all the rules and protocols about wish-making. These were rules that Henry had never heard of before. Henry didn't know if Augie just made that stuff up off the top of his head or if he had access to some sort of established, arcane folklore; but it didn't matter because it was fun to go along with Augie, because…well, just because Augie was being Augie. Augie's whole manner of being seemed to be light-hearted and carefree and it was fun to be a part of all that. This was a new experience for Henry, being with someone who put his worries aside and just enjoyed life, savoring the present as it unfolded and not worrying about tomorrow.

At that moment, a woman wearing an apron and carrying an order pad and pencil approached their booth. Henry assumed that she was the waitress. Of course, Augie knew her.

"Hi Marcy; you're just in time, Henry and I are ready to order. Henry, this is Marcy. She is the best waitress in all of Brooklyn. What am I saying? She's probably the best waitress in all of the world. And she's quite a looker, isn't she?"

When he said that, Augie reached over and put his arm around her waist in an affectionate hug. Marcy accepted the hug as if she were used to it, but at the same time made a mild, token protest.

"Oh Augie, stop it! He's always teasing me."

"I can't help it Marcy, it's because you're so cute. Oh hey, Marcy, I want you to meet a good friend of mine. This here is Henry Gainsvort."

"Pleased to meet you," she said.

Henry nodded and murmured some sort of greeting in response and at the same time he looked at her. She wasn't, as Augie claimed, a "looker", but she was kind of attractive in a plain sort of way. She was short, about five-three or maybe four, and had an acceptable figure. Henry judged her to be somewhere in her thirties. She had a mop of reddish-brown hair that was cut short in a page-boy style. Her hair wasn't disheveled, but it wasn't exactly neat either, but somewhere in between. Her face was pleasant, but not especially beautiful, and she had freckles on her cheeks and two big, brown eyes. When she smiled or opened her mouth, Henry could see that she had a more than an ample supply of teeth. In fact, it looked like she had too many teeth to fit in her mouth, because a few of her teeth overlapped each other. But, all in all, Henry judged Marcy to be a nice, working-class girl making an honest living waitressing in the neighborhood bar and grill.

"You guys know what you want to order, or do ya wanna see a menu?"

"Menu, shmenu!" said Augie in mock contempt. "Who needs a menu? We know what we want, don't we pal?"

Henry looked back at Augie in disbelief. This was the first time that he had ever set foot in Gallagher's. He had no idea what kind of food they served here and he had no notion of what he wanted to eat. He was about to voice his concern, but he could see that Augie was going to order regardless of what he said, so Henry kept his mouth shut and let Augie run the show.

"Okay let's have two burgers. Oh Henry, you're gonna like the burgers that they have here. Really delicious! Trust me on this. And put everything on them, tomato, lettuce and a pickle on the side."

"How do you want those burgers?"

"Medium. Not too rare, but still with a little pink, just so they're juicy. And we'll have an order of fries with those burgers. We'll split an order, okay Henry? Unless of course you're real hungry then we can each get an order. I hope that you're not the type that puts ketchup on his fries because I don't like that. I like my fries plain, just with salt. I hope that's okay with you."

Henry assured Augie that he wouldn't put ketchup on the fries.

"Okay, so we'll just have one order of fries. Oh! And let's get an order of fried onion rings. You like onion rings don't you Henry? What am I asking? Everybody likes onion rings, right? Yeah, of course they do. So, we'll have one order of onion rings. We can split them between us."

Henry didn't say anything to that because by now he had come to accept the fact that whenever Augie went into one of his running monologues, his mind was already set and anytime he asked a question it was purely rhetorical and he really wasn't concerned about what Henry's response would be. He just assumed that Henry felt the same way that he did. So, Henry just went along, nodding now and then to show that he was still alive while he let Augie do his thing.

"You guys want something to drink with your food?"

"What?" asked Augie in theatrical surprise. "You have to ask? We're in Gallagher's ain't we? People don't come into this place unless they want to drink. Isn't that right Henry?"

Henry nodded, although he couldn't say with authority why anyone came into Gallagher's because he had never set foot in the place before this evening.

"Of course, we'll have a couple of beers."

"In bottles or from the tap?"

"What do you have on tap?"

"Augie," said Marcy in a tone of exaggerated exasperation, "you ask me that every time you come in here and every time it's always the same thing."

"Yeah, I know, but I just like to hear you rattle off the names."

Marcy let out a sigh as if to broadcast that a woman's work is never done, then she started to recite the name of the brews on tap. "We got Budweiser, we got Miller Lite, we got Brooklyn Brewery, we got—"

"Brooklyn Brewery. We'll have two glasses of that. You ever had Brooklyn beer, Henry?"

Henry confessed that he hadn't ever tasted the beer.

"Well then, you're in for a treat. The stuff is really good. You know why? Because it's made in Brooklyn, that's why. Everything made in Brooklyn is great. That's why Marcy is such a hot number, because she was born in Brooklyn."

"Yeah!" said Marcy sarcastically. "I'm so great. That's why I get to work in a joint like this. I'll get your beers."

Marcy walked away and Augie clasped his hands behind his head and leaned back against the wall.

"This is the life, huh, kid?"

Henry looked at Augie and saw the broad smile on the little man's face and at the same time he could feel the sense of contentment that the little man effortlessly radiated. As he looked at Augie, Henry thought to himself that, at that moment, for Augie, that wasn't just an idle expression; the little guy was genuinely happy. For him just coming to the neighborhood brew house and ordering simple fare was enough to make him relax and smile and put him into a state of mild euphoria, and at this moment, *this really was the life.*

Henry looked at Augie with a feeling of admiration and even envy, because Henry realized that Augie had genuine *joie de vivre*. As Henry reflected on this, he realized that sometime in his life he, Henry Gainsvort, had lost that ability to relax and enjoy life as Augie could. He had lost the knack of taking time out from the daily grind to just sit back, relax and just be happy. But now as he looked at Augie's big smile and sunny expression, Henry realized that he too was happy—maybe not as happy and contented as Augie, but still happy nevertheless—and that surprised him. It surprised him because up till now, Henry always believed that happiness only comes with success and achievement and monetary security. But here he was sitting in the back room of a bar, waiting for hamburgers and beer with a little man that he had only met an hour ago and he, Henry Gainsvort, was unexpectedly, but decidedly happy. He was happier than he had been for a long time, and that was a good feeling.

CHAPTER 13

Marcy came back and put two glasses of beer on the table before them. "Your food'll be out in a few minutes." Then she disappeared leaving the two of them sitting facing each other with two beers between them. Augie picked up his glass.

"What'll we drink to?"

Henry looked back at Augie and drew a blank. It hadn't occurred to him to drink to anything, and he found himself at a loss for what to suggest. But it seemed that Augie was never at a loss for words or inspiration. He raised his glass and said, "Here's to friendship."

Henry looked at him and thought to himself that this was, indeed, the perfect toast. *To friendship!* A true friendship was something that had eluded Henry for most of his life. He had gone for so long without having a close friend that he had come to accept solitude and loneliness as his lot in life; but now here he was, sitting in the same booth with a little guy who was a total stranger yesterday, but now, today, had become his friend. Henry had suddenly, and without premonition, found a friend.

Henry raised his glass and said, "To friendship." They clinked their glasses and each took a swig. The beer hit Henry's palate and it tasted good, really good. He didn't know if it tasted so good because it was made in Brooklyn as Augie had said, or because it was flavored with friendship, but whatever the reason it was good.

They settled back and Augie pulled out a cigarette and lighter, then he lit up.

"Are you allowed to smoke in here?"

Augie shook his head. "Not really; but I sit back here in this corner booth where there's a window. I keep the window open a crack and it pulls out the cigarette smoke. Nobody notices, so they let me get away with it. It's a good thing too, because I gotta have my cigarette. I'd die without it."

Henry thought to himself that, considering how bad cigarettes are for your health, and how much he smoked, then someday Augie would probably die with his cigarettes; but he didn't say anything. Augie was old enough to know what he was doing. If he wanted to smoke, then let him. It was his life, so let him live it as he saw fit.

Augie took a drag and settled back against the window. "This is some place isn't it?"

Henry nodded. "Yeah it is. It's truly amazing, and to think that it's only a few blocks from where I live and I've never been in here before." He paused for a minute as he looked around at the walls. "There are so many great, old pictures on the walls."

"You recognize anyone in them?"

Henry looked around again. "There's Joe DiMaggio batting at the plate."

Augie nodded. "Yeah, the 'Yankee Clipper'. The great Joe DiMaggio hisself. He was probably the best baseball player who ever lived. Ya know, he hit safely in fifty-four consecutive games. Imagine that! Fifty-four games in a row and always getting at least one hit. That's a record that still stands."

"You ever see him play?"

Augie shook his head. "Not in person. He was before my time. But I did see films of him. Newsreel footage. Man, he could really swing a bat. I mean he could really hit. Ted Williams was like that too. Ted Williams, 'the Splendid Splinter'. I mean, both of them, natural hitters. They don't make ball players like that anymore."

Augie paused to take another long drag, then he pointed to a picture on a nearby wall.

"There's another great slugger."

"Where?"

Augie pointed. "Over there behind you. Only he wasn't a ball player. He was a fighter. One of the best. That's the great Rocky Marciano, the 'Rock' they called him. He was like a solid wall; punches didn't seem to stun him.

"There he is slamming Jersey Joe Walcott. Man, that guy could hit. Look at Walcott's face. It looks like a squashed prune. Something about Marciano that maybe you didn't know, but the guy was short. I don't remember how short. Probably not as short as me, but short for a fighter. Sometimes, in order to land a punch, he had to jump at his opponent. Can you imagine that? I mean landing a punch in midair."

"No, I didn't know that."

"I think that fight was in the Garden. I mean the old Madison Square Garden, the one that used to be on forty-ninth` street and eighth, not the new one on thirty-third street. That old Garden was great, it had character; not like the new monstrosity they have now. You ever been to that old Garden kid?"

"No, it was before my time."

Augie nodded. "Yeah, mine too, but my old man went to lots of events before they tore the place down. He said that it was some place. He went to see a lot of fights. I don't remember all the bouts that he told me about. Most of them weren't big-name bouts. The place was great. The audience was filled with men—there may have been a couple of broads here and there, but it was mostly guys, and the air was filled with cigarette and cigar smoke and you could actually smell the sweat of the fighters—although some of that smell may have come from the crowd, because back in those days there was always a lot of bums in the audience. You know what I mean? But anyway, that didn't matter because it just added to the atmosphere. I mean it was a real gutsy scene. Really great. You know what I'm talking about?"

Henry nodded although he really didn't really have any conception of what Augie was talking about—at least he never had any kind of personal experience quite like that because he had never gone to any professional sporting events, much less a boxing match. So, he really had no idea what it was like to sit in a closed environment where men smoked and smelled and probably spat on the floor.

Actually, as he thought about it, Henry realized that the only games he had ever been to were those he saw in high school and college, and in thinking about it, he came to see that he'd always led a kind of sheltered life. He'd never experienced the kind of manly, working-class type of event that Augie was talking about. A prize fight was not the type of thing that he would ever have gone to because he had the impression that those events were always noisy and noxious, populated by boisterous and ill-mannered people. None of his classmates—the few vague friends that he had in his youth—would ever go to prize fights either. They were all kind of sheltered like himself.

So, he never went gone to a prize fight, or hockey match, or horse race, because he always thought those were the kind of rough-and-tumble events that attracted a seedy element. But now, listening to Augie talk of the good old days in the Madison Square Garden that once was, he began to wonder if maybe he had missed out on something.

"Yeah," continued Augie, "those were the good old days when you had real men fighting. Guys who could climb into the ring and really move around and mix it up. I mean they were really tough back then, and real athletes. Not like today."

"You don't think today's boxers are as good as those in the past?"

"They could be, if they concentrated on fighting. But the fight game has changed so much nowadays. Today prize fighting is a media event. All the fighters care about today is getting their name in the news and their faces on TV and making as much money as they can. Some of them don't fight for a year or two. They sit out the months between fights just to give the promoters enough time to work up the bout into a splashy media event. In the old days the fighters were always training for an upcoming bout."

While Augie was talking, his ever-present cigarette was dangling from his lower lip. Henry was practically mesmerized by the fact that the cigarette would stay fixed to that lower lip no matter how much Augie talked. And it seemed that Augie was always talking.

"Today, when the big fight finally does come around, they hold it in some humongous arena somewhere that's got lights and music and bells and whistles. And the crowd they attract is a bunch of weirdos. They come in wearing their furs and fancy clothes with flashy jewelry—and these are the guys that I'm talking about, not just the broads. No, it's not the same as it was back in the good old days."

At that moment Marcy walked up with the food. Henry noted that she managed to carry the four plates without a tray, just holding two plates in her hands and balancing the other two on her forearms. She put the food on the table then asked, "You guys want anything else?"

"Yeah!" said Augie. "Why don't you bring us two more beers while you're at it. We're gonna need refills soon."

Henry looked at the two glasses on the table. He had only taken a few gulps from his, but Augie's glass was almost empty.

"Drink up kid! We got two more coming and the night is still young."

Henry raised his glass and took a manly gulp. At the same time, it occurred to him that Augie had taken to calling him, "kid". Henry didn't mind that he had suddenly become the *kid*. In fact, he kind of liked it: he felt that this new sobriquet made him a part of Augie's world.

Marcy started to walk away but then turned back to Augie. "Hey Augie! You know you're not supposed to smoke in here. It's against the law."

"Oh yeah! You're right. I'm sorry, I musta forgotten about that."

"You didn't forget; you just don't have any respect for the law."

"No, gee, Marcy, that ain't so. I do respect the law. And I'll put out my cigarette right away. I will."

"Just see that you do."

With that Marcy turned and walked away. Henry looked at Augie to see him extinguish his cigarette, but to his surprise, Augie continued to smoke. Augie looked at Henry and knew the question that was forming in his mind.

"It's kind of a game that we play. She tells me to put out my cigarette and I say I will. Then she walks away and I continue to smoke and she don't bother me no more. I'm way in the corner here. Who's gonna see me smoking? And if some joker comes over, I can always flick the butt out the window before he gets close enough to say anything. Then there's no evidence and nobody can say nothing. Clever huh?"

Augie picked up his burger. "Dig in kid, while the grub is still hot." He took a big chomp out of his burger and was still chewing when he started to talk again.

"Now as I saying, the fight game ain't like it used to be. Naw! Not at all. Why I hear that they're even letting broads into the ring. Can you imagine that? I mean, a couple of dames slugging it out in the ring. No way! Now don't get me wrong, I like to see dames fight; but they should do it like broads fight naturally, with kicking and scratching and tearing out hair. That's the way broads were meant to fight. I mean who wants to see a couple of broads throwing leather at each other and sweating in the ring? I mean that's disgusting."

Marcy came back with two more beers. Augie spotted her coming with the beers and put his smoldering cigarette on the window sill. Either Marcy didn't notice the butt or else she chose to ignore it, because she said nothing about it as she put the glasses on the table.

"Here, this oughta hold you guys for a few minutes."

"Yeah," said Augie. "That oughta hold us for now. But we'll probably want some more brewskis later. Right kid? I'll give you the high sign when we need refills."

Marcy nodded then walked away.

"Now, where were we? Oh yeah, we were talking about broads fighting. I'll tell you that there is really one place where the dames really put on a good fight and when they go at it, they put on a great show. Know where it is?"

Henry shook his head. "I have no idea."

Augie leaned closer across the table as if he were about to disclose some state secret and he didn't want anybody but Henry to hear it.

"Politics!"

"Politics?"

"Yeah! You ever see when two broads are running for the same office, and they get up and give press conferences and start attacking each other. Man, then they start to get vicious. The next day you see them in the newspaper pictures, and do they ever look mean and wild. You can practically see their fangs and claws.

"I just love it when two dames are running for the same office. In fact, I wish more women would get into politics. Can you imagine what it would be like if two dames ran against each other for President? Man, that would be the cat fight of the century with fur flying all over the place."

Augie took another chomp on his burger then looked back at Henry. "Hey, whatsa matter, kid? You're not eating."

It was true. Henry had become so engrossed listening to Augie ramble on, that he had forgotten about eating. He sat there holding his burger between his two hands, elbows resting on the table, looking and listening to Augie but not taking a bite.

"Something the matter with the food?"

"No," said Henry. "It's just that I...well, I got so caught up listening to you that, I just forgot about eating."

"What? Hey, you can listen and still eat. That's easy. After all, I'm talking and I'm eating. So, you can listen and eat; so, eat!"

And that was also true. Augie was talking and eating, doing both at the same time. So, Henry started eating while at the same time he listened to Augie go on about this and about that jumping from one subject to another without pause. Augie talked on and on, and it amazed Henry that Augie could eat, drink, smoke, and talk at almost the same time without missing a beat. For Augie it was one, long stream-of-consciousness monologue delivered while chomping and drinking and taking a drag.

Henry hardly said anything. He just sat there trying to eat as he listened to the little man sitting across from him. As Augie rambled on and on, he generated an enthusiasm, an unpretentious warmth and friendliness that was spontaneous, infectious, and captivating. He seemed to have an opinion about everything and as he talked, Henry soon felt a genuine liking for this little guy, his new-found friend, Augie Martello.

After a while they finished eating, but not drinking. They continued to drink their beers and when they each finished a glass, Augie gave the high sign to Marcy who brought over two more glasses of Brooklyn Brewery. During all this, Augie continued to smoke and drink and talk. He pointed to another picture.

"Take a look at that picture over there."

Henry looked around to see where Augie was pointing. "Which one?"

"That one there."

"You mean the one of the horse?"

"Yeah, but that's not just any horse. That's a special horse."

"Who is it, Man O' War?"

"Good guess, but no cigar. No, that's Secretariat. 'Big Red' they used to call him. That's him coming across the finish line at Belmont. I saw that race on a TV special. That's when he won the triple crown. Look at that, he was way ahead of the other nags when he crossed the finish line. You know how far out he was?"

Henry shook his head.

"Thirty-one lengths. Can you imagine that? I mean thirty-one lengths."

"That's amazing," said Henry but he said that just as response. There wasn't much enthusiasm in his voice because he wasn't sure how far thirty-one lengths covered; but judging by Augie's enthusiastic tone, Henry figured it must be quite a distance.

Augie continued. "He left the other ponies in the dust. Man, he was magnificent! That horse could really run. The jockey was Ron Turcotte."

Augie paused a minute to take a drag followed by a gulp of beer. "You ever been to the track kid?"

"You mean Belmont?"

Augie shrugged. "Belmont. The big A. The Meadowlands. Any track, anywhere. You ever seen the ponies run? I mean live, in the open air, not on television or in the movies."

Henry shook his head. "No, I've never been to a horse race anywhere."

"Oh man, you should go. I tell you, there ain't nothing so great as watching your horse come over the finish line. Especially when you got a few pennies on its nose. That makes it all the more sweeter."

"You go to the track often?"

"I don't know what you'd call often. I like to go to the track at least a couple of times a month, maybe more. In the summer I go two, maybe three times a week. It's a good way to get out of the house. I especially like to go when I get a hunch. I like to play hunches." He paused they looked back at Henry. "You ever get hunches, kid?"

Suddenly that question struck a chord in Henry's alcohol-befuddled brain and roused him from the mild state of euphoria that he had lapsed into. To Augie this was a simple enough question, but it struck a note of fear within Henry. How to answer that question? After all a hunch is kind of like a vision and Henry had promised himself that he would never, ever talk about his visions.

Up till now he had been enjoying this evening. He had unexpectedly found a friend he enjoyed being with, but he was suddenly afraid that if he owned up to the fact that in his life he had those instances when he had visions of the destiny, times when he looked into tomorrow, then maybe all this merriment would come to an end.

Suppose now he told Augie about his visions, then would he, like all those other people in the past, suddenly look at Henry with suspicion and distrust? Would little Augie shun him just as those others had done in the past? Henry decided that it was better not to chance it. He simply said, "No. No, I never get hunches."

"Never? Gee, imagine that! I thought that everybody got hunches; but I guess maybe not. Oh well, that's a shame because it makes it more fun to play the ponies. Although as I think about it, maybe you have to go to the track a few times to get a feel for the horses and how they run. Maybe then a hunch will hit you. Oh well, never mind, that time will come."

Augie was silent for a few minutes, then he spotted another photograph on the wall. This one was of former New York City mayor, Fiorello LaGuardia and it proved to be that catalyst for another of Augie's monologues. He immediately started to talk about the politics of New York City contrasting the administration of Jimmy Walker to that of LaGuardia. And Henry breathed a silent sigh of relief; he had been able to sidestep the issue of premonition and thus keep his secret hidden from Augie.

Henry was able to relax again and let Augie talk on. As he listened to Augie talk, Henry noticed that he would just ramble on and, and even though Augie asked an occasional question, he never waited for a reply. It was as if he knew that his listener was going to respond as he expected, so he didn't feel the need to pause and interrupt his train of thought. The conversation was largely one-sided with Augie doing all the talking and Henry doing all the listening.

Augie continued talking, stopping now and then to light up a fresh cigarette or order another round of beer. As the evening wore on, Henry lost track of how many beers he had consumed. There was no way for him to check the count because Marcy had taken away the empty glasses with each new order. But as the evening wore on, Henry could feel that he was getting inebriated and tired. He didn't know which was getting the better of him, the fatigue or the alcohol—although it was probably a combination of both. He only knew that he was fading fast and couldn't stay awake much longer.

Yet as he looked at Augie, he saw that Augie was still going strong, still talking, still smoking and drinking, apparently unaffected by either the many beers or the lateness of the hour. Henry marveled that Augie could put away so many beers and yet remain unphased by it all. *How many brewskies had they had anyhow?* Henry wondered how much longer Augie could go on. Then abruptly Augie looked at his watch.

"Hey kid! Do you know what time it is?"

Henry shook his head.

"It's after one. Maybe we should call it a night."

Henry nodded in agreement and Augie called Marcy over for the check. She came over, figured the total then left the slip of paper on the table. Augie reached for it, then leaned forward to share it with Henry. Augie looked at the total and did some mental calculations and announced what Henry's share should be. Henry accepted Augie's calculation without argument, because he was too tired to go over the figures himself. He reached into his pocket for his wallet and pulled out the necessary bills which he deposited on the table. Augie added his money to the pile and they left it there as they got up and made their way out of the place.

They walked along back to their apartment building, with Augie walking and talking and still seemingly as fresh as when they started out. Henry walked beside him trying to maintain the appearance of alert sobriety and walk without staggering or stumbling.

They got to the apartment house, entered the foyer and climbed the stairs to the second floor where they stopped at the door to Henry's apartment.

"Well kid," said Augie. "It's time to say goodnight. Thank you for coming with me. I had a good time. I hope you did too."

"Yeah, Augie I did. It was great. Really great!"

"Well, good! Then maybe we could do it again sometime."

"I'd like that, Augie. I really would."

"So good!" said Augie with enthusiasm. "So, let's plan on doing it again soon. Hey, and who knows, but maybe we can try something else."

"Yeah, Augie, sure. I'm up for almost anything."

"Great! So, we'll do something soon. In the meantime, I'll say goodnight kid."

With that Augie turned and went up the stairs to his apartment. Henry groped through his pocket for his keys. When he found his keys, he fumbled to find the right one and struggled to fit the key in the lock and turn the cylinder. All this took a lot of time as he went through trial-and-error to get his door open; but eventually he did manage to unlock the door and push his way into his apartment.

He locked the door behind him then pulled off his jacket and threw it to the couch. Unfortunately, it missed and slid off onto the floor, but Henry was too tired and drunk to pick it up.

Next, he made his way into the bathroom where he splashed his face with water then brushed his teeth. Then he staggered into his bedroom. He pulled off his shoes, dropped his pants, and struggled out of his shirt then he fell back onto the bed in his underwear and socks.

As he lay there on his back, looking up at the ceiling with the room spinning around about him. He saw a big brown water bug hanging motionless on the ceiling, but he was too tired to get up and swat it. Instead he lay on his bed and he thought over the whole evening. This night he made a new friend and he had a good time with that friend. It was the best time he had in so many, many years. Maybe it was the best time that he had ever had in his whole life.

As he thought back over the evening, Henry remembered the wish he made, "I wish that all good things would come my way from now on", and he thought that maybe with this wish he had reached a turning point in his life. Maybe good things were starting to come his way, and maybe they would follow from now on. If only that would happen. If only good things would continue to come his way. Well, there was no reason to believe that they shouldn't happen—if only he could keep his visions to himself. If he could just do that, then he would be just like any other guy and everything would be okay. With those mellow thoughts dancing in his inebriated mind he soon fell into a deep sleep.

CHAPTER 14

After that first evening at Gallagher's, Henry and Augie began to see more of each other. They met frequently and usually went to Gallagher's but often they did other things as well. It wasn't long before Augie and Henry were the best of friends. For Henry this friendship was like a breath of springtime; now, at long last, he had a tried-and-true good buddy, someone he could talk to, drink with, laugh with, and hang out with.

Henry noted that Augie had started calling him "kid" on their very first night at Gallagher's. Afterward whenever he addressed Henry, he used this appellation so that now Henry came to think of himself as "the kid". This didn't bother Henry; in fact, it amused him. He kind of liked his new nickname because it made him feel like he was a special person in Augie's world. And for Henry it was a wonderful feeling, being part of Augie's world.

As the weeks progressed, Henry and Augie did a lot of things together. Of course, they frequented Gallagher's often, but sometimes in the evenings, they took walks along the promenade deck at Brooklyn Heights where they had good view of the Manhattan skyline. Other days they wandered and explored other neighborhoods around the city.

And no matter what neighborhood they walked in, it seemed that Augie knew a bar that they could drop into for a brew. And whatever bar they walked into, it seemed that the bartender knew Augie and Augie always knew a couple of the patrons.

Sometimes, when the weather was bad, they got together in Henry's dingy apartment, and they would often spend the long evening there talking together. At first Henry was reluctant to invite Augie into his pad because he felt it was dreary and dismal and infested with roaches and mice and he was ashamed to show anyone where he lived. But as he thought about it, he figured that if Augie lived in the same building as he, then it figured that he probably had a similar atmosphere with no sunlight and he faced the same problems with mice and roaches. So, one evening when the weather was particularly foul, Henry suggested that the Augie come down to his apartment where he had beer in the fridge and where they could call for a pizza delivery. Augie readily agreed.

When the pizza came, they brought it into the kitchen and opened a couple of beers. Henry really didn't like hanging around in his kitchen at night because the only lighting was an overhead fluorescent fixture that cast a ghostly, artificial blue light on everything and gave the room a kind of unnatural, sterile look; but there was really no other place to sit and eat in his apartment, so they settled in the gloomy kitchen to eat and drink. Of course, Augie had to smoke also. In spite of the food and beer, Henry still didn't like the eerie glow of the room, but Augie seemed indifferent to it.

Indeed, that was something that Henry noticed about his pal; Augie never seemed to mind any of life's minor annoyances. Henry found that no matter what circumstances the two might find themselves in, no matter how unpleasant or uncomfortable, Augie seemed indifferent and blasé about the little irritants that would drive most people up a wall.

And he never complained. Augie had an opinion or comment about everything in the world but he never carped about his lot in life. He just accepted his circumstances for what they were and went through life without complaining or grumbling. This blanket acceptance of life was one of Augie's most endearing charms and Henry truly admired that trait in his friend.

That stormy evening, for example, as they were eating pizza in Henry's cheerless kitchen, a big, brown roach scurried across the kitchen counter. Henry looked at it in revulsion and jumped up to squash it, but Augie only gave it a momentary look and said, "Let it go. He's probably just passing through."

Henry paused, then sat down again. He looked at Augie who had now turned his attention back to his slice of pepperoni pizza with extra cheese, and he silently wondered to himself if maybe Augie had some secret reason for letting the roach live; like for example, that he knew and recognized that particular roach. Maybe it was some sort of quasi-pet or maybe Augie thought of it as a friend of some kind. After all, he knew everyone else in the neighborhood, so why not the cockroaches and mice too? Well, whatever the reason, Henry followed Augie's advice and let the ugly brown roach pass by without attempting to flatten it into oblivion.

This relatively minor incident later gave Henry pause for further thought. It made him search his conscience and ask himself why he ever started to kill those big brown bugs in the first place. Up till now he had always squashed them and laid out traps for them without giving his actions a second thought. He just assumed that it was natural to kill the insects because…well, because they were insects. He just killed those big brown creatures because they were ugly and vile and it was it was natural to want to exterminate them; but, now on reflection, he wasn't so sure of himself. *Why not just live and let them be?* He didn't have an answer to that, but he would think about it.

As that evening turned into the night, they continued eating and drinking and talking. Augie told a number of stories about sports and life in the good old days. He peppered his many stories with his opinions and insights—of which there were many—but he also told Henry something of his past. Henry learned that his friend had been a career man in the Navy. He served for almost twenty-five years in the service mostly on board an aircraft carrier and he rose to the rank of chief petty officer before he retired from the Navy.

Now that he was retired from the service he was living off his pension, but he continued to work at odd jobs here and there just to make extra spending money. He told Henry that sometimes he got jobs as a messenger or a night watchman. One time he even took a job where he dressed up in a chicken suit and handed out flyers in Times Square to advertise a fast-food chicken restaurant that was about to open in Manhattan. When he wasn't working at these odd, piece-meal jobs he spent most of his time in bars or at the track.

Augie talked on for most of the evening and Henry listened. During all this they munched on the pizza and consumed numerous bottles of beer and Augie puffed away on his ever-present cigarette. Augie did almost all of the talking, but then around about midnight, after all the pizza was consumed and they were working on the last few bottles of beer, he sat back, smiled and he said to Henry, "Go ahead kid, now it's your turn."

Henry looked back in surprise. They had had many conversations during the past few months, but it seemed the Augie always did most of the talking with Henry only asking an occasional question or throwing in a comment here and there. Now, suddenly, unexpectedly, it was as if Augie had handed him the microphone and stepped aside. Henry found himself in the spotlight and was totally unprepared.

"My turn? What do you mean?"

Augie smiled his broad benevolent smile. "Tell me about yourself, kid. It seems that I'm the one who's always doing all the talking. Let's hear about you for a change."

"Well, I'm not sure what to say. I mean, I don't know where to begin. I really haven't done much of anything."

That was true; Henry didn't really know what to say because it seemed that no one had ever been very interested in him, so he never really had the opportunity to talk about himself. Well, that wasn't entirely true; there was Doctor Wolfgang Holtz way back when Henry was in the seventh grade. At the time it seemed as if he was interested in Henry; but that was different. Doctor Holtz was a psychologist. It was his job to be interested in people. He was getting paid to listen.

Other than Holtz, however, no one ever seemed to want to know anything about Henry. Henry had always been someone who just hung around and people accepted him as one of life's fixtures, like human wallpaper. Now, suddenly, Augie was asking Henry to talk about himself and he didn't know where to start. Also, he was reluctant to talk about himself, because he hadn't done much in life and he felt that his experiences were dull when compared to those of his friend, Augie Martello.

Augie sensed Henry's awkwardness and inability to talk about himself.

"Start at the beginning kid. Where did you grow up? Where did you go to school?"

Prompted by Augie's questions, Henry began to talk about himself. Slowly at first with sentences that were hesitant, tentative and unsure, but once he got his narrative ball rolling he found his voice and talked with more confidence. Augie sat back and listened, smiling and smoking. Whenever Henry paused as if unsure what else to say, Augie asked a question to jump start the narrative.

And so, Henry told about himself. He told about his childhood in Jersey City and his grammar school and his high school. He told about going to college. The beer acted as a lubricant and put him in a mellow mood. He soon forgot his inhibitions and he talked freely about everything.

Almost everything. There was one topic he could not bring himself to talk about—one subject he avoided. Henry reminded himself that years back, he vowed never to talk about his uncanny visions where sometimes destiny came alive as a scenario that only he could see—that he had the ability to sometimes glimpse into the future. He had learned from painful experience that this was a subject that he had to keep hidden and avoided at all costs.

It wasn't that he wanted to deceive Augie and he wasn't trying to be dishonest about himself. It's just that Henry was afraid. Henry remembered from the past how people reacted when they found out that he could sometimes, at odd moments, here and there, see into the future. He still had those unpleasant memories of his former friends who suddenly changed their attitude and avoided him when they found out about his strange visions. He remembered how he suddenly became a freak in their eyes and how they moved away from him.

Henry knew from past experience that many a friendship was destroyed because people didn't trust this strange quirk of his and he didn't want that to happen this time with his friend, Augie. Augie was his good friend and he didn't want anything to come in the way of their friendship—not now when it was going so well. Maybe Augie would react differently than all those others; but then again, maybe not. Henry wasn't about to risk this friendship, so he said nothing about the many visions that he had seen during the course of his life. He was determined to keep them a deep secret no matter what. It was the one thing in his life that he would keep under wraps. The one part of his life that he would never tell Augie about.

Unfortunately, the best-laid plans of mice and men often come to naught even in the face of solid determination; and although Henry tried hard to keep his uncanny ability a secret, Henry's ability was such that it was bound to surface in spite of his best efforts. One day, in an unguarded moment, Henry's clairvoyance revealed itself. This is how it happened.

After an evening of eating, drinking, and talking at Gallagher's, just as the two friends were about to part company at Henry's door, Augie abruptly asked, "Hey kid, if you've got nothing on the fire for tomorrow how's about you and me going to see the Cyclones tomorrow evening?"

Henry looked at Augie in puzzlement. "The Cyclones. What are the Cyclones?"

"What? How long you been living in Brooklyn now? What did you tell me? Almost two years? You've been living here that long and you don't know who the Cyclones are? That is hard to believe."

"No Augie, I don't think I've ever heard of the Cyclones. Who are they?"

"Why the Cyclones are Brooklyn's baseball team."

"I didn't know Brooklyn had a baseball team anymore. I mean, I heard of the Brooklyn Dodgers, but they moved to L.A. in the sixties. When did Brooklyn get a new ball team?"

"A few years back. I don't remember exactly when. The Cyclones are the Mets' farm team. They used to play somewhere else but the Mets brought them here to Brooklyn."

"Oh, I never heard. Where do they play?"

"There's a stadium in Coney Island."

"There's a baseball stadium in Coney Island? I didn't know that either."

"Oh kid, I can see your education has been sadly neglected. We're gonna have to do something about that. So, how's about tomorrow night? We'll hop the subway and ride it to Coney Island tomorrow and take in a game. That is unless you've got something else cooking."

"No Augie, I've got nothing else. Do you think we'll be able to get seats? I mean, don't we have to book ahead?"

"No kid! There's always room. Trust me; we'll get seats and you'll have a good time. Trust me!"

"Sure Augie, whatever you say. I'm up for it"

The next evening, they took the train down to Coney Island and went to the stadium to see the Cyclones play. They got good seats where they had a clear view of the playing field. Well, that wasn't too difficult because the stadium isn't large and there's a good view of the field from almost every seat.

That particular evening was a good night to watch an outdoor ballgame; the air was clear, the temperature just right, there was no humidity, and overhead the stars and moon were shining.

Augie and Henry found their seats and settled down. They ordered hot dogs and beer watched the game together. It was a good game with several outstanding plays, a few exciting moments, and one home run. The players weren't exceptional because, after all, this was the minor leagues and one couldn't expect these players to be in the same class as those in the majors. So, there were a lot of errors; but that was the fun of watching because this wasn't slick, precision baseball. It was a game with human foibles and missed chances, where you never knew what was going to happen next.

It was now the bottom of the seventh and the Cyclones were at bat. There was a man on first and one out. The Cyclone's left fielder came up to bat.

Augie leaned over to Henry. "The trouble with this guy is that he always hits into a double play. You watch, he'll smack the ball to one of the infielders and they'll turn a double play."

But Henry didn't see it that way. A sudden vision flashed in his mind's eye and he saw that something else was about to happen.

"No, not this time. You watch. The shortstop will bobble the ball and they'll only get the runner out. The guy on first will get to second before the throw."

At that moment, Henry realized what he had done. He had let his guard down, and without thinking blurted out his latest vision. He knew that he shouldn't have said it, but he had gotten caught up in the game and he totally forgot his resolve. Now he had revealed a vision, and there was nothing to do but see how the game would play out.

The pitcher threw the ball, the batter hit it to the shortstop, and the rest happened exactly as Henry said it would. When the play was completed there was one runner out and the other safe on second. Augie looked from the field back to Henry.

"Hey kid, you called it. It happened just as you said."

Silently, Henry cursed himself for having made the slip. Suddenly he was on the spot, his secret was out and there was no way to cover it. *What kind of explanation could he give for having predicted the play before it actually happened?*

He was trying to think of some sort of rationalization when Augie said, "You had a hunch right?"

"Yeah Augie, I guess I did."

"I thought you said you never get hunches."

"Did I say that? Well I never did before, but I guess I just got one this time."

"Well that's good, kid. Whenever you get a hunch you should go with it. Hunches are good things. I oughta know, I won some nice moola when a pony paid off on one of my hunches."

So, Henry had another vision—one that he inadvertently blurted out—but it was innocent enough and Augie dismissed it as a mere hunch. Henry breathed a sigh of relief and thanked his lucky stars that he still able to keep his secret hidden from his friend Augie. But that wasn't the end of it, because there was another incident a few months later.

CHAPTER 15

The next time Henry had a vision the explanation wasn't so easy. In fact, there was no explanation other than the real thing. It happened like this.

Augie and Henry were standing on the edge of the curb in Manhattan and were about to cross fourteenth street and go into Union Square Park as soon as there was a break in the traffic. Augie saw an opening and stepped off the curb, but before he took another step, Henry extended his arm across Augie's chest and blocked him from further advance. Augie looked up at Henry in puzzlement. Henry pointed to a place before them in the middle of the street.

"That manhole is gonna explode," he said.

Augie thought this strange and looked from Henry out to the street at the manhole. Then he looked back at Henry and he was about to ask Henry what he was talking about, when, at that very moment, there was a loud explosion; a bright yellow-orange flame shot out from the manhole and the heavy metal cover went flying high up into the air, flipping end-over-end, like a coin spinning in the air. It came crashing down to the black-top street and buried itself half-way up into the asphalt.

Augie looked from the street to Henry. For a long minute neither of them said a word. Then finally Augie's eyes narrowed as he looked at Henry and he asked, "How'd you know? How did you know that was gonna happen?"

Henry gulped. Suddenly he realized that he had blurted out another vision. Up till now he had tried so hard to keep his visions an inner secret, but now, without thinking of it, in an unguarded moment, he had inadvertently let out his latest vision and he realized that he had just made a serious mistake. He tried to backpedal and cover his tracks.

"Well...er...Augie, it was just...I mean...it was just a hunch. Yeah, that's what it was. It was a hunch that I suddenly had."

Augie's eyes narrowed and he looked at Henry and slowly, knowingly, shook his head.

"No, kid. That was no hunch. I've had many hunches in my life. I've been around hunch players and I know a hunch when I see one. That was no hunch. You knew that was gonna happen just like it happened. You knew it. How? How did you know that it was gonna happen before it did?"

Henry suddenly felt very shaky. Up till now he had tried so hard to keep his strange clairvoyance from his pal Augie. He wanted to do that because he harbored a deep-seated fear that once Augie found out, he would desert him like all the others had before. Now, however, in spite of all his efforts, his secret was out and there was no way to hide it again. Henry didn't want to talk about it, but as he looked back at Augie, he saw there was no way around it. The time had come when he would have to tell all.

"Well..." he began weakly.

But just as he was about to tell his story, Augie grabbed him by the arm.

"No, kid; not here. This is too crowded and too noisy. I have a feeling that this is going to be a long story and we should go someplace quiet. Come on, I know a good bar near here. We can talk there."

It figured. No matter where in New York City they were—no matter what neighborhood—it also seemed that Augie knew of a good bar close by. So, Augie led Henry across the street, through the park, across another street and down the block to the Old House Tavern near eighteenth street.

They entered the place and walked up to the bar where Augie ordered two glasses of beer for the table. While the bartender was pouring the brew, Henry looked about. This bar was old and it was quiet. There weren't many people in the place and there was no television blaring with some loud game. This seemed like a nice, quiet place. If Henry had to tell his story, then this seemed like the place to do it.

They took their glasses and settled into a back booth.

Then Augie said, "Okay kid, tell me what's going on. Tell me the whole story; I'm all ears."

Henry realized that he had no choice. His back was to the wall, and there was nowhere to go, no room to maneuver. It was time to 'fess up and tell Augie all about himself and of his many strange visions. So, Henry launched into the story of all his visions. He told about his first vision when he was walking along Stevens Avenue with his mother and he saw the car crash before it actually happened. He continued with the visions he had in childhood and in grammar school and the vision he had in high school. He told about all his visions, and he told of the reaction that he got from his friends and classmates.

He told of his encounter with Judson Blaine. Then he told about his first job as an accountant and how he saw the demise of the mighty Entrac empire and how he tried hard to warn people about what was coming.

He told Augie all of that and more, and he held nothing back. And while he was talking, he continued to look at Augie for some sort of reaction, but there was nothing. Augie just sat there, looking back at Henry, without comment or expression, just absorbing it all.

When he had finished his tale, Henry breathed a silent sigh of relief. Finally, he had confessed all, and at the same time, he had unburdened himself from the heavy emotional weight that he had been lugging around by withholding his dark, inner secret from his best friend. Now it was out and with that revelation, Henry felt a release from the inner tension that had pulled at him for so long.

But he still wondered how Augie was going to react to his story. After all, in the past, everyone else had always parted company with him whenever they found out about his visions. He remembered how so many times before, he had suddenly become a freak in the eyes of his friends just because he could see things that they couldn't. *Would Augie see him as an oddball too? Would he just get up and walk away? Was their warm, close friendship about to come to an end?*

Henry wasn't sure and he looked back at Augie and searched his face for some kind of reaction, some response; but there was nothing. Augie just sat there leaning back against the wall of the booth looking intently at Henry. He looked at Henry for the longest time, and it was such a strange look. Henry could tell that Augie was scrutinizing him and at the same time thinking. *But what was going through Augie's mind? Henry couldn't tell.*

Finally, Augie leaned forward and put his face close to Henry.

"Tell me kid," he said, "about these…what d'ya call them, 'visions'… yeah? Have you ever tried to make money with these visions of yours?"

Henry looked back at Augie in surprise and puzzlement.

"I don't understand. How could I make money with my visions?"

Augie shook his head. "I'm not sure, but I think there's something there, some sort of angle. And wherever there's an angle there's a way to make money."

"I don't see how."

"I'm not sure either, at least not yet. Tell me something about your visions. Yeah, tell me about them. How often do you get them?"

"I don't know, I never really thought about it. Sometimes I get three or four a year, sometimes more, sometimes less. One time I went almost two years before I had one. At that time, I thought they were gone forever and I outgrew them, but then they came back."

"And now they keep coming back?"

"Yeah, I guess so."

"And when you get them, what'd ya see?"

"I don't understand what you mean."

"I mean what happens when you get a vision. Does everything go dark and suddenly this picture pops up like a television screen? Or do you see strange lights and colored beams?"

Henry shook his head. "No, it's nothing like that. It's more like... let me see how can I describe it. Well, it's kinda like when you tell a story. Yeah, it's like that. Imagine that you're telling me a story about Ted Williams or Mickey Mantle hitting a home run. You're looking at me, and you see me, but at the same time you see a picture in your mind of Williams at the plate in the stadium and he swings at the pitch and knocks it out of the park. Yeah, you're looking at me and at the same time you're having a picture of Williams at the plate. That's what it's like."

Augie's face lit up with recognition. "Okay, I get it. It's like you're running the picture in your mind's eye while your two front eyes are still seeing everything around you."

Henry nodded.

"And do you have to be there to see your vision?"

"What do you mean?" asked Henry.

"Well, can you be sitting in your living room when suddenly you get a vision of a fire happening downtown around wall street?"

Henry shook his head. "No, I have to actually witness the scene. Sometimes I can get a vision of a play when I'm watching a ballgame on television, but otherwise I have to be there—right at the scene—in order for me to see what will happen."

Augie nodded. "Yeah. It sounds like maybe there's something there in the atmosphere around you that kind of triggers your visions."

"I don't know. I guess that's logical, but I don't know. I never gave it much thought before."

"And how far into the future can you see? I mean can you see something that is going to happen, say, next year?"

Henry shook his head. "No, most of the time the things I see happen in the next few minutes after I see them. Sometimes it takes longer."

"How much longer?"

"I'm not sure exactly. I never really kept track of when I saw something and when the event actually happened, but I think the longest time interval was about two weeks."

"And can you make these visions happen, or do they just pop up unexpectedly?"

"They just pop up. I have no control over them."

"How do you know? Have you ever tried to look into the future? I mean really tried."

Henry paused for a minute to think about it. "No, I never tried. I just assumed that they would come when the time was right. It never occurred to me to actually try and see into the future."

"Well, why don't you try now."

"How? I have no idea as to how to go about it."

"Well, look at the bartender back there. Look at him and try to see what's going to happen to him…oh, say, tomorrow. Yeah, just look at him and concentrate. Try to think about what's going to happen to him in the day or two."

Henry turned around and looked at the bartender. He was skeptical about this approach but at the same time he figured that he had nothing to lose by trying and maybe it might be interesting to find out if he really had the power to actually see into the future whenever he wanted. He stared at the bartender and at the same time he tried to keep his mind a total blank allowing any random thoughts or visions ample opportunity to pop up spontaneously; but at the end two minutes of concentrated effort nothing happened. He turned back to Augie.

"No, I'm sorry Augie; I'm not getting anything. It just isn't working."

"Don't be sorry kid. It ain't your fault. Well, at least now we know that your visions have to come of their own accord and there's no way to make them happen."

"Is this getting us anywhere? I mean what difference does it make how I get these pictures?"

"It makes a big difference. See kid, you have a power that no one else has. If we can figure out how that power works then maybe we can harness it and make it work for us. I'm telling you kid, that there's a way that you can make money with your visions; all you gotta do is find it."

"Sure Augie," replied Henry in frustration, "but how? How can I make money by seeing these events before they actually happen?"

"I don't know kid, but I'm working on it. I'm thinking about it now."

There was a silent pause in which neither of them said anything. Henry just sat there and let Augie stare up at the ceiling and think. After a few minutes Augie looked back at Henry.

"This is no good. I can't think here. The trouble is that I can only think when I have a cigarette and they won't let me smoke in here. I tell you what. Let's go outside and walk back to the park. I can have my cigarette there and then I can do some serious thinking."

So, the two men left the Old House Tavern and walked back to Union Square Park. They found an empty bench in a quiet section of the park and sat down. Augie immediately pulled out a cigarette and lit up. He took a few puffs and Henry could see his friend relaxing and enjoying his smoke. There were a few moments of silence when neither man spoke. Augie just sat there smoking his cigarette and staring into empty space before him, and Henry sat there looking at his friend and wondering what Augie could possibly be thinking about.

Finally, Augie turned to Henry with a slight smile on his face.

"Say kid, I think that maybe we should visit a casino."

CHAPTER 16

So, Henry and Augie took the bus to Atlantic City and this is what happened when they got there. The bus pulled up into a parking lot and everybody got off. Augie and Henry walked to the nearest casino.

They entered the casino and Henry was immediately transfixed by the glamor and glitter of the surroundings—the constant medley of whistles, beeps, bongs, of bells ringing and coins splashing together. The big room was a vibrant, dazzling spectacle of mirrors, chrome and sparkles brightened with flashing lights, a galaxy of LED's and miles of neon. There was something strange and wonderful about the place. It was strange because there were no windows anywhere. It was wonderful because it was a vast surreal, artificial environment isolated from the cares, tribulations and grime of the outside world.

Suddenly there was a cry of jubilation—obviously somewhere in the big room, someone had just hit a jackpot.

Henry looked about him in wonder.

"Wow!" he said. "I've never seen anything like this."

"What? You've never been in a casino before kid?"

"No, this is my first time."

"Well, then you get to make another wish. Go ahead, make one."

Henry stopped walking and closed his eyes tight. Then he thought to himself: "I hope that this works out. I really do."

Then he opened his eyes. Augie was standing there looking at him.

"You made your wish?"

Henry nodded.

"Okay, then let's wander around for a bit."

So, they walked about the huge room. Eventually they came to a section where there were rows and rows of slot machines.

"Let's try this on for size," said Augie.

They walked up and down between the corridors of slot machines.

"What are these machines, Augie?"

"They're slot machines, kid. They used to be called one-armed bandits 'cause at one time they had a lever on the side that you pulled to activate the mechanism. Now most of them are electronic and all ya gotta do is push the button."

"How do they work? I mean how do you play one?"

Augie looked at Henry and grinned. "Boy you are green if you ya don't know how to play one of these babies. Look, all ya gotta do is put your money in the slot and push the button. Then, you see the little window there? When you push the button, little pictures appear in that window, and, depending on the combination of pictures that come up, you either win or lose. I can't believe that you didn't know that."

Henry felt a little embarrassed and ashamed at his ignorance. "No, I didn't. I'm sorry, but I guess I never really traveled much."

"Don't be sorry kid. You didn't do anything wrong. And relax, you're here to learn, and I'll be your teacher. I'll teach you all you need to know."

"Okay, so what do we do? Do we put our coins in and play one of the machines?"

"No, that would be throwing our money away. Right now, we don't do nothing. We just wander around to get the lay of the land. We walk around and listen and look. We wait to see if you get one of your visions."

So, they walked around. They walked up and down the aisles, between and around the slot machines. This was a totally new experience for Henry; he had never been in a casino before so he never really saw slot machines except maybe on television. He stopped and watched a silver-haired lady pump coins into the slot and push the button. Pictures spun into the little windows at the top of the machine, then stop. It seemed like nothing happened. Henry watched the lady repeat the procedure time and time again without ever tiring of it.

He continued to watch as the pictures of cherries and lemons and bells and bars came whirling into place in the little windows. He had no idea what any of those symbols meant or why a buzzer would unexpectedly sound and coins would come pouring out of the machine into the tray. As Henry stood there, just looking, he was fascinated by the action that these strange, gleaming machines generated. He was tempted to go over and put a coin in the slot himself, but Augie had said to wait, so Henry waited.

Augie stood there beside Henry, saying nothing, just watching. He looked at Henry and tried to see if maybe his friend was seeing something, something more than he was seeing. Finally, he asked, "You getting anything, kid?"

"No, Augie I'm not seeing anything, but these things are amazing. To me it's very exciting just to stand here and watch them and see how they work."

"Yeah, but that don't pay the rent."

"Gee, I'm sorry Augie, but I'm just not seeing anything. Nothing at all. I'm really sorry."

"Don't be sorry kid, it ain't your fault. Maybe the slots don't put out the right vibrations. Let's try something else. Come on, let's wander over there."

They ended up standing by the blackjack table watching the play.

"How does this game work, Augie?'

"Well kid, the player has to get a twenty-one before the dealer does."

"How does he do that?"

"It's in the cards kid. He's got to get the right combination of cards. If he gets a ten and…"

At that moment Augie paused and looked at Henry. "You know, I think this may be too complicated, and besides you gotta be in it to win. I think we should look at a game that's a little less difficult and where we can stand on the side, watch, and place our bets without having to do anything else. We should find a game that needs less participation on our part. You know one where we only have to put our chips down without actually doing anything else."

Augie looked around.

"Ah, the craps table. Now that may be just what we're looking for. Come on, let's go over there."

There was a small crowd of people standing around the craps table. The stickman was positioned at the center and one man, the shooter, was at the end. He was shaking the dice in his right hand getting ready for a throw.

"How does this game work, Augie?"

"You don't have to know that kid. All you gotta know is that there are two dice and that they can show numbers from two to twelve. Now what we want to find out is if you can see what number comes up before the dice stop rolling. So, let's just stand here and watch for a bit just to see if you get anything."

So, they stood there, not far from the table, and they watched while the shooter shook his fist and blew on the dice and said something inane like. "Come on little babies, be kind to papa!"

Then he threw the dice against the backboard of the table. The two cubes bounced off the cushioned surface and rolled out onto the green-baize table top. When they came to rest there was a two and a three looking up at the ceiling.

"Five is the point," said the stickman and he raked in the dice and handed them back to the guy at the end of the table. The man repeated his ritual of blowing on the dice, shaking his fist, and uttering an incantation, then he launched the bones against the far wall of the table. The dice rebounded off the padded surface and rolled out onto the table. When they came to rest, the number nine came up.

Again, the stickman picked up the dice and handed them back to the shooter who repeated his throwing routine. He sent the dice flying against the backboard and this time after they bounced and rolled and came to rest, six was the number facing skyward. With each throw Augie looked up at Henry for his reaction—to see if maybe Henry was getting some kind of vision, but Henry just stood there mute and expressionless. There were two more tosses but Henry still remained unmoved and silent.

On the next toss however, just as the dice ricocheted off the wall cushion, Henry said, "eight." That one word was all he said.

Augie looked up at Henry in surprise then quickly looked back to the table. The dice rolled to a stop and there were a pair of fours looking up at the spectators around the table.

"Eight!" exclaimed Augie. "You called it kid! You said 'eight' and the guy rolled an eighter from Decatur. You did it, kid!"

Henry looked back at Augie. He had been so intent on watching the play that he didn't even realize that he had called out the number. He was about to say something but Augie held up his hand and pointed. The shooter was about to make another toss. Both men looked back at the table.

Again, the shooter shook his fist, blew on the dice and said, "Come on, baby needs a new pair of shoes." Then he threw out the dice.

The small cubes hit the far wall and rebounded back onto the table, but before they came to a stop Henry said, "twelve."

The dice rolled and stopped in the center of the table. Two sixes were showing their faces to the world.

"Hot dog!" said Augie. "Boxcars! You did it again kid! You called the number."

"Yeah, I guess I did; but Augie is that really any good? What I mean is that this game is going so fast that I only see the number on the dice just before they stop rolling. It seems that then it's too late to make a bet. I mean, that doesn't really help us, does it?"

"Kid, all we're doing now is getting our feet wet. We're just testing the waters to see what's what. The most important thing is that you've called the right numbers before they came up. You're doing it kid. You got the talent, the hot touch, the knack, and that's the big thing.

"But you're right when you say the game is too moving fast. This doesn't look like the right game for us. Now what we need to do is to find a game where the action is a little slower. A game that will allow us the time to get in and lay down a bet before you get the big vision."

Augie looked around the big casino. After a minute of surveying the room, he said, "And I think I may have found the perfect thing for us. Let's go over there."

Augie led the way and Henry followed. They walked across the room to the far side where the roulette wheels were spinning.

"Now this is more like it," said Augie smiling as he looked at the table before them. "The little white ball rolls round and round in the big wheel and finally lands on a number. The number pays off thirty-five to one. All we gotta do is pick the right number."

So, the two of them stood near the roulette table and watched as the players placed their chips on the number layout of the big, green felt table. Henry was immediately taken with the beauty and color of the game. The long table was covered with a brilliant green-baize cloth that had a fascinating layout of lines and numbers in red, black, green, white, and gold.

The big wheel at the end of the table was magnificent. It was made of dark, mahogany, smooth and polished so it gleamed under the overhead lights. In the center of the wheel was a large chromium disk with number pockets separated by frets. As the wheel spun, making slow, lazy turns around and around, the colored numbers seemed to dance and glitter under the bright lights of the room. The gaily colored chips stacked before the dealer and scattered around the table before the players and on strategic spots on the table layout all added to the enticing picture of color, texture and glitter.

The croupier took the little white ball and sent it spinning around the inner rim of the mahogany wheel. The wheel was turning slowly, smoothly in a counter-clockwise direction, the white ball was whirling like an electron in the opposite direction. The croupier called out, "No more bets!"

After a few revolutions the ball lost momentum and dropped toward the center of the wheel where it bounced and ricocheted off the frets until it finally nestled in one of the number pockets.

"Seventeen, black!" called out the croupier.

There was one winner, the rest of the players muttered a quiet word of disgust at having made losing bets. The croupier placed a crystal cylinder on the winning number and then raked in all the losing bets. Then he paid off the winner with a stack of chips.

VISIONS OF DESTINY

The croupier called out, "Place your bets!" and it was time for another round of wagering. Henry watched with interest as the various players positioned their chips on the table layout. Most of the bets were straight forward, either directly on a number or on one of side panels like red or black or odd or even. Some of the chips, however, rested in between the numbers. This puzzled Henry a little and he asked Augie about it.

"They're line bets, kid. The player places his chips on the line between the numbers. If either number comes up, he wins. That gives him a double shot at winning, but the payoff isn't as big as betting on a single spot."

Henry nodded in recognition, at the same time he felt a little stupid. After Augie had told him that, Henry realized that the answer was so obvious that he should have been able to figure it out by himself. He was, he realized, a real babe in the woods when it came to gambling and casinos and betting, and he was happy that he had a pal like Augie to guide him through this strange new world.

After a few moments, when the players laid their chips in place, the croupier sent the white ball whirling around the wheel. He then announced the end of betting. Henry watched the spinning ball and said quietly, "Thirty red." When the ball lost momentum and bounced in the chromium center disk and finally stopped, it was nestled in the thirty-red chamber. Augie looked back at Henry with a broad smile but said nothing.

The croupier cleaned the table and paid off the winner and another round of betting commenced. Augie and Henry continued to stand by the table as spectators, never laying down a bet, but just watching… watching as the game went on… watching to see what number would come up. Each time the play was repeated and each time Henry predicted the outcome before the white ball found its resting place on the big wheel.

This continued for another hour with the players making bets, but with Augie and Henry remaining on the sidelines. And with every play, Henry softly called the number that was about to come up, always before the ball fell into place. Each time, it happened exactly as he called it and he never missed. By now Augie was so excited that he could hardly keep from jumping up and down and slapping Henry on the back.

"Come on kid, I wanna buy you a beer. Let's go over to the bar where we can talk about this."

They walked over to the bar where Augie ordered two glasses from the tap, and they sat down on two stools to sip their brews.

"You got it kid. You're a natural. Man, with your talent we can really clean up."

"But Augie," cried Henry. "I always see the numbers after the dealer stops the betting. What good is it if I see the numbers after it's too late to put our money down? I mean, how can we make any money if we can't bet? And how can we bet if I don't see the numbers until it's too late?"

Henry was genuinely concerned that he was failing at what they had set out to do, that is, make money with his visions. Augie, however, didn't seem to be at all discouraged.

"Listen kid, let's not worry about that now. We only came out here to see if you get any visions in the casino. Now we know that you can do it. You got the touch kid, I tell you it's there.

"Okay, it's true that your visions come a little late in the game, but I have a theory about that. I believe that all you gotta do is fine-tune your skills. After all, remember that this is only the first time that you've ever been in a casino. I think that if we keep coming back, you'll get better and better at picking up the vibrations in the air, and who knows, but soon you'll be seeing the numbers before the dealer starts the little ball rolling. I'm sure it's only a matter of time before we're in the money."

Augie leaned back against the bar and sipped his beer.

"So, we're going to keep coming back here?"

"Yeah, we keep coming back." Augie said that vaguely and Henry could see that he was staring out into space apparently thinking about something else. After a few moments of silent thought, Augie looked back at Henry.

"Yeah, we'll keep coming back here, now and then; but you know, I think that it might be good if we also spread our net a little wider. Yeah! Maybe we should also take a bite of the big apple."

Henry had no idea what Augie meant when he said they were going to bite the big apple, but he didn't ask because he knew that in time Augie would explain everything, and two days later, he did.

CHAPTER

Mention the "Big Apple" and most people immediately think of New York City; and it's true that now that sobriquet does apply to all of New York City. However, that moniker really started in a small part of the city. It came into being in New York City's only racetrack, the Aqueduct.

Sometime in its early history, the Aqueduct came to be called the big A. Then in the twenties, jockeys visiting the big A started calling it the Big Apple. Well, the name stuck and eventually it was applied to all of the surrounding city, but it started at the Aqueduct racetrack.

This is what Augie meant when he said that they were going to take a bite of the Big Apple. About a week after their casino experience, Augie suggested that they go to the Aqueduct race track and watch the races. That's what they did, and this is what happened when they visited the big race track.

One fine morning they got on the subway. They boarded the R train because that was closest to their apartment and later they had to transfer to get to the A train. The A train took them right to the Aqueduct.

When they entered the main building, Henry said, "This is my first time coming to a real race track. The closest that I've ever come to any kind of horse race was in the movies."

"Well kid, you know what you get to do when you come to a new place, one that you've never visited before."

Henry nodded because he knew that it was time for another wish. He closed his eyes and he thought to himself, "I hope this works out. I really want it to, and I hope that I can really see good things this time."

While Henry was making his wish, Augie went over to a nearby rack and grabbed a couple of racing forms. He handed one to Henry.

"Here kid, take a gander at this."

"What is it?"

"This is the daily racing form."

"What am I supposed to do with this?"

"Look at it and read the names. It has each race listed and it shows which horses are running. Read it over. Start with the first race see which nags are in the lineup. Just read through the names and see if you get anything."

Henry dutifully looked at the form and read each name. He read the names of all the horses in the first race, then reread the names again. Finally, he looked back at Augie.

"Anything?" asked Augie.

"No Augie, I'm sorry but I'm not seeing anything."

"Don't be sorry kid. Maybe the printed page don't give off no vibrations that you can pick up on. Maybe seeing the ponies run will give you a vision. It's too early for the first race so let's mosey around a bit before we go over to the track. Who knows but maybe something will come to you."

They wandered around the facilities for a little while, just to acquaint Henry with the layout. After a little while Augie looked up at the wall clock.

"The first race is about to begin. Let's go someplace where we can see the action."

Augie and Henry took up a position at the rail where they had a commanding view of the starting gate and the final stretch to the finish line. They stood there waiting in anticipation of the start. It wasn't long in coming. The bell sounded, the starting gates sprang open and the horses bolted from their compartments onto the track.

At first, it was just a clump of equine heads, fluttering manes, flanks, galloping hooves and multi-colored jockeys all packed together in one mass with each horse straining and jostling to take the lead. By the time the pack reached the end of the stretch and were entering the first turn, it had lengthened out and the horses were falling into a recognizable order with a leader, a middle line-up, and one horse bringing up the rear.

The leader was Bright Boy. As the horses entered the back stretch that horse was ahead by a length.

"Looks like Bright Boy is gonna run away with this," said Augie.

But Henry didn't see it that way. He was watching the race and his eyes were seeing the race happen as it happened, but in his mind, he was seeing a different picture. His mind picture had already played the whole race to finish, then it started to replay the race again, and again—always with the same result.

"Lil Diamond's gonna win it," Henry said.

Augie looked back at Henry in surprise. "What? Are you kidding or what? Lil Diamond is in the rear. That horse is eating everyone's dust. No way is he gonna overtake the pack. No way!"

But the pictures were still running in Henry's mind and he was seeing what was going to happen right to the very end. He had already seen who was going to cross the finish line.

"Lil Diamond is going to win and he's going to make his break...right about...Now!"

At that very moment, a split second after Henry said it, Lil Diamond made the move forward and started to gain ground. A quarter way into the back stretch he was no longer last, but now tied for last place and still gaining turf. He was moving up when the horses entered the final turn. The pack hugged the inside rail, but Lil Diamond swung wide.

"Uh Oh!" said Augie. "That was a mistake. That jockey should know better. The horse is too far out. That wide turn will cost him and he's gonna lose ground. He's dead meat now."

At first it seemed that Augie was right, for Lil Diamond did, in fact, fall back and lose position making that wide turn, but that proved to be only a temporary set-back. While the rest of the horses clumped up along the inside rail, crowding and nudging each other, and fighting for position, Lil Diamond had a wide berth and was running strong. The horse quickly made up the lost ground, and coming into the final stretch, Lil Diamond had a clear field. It was at that moment when the jockey slapped Lil Diamond on the rump with his whip and the horse shot forward with astonishing speed.

The horses were running hard into the stretch but Lil Diamond was running harder and faster than the rest. He started moving up. He was in fourth place and gaining ground. In an instant he was moving into third place. Next, he was challenging for second, then he was in second place. Bright Boy was still in the lead but Lil Diamond was coming on strong and as the horses approached the finish line it was Bright Boy and Lil Diamond. Bright Boy and Lil Diamond. Bright Boy and Lil Diamond were running neck and neck. Then it was Lil Diamond by a nose with Bright Boy a close second. As the horses thundered across the finish line, it was Lil Diamond the winner by a half-length.

As the horse ran across the finish line, Augie jumped up and down with excitement.

"Ha, ha!" he shouted. "What a race that was. It was one of the best that I ever saw. Man, that horse was on fire; he burned up the track. Hey, and you called it kid. You called it and it happened just as you said. Oh kid, have you got the golden touch."

"Yeah, but Augie, I didn't see the winner until the race was half way over."

Augie shook his head. "Don't make no difference, kid. Not now anyways. Right now, all we are care about is you getting your pictures and seeing the winner before he gets to the finish line. Later when you get your machinery tuned up, you'll be seeing the winners even before the race starts.

"Trust me on this kid. I got a real strong hunch on this one and I know that it's gonna happen. In time, it will happen, believe me. For now, let's just be patient. Okay, let's see what happens in the next race."

So, they waited for the next race. Augie was eager with anticipation. Henry was rather apprehensive because he wasn't sure what would happen; suppose during the next race he didn't have a vision? *What then?* They stood there and waited for the start of the second race.

They watched as the horses took their positions before the starting gate. After a few minutes the horses were all in place and enclosed, then the bell sounded, the gates flew open and the horses thundered out onto the track. Immediately one horse, Slippery Dan, took the lead and he held that position through the stretch and into the first turn.

As the horses were running along the back stretch, Henry was getting another vision. He was seeing he entire race and he was seeing the horses as they crossed the finish line.

Augie said, "Slippery Dan is going to win this."

Well, that was no surprise to anyone because Slippery Dan was the favorite and at that point he was leading by two lengths and still gaining ground. But Henry's next statement was a bit of a surprise. His mind was replaying the finish of the race and as he was seeing the horses crossing the finish line, he called out their names in the order that they came across the line.

Augie listened and immediately penciled in the finishing order on his form just as Henry recited it; then he waited. He waited and watched to see how the race would finish. He wanted to see the final order and see how accurate Henry's prediction would be. Augie looked back to the track. The horses were coming into the final stretch and Augie looked from the track to his form and back again. Slippery Dan was still in the lead but the rest of the order was still in doubt; some of the horses were moving up, others were falling back. Some were tied for positions. It was still a toss-up as to how they would finish.

Augie's eyes were glued to the horses on the track. As they crossed the finish line, he glanced down at his form to check Henry's call against the finish. Henry's prediction was exactly on the nose. Each horse finished in the order that he said they would.

Augie looked up at Henry. "You did it again, kid. You got it right."

"Yeah, I guess so," said Henry absently.

"Guess so? Guessing had nothing to do with it. You saw it, and you knew, and you got it right. Man, but you are good. Good? You're great!"

They continued to stand there until soon it was time for the next race. Augie and Henry were standing as before. They watched the horses move into the set-up and when the bell sounded, they watched as the horses bolted from the starting gate. Their eyes were glued to the track. Almost from the beginning, one horse, Wisdom's Child took a commanding lead and as the horses entered the back stretch, it he seemed like the obviously winner.

"Wisdom's Child is going to run away with this," said Augie. "It's in the bag. None of the other nags can touch him."

Henry was having another vision and he shook his head. "He'll never finish the race. Fran's Favor will take it."

Augie looked back at his companion. He wasn't sure if he heard Henry correctly. *The horse will never finish the race? Now how was that possible? It's one thing for a horse to lose, but how can it not finish? After all, every horse has got to come across the finish line in one place or another, right?* That, of course, was the obvious conclusion, but Henry was seeing something else, and as the horses came out of the turn, Augie watched to see Henry's prediction come into being.

Wisdom's Child, the horse that had such a commanding lead, suddenly had a problem. It stopped running and started hobbling. Obviously, it had injured itself somehow, and now it was limping, favoring its back leg. The jockey pulled the injured horse over to the side and the other horses ran past the side-lined horse. Fran's Favor ran on to cross the finish line in first place. Once again, it happened as Henry said it would. Later an announcement said that Wisdom's Child had broken its leg coming out of the turn and was now in the care of the veterinarian. When Augie heard that he marveled to himself at just how good Henry was.

Augie and Henry stayed at the Big A for the rest of the afternoon. They watched all of the races and each time, as the horses galloped around the track, Henry had a vision. He saw each race as it was happening and also in his mind's eye; and he saw the winners and those in place and the show positions and he saw everything before the race was over. As Augie had said, he had the knack for picking the winners. The only problem was that he saw the winners after the betting windows had closed, when it was too late to make a bet and reap the rewards from his uncanny visions.

This, of course, bothered Henry because he felt that he wasn't achieving very much. Augie, however, remained undeterred. He was sure—right down to his toes—that with practice and perseverance, Henry would see his visions before post time. All they had to do was keep coming back to the track on keep watching the races.

When the last race was finished, Augie and Henry took the subway back home. In the subway car going back to Sunset park, Augie was euphoric.

"Kid you got the talent. No doubt about it. Once you fine tune your visions, you'll start seeing winners before the betting window closes, then we're gonna clean up. Yes sir, there ain't no stopping us now."

At that moment, however, Augie suddenly fell uncharacteristically silent and his face unexpectedly and strangely turned from a beacon of joy to a visage of sadness. Henry looked at his companion and wondered what had happened to bring about this abrupt and dramatic change.

Augie looked back at Henry and anticipated his question.

"I just thought of something," he said. "Once you start picking winners and raking in all the dough, you won't need me anymore. You'll be able to do it all by yourself. I guess I'll be headed out to pasture."

Henry was horrified by that thought.

"Oh Augie, don't say that, not even in jest. You're my pal. I'll always need you. We're friends and we're going to stick together right into the big money."

Augie smiled again. "Thanks kid! I was hoping that you'd say that. I know that if our positions were reversed, I'd say the same thing about you. Yeah, we're pals and we'll be pals until the end."

They both smiled together because they both knew it was true; they were pals, tried and true buddies, and they would remain so until the end. The only problem was that the end was a lot closer than either of them could imagine at that moment.

CHAPTER

For the following few weeks, Augie and Henry made periodic visits to Atlantic city and to the Aqueduct. During these excursions, they didn't lay down any bets. Their visits were more like reconnaissance trips to test the power of Henry's visions. Augie just wanted to see if Henry's timing was getting any better; that is if he could see the winning number or pick the right horse in time to put some money on the outcome. So, they went and they watched and Henry continued to see the winning number before the little white ball dropped into place and he always saw the horses as they crossed the finish line. He saw all of that before it happened, and he was right every time without one miss.

There was no doubt about it, Henry could pick the winners. So that was the good part. The bad part, however, was with Henry's timing. He still couldn't see things before the window of opportunity closed on them. He only got those winning mental pictures after the action started when it was too late to place a bet.

All this created a kind of ambivalence for Henry because, for the first time in his life, it seemed that his visions were actually serving some sort of useful purpose and he felt good about that; and yet at the same time, it was frustrating for him because they couldn't profit from the things he saw. It seemed like they were so close and yet so far from their goal. It was as if the big rewards were in sight but still just beyond their grasp.

Henry may have been a little perturbed but Augie wasn't. Augie felt that even if they weren't hitting home runs, then at least they were in the ballpark. Sooner or later, Augie believed, Henry would fine tune his perceptive mechanism and he would begin to see things in time to capture the big money. After all, hadn't Henry said that sometimes he got a glimpse of an event two weeks before it actually happened? Well, maybe then with practice, that would happen to Henry at the casino and at the track. All Henry had to do, Augie believed, was adjust his antenna to capture all the vibrations in the atmosphere and that would eventually happen with continued exposure. In the meantime, they could be patient. They could afford to wait until Henry's ability sharpened and everything fell into place.

They had time. Well, that's what both Augie and Henry believed back then, but what they didn't know was that time was running out for them. Augie didn't it know it then, and neither did Henry until he had another vision. In this vision he saw the end of everything they were working for. It happened like this.

On Tuesday, they had just come back from another excursion to Atlantic city where they had spent most of the day standing and watching the roulette wheel and that mischievous little white ball as it spun round and round. On this last outing it seemed to Augie that Henry's timing was actually getting better; his predictions and visions were happening almost before the croupier called out to stop the betting. Augie was sure that with a few more visits Henry would see the magic number in time to place a bet. They seemed to be getting closer to their goal, and if so, winning and rewards were just around the corner.

So, Augie was in a euphoric mood when they arrived at the door to Henry's apartment that evening.

"Well kid, it's time to say goodnight. This was a good day for us. You did good, and ya know, I think that soon it's really gonna happen for us. Another few trips should do it for us. Yes sir, I can almost see the money in our bag."

With that he beamed his broad smile and extended his hand. Henry smiled back and took hold of Augie's outstretched hand. As they shook hands and said good night, a vision flashed in Henry's mind. It was the most frightening vision that he ever had and a look of alarm flashed across his face. Augie didn't see the change in Henry's expression because he was lighting up another cigarette. When he looked up, Henry had managed to mask his gloom with a weak smile so Augie never suspected that something was amiss.

The two friends parted and Augie climbed the stairs to his apartment while Henry turned and unlocked the door and entered his vermin-infested domicile. Once inside his dark abode with the door safely shut and locked behind him, Henry shuddered. He shuddered and trembled because he recalled the vision that had just flashed in his mind at the moment when he shook hands to say goodnight to Augie.

The vision he'd had was one of Augie lying with his eyes closed, a vision of peace and tranquility, just lying there quiet and unmoved in a coffin. Henry knew that he had just seen a vision of his best friend in death. Henry walked into his dark living room and sank down on his couch. He buried his head in his hands and he hoped, and he prayed that this vision would never come true.

For the next three days, Augie and Henry didn't see each other. Henry had a freelance bookkeeping job in lower Manhattan and Augie was working in a mail room somewhere in midtown. The weekend came and Henry and Augie connected to go to Gallagher's for burgers and beer. All the time that they were there, sitting across the table from each other, Henry eyed Augie.

He scanned Augie's face, looking carefully, searching for any telltale signs that might indicate the reason for his recent vision of death. He tried not to stare in an obvious manner but at the same time he made a careful, surreptitious effort to examine Augie's physiognomy to see if maybe there might be something, some sort of telltale clue, that could possibly suggest a hidden illness or malady in his friend; but Henry saw nothing out of the ordinary. Augie was his usual effervescent self, talking, drinking, smoking and eating. Everything seemed to be all right with Augie, so Henry relaxed a little; but still in the back of his mind he remained wary because that vision of Augie lying there in a coffin stayed with him, mostly in his subconscious but occasionally it popped up to the forefront of his mind and it continued to haunt him.

Well, a week went by, followed by another and yet another, but still Augie looked and acted great, and he seemed to be in the pink of robust, good health. For Henry this was unusual; never before did he have vision that didn't come into being within two weeks after he saw it. This time, however, a full three weeks elapsed after he had that dreaded vision of his pal Augie in death, and still there was no indication that the frightful forecast would come to pass.

By the fourth week, Henry began to relax and he breathed a little easier. He thought to himself that maybe this was a sign of change in him. Perhaps his ability to see into destiny was at long last beginning to fade away. Maybe now, at long last, he was on the verge of becoming normal just like everyone else. Maybe soon, he would see only events as they happened and not before. Then with his precognitive powers gone, he wouldn't have to worry about being a weirdo in the eyes of society.

True, he might also lose the ability to predict winning numbers or see triumphant horses crossing the finishing line, but at the same time he wouldn't have to see accidents, and losers, and tragedy where no one else could. And maybe if he lost the ability to make money by picking winners then at least he would gain a sense of inner peace because he wouldn't see disaster before it happened. So, with that thought in mind, Henry felt as though a burden was about to be lifted from his shoulders.

The next day Henry was on his way to work. This time it was a job doing data entry work for some small firm in downtown Brooklyn. Henry had just emerged from his apartment and was locking the door behind him when Augie came bouncing down the stairs. It was eight o'clock in the morning and Augie already had his trademark cigarette in his mouth.

"Hi ya kid! Off to work this morning?"

"Yeah, I got a temp job with some small rinky-dink company downtown. I don't imagine it will last too long and I should be through by Thursday. So, if I don't have to work on Friday, maybe we can go to the track."

"No, we can't do it Friday. I have a doctor's appointment at the VA in the afternoon."

At the mention of the word *doctor* Henry's heart skipped a beat and he looked at Augie with alarm.

"You have a doctor's appointment? Why? Is something wrong?"

"Relax kid! It's nothing to get worked up over. I have a small hernia that needs to be taken care of. It's nothing. The doctor will do the whole job and I'll be home by supper. It's a minor thing, nothing to get your glands in an uproar about."

"Well, do you want me to go with you? As I said, I may not have to work that day."

"Naw! Don't trouble yourself. I'll take the train to Bay Ridge and walk to the VA. If I don't feel so good after I see the doc, then I'll call for a cab. I tell you, it's nothing. I'll be fine."

"Okay Augie, if you say so."

"Sure kid, but I appreciate the offer. Well, I gotta run. I got mailroom duty with a firm uptown. Catch you later."

With that Augie turned and bounded down the stairs and out the front door, leaving Henry standing on the landing looking after him and wondering if, in fact, the upcoming procedure at the doctor's office would be as simple as Augie said it would. And Henry had to wonder if that chilling vision of his might yet come true.

Well, there was nothing to do but wait and see, so Henry went off to his small rinky-dink company in downtown Brooklyn to do his mundane data-entry tasks. He worked that Monday and Tuesday and Wednesday and Thursday. He even had to come in for half a day on Friday.

That Friday, as soon as he got off work, Henry rushed back to his apartment building. He ran up the steps to the third floor and knocked on Augie's door, but there was no answer. Henry waited a few moments and knocked again, but still no answer. He figured that Augie was probably still at the hospital. Well, nothing to be alarmed about; after all didn't Augie say his appointment was in the afternoon? Now it was barely two o'clock. Most likely Augie was at the VA and probably just getting to see the doctor.

As Augie had said, it was nothing to get worked up about, but still Henry had an uneasy feeling in his gut. Well, for now there was nothing to do but wait for Augie to come home. So, Henry returned to his apartment and waited there alone, with only scurrying cockroaches and a lone, cautious mouse to keep him company.

There wasn't much for Henry to do in his cheerless apartment. He didn't feel like watching television nor reading, and somehow, he wasn't in the mood to squash bugs or put out more glue traps. All he could do was sit and wait in the dim light for Augie to come home.

Eventually Augie did return. Henry heard him coughing as he opened the door to his apartment and he heard the sound of footsteps as Augie entered and walked across the floor. Immediately, Henry grabbed his phone and called upstairs.

Henry could hear the upstairs phone ringing and Augie's footsteps coming across the room. Then there was a voice on the line: "Hello."

"Hi Augie. I heard you coming in. How did everything go?"

"Fine kid. It was a piece of cake. Just like I said it would be. The doctor fixed my hernia and took a tissue sample for a biopsy then sewed me back together. As I said, it was nothing to get worked up about."

Henry breathed a silent sigh of relief and said, "Say I'll tell you what. Let's go to Gallagher's tonight for dinner. It'll be my treat."

"Thanks kid; it's a nice offer, but I tell you I'm a little tired. I guess it's the after-effects of the anesthetic that the doc gave me. I think maybe I'll turn in early tonight. But I tell you what, if your offer is still up for tomorrow night then it's a date."

"Sure, Augie, my offer stands for tomorrow night. We'll do it then. Good night and sleep well."

"Thanks kid. See you tomorrow. Until then, good night."

The next night they did go to Gallagher's and had a grand time together. Augie seemed to be fully recovered from the previous day's experience with his doctor. He was in good spirits and it seemed like old times again. On the following evening the two went for a walk along the promenade near Brooklyn Heights. There they had a breathtaking view of Manhattan with all its many tall buildings lit up so that the many lights looked like gems sparkling against the dark blue of the evening sky.

The bright moon was low in the horizon and as Henry looked out over the cityscape he thought to himself that the evening was lovely and that life was wonderful. At the same time, he glanced over to the West and saw that there were dark clouds gathering over New Jersey. Eventually they would come this way; and as Henry looked at them, he wondered if maybe they were an omen of dire things to come.

CHAPTER 19

On Sunday the pair of friends took the bus down to Atlantic City and did some more casino reconnaissance work. As usual Henry was red hot and he picked every winning number, but he was still not hot enough to get the vision before the croupier called a halt to the betting. But as the day progressed and Henry watched the wheel making lazy turns with the little white ball bouncing around the inner disk, he began to grow in confidence. Something inside of him told him that his timing was improving and that he was closing in on seeing the magic number in time to lay down the chips. He was getting closer to that elusive goal—he was sure of it.

So, riding back to Brooklyn on the cruiser bus, both Henry and Augie were jubilant and in fine spirits. Henry leaned back against the headrest and smiled to himself with satisfaction and he was able to forget about Augie's health and that alarming vision that he had five weeks previous.

For the next three days, Henry was occupied with another mindless job at another non-descript company in Manhattan. On Thursday, however, Henry had nothing in the mix so he slept late. After a good night's sleep, he woke up feeling bright and chipper. After getting dressed and having breakfast, he went up to the third floor and knocked on Augie's door. After a few minutes Augie opened up.

"Hi ya kid!"

Henry noticed that Augie seemed more subdued than usual, but he attributed that to the fact that it was still morning and maybe Augie hadn't had his third cup of coffee and his morning cigarette yet.

"Say Augie, I was thinking that today is such a beautiful day, and I don't have to go to work. Well, I thought that if you don't have anything doing then maybe we could go to the track together."

Augie was slow to answer. He finally said, "Thanks kid, but I think not. Not today. In fact, I think that maybe our trips to the casino and the track will have to be on hold for a while."

Henry now took a long look at Augie and he noticed that his friend's face seemed drained and that his eyes had lost their sparkle and glint. At that moment, Henry could tell that something was wrong. He suddenly felt scared and was almost afraid to ask the next question for fear of what the answer might be. At the same time, he knew that if there was a problem he had to find out what it was.

"Why do you say that, Augie? Is something the matter?"

"Yeah, I guess you could say that."

There was a pause while Henry waited, expecting Augie to say more and elaborate on his last statement; but Augie just stood there without a word.

Finally, Henry asked, "Well, what Augie? What's the matter?"

"You remember when I told you the other day when I had my hernia fixed that day in the doctor's office?"

"Yeah."

"And you remember my saying that the doctor took some tissue and sent it to the lab for a biopsy?"

"Yeah."

"Well yesterday, the doc called me with the results."

"And?"

"The doc called to say that I've got cancer."

"What?" Henry felt like he had just been hit in the guts with a pile driver.

"Yeah kid; it doesn't look good. The doc told me that I gotta begin chemo treatments as soon as possible. I'm going down to see him later today."

"You want me to go with you? I mean for moral support or something?"

"No. Thanks kid, you're a pal; but I kinda think this is something that I gotta do on my own. But I appreciate the offer. You go to the track by yourself and try picking the winners. And when you do, imagine that I'm there beside you, cheering you on."

Henry was completely stunned by Augie's announcement and he didn't know what to say or do. He nodded and backed away, slowly retreating down the stairs. Then he went back into his apartment, sank down on the couch and let his head fall into his hands. This was tragic news and to Henry it seemed as if his unsettling vision might come true after all.

Henry didn't know what to do with himself for the rest of the day. He knew he couldn't hang around his apartment waiting for Augie to return. He needed to do something to occupy his mind, something to distract himself so he wouldn't keep worrying about Augie; but what? He didn't feel like going to a movie; there wasn't any picture that he wanted to see. And he didn't feel like reading or going to the track or doing anything else for that matter.

But he knew that he had to get out of his gloomy apartment and into the sunshine or else he would start climbing the walls; so, he went outside and just started walking. He walked and walked, aimlessly, without any particular destination in mind. His object was to simply walk and tire himself out. He wanted to get so tired that his brain would be numb and he wouldn't be able to hold a thought in his mind and he wouldn't be able to think about poor Augie or recall that chilling vision of his friend in death.

So, he started walking along fifth avenue. He walked to Park Slope then hit Flatbush avenue and he turned and walked to Brooklyn Heights then turned and started back by a different path. He stopped twice to get something to eat, but other than that, he kept on walking. It was a very long walk and after a while it wasn't like he was really walking, but more like he was just putting one foot in front of the other and pulling himself forward. He went all day and into the evening before he returned home.

The long walk had its desired effect: Henry was exhausted when he finally returned to his apartment. His feet and legs were aching, his back and shoulders were stiff and sore, and his mind was a blank. He wanted to just throw off his clothes and fall onto his bed, but he thought that maybe he should call upstairs to find out how Augie was.

Henry picked up the phone and dialed Augie's number. He listened to the receiver with one ear and heard the ringing sound coming out of the earpiece. With the other ear he could hear the phone ringing in Augie's apartment through the ceiling above. Augie's phone rang at least a dozen times, but there was no sound of anyone above walking across the floor to answer it.

Henry stood there, holding the phone, listening while it rang and rang; but there was no answer. Finally, he decided that Augie wasn't home. Maybe that was something he should worry about because maybe it was a bad sign of something or other; but at that moment Henry was simply too tired to do anything or even think about it. He put the phone down then made his way into his bedroom where pulled off his clothes, collapsed on the bed and quickly fell into a sound sleep generated by pure exhaustion.

The next day Henry awoke but was unmotivated to get up and move about, so he lay there and from his bed and he looked out the window at the sky above. It was an overcast sky, a continuous sheet of dull gray without a hint of white or blue or any vestige of sunlight. For a long while, Henry just lay there looking up at the ceiling and occasionally glancing out the window at the dreary sky. It seemed like a gloomy start to the day, and he wondered to himself what he was going to do for the rest of the day, how he was going to pass the time. There was no job to go to. He didn't want to go to a casino or the track by himself because somehow it didn't seem right to go to those places without Augie.

Eventually, Henry did roll out of bed and when he did, and tried to stand up straight, his body telegraphed a whole collection of aches and pains and stiffness from every joint, limb, and extremity. When he tried to set his body in motion, he felt even worse and he knew that he was paying the price for his long, strenuous walk the day before. He managed to hobble to the bathroom—this was a painful little walk, because his feet were incredibly sore—and turned on the hot water faucet in the bathtub. When the tub was full, Henry sat in it, and let the hot water soak away the aches and pains and stiffness in all his muscles.

While he was soaking in the water, slowly getting his body parts back into working order, he thought about Augie. Somehow, he had to find out what had happened to his friend. After an hour in the hot tub, Henry got up and toweled off, then he shaved and brushed his teeth. After getting dressed and making a breakfast of cold cereal, Henry went upstairs to Augie's apartment. He knocked on the door and softly called out Augie's name; but there was no answer. Augie still had not returned home.

Henry spent most of the morning doing odds-and-ends chores. He went out and did some grocery shopping. After that he worked at cleaning and straightening his apartment. Funny thing, but no matter how much Henry cleaned and straightened his apartment it never looked any different. It always looked dull, and gloomy and depressing no matter how much effort he put into it.

Around one o'clock the phone rang. Henry answered it.

"Hello," he said.

"Hello," said the voice on the other end of the line. "I'm calling for a Mister Henry Gainsvort."

"This is he."

"Well, I'm Nurse Ferdinand and I'm calling from the Brooklyn VA hospital. I'm calling on behalf of Mr. August Martello."

Henry's heart skipped a beat. "Yes? How is he?"

"Well he came in yesterday for his first chemo-therapy treatment and unfortunately he had a severe allergic reaction to it. We had to keep him here overnight."

"Well, how is he now?"

"Better. The doctor prescribed medication for him and he had an uncomfortable night, but he seems to be better this morning."

"Is it possible for me to come and see him sometime soon?"

"Yes, that's possible. You can come today if you want. The visiting hours are until eight tonight."

Henry said goodbye and hung up his phone. He was suddenly relieved and elated at this recent news about Augie. Yes, it was bad news that Augie's chemo-therapy treatment knocked him for a loop, but at least he was alive and getting better and was now able to have visitors.

Henry put on his jacket and went the subway which he took to Bay Ridge. On the train he thought to himself that maybe he shouldn't visit empty handed; maybe he should get a little something as a get-well present for his friend. *Yeah, good idea, but what?* He didn't think that Augie would appreciate flowers, and he couldn't smuggle a six-pack of beer into the hospital and cigarettes were definitely a no-no. *So, what was left?* Henry thought about it for a while then he came up with the perfect gift idea. He took the train to eighty-sixth street and walked to the VA hospital Along the way, he stopped at a newsstand and bought a present for his pal, Augie.

Henry entered the hospital and was surprised to see that he had to go through a security check. There was an x-ray machine with a conveyor belt for parcels and bags, and he had to walk through a metal detector before he could even get to the information desk. At the desk, he inquired about the number and location of Augie's room. The receptionist told him that Augie was on the seventh floor, in room seven-fourteen. Henry took the elevator up and walked down to hall to find Augie's room.

He walked in. There were four beds in the room, two positioned on one side and the other two on the opposite side. Augie's bed was in the far corner by the window. Augie didn't see Henry come into the room because he was watching a television that was suspended from a ceiling bracket. It wasn't until Henry got to the foot of his bed that Augie looked away from the screen. He was clearly elated by Henry's sudden appearance and he immediately used his remote to turn off the TV.

"Hey! Hi ya, kid. This is a surprise. Boy, are you a sight for sore eyes. Come over here and sit down on this chair by the bed."

Henry walked around and took up a position in the solitary chair at bedside. As he did so, he had a chance to look at his friend in the bed. Augie looked much the same as always, except that today he looked tired and worn, as if he had been pulled through a knot-hole backwards. Obviously, his first chemo treatment had hit him hard. Still, upon seeing Henry, Augie's mood brightened and he managed to smile; it wasn't his usual one-million candle-power smile that he always flashed. No, it was weaker than that, but it was a smile nevertheless.

As Henry sat down he handed Augie the present that he bought. It was a newspaper, but it wasn't just any ordinary newspaper. When Augie unfolded it, his mood brightened even more.

"Hot dog! You brought me the Daily Racing Form. This is just what the doctor ordered. Gee, what a pal you are."

"Well, it's not much, but I thought it might help pass the time while you're here." Henry tried to act up-beat and cheerful, but he was aware that his friend was seriously ill and he found it difficult to be nonchalant and jovial. After a minute he asked, "How are you feeling?"

"I'm okay kid. It was rough going for a little while, but now I'm feeling better." Augie said that, and maybe he meant the part about feeling better, but somehow his voice seemed a little hollow. Well, maybe he was still tired from his previous ordeal.

"How long are you going to be in here for?"

"Not too long. The doc talked to me this morning and said that I'll probably be able to go home tomorrow."

"That's good."

"Yeah, it is. I'll be able to go home and get back to normal." Augie now looked at Henry and then his manner changed. Gone was the effervescent, blustery charm, gone was the countenance of unbridled optimism. There was no smile, no twinkle in the eyes; these were replaced by a grave seriousness.

Augie continued. "But then later, I'll have to face another chemo-treatment. I don't mind telling ya kid that this thing has got me running scared. When I came in here yesterday, I figured the whole thing would be a piece of cake. You know, one shot and I'd go home. But wow! That first treatment sent me to the canvas. I felt like a horse whose been hobbled out with an injury and can't make it to the finish line."

Henry noted to himself that Augie was mixing his sports metaphors but he didn't say anything because he saw how genuinely concerned Augie was by the seriousness of his illness. He could see that Augie was scared by the prospects that lay before him and Henry wished that he could do, or say, something to somehow give Augie a glimmer of hope and lighten his mood.

Then just off the top of his head, Henry said, "Augie, you don't have to anything to worry about. You know why? Because coming over here I had another vision. That's right! In my vision I saw you back in good health, and us going to the track and me picking a winner and the two of us cashing in on my pick. Yeah! I saw that. So, there's no need for you to worry."

"No kidding? I mean you really saw that? You saw me getting better and beating the big C?"

Henry nodded and Augie's mood instantly brightened. He seemed relieved and his mood changed from grave seriousness back to his former disposition of bubbly good cheer. It was as if the demons of illness and the specter of death had suddenly been banished from within to allow the flippant, good-time Augie to reemerge and Henry was pleased with the change in his friend.

Henry sat with Augie and the two of them talked until the end of visiting hours, then Henry said goodnight and walked to the elevator. Alone in the elevator Henry thought back over his visit with Augie, and he felt a sudden pang of guilt. He felt this because he remembered that he had lied to Augie about having a vision of recovery and a return to good health. In fact, he had never had such a vision, but on the spur of the moment, when sitting there at bedside looking at Augie, who was depressed and defeated, he had lied because it seemed like the only way he had of cheering up his friend.

And it worked; it did make Augie feel better—at least for the time being. So maybe it was all right to tell a lie if it helped to make someone feel better. And who's to say that the vision he lied about might not just come true? As Henry thought about it, he realized that many years back he wondered to himself if his visions happened because he saw them or because he told about them. In other words, did talking about his visions actually make them come true? He had asked himself that question once before and never found the answer. Maybe now he would find out.

CHAPTER 20

Well, Augie came home from the hospital and within a few weeks, he started to get better and it seemed like he was back to his old self again. Henry began to believe that maybe his lie had worked and that maybe the invented vision, concocted in a moment of desperation, would actually come to pass as he had described it. Augie truly believed in Henry's fabricated vision and it seemed like he was on the road to recovery. He had to undergo more chemo-treatments of course, but he got through them with no ill effects—well almost none. He began to lose his hair, and he dropped some pounds from his frame, but he managed to conceal these flaws with an imaginative wardrobe.

To cover his balding pate, he took to wearing a fedora which he set on his head at a jaunty angle. It gave him a kind of continental, rakish charm. He also found an old double-breasted sport coat in a local thrift shop. The coat was amazing in that it had an unbelievable amount of shoulder padding; and when Augie put it on, it effectively masked his thinned-down frame and it actually looked good on him. On anyone else this combination of fedora and overstuffed sportscoat would have looked ridiculous, but it suited Augie because he carried off the look with an air of self-confidence and bravado. In fact, his new wardrobe gave him an engaging, smooth, debonair quality that went naturally with his out-going personality.

And so, for the next four months everything seemed to be getting better for Henry and for his pal Augie. Once or twice during the week, they went to Gallagher's for their usual beer-and-burger evening. On other evenings they met in Henry's apartment for pizza and beer. They still made their periodic visits to Atlantic City and to the Aqueduct although not as often as before, because even though Augie tried to maintain the image of his former self, it was obvious that he didn't have the strength or endurance that he had in the past. On some days he tired more easily than on others.

One night, for example, he said that he wasn't up to going to Gallagher's because he was tired; and he said that he even felt a little too bushed to come down to Henry's place. In response, Henry suggested that maybe he could bring the pizza upstairs and they could make merry in Augie's pad. That seemed agreeable to Augie; he felt that he could manage that. Augie said he had beer in the fridge, so Henry went to a neighborhood joint and got a large pie from which he brought up to the third floor.

This was the first time that Henry had ever been inside of Augie's apartment and he was surprised when he entered and looked around. Augie's apartment was in the same building as Henry's so naturally the layout of the rooms was the same. Both apartments had the same window configuration and the same number of ceiling fixtures, so both were equally dark and gloomy.

But there was also a subtle difference between the two dwellings. Augie's apartment was sparse with little in the way of furniture or accessories—only the things that were really needed. There were no drapes or shades on the windows and no books or magazines about; in fact, there was nothing except a television to indicate how Augie spent his leisure moments. Augie's apartment seemed Spartan and austere in the extreme.

But as Henry looked around Augie's place, there was one object that caught his attention. It was the one thing that shone out from the shadows—the one jewel in an otherwise gloomy atmosphere. It was a bronze statue of a racehorse and jockey mounted on a gray marble base. It sat on the window sill in the living room. It was so different from everything else in the apartment that it seemed to stand out like a small beacon of magnificence in an otherwise lifeless, drab atmosphere. When he first noticed it, Henry felt immediately drawn to it and he crossed the room to have a closer look at it.

The window sill was low, so Henry had to kneel down to look at the statue from eye level. The piece stood about ten inches high and was about twelve inches long and it had an engaging quality about it. It was a statue of a thoroughbred in full stretch as if it was just about to cross the finish line. The jockey was rising out of the saddle and wielding his whip as if he were trying to get every last ounce of energy from the horse. Henry was completely captivated by the statue and for a moment he just knelt there looking at the miniature bronze figure, oblivious to all around him.

"You like that?" asked Augie.

Still kneeling before the statue, Henry turned to look at Augie. "It's really quite beautiful. It's like you're actually looking at a race, but it's like a minute in suspended animation. It's like you're seeing the exact moment, in a single frame, just when the horse crosses the finish line."

"Yeah. That belonged to my old man. I don't know where he got it, but he had it as long as I can remember. When he died, I got it. I keep it for a number of reasons: first because it reminded me of him. Also, because it's probably the closest to art that I'll ever get. But I also like to look at it from time to time because when I look at it, I see the glory moment. And I think to myself that what's it like to be a winner. Who knows but if I look at it long enough and think about it enough times, maybe I'll be a winner someday too."

"You will Augie. We're getting close and soon you'll be a winner."

"You think so kid? Well maybe someday; but right now, the pizza's getting cold. Let's chow down."

They ate and drank and talked and the evening seemed like old times again—except for two things: Augie didn't smoke and around ten o'clock he announced that he was getting tired. They put the empty pizza box and beer bottles in the trash and called it a night. Other than that, well, it was like old times again.

They still made their periodic visits to Atlantic City and to the Aqueduct and Henry continued to see winners whenever they went. Henry was getting to the point where he could see the winners almost in time to lay down a bet. He was almost at that point, but not quite there, not just yet. Nevertheless, it seemed that for Henry and Augie, success was just around the corner; but then the bottom dropped out from them. This is how it happened.

Sometime in November, Augie went for another chemo-treatment and he had another reaction to it. This shot hit him harder than any of the previous ones and it landed him back in the hospital, but this time it wasn't just an overnight stay. He was in for a week and he was getting care, but it didn't seem like he was getting any better.

Henry visited his pal almost every day, but these were sad experiences for him because with each visit he could see his friend slowly slipping away from life. In the hall, he talked to Augie's doctor, hoping for some word of encouragement about Augie's condition, but the doctor only said that he should make sure Augie's affairs were in order. Henry took that to mean that Augie was in the back stretch and the finish line was in sight.

In the middle of the second week, Henry went to the VA hospital to visit Augie again. Henry brought the latest edition of the Daily Racing Form and when he got to the bed he handed it over to his pal. Augie glanced at it briefly but didn't open it. He wasn't in the mood to read; in fact, he wasn't in the mood to do much of anything. All he could do was lay there with his head propped up against the pillows with his eyes half open looking out into space.

"How are you feeling, Augie?"

"Not good, kid. I think I'm facing my third strike and this is my last chance at bat."

"Oh, don't say that, Augie. You're going to get better. I know you will."

Augie made a feeble attempt to shake his head. "Not this time kid. I think this is the final inning for me."

Henry didn't say anything to that, because he suspected that Augie was right. He wanted to say something, something upbeat, something to cheer Augie up and give him encouragement, but he could think of nothing. He sat there at bedside to keep his pal company. After a few minutes of silence, Augie spoke again.

"Kid, I don't have much to leave anyone. If you look in the top of my dresser drawer you'll find my insurance policy. I made you out as the beneficiary. It's not a big policy but you can use the money to get me a decent burial. Keep what's left for yourself."

Henry wanted to say something to that, maybe to make some sort of token protest that there was no need to be pessimistic and talk about burials, but it suspected that such protestations would be futile. He just nodded and was silent. Augie didn't say anything either. For a long while he just lay there looking into the space before him. Thus, there was silence between the two men, until after about ten minutes Augie spoke again.

"You've been a pal kid and I'd like you to have the one really good thing that I've got. I want to you take my statue of the horse and jockey. You know, the statue on my window sill, the one my old man left to me. Take it, and when you look at it, think of your old pal Augie Martello. Who knows but maybe it will bring you luck."

"Sure Augie, I'll take it. I'll take good care of it too. But there's no need to talk about this now, because you're gonna get better and so you're gonna hang on to it."

Augie made another feeble attempt to shake his head. "Not this time kid. Not this time."

This was followed by another long period of silence with Augie lying in the bed, motionless and with Henry sitting in the single chair at bedside. After about twenty minutes without either one saying or doing anything, Augie spoke up.

"Kid, you remember when I was here in the hospital after I had my first treatment and you came up to see me?"

"Yeah?"

"You told me that you had a vision of me getting over this and getting better. You remember that?"

"Yeah Augie, I do."

"You never really had that vision, did you? I mean, you made it up."

Henry gulped and was silent for a minute before he answered. The he confessed timidly. "No Augie, I never had that vision. I just made it up. I'm sorry, but I only said it because—"

"No need to explain, kid. I know why you did it. You said it to make me feel better. That's what friends do for one another. You're a real pal kid."

"I try to be Augie."

"You are, kid. In fact, you may be the best friend that I've ever had."

"Thank you for saying that Augie."

"It's true, kid. Now if you don't mind, I'm kinda tired. I think I'll shut my eyes and rest a little."

"Yeah sure, Augie, you do that. You get some rest."

So, Augie Martello closed his eyes, and he never opened them again.

Henry took charge of making the funeral arrangements for his pal Augie. He wasn't completely alone in this; Marcy, the waitress from Gallagher's, came around to help him and together they found a funeral home and picked out a casket and scheduled the wake.

The wake turned out to be a very busy affair, because Augie had a lot of friends in life and they all came to pay their respects to their little buddy in death. Marcy and Henry knew most of the visitors because they were regulars at Gallagher's, but there were a few strangers, people who had worked with Augie in Manhattan and some friends from the past. One woman who showed up claimed to be a former high school classmate. Another fellow came in from New Jersey and said that he and Augie had served together in the Navy.

Most of the visitors were quiet and respectful, but three guys who came in were plastered to the gills. At first Henry was a little annoyed with their inebriated condition, but then he thought to himself that these were the kind of friends that Augie had had in life, and he would probably have understood and even approved of their need to get liquored up just to face a morbid affair like Augie's wake. So, Henry dismissed his righteous indignation and welcomed the intoxicated trio because he recognized that their intentions were good even if their manners were a little tattered.

In the evenings in the funeral home, when visiting hours were over and the doors to the room were closed, Henry sat by himself in the first row in the room. He sat there just looking at Augie lying peacefully in the coffin with his eyes shut. And as he looked at Augie, Henry knew that he was looking at that very image that he saw in his fateful vision six months previous when he and Augie were parting outside of his apartment. This was the vision that came into reality, not the fictitious one that he had made up in the hospital. So now he knew—his visions came true only when he had them. It didn't matter what he said or did, it was only the visions that popped into his mind's eye that would come true and nothing he did or said could change the way they turned out.

When he left the funeral home and went back to his apartment and was all alone, Henry cried. He cried because he remembered Augie and the many good times that they had had together and he realized that now he would have to carry on without his good, little friend. Henry cried because he had just lost his best friend, the only true friend that he had ever known.

The burial took place in Greenwood Cemetery in Brooklyn. Strictly speaking it wasn't really a burial because the casket was not put into the ground. Henry and Marcy had selected a mausoleum in which to put Augie's remains.

Along with Henry and Marcy, a lot of Augie's former friends came to watch as a priest said a few words over the casket. Then a cemetery worker operated a hydraulic jack which raised the coffin and pushed it into a compartment three rows up on the second floor of the mausoleum building. Once the casket was inside, the worker withdrew the jack then stepped up to seal up the compartment. He drew a bead of caulking compound around the opening of the compartment, then he placed a panel over the opening and bolted it in place. With that, Augie was safely sealed away for the ages.

Once the funeral service was over the people departed. Marcy and Henry lingered a bit until they were the only two remaining. They stayed behind to take one last look at the place where Augie was going to spend the rest of eternity.

Augie's burial niche was just like all the rest in the big mausoleum, sealed with a marble panel—one marble panel among hundreds of others. On the panel was a rectangular brass plate with Augie's name and the dates of his existence engraved on it. It was all there was to remind the living world that at one time a happy-go-lucky fellow by the name of Augie Martello lived in Brooklyn and in his inimitable way, made a lot of people happy. A small brass plate with a name and dates but nothing else to describe the remains of the man inside nor tell what a cheerful little person he was.

Henry and Marcy decided to walk from the cemetery back to Sunset park. It was a pleasant day and the walk back was a little less than a mile and they felt that the walk would do them both good so they left the mausoleum and walked together along the road that winds through the cemetery

Greenwood Cemetery is large and it took them about ten minutes to walk from the mausoleum to the main gate on Fifth avenue. Now the main entrance to Greenwood Cemetery is an impressive structure. It is a Gothic Revival tower with three pinnacles, all carved from brown sandstone. On ground level of one tower is a small chapel, on the other is the cemetery office.

Before they passed through the tower gate, Henry paused and looked up. Marcy looked up also, but she didn't see anything.

"What are you looking at?" asked Marcy.

"Those towers. Augie once told me that over a hundred parakeets live there."

"Parakeets in Brooklyn? Aren't they supposed to be tropical birds?"

"That's what I always thought, but Augie told me that sometime way back, somebody's pet parakeets flew out the window and made a nest in that tower. He said that eventually they multiplied until now there are over a hundred up there."

They stood for a few minutes looking up at the tower.

"I don't see any parakeets," said Marcy.

"Neither do I, but they're supposed to be in there. Well, we might as well go home."

And so, Marcy and Henry left Greenwood Cemetery and the small site where Augie was laid to rest. They parted company in front of Henry's building and Henry went upstairs into his apartment. He sat down on his couch. For a long while he just sat there thinking of nothing; his mind was a blank. Then by chance he looked across the room and he saw the statue of the race horse and jockey that Augie had left him. And as he looked at that little figurine, he thought of the many times he had spent with Augie and he realized that Augie had been the one and only true friend that he had ever had. Now, however, little Augie was no more and Henry wondered to himself what life was going to be like without him.

CHAPTER 21

Well Augie was gone and with his passing, it seemed that the meaning and purpose had gone out of Henry's life. Indeed, when Augie was alive, he was so full of life and always fired with energy and gusto so that with his death, Henry was left with a big, black void that he had no initiative to fill. Henry simply went through the motions of living, but it was a vapid existence—just going from one day to the next without much caring about what he was doing or why he was doing it. It seemed that when Augie died, the zest and enthusiasm of life died with him.

Henry actually lost his desire to continue living and he wished secretly that something would come along to end his existence and put him out of his misery. As much as Henry wanted to end his life he could not bring himself to take that drastic step on his own. That would be suicide and Henry knew it was wrong and immoral and that if he took his own life he would probably spent the rest of eternity burning in hell. If he was to die, it would have to come from somewhere other than his own hand. He silently wished that something would come along, some accident, some unforeseen calamity and end it all. Maybe it might happen when he was walking down the street; a loose brick would fall from a building and clunk him out of existence; or maybe on some dark, rainy night, a drunken driver would lose control of his vehicle and run up on the sidewalk where Henry was walking and squash him into the pavement.

However, Henry had no such luck. There were no falling bricks in his life nor reckless drivers. Henry had a strong death wish, but for some reason, providence seemed reluctant to fulfill it, and Henry had no choice but to keep on living. During this time of loneliness, despair, and desolation, Henry found one thing to give him a glimmer of purpose and it sat in his apartment on top of his bookcase. It was the bronze statue of the horse and jockey that Augie had given him.

On some quiet evenings when Henry returned home from a boring day at work or from aimlessly wandering the streets of Brooklyn, he would go back to into his kitchen and pull a beer from his fridge. Then he would quietly plop down on his sofa and watch the roaches scurry across the floor. Occasionally he would look up and let his eyes wander about the room until by chance, they settled on that statue.

Then he would reminisce about Augie and the many good times they had together. And during these recollections, Augie's words would come back to Henry: "There's a way to make money with your visions, kid! All you gotta do is find it."

Maybe there was a way to make money with his visions—but how to do that? How indeed? Maybe the path to rewards lay in the casinos or at the racetrack, but Henry knew that he couldn't go back to either of these places ever again. He couldn't go back to either of them because they were filled with the memories of the many times he spent with Augie at his side. Somehow it wouldn't seem right to go back to them without his faithful companion, his tried-and-true buddy, Augie.

If there was a place to have his paying visions it would have to be somewhere other than a casino or a racetrack. *But where could that be?*

Well, Henry didn't know it at the time, but he was about to find the answer to that question. He was soon to find that hidden path to riches that had eluded him for so long. His inspiration would come in an unguarded moment, when he least expected it. This is how it happened.

Henry had just come out of the office of a small clothing firm in midtown Manhattan. He had spent the last week there working on the books and doing financial statements. He finished the job Friday afternoon and was walking from the office to the nearest subway station, but it was the height of the rush hour and he didn't relish taking a crowded subway car where he would be packed like a sardine with all those other weary commuters. He looked around for someplace quiet where he could sit in peace and wait for an hour until the crush of the rush hour had subsided.

There was a Starbucks on a distant corner and it seemed like the ideal place to waste an hour in quiet solitude while the mad pack of commuters made their way home. He crossed the street and walked down the block and entered the place.

Inside, he ordered a tall coffee and a crumb cake then he walked over to a vacant table and sat down. He was quietly sipping his coffee and munching his crumb cake while at the same time he glanced around at the walls, and ceiling, and the other people in the place; that's when he spied what looked like a tabloid newspaper lying on an adjacent table. He reached over and grabbed it, figuring that he might as well read the news while he waited and sipped and munched.

He expected the tabloid to be either the *Daily News* or the *New York Post*, but when he turned it over, he was surprised to see that it was a recent edition of *Barron's*. At that point, he remembered that afternoon he'd spent in the Hamptons at the Blaine summer estate. He remembered the lunch when he talked with that curious old gentleman, Mr. Sinclair.

He recalled Mr. Sinclair's words, "Subscribe to *Barron's* and read it faithfully, cover-to-cover. That will give you the background knowledge that you need to navigate in today's cutthroat business world."

Back then, Henry dismissed the old man's advice as meaningless because he didn't know what *Barron's* was. Now he was holding a copy of that very publication in his hands. Curious as to what it might possibly contain, Henry started to read through it. The first few pages were dull and uninteresting to Henry. The articles were about a bank merger and an attempted take-over of a major airline. Henry continued to read the pages because it was a way to pass the time while waiting for the rat race to wind down.

He continued to turn the pages and scan the articles until he came to a piece on page thirty-two that unexpectedly caught his attention. It was only a small article—just three paragraphs long—about a mining company in Colorado. The company was The Colorado Mineral Research and Discovery Corporation. Now Henry had never heard of this company, but for some unknown reason he found the article interesting and he read and reread the text.

The article said that The Colorado Mineral Research and Discovery Corporation was headed for certain bankruptcy because their mines had played out and recent geological explorations had proved fruitless. Analysts predicted that with no incoming revenue the company would fold in less than two months' time. Henry found the article intriguing—although he had no idea why because he'd never had an interest in mining. He started to read it for the third time. That's when he had a vision.

In his vision he saw that The Colorado Mineral Research and Discovery Corporation had a sudden, and totally unexpected breakthrough. One of their exploration teams hit pay dirt. They discovered a rich source of copper ore in a remote part of Alaska. This discovery would make The Colorado Mineral Research and Discovery Corporation solvent and prosperous again. Henry realized that with this vision he was seeing an opportunity in the making, and his first thought was to get home as soon as possible to his apartment where he could plan a strategy to capitalize on his vision.

He folded the paper, tucked it under his arm and raced for the subway. The rush hour crowd hadn't subsided yet, but Henry didn't care. He just wanted to get home and if he had to travel like a sardine in a steel tube to get there, then that was all right with him. So, he endured the long, hot subway ride home to his neighborhood, where he walked back to his domicile.

In the quiet recesses of his dungeon-like apartment, surrounded by crawling roaches and sneaking mice, Henry reread that article and once again the vision of an unexpected corporate turn-around replayed in his mind. And with that vision, purpose and meaning had suddenly come back into his life. It was as if opportunity was knocking at his door and this time he knew just how to answer it.

The next day, Henry searched the internet and found a mid-sized brokerage firm in Manhattan, White, Canton & Beck. He called the number listed and made an appointment that very day to drop into their office and sit down with a broker. Henry went for his appointment and he brought his checkbook with him.

At the brokerage office, he met Paul Linderman. Linderman had been a broker with White, Canton & Beck for the better part of two decades. He was a competent, if not inspired broker who had a modest list of clients. He offered his clients advice and counsel as to safe and reliable picks in the stock market and handled all of their transactions. None of his clients were wealthy, but they all had secure and sturdy portfolios of solid, comfortable investments, based on the recommendations of Linderman.

Linderman was not a risk taker. He knew that the market could be volatile at times, so he always advised his clients to take a safe and steady path investing only in tried-and-true companies with proven track records; and his clients always accepted that advice without question. Well, all that was about to change. Paul Linderman couldn't know it at the time, but Henry Gainsvort was about to enter his life and upset the equilibrium of his financial apple cart.

When Henry arrived at the office of White, Cantor & Beck, Paul Linderman met him at the reception desk and escorted him back to his cubicle. They sat down and exchanged meaningless chit chat about the weather as a way of establishing a rapport between them. Then Linderman cleared his throat and commenced to talk about some safe, choice picks he had in mind for the prudent investor. He was just warming up to his subject when Henry held up his hand.

"Thank you, Mr. Linderman. I'm sure you know what you're talking about and I'm sure that all your suggestions are sound and reliable, but I already know what company I want to invest in."

Linderman was a little surprised. "Oh, you do? Well what company do you have in mind?"

"I want to buy shares of The Colorado Mineral Research and Discovery Corporation."

Linderman looked back at Henry with skepticism. He had never heard of The Colorado Mineral Research and Discovery Corporation so he didn't quite know what to say. He reached up to the shelf above his desk and pulled down a black binder. The binder contained reports by financial analysts, who had researched and reported on the companies listed on the big board. He flipped through the pages until he came to the report on The Colorado Mineral Research and Discovery Corporation. Linderman read the report carefully and he didn't like what he read. He looked back at Henry.

"Mr. Gainsvort, I don't know how you heard about The Colorado Mineral Research and Discovery Corporation, but I have to warn you that company is really a disaster waiting to happen. You could not have picked a worse stock to buy. According to our reports, that company is headed for bankruptcy."

"Nevertheless, that is the stock that I want to buy."

"But Mr. Gainsvort, that company is about to fail. Its stock will become worthless. You would actually be throwing your money away if your bought into that company."

"I thank you for your warning, but my mind is made up. I want to buy shares of The Colorado Mineral Research and Discovery Corporation."

"May I ask why?"

"Well I like the name of the company and I have a hunch that it's going to go someplace."

Linderman shook his head. "Mr. Gainsvort, I've been a broker for almost twenty years and I can tell you from experience that playing hunches only leads to disaster. Buying a stock takes time. You can't simply pick a stock because you like the name of the company. You have to research the company carefully before you put your money into it. Now our experts have looked into the assets and management of that particular company and they report that it is in very bad shape."

"Mr. Linderman, with all due respect, I do appreciate your warning, but my mind is made up. I want to buy shares of The Colorado Mineral Research and Discovery Corporation. I'm not interested in anything else. If you won't make the purchase for me, then I'll go someplace else."

Linderman looked hard and long at Henry. At first, he thought to himself that Henry must be some sort of nutcase, but as he looked at Henry's face and gazed into those two big, clear hazel eyes, Linderman saw a look of sincerity and intelligence that he could not discount and he was divided as to what to do.

On one hand he had his reputation to consider. He was broker who always advised his clients to take the safe, steady investing path. What would happen to that reputation if word got out that he allowed one of his clients to invest in a junk company like The Colorado Mineral Research and Discovery Corporation?

On the other hand, there was his commission to be considered. It was his job to service his clients and cater to their wishes. Was he to be held responsible if one of his clients was a lamebrain who wouldn't listen to reason? And then again maybe this Gainsvort guy wasn't simply a lamebrain and maybe he had some obscure but justifiable reason for this irrational obsession with The Colorado Mineral Research and Discovery Corporation. Well if so, what could that reason possibly be?

Linderman bounced that polemic around in his mind for a good, long minute, then at last he said with a deep sigh, "All right Mr. Gainsvort, if you insist, I'll buy the stock for you. Write out a check and I'll place the order, but don't say I didn't warn you."

"Yes Mr. Linderman, you did warn me, and I appreciate that; but this is something that I feel I must do."

Henry wrote out his check and handed it to Linderman. They shook hands and Henry departed. After Henry had left, Linderman shook his head and let out a soft, almost inaudible moan. What would his colleagues say if they knew that he, Paul Linderman, the cautious, play-it-safe broker, was placing an order for the stock of some obscure mining company that was about to go belly-up? Still, he had to respect his client's wishes no matter how bizarre, so turned to his computer and sent in the order.

Later that afternoon, Linderman called Henry to say that he bought the stock as Henry requested. At that point it was done; Henry's money was riding on some shaky company that according to all reports hadn't a ghost of a chance for survival; but Henry's vision had told him otherwise and he was willing to gamble his money on the strength of that vision. Well, it was done. The money was spent and all Henry could do now was wait for the outcome.

Two weeks later Linderman called Henry to report that The Colorado Mineral Research and Discovery Corporation had scored an unexpected and dramatic turnaround. Their exploration team had uncovered a rich source of copper ore in a remote part of Alaska. The company was suddenly solvent and prosperous. Almost overnight Henry's stock had doubled in value.

Soon other investors were jumping on the bandwagon and the value of Henry's stock doubled again. In just three weeks, it seemed that The Colorado Mineral Research and Discovery Corporation had become the success story of the year and now analysts were predicting that the stock would go through the roof.

But Henry didn't see it that way, because by then he had had another vision. This time he saw that the rich vein of copper ore was not nearly as deep and wide as original reports estimated. In addition, environmentalists were all lining up to put a stop to any mining operations in the precious, unspoiled wilderness of the Alaskan wilds. Henry saw that The Colorado Mineral Research and Discovery Corporation was about to have another turn around and this time it would go belly up. He immediately put in a call to Linderman.

"Mr. Linderman, I've decided that I want to sell all my shares of The Colorado Mineral Research and Discovery Corporation."

"But why Mr. Gainsvort? The stock is doing so well. It seems a shame to liquidate just when you're making such a good profit on your investment."

"Yes, I realize that but…well…I'm getting tired of it and I'd like to sell it."

Linderman let out a long, deep sigh. Henry could tell from that expression that the broker thought he was a capricious, lunatic investor, but Henry didn't care. He knew he had to get out of his investment before it turned sour, so he held his ground.

"Okay Mr. Gainsvort, I'll do as you wish. I'll sell your shares today."

Later that day, Linderman called to say that he had completed the transaction and Henry was fully divested of The Colorado Mineral Research and Discovery Corporation. That transaction happened just in time, because two days later, just as Henry's vision foretold, the news came out about the company's latest misfortune and the stock plummeted. All those investors who held The Colorado Mineral Research and Discovery Corporation securities lost their shirts. All except Henry. Henry walked away from the deal with a fat profit, because his visions had told him when to buy and sell. Henry knew at that point it was just the beginning and that from now on he was going to ride his visions to success and there could be no stopping him.

For the next six months it seemed that Henry had become the unstoppable force of Wall Street. He had a continuous series of visions where he saw obscure companies and stocks suddenly and unexpectedly make big surges. He saw stocks rapidly shoot up and he saw just when the bottom was about to drop out of those same investments. When it came to racing or gambling Henry couldn't master the timing but in the stock market, his timing was perfect, and here he was able to capitalize on all those visions in time to make money.

Henry was feeling elated by his recent success, but unfortunately, he had no one to share his success with. On a whim, he thought that maybe there might be a way to share his triumph with Augie; so, one bright sunny afternoon he paid a visit to a neighborhood flower shop and had the florist make up a flower arrangement in the form of a big horseshoe. He took this to the Greenwood Cemetery, to the mausoleum where Augie was resting. He laid the flowers on the floor beneath Augie's compartment.

Then he stepped back and said quietly, "You were right Augie. You said that there was a way that I could make money with my visions and I finally found it. I only wish that you were here to see me make it happen. Well, maybe you are someplace where you can see it happening. I hope so. Thank you for your faith and guidance." Then Henry left the mausoleum and walked home from the cemetery.

CHAPTER 22

It now seemed that Henry had at long last found a way to make his visions pay off. Indeed, he had, for within six months he had managed to accumulate over one-hundred-and-fifty-thousand dollars. Henry thought that now he could afford to move out of his dungeon-like apartment and relocate in Manhattan. Maybe now he could move up to a luxury place that he wouldn't have to share with mice and roaches. He was seriously thinking about going to a real estate agent and start looking into the possibilities, but he hesitated; some nebulous feeling in his gut told him that maybe he should wait a bit just to see if his good fortune would continue.

That turned out to be a sound tactic, because although Henry was now riding the gravy train to the land of wealth and success, fate had something else in mind for him. He didn't know it at the time, but his gravy train was about to become derailed and his dreams of unlimited wealth were soon to evaporate. This is how it happened.

Paul Linderman had been handling all of Henry's stock transactions from day one. His first impression of Henry, gleaned during their initial meeting, was that Henry was just some crackpot off the street who had no savvy at all when it came to picking stocks. But later, after Henry maneuvered his positions in the market and scored a succession of bullseyes, Linderman began to sit up and take notice. He recognized Henry's amazing success and modified his opinion of Henry. He no longer thought of his client as a crackpot, but he still didn't believe that there was any real thinking behind those investment choices. Linderman thought that Henry just made a brief series of lucky guesses here and there and they paid off. Linderman, however, was sure that soon Henry's luck would run out and he would choose rubbish stocks and lose his money.

But after more successes followed, Linderman changed his thinking again; he saw Henry in an entirely new light. He saw Henry as a studious and perceptive investor who had special insights into the marketplace. But later, after seeing Henry's steady and unparalleled successes in an unbroken, six-month run, Linderman began to grow suspicious and uneasy.

It seemed impossible that anyone could be that lucky or even that perceptive. After all, even the smartest investor has to stumble occasionally, but in Henry's portfolio there were no stumbles, no errors, no bad choices, and no losses. Linderman began to feel that there had to be something more to all this. The more he thought about it, Linderman came to feel that there was something very strange and dubious about Henry Gainsvort and his investment activities.

With each transaction, Linderman grew more and more suspicious of Henry Gainsvort's meteoric rise to wealth and he had the mounting feeling that there was something very unnatural, irregular and possibly illegal with the way Henry Gainsvort was trading in the market. Unfortunately, he couldn't say exactly what it was about Henry that was wrong; he only knew that something didn't *feel right*. After six months of handling Henry's transactions, Linderman was in a quandary about what to do and he felt that maybe he it was time that he talked to someone else about his client. Paul Linderman decided to have a chat with the big boss, A.J. White.

Now, A.J. White had been a stock broker since he graduated from New York University and he had been trading on the big board for over fifty years. His full name was Ahab Jonah White. That was a terrible name to be saddled with as a youth because all the kids in school who had read *Moby Dick* teased him about being the mad whaler in search of the great white whale. The fact that his middle name was Jonah didn't help either and in college Ahab Jonah became known as the "old salt of the campus".

A.J. couldn't understand why his parents chose to call him Ahab Jonah, but he suspected that at the time of his birth they must have been in some sort of a nautical mood and those were the names that they came up with. Unfortunately, he had to live with, and endure the results of his parent's capricious whim. In high school and college, he accepted the kidding of his school mates but when he entered graduate school he figured that enough was enough and he dropped the Ahab Jonah in favor of the initials. After that, the teasing stopped and he stuck with the abbreviation ever since. From then on, he kept his name a secret and he never had to put up with the compendium of tired whaler and nautical jokes that plagued him in his earlier days.

White was a shrewd and savvy broker who weathered many a bear market and had profited from many a bull market. As a wall street veteran, he was a man of considerable experience; he had seen all the trading strategies, schemes and scams that could possibly take place on the trading floor, in the board rooms, or in brokers' offices. Moreover, he was an easy man to talk to. It seemed that he would always make time to listen to a colleague's concerns and offer sage advice when asked.

Paul Linderman felt that A.J. White was the ideal man to consult on the issue of Henry Gainsvort, so he walked around the office corridor to White's office and knocked on the door. White bid Paul to enter and the two men sat down to talk about the mysterious Mr. Henry Gainsvort and his extraordinary performance in the stock market.

Linderman began with the story of his client's obsessive demand to buy shares of The Colorado Mineral Research and Discovery Corporation at a time when the company seemed headed for financial disaster and oblivion. Then he described the killing that Gainsvort had made when the company rebounded with spectacular results. He told White about Henry's abrupt decision to sell the stock when it seemed to be climbing up the charts and how that turned out to be a smart, if unwarranted—at least at that time—decision. Linderman then went on to tell of Henry's other successes, a perfect trading record with many hits and no failures.

At first White said nothing; he just listened to everything Linderman had to say. Then, at last, after Linderman had laid out the whole story for him, White spoke.

"Where is he getting his information from? I mean how does he find out about these companies?"

"That's just it, I don't know. He says that he's just playing hunches. And well, for the first few picks I accepted that; but now I have to wonder, because he always seems to know just when a stock will take off and just when it will turn sour. And he never misses. That's the really strange part. He's always right, all of the time. It just seems incredible that he can have such a long string of right hunches without one lemon."

A.J. listened attentively and nodded. "Yes, it does seem implausible."

"I mean, I've never seen anything quite like this. Have you?"

White shook his head. "No, come to think of it, I haven't. Your client seems to be an extraordinary trader."

"Yes, he is; and that's the part that makes me nervous. Nervous and suspicious. It seems that he's too extraordinary to be on the level."

White nodded but said nothing. He was trying to weigh all the possibilities in his mind. After a few minutes of silent deliberation, he concluded that Linderman was right; something just didn't jive.

"What do you think I should do?" asked Linderman "You think maybe I should stop handling his trades and tell him go somewhere else?'

"No, don't do that; as far as we know, Mr. Gainsvort isn't doing anything illegal. But on the other hand, we don't know, do we? I think that just to be on the safe side, maybe I should put in a call to the Securities and Exchange Commission. Maybe someone in the Commission might be interested in how Mr. Gainsvort is getting his information."

So later that day, A.J. White put in a call to the Securities and Exchange Commission to tell them about Henry Gainsvort and his extraordinary successes in the stock market. He talked to Jackson Ellis. Ellis thanked Mr. White for his heads-up information and said that indeed he was interested in the extraordinary Mr. Gainsvort."

A few minutes after he concluded his conversation with A.J. White, Jackson Ellis made a call to Henry and asked him to come by for an informal conversation, but he didn't specify what he wanted to talk about. Henry of course was surprised to get a call from someone at the Securities and Exchange Commission, but dutifully accepted the invitation to come to the office to speak with Jackson Ellis.

On the morning of his appointment, Henry took the subway from Sunset Park to lower Manhattan. He walked from the Manhattan subway station to the offices of the Securities and Exchange Commission. Now the New York offices of the Securities and Exchange Commission are located near the site where the attack on the World Trade Center happened.

When Henry approached the site of the attack, he stopped to look at the place where the Twin Towers once stood. At one time those Towers stood proud and tall and punctuating the Manhattan skyline with gleaming steel and glass. However, one quiet morning, two planes piloted by terrorists crashed into the towers and brought them to the ground as broken, flaming wreckage. In addition to the destruction of the towers a large part of the area was laid waste.

Now the area was largely rebuilt with newly-constructed office buildings and a ground-zero memorial. Ostensibly, all traces of the disaster have been erased, but for many the memory of that terrible day still lingered. As Henry surveyed the site, a sudden and strange thought clouded his conscience. He wondered to himself if there was still something in the atmosphere, some sort of negativity, some invisible damaging karma, some vestige of that disaster that was still hovering in the environment. If that was the case, then he might be exposing himself to it just by standing nearby. Maybe there was an omen, a portent of a dark cloud that was about to materialize and change his destiny. For the first time in his life, he was doing well, but now he wondered if maybe his luck was about to change.

Henry stood there looking across at the ground-zero site for a long time, lost in that thought, then he came back to the present moment and reminded himself that he had appointment to keep. He walked into the building where the offices of the Securities and Exchange Commission were located. He signed the visitor register in the lobby and a guard directed him to take the elevator to the sixth floor. When he got off the elevator and entered the offices of the Securities and Exchange Commission, Henry walked up to the receptionist and identified himself. He explained that he had an appointment with Mr.

Ellis. The receptionist put through a call, and soon Jackson Ellis came out to greet Henry.

Jackson Ellis was wearing slacks, a white shirt and a striped tie. He was a pleasant looking man somewhere in his mid-forties. One couldn't really say that Ellis was overweight—well not by much—but he did have a slight bulge over his belt. He had thin brown hair that he slicked back and his scalp showed through the meager fibers on the top of his head. He wore glasses. Henry thought that he looked like an insurance salesman or a car dealer.

Ellis led Henry back to his office where they sat down. Without beating around the bush, Ellis explained that he was aware of Henry's amazing trading record in the recent months. Ellis said that he just couldn't understand how one individual could pick so many doubtful stocks—stocks that professional analysts had previously condemned as poor investments—and ride them to profitability. One or two picks was in the realm of plausibility but not the dozen hits that Henry had captured. With a blunt, point-blank question, Ellis asked Henry how he did it.

Henry was a little taken aback with Ellis' direct manner, but after a moment of consideration, decided that there could be no harm in telling Ellis the truth. So, Henry told all about his visions. He briefly summarized how they started when he was a little boy, and how he continued to have glimpses into the future throughout his life. He then told how he had visions of stocks and of companies and of the numbers on the big board when he looked through *Barron's*.

Ellis listen politely to Henry's story with interest and skepticism. In his mind, he could not believe that anyone could see into the future—well certainly not a man like Henry Gainsvort who seemed like a typical, mild-mannered, unassuming fellow and not some dark, mysterious sage who dabbles in the occult arts. As Henry was talking about his visions,

Ellis searched his face to see if maybe this tale of visions of tomorrow was really some sort of put-down, some hoax conjured up to disguise a more sinister method of trading. But when Ellis looked into Henry's big, bright hazel eyes he saw no traces of guile or deviousness, but only an honest, unaffected sincerity. Ellis had to believe that Henry Gainsvort was telling the truth as he truly believed it to be.

After Henry told about his past and his visions, Ellis asked questions. He asked a lot of questions, ostensibly to clarify some points of interest but also with a subtle intent to try to trip Henry up and possibly expose any pretense or fakery on Henry's part. After an hour of dialogue, Ellis accepted that he had the whole story and that Henry Gainsvort was neither a lunatic nor a conman, and Jackson Ellis was left with the unavoidable conclusion that Henry Gainsvort really could see into the future.

After hearing all that Henry had to say, Ellis thanked him for taking the time and trouble to come down to the offices of the Securities and Exchange Commission. He added that Henry's input had done a lot to shed light on the mystery of his recent trading success. Ellis accompanied Henry back to the reception area. The two men shook hands and they parted company.

Henry walked out of the offices and went into the hall where he waited for the elevator. As he was descending in the elevator, he thought to himself that his session with Jackson Ellis had been interesting and it seemed that Ellis was satisfied with the explanation that Henry had put forth. Henry assumed that the matter was closed and he would hear no more about it, and he was confident that he would be able to continue trading in the stock market as he had done before.

CHAPTER 23

Henry couldn't know it at the time, but the matter was far from being closed. Back in his office Jackson Ellis was very concerned about all that Henry had just disclosed. He felt that Henry was basically honest but that still there was something wrong about how he was trading in the stock market. Jackson Ellis felt that there was a definite problem here, but he wasn't sure exactly what it was or what he could do about it. He decided that maybe he should talk it over with one of his colleagues. So, he went down the hall to visit William "Bill" Hirsch in his office.

Ellis told Hirsch all about the remarkable Mr. Henry Gainsvort and the two men sat together and hashed over the whole situation. After an hour, they both concluded that there was something improper with Gainsvort's trading methods but they didn't know how to handle the problem. They decided to consult with their supervisor Mackland Engel.

Mackland Engel had been with the Securities and Exchange Commission for almost forty-five years. He joined the Commission almost immediately after he graduated from law school. He was a tall man with a head of thick, wiry, gray hair, bushy eyebrows and a thick mustache that looked kind of like an elongated Brillo pad that he had pasted on his upper lip.

He was a little surprised when Ellis and Hirsch appeared together at his office door, but he knew that if both men were coming to see him then something important must be in the air. He invited the pair to take up chairs in his office and tell him what was happening. At first, Jackson Ellis did all of the talking because, after all, it was he who had interviewed Henry Gainsvort; then Bill Hirsch added his impressions based on what Ellis had told him. After both finished, the trio sat in silence for a few minutes. Jackson and Bill remained mute, waiting to see what Engel was going to say.

At first Mackland Engel didn't say anything. He just sat there leaning back in his chair with his lips pursed as he looked up at the ceiling. After a long pause, he snorted through his mustache. Ellis noted that whenever Engel was about to say something significant, he first snorted through his mustache. To Ellis, this sounded like a bull who was about to charge. After the snort, Engel said, "It seems obvious that Mr. Engle is engaging in insider trading."

Both Jackson and Bill exchanged glances. Each man had secretly been thinking the same thing, but hadn't wanted to voice that thought because neither was sure that Henry's Gainsvort's precognitive visions could, in fact, be called insider trading. But now their boss, Mackland Engel had said exactly what they had both been thinking: Henry Gainsvort was doing insider trading.

Bill Hirsch cleared his throat, then spoke. "Okay, assuming for the sake of argument, that Gainsvort is doing insider trading—"

"Not assuming," interrupted Engel, "we're not assuming anything here. Make no mistake, Gainsvort is doing insider trading. He has gained access to information that is denied to other investors. That is insider trading."

"Okay," said Hirsch. "So Gainsvort is doing insider trading. Well, what do we do about it? We can't very well bring him into court and tell a judge and jury how he's doing it. It would sound like we're trying to prosecute a fortune teller or a soothsayer. They'd laugh us right out of court."

"Bill's right," said Ellis. "We only have Gainsvort's word about how he's getting his information. Suppose he denies that he has these visions when he's on the stand? We have no way of proving otherwise and we'd lose our case."

Mackland nodded, paused for a minute, then snorted through his mustache. "Yes, all of that is true, but suppose Gainsvort doesn't know any of that? From what you've told me about him, I'm willing to bet that he probably doesn't, and I believe that we may be able to work Gainvort's ignorance to our advantage. Yes, I think we may be able to throw a scare into Gainsvort and settle this whole thing without going to court. Jack, why don't you give Mr. Gainsvort a call and ask him to come by our offices early next week."

The next day, Henry got another call from Jackson Ellis at the Securities and Exchange Commission. He was surprised by this second call, because he thought that he had explained everything to Ellis' satisfaction and that the matter was closed. "What now?" Henry asked himself. "What else did the man want to know?"

There was only one way to find out, and that was by returning to the offices of the Security Exchange Commission and going through another dialogue with Jackson Ellis. Henry agreed to a return meeting and a second round of explanations. They set a date and time for the next appointment. This is what happened when he met that appointment.

Once again, he retraced his path from his apartment to the office building that he had visited before and again he signed the visitor register and took the elevator to the sixth floor. And again, Jackson Ellis came out to the reception area to greet Henry, but this time they didn't go back to Ellis' office. This time Ellis led Henry through the corridor to a conference room.

When they entered the conference room, Henry was surprised to see two other gentlemen sitting at the far end of a long table. Ellis directed Henry to sit at one end of the table and he walked to the opposite end to sit with the other two. Henry sat down and waited wondering what was coming next.

For a minute no one said anything, they just sat there with the three men at one end of the table looking at Henry, and with him sitting at the other end looking back at them. Henry felt a distinct chill in the air. He sensed that there was something ominous in the atmosphere. His instincts told him that this meeting was not going to be a pleasant one.

Henry waited for someone to say something, but the three men at the other end of the table continued to sit there in silence, just looking at him, studying him. Henry felt like he had been called before a tribunal, an inquisition, but he couldn't imagine why; after all he hadn't done anything wrong—well, at least as far as he knew. He hadn't a clue as to what this meeting was all about, but he had the uneasy feeling that these men were out for his blood and his gut feeling told him to expect the worst.

Finally, the man with the bushy mustache spoke. He introduced himself as Mackland Engel and he introduced his college, Bill Hirsch. Then he got down to brass tacks.

"We've been looking over your trading record Mr. Gainsvort and I must say that it is extraordinary. You've managed to make a number of killings by picking the dark horses of the market. That's really quite amazing. Now, Mr. Ellis tells me that in a recent interview you had with him, you claimed to be clairvoyant and you said that you had visions where you saw phenomenal market turnarounds. He said that you claimed to be able to look into the future."

Mackland Engel had made that brief introduction in a quiet, almost avuncular manner, but Henry was still wary. His instinct told him that Engel was deliberately attempting to be disarming in an attempt to throw him off his guard. Henry suspected that behind that calm, benevolent façade of Engel was a predator posturing for a strike. Henry decided that in this dialogue he would have to play his cards very close to the chest. If Engel could put on a front, Henry figured then that he could also. He managed a warm smile and tried to appear nonchalant and relaxed.

"I think Mr. Ellis is mistaken. I don't think that I ever said that I had visions where I looked into the future."

"Oh, but you did. You told me that you had these visions all of your life," interjected Jackson Ellis hastily.

"Did I? I think not. You probably misunderstood me, or else it was a poor choice of words on my part. I never meant to imply that I could really look into the future. I don't remember having used the word *visions* either, I think I said that I had insights into the market. Yes, *insights* was the word that I used."

"That's not true. You did tell me that you had visions of what was going to happen before it really did happen."

Henry paused to refresh his smile. "I'm sorry, but I really don't remember ever having said that. What I meant to say was that I get insights, little hints, from reading the financial sections. I'm sure that I never claimed to be clairvoyant."

Henry could see that Ellis and the other man, Hirsch, were a little perturbed at the turn that this interview was taking; obviously they weren't hearing the answers that they had expected. Henry also saw that Mackland Engel remained unruffled. Engel smiled, but it wasn't a warm, friendly smile. No, it was a closed, tight-lipped, sinister smile, like a crocodile that is very sure of itself and is now maneuvering to pounce on its prey. Henry saw in Mackland Engel's eyes a look of determination and that look made Henry very apprehensive. Henry recognized Engel as a supreme predator with a single-minded purpose; this was a hunter who was resolute in bringing down his prey.

Sure enough, Engel spoke next. "Well why don't you tell me about your insights. I'd like to hear more about them. About how you arrive at them and what form they take."

Henry felt that he was in tight corner. He improvised an explanation of his so-called insights. He said that he read all the papers and as many financial reports that he could, and the articles that he read somehow gave him inspirations for trading opportunities. In his ramblings Henry tried to make it seem as if all his reading was just fodder for intuition and grist for his hunches. He reiterated that he never actually saw what was going to happen in the future, but only that the items he read sparked his imagination and inspired him to take risks in the market, and that was all there was to it. Henry tried to make out that he was just an avid reader who had a lot of lucky hunches.

Henry said all that while trying to project an air of self-confidence and an image of authority. The problem was that he wasn't sure any of the men at the end of the table were buying into his spiel.

While he was saying all of this, he avoided making direct eye contact with the others. He looked down and with his index finger he traced imaginary circles on the polished surface of the table. He did this to appear casual but also it was a ploy to allow him to focus his eyes on something and thus shield his face from the three men at the opposite end of the table. He was afraid that if he looked directly at them, some facial expression or something in his big eyes might give him away and reveal the falsity in the details of his explanation.

When he had finished, he looked up. No one said anything and the room remained engulfed in silence for a long time. To Henry it was a pregnant pause. He looked up at the men and he could see that they were unsettled by his explanation. It wasn't what they expected to hear, but they had no way to refute his claims or poke holes in anything that he had just said. It was as if he had thrown them off their established game plan.

Henry felt a mild glow of victory. He felt that his subterfuge had worked. At the same time, he could see that his battle was not over. Even though his three adversaries were stymied, they were not defeated. He sensed that they were only pausing, just long enough to regroup and launch a fresh attack. Henry was particularly unnerved by the cold look in Mackland Engel's eyes. He knew that Engel would counterattack, but all Henry could do was sit there and wait to see what the man would come up with next.

Henry didn't have to wait long, Mackland Engel broke the silence.

"Well, Mr. Gainsvort," he said with another unctuous smile, "that was a very imaginative explanation, but I don't believe a word of it. I do believe what Jack said that you originally told him, that you can see into the future. He said that you told him that you see changes in the stock market before they actually happen. That is what I really believe you said, and what I believe that you actually do. If that is truly the case—and I believe it is—then that kind of information constitutes insider trading and it is illegal."

Henry knew that the game had taken a turn. They had taken off the kid gloves and were playing for keeps now. His face hardened and he dropped his cavalier attitude.

"Well of course, you can believe what you want Mr. Engel, but you can't verify any of it. There is no way that you can possibly prove that I have ever had a vision of future. And as for me telling Mr. Ellis that …well …it's his word against mine and I deny ever having said any of that."

At that point Jackson Ellis must have felt that his credibility was being undermined and he leaned forward to speak, but Engel waved him back to the silent sidelines.

"Yes, you're right when you say we can't prove any of it, Mr. Gainsvort, but fortunately we don't have to. There is another approach that we can take."

When Engel had said that, Henry was gripped with an icy fear. It was as if the predator had found a weak spot and suddenly and unexpectedly struck and sank his fangs deep into Henry's heart. Henry wasn't sure what Engel had up his sleeve, but he knew that he wasn't going to like it.

"You see, Mr. Gainsvort, we know a great deal about you. For example, we know that you are an accountant and that you have many free-lance clients. Now it is entirely possible that in the course of your dealings with your many clients you have gained access to information which has enabled you to make trades in the stock market. Profiting from such information would, of course, be illegal."

"But," protested Henry, "none of my clients are in any way related to the companies that I bought in the stock market. There was absolutely no connection between them."

"Yes, ostensibly that is so, but it is possible that those companies, your clients, may have had business dealings that in some subtle way related to the companies that you bought into. Now, they didn't have to be solid connections, just enough to give you a slight edge here and there."

"But there was nothing like that. I swear to it. You just look. You look, and I guarantee that you won't find anything."

"Oh, we'll find the evidence that we need Mr. Gainsvort. Make no mistake about that. You see, we are in position to place certain information within the files of your clients to establish the connections that we are talking about."

When he heard this, Henry was stunned. "Wait a minute! You mean that you'd frame me?"

"Let's just say that we'll structure the evidence to fit the crime."

"But that's illegal."

"So is insider trading."

As Engel said that, Henry detected a sinister tone of delight in the man's voice and he could see that Engel was very pleased with himself. It was as if victory was in his grasp and he was already gloating over his triumph.

They sat there for the longest time, with no one saying a word.

Once again Engel broke the silence.

"Now Mr. Gainsvort, we are not going to prosecute you for the trades that you have made. As far as we are concerned, that's water under the bridge. And you can keep all of the money that you earned. All we want is for you to stop trading. As far as the stock market is concerned, it's over for you Mr. Gainsvort. You made your last stock deal and it's time for you to liquidate your portfolio and relinquish your position in the market. We'll be satisfied if you do that. If you do, then we're willing to drop the whole matter. Okay, Mr. Gainsvort?"

Henry was stunned and said nothing at first. It was as if he had just been impaled and gutted and he was still numb from the experience. There was a long silence and Henry just sat there without a word. *What could he say to that?* He knew that he was looking into the big guns of the federal government and he saw that they were determined to stop him—to stop him at any cost and there wasn't a thing he could do about it. As he sat there thinking about his situation, he felt so small and so very impotent. He was facing annihilation and all he could do was cringe and take it.

Finally, Henry nodded. The three men looked at him then they exchanged glances of satisfaction and they smiled. The meeting was over and they all got up to leave. Ellis escorted Henry to the exit and Henry followed his lead walking in numb stupefaction.

Henry left the offices of the Securities and Exchange Commission and took the subway back to his apartment. He was defeated, crushed and deflated. Once again, his visions had gotten him into trouble. Once again, he renewed his resolve that no matter what, he would never, ever, talk about them again—not to anyone. He knew that there was no way to stop his visions from popping up, but he was determined never to reveal them to anybody.

CHAPTER 24

The incident at the Securities and Exchange Commission convinced Henry that following his visions would only lead him into trouble and he resolved that from then on, he would do his level best to ignore them. At the same time, he knew that there was no way he could prevent his visions from coming, but he could at least keep quiet about them. Let them happen but don't talk about them; that was his mind set. As long as he never said anything about them, then no one need ever know that he had these glimpses into destiny. And if no one knew about them, then they couldn't laugh at him or criticize him or ostracize him or call him a freak, and the authorities couldn't bug him.

For the next year, he stayed true to his purpose. He continued to have visions—they popped up now and then at odd moments—but they were narrow windows into small, inconsequential scenes. He saw a couple of car accidents, and the final results of a few ball games, and he saw a prominent politician's career come to ruin when the newspapers found about his financial chicanery; but these were minor events and Henry could easily put them out of his mind. Thus, it was relatively easy for Henry to keep his resolution about never, ever revealing the content of his visions and no one ever suspected that he was even having them.

During the course of that year, he had actually come to believe that he could forever remain mute about his visions of destiny and he even convinced himself that he would never waver from his resolve. But Henry should have known better, because in the past, just when he seemed so sure of himself, fate had always stepped in to undermine his iron-clad determination and topple his rigid structure of self-confidence. Unbeknownst to Henry, fate was about to step in again and play another hand. This is what happened when it did.

Soon after that depressing meeting at the Securities and Exchange Commission, Henry had done as he'd been instructed: he divested himself of his position in the Stock Market and he quit trading. Making money in the Market was the one chance that he had to make his visions pay off, and when he could no longer do that, he felt that he had failed. In his mind he had failed himself and he had failed his deceased friend Augie. With that realization, it seemed that once again the very purpose of life had been drained from his existence.

He continued to live in his hovel-apartment and he all abandoned thoughts of moving out and finding a better place. He stayed where he was, and for a time, he still put out the roach bait and mouse traps; but then, after a while, his attitude changed and he stopped laying down these things. He stopped killing the roaches and the mice because he began to see himself as another one of life's creatures no better or worse than any other. As Henry came to see it, he was like the other beings of the earth, just passing through life, just trying to get by and make a living. As long as those little critters weren't harming him, then why bother to smash them into oblivion?

During this time, Henry continued to do his freelance accounting and bookkeeping jobs. He wasn't working so much for the paycheck—because he had the money that he made in the stock market—but going to odd jobs here and there gave him something to do, a reason to get up in the morning and someplace to go to that would take him out of his dingy apartment. Moreover, reporting to a job now and then, occupied his mind and passed the time and gave his life some semblance of variety and a dim purpose in life.

Every day he got out of bed and bathed and shaved and dressed himself and went about his chores and sometimes went to an occasional free-lance job. He was essentially drifting through one day and into the next, going through the motions of living without any real meaning. Henry's life at this point had been distilled down to sleeping, eating, going to work and returning home. Often there were times when he was alone in his apartment and he pondered the big questions:

Why was he doing any of this? To what end did his life serve here on earth, and moreover why was he cursed with these strange visions? What purpose did these visions have? Why him and no one else? If he couldn't change fate, or profit from his visions, then why have them at all? Those were the big questions, and each time he asked himself, Henry had no answer and he came to doubt that he would ever find it.

On some evenings, when his apartment seemed particularly morbid and depressing, Henry would go out to Gallagher's. Returning to Gallagher's wasn't as cheerful and uplifting as in the past when he frequented the place with Augie, but it was still better than sitting within the confines of his dreary, dungeon-like apartment.

Whenever he walked into Gallagher's, Henry circulated around the bar and tried to greet of all the guys like he did when he was with Augie. He did this in an attempt to be friendly, but it wasn't easy. Somehow, Henry found that he couldn't make small talk or show real interest in those men the way Augie did. Still, Henry made a sincere effort to be one of the gang by going around and greeting everyone in sight. He did all of that because those guys were friends of Augie's, and by association they were his friends also, and Henry felt that...well...doing the good-buddy bit was something that was expected of him so he tried his best to do it, but his heart wasn't really in it.

After greeting everyone at the bar, Henry retreated to the back room and took up a position in the far corner booth. This was the same booth that he and Augie always occupied together. He liked it because it reminded him of the many times that he and Augie would come in and sit together and eat and drink and talk. He liked this booth because when he sat in it and looked around at the many pictures on the wall, he could almost see Augie sitting across from him.

As Henry looked from photo to photo, it was almost as if he could hear Augie telling him stories about the glory of sports in the bygone days. In that way, at least in Henry's mind, Augie wasn't really dead—at least not in spirit. And as long as Gallagher's continued to stand, Augie would always be there, in that back room with all those old photographs.

That was the main reason that he chose the booth, but he also liked it because it was in the far corner and he could sit in quiet seclusion without having to make human contact with the others in the place. In his cloistered booth, Henry would order a hamburger with onion rings and a beer and sit there alone and relive those happy moments that were long gone.

Marcy was still working the backroom as a waitress and she always waited on Henry. At first, she treated him like any of the other regulars, but then one night, she took a good look at Henry sitting all by himself and she sensed his loneliness and her heart went out to him. After that, whenever there was a slow period with only a few customers to wait on, Marcy took a break and went over to Henry's booth to sit down and chat with him. She did this many, many times and gradually they formed a friendship, although it was a relationship that existed only within the confines of Gallagher's.

Henry soon found himself going to Gallagher's solely to meet and talk with Marcy. She became the only bright spot in Henry's world of gloom and depression. She was his only friend. During the course of their many sessions together, they talked about a lot of things. Henry liked talking to Marcy because she seemed interested in him and she was a good listener. He told her about himself, his youth in Jersey City, his college, and the kind of work that he did.

Henry felt relaxed and comfortable around Marcy, so he opened up and told her everything—well almost everything. There was one thing he didn't talk about. He never mentioned—nor even hinted at—his visions. That was the one subject that Henry kept under wraps. Henry promised himself that he would never talk to anyone about those secret looks into the future and he was bound and determined to keep that promise and he never told Marcy about his visions.

Henry had now settled into his mundane, routine existence and he accepted the fact that this was the way he was going to live out the rest of his life. And indeed, it seemed that his life would continue in this manner to his final day on earth; but then all that changed. It changed because he had another vision. This vision was different from all those others that he had in the past. It was the biggest one that he had ever had. It was so big and so horrifying that he couldn't put it out of his mind and, try as he might, he just couldn't ignore it. This is how it happened.

One afternoon, Henry was sitting outside on a bench in the small triangular park across the street from the big Federal Reserve Bank in the financial district of lower Manhattan. He was just sitting there, sipping a Coke and eating his lunch, a ham and cheese sandwich on rye bread with lettuce and a wedge of pickle on the side. His mind was a total blank as he sat there, munching and sipping just looking across the street at the big bank building.

Previously, he had read a bronze plaque affixed to the outside wall of that bank building; it described the building. It said the structure was designed in neo-Florentine Renaissance style using rusticated Ohio sandstone. As he sat there looking, he admired the massive façade of the building and the huge, elegant, wrought-iron lanterns that were mounted on the wall and extended out over the sidewalk. He looked at sturdy grillwork on the windows and he thought to himself that this building was unlike any other in the area. It was as if a little piece of Renaissance Italy from the time of the Medicis existed in the heart of Manhattan.

The place was built like a fortress—with good reason, for some five stories below the ground level, in the bowels of the earth, the gold reserves of the international banking community were stored. Or so he'd heard; Henry had never seen them because the subterranean vaults were not open to the general public.

For the next twenty minutes, Henry continued to sit there, quietly munching his sandwich, nibbling his pickle, and drinking his soda, while looking at the monumental bank building across the street from him, admiring the many nuances of its architectural details. His eyes moved from the ground level up the sides of the façade to the edges of the roof. He surveyed the roof details, mentally capturing the niceties of the perimeter ornamentation. Then he looked above to beautiful cloud-studded sky.

His mind was a virtual blank slate. He wasn't thinking about anything in particular, just looking at the edifice and the sky because they were there and he had nothing else to do and the building and the blue sky gave his eyes something to focus on. He continued to look upward at the roof, and that's when he saw them. He saw big, dark objects sailing across the sky from adjacent buildings to the roof of the Federal Reserve Bank. And as he saw the vague shapes, one after the other—five in all—Henry knew that he was having another vision.

The objects, whatever they were, weren't really there—they were a vision in his mind's eye—but he knew that sometime soon, in the near future, they would come into being. However, at that moment, his vision was just forming, and he couldn't tell what those strange shapes were because they were still vague blurs. He knew, however, that in the next few minutes that would change. Everything would come together and the vision would become crystal clear. That was always the way with his visions. They just appeared, vague at first, then they suddenly came into focus.

Henry just sat there, calmly eating, silently finishing his sandwich, staring up at the roof with the vision of the future running in his mind. In less than a minute, everything was revealed and he saw the entire story in all its horrifying details. The shapes were crystal clear now, and he saw that they were hang gliders. Hang gliders piloted by terrorists who launched themselves from the rooftops of the taller neighboring buildings and sailed over to the top of the Federal Reserve Bank.

For all intents and purposes, the building was a virtual impenetrable stronghold impervious to outside attack. Well it was that—at least on the ground level. But the cunning terrorists had found a weak spot in the Bank's defense. No one had thought to safeguard the roof, because it was thought to be impossible to get to. And it was—until now.

In his vision, Henry saw that some villainous minds had devised a plan to attack the Bank from the air with an ingenious and daring raid. Once on top, the terrorists would use explosives to blow a hole in the roof then descend inside. Their plan was diabolical in the extreme: once inside, they would force their way through the bank, throwing nerve gas canisters ahead of them, to get to the vaults below. The security guards within would be caught totally by surprise. Once they gained entrance to the vaults, the raiders planned to explode a dirty nuclear device that would wreak havoc with the vaults and contaminate all the gold reserves within.

It was a bold plan, but it would eventually fail because the Bank's security force would ultimately rally and hold off the attackers until reinforcements arrived. But before that happened a vicious battle would ensue and many would die in the conflict. Henry saw the fighting, the blood-spattered walls, the dead bodies lying in halls, the many injured people, and the carnage that was yet to come. Yes, the terrorists would eventually fail to detonate their bomb, but they would succeed in showing the world that they were a force to be reckoned with. A potent, secret army that could strike anywhere whenever it had a mind to. And the people of the United States would come to realize that they were not safe even in their own backyards.

Henry sat there seeing the violence, death and destruction vividly in his vision as if it was actually happening at that very moment. When he could endure it no more, he got up threw his crumpled-up lunch bag and empty soda can into a nearby trash receptacle, then walked to Fulton street where he got the subway back to Brooklyn.

For two days, Henry thought about that vision. Up till that moment, he had never had a vision with killing and carnage in it. This was the most frightening vision that he had ever had, and he debated with himself if maybe he should break his self-imposed vow of silence and say something to somebody about it. On one hand, he felt that he should sound the alarm and tell someone, the authorities maybe, that an insidious, diabolical plot was in the making; but on the other hand, he reminded himself that in the past, after he told of the things he saw, the consequences of his revelation always came back to plague him. Every time he told anyone about one of his visions he found that they just didn't understand and they didn't believe.

People just didn't understand, because they couldn't see what he saw. When he tried to describe his visions, they didn't believe him or maybe it was just that they were afraid of the future. Whatever the reason, they viewed him with skepticism and maybe even a little fear. Maybe they were afraid because he possessed a power that they didn't. Henry never understood the reason for their fears and skepticism; he only knew that once he told about his visions, it seemed that everyone distrusted him and shunned him—well not everybody.

There was Augie. Augie was different. He understood and he accepted Henry for what he was. With Augie, Henry could open up and at the same time feel safe, knowing that he wouldn't be looked on with apprehension and distrust. Yes, with Augie it was different; but now Augie was gone and once more Henry was all alone, this time with a deep, dark secret and there was no one to talk to.

No one? Maybe there was someone out there who was like Augie and who would accept this latest vision and try to help him to do something about it. Maybe there might be someone who would lend a sympathetic ear, but trying to find that someone was next to impossible. Experience had taught Henry to be wary. And he suspected that if he went out now and told people of his latest, most frightening vision, they simply would not understand, and once again he would be seen as the village idiot.

So, he kept his vision to himself and tried to go on with his life as if that horrible mental picture had never appeared. But, try as he might, he just could not get the sights and sounds of that bold and vicious attack out of his mind. He thought about the terrifying scene during the day, and it continued to haunt him into the night. He didn't eat or sleep well.

Yet some spark of conscience in the back of his mind told him that he had to tell someone about what was coming. An ethical voice deep within him told him that he should try to sound an alarm; but a gut feeling told him that if he did, he would meet the same stone wall and the same skepticism and hostility that he had faced so many times before. Henry was fighting an intellectual-emotional tug of war, that was gnawing at his insides.

CHAPTER 25

Henry spent the next three days confined to his miserable, vermin-infested apartment with its dark, dingy atmosphere. He tried to pass the time reading or watching television, only going out to get provisions in the small, neighborhood Key Food supermarket across the street from his place. After three days of self-imposed, solitary confinement, he couldn't endure the loneliness anymore; he had to get out and experience the company of other human beings or else go mad sitting around in his cave with only mute bugs and mice for companions.

Henry went out and walked to Gallagher's Bar & Grill. Inside, the place was relatively empty because it was still early in the afternoon and most of the regulars hadn't gotten off work yet. There were two men standing at the bar but Henry didn't know them. This was a good thing, because on that particular day Henry wasn't up to doing the glad-hand bit. So, when he entered, he just waved and offered a weak smile to the bartender then immediately walked into the back room where he took a seat in his usual booth. He sat down and waited patiently for Marcy to come over and take his order.

Marcy saw Henry come into the room and she immediately noticed that there was something different about him. Even though he tried to give a cheery wave to her, she could see that he was not his usual self; his eyes were dark and his face was drawn. She suspected that he was troubled about something. She waved back, but at the same time she watched him as he walked across the room and sat in the corner booth. For a long minute she continued to stand in place looking at Henry in the far booth and she could tell by his manner and expression that he was deeply concerned about something.

She walked over and took his order and tried to engage him in light banter, hoping that maybe she could cheer him up, or that maybe he would open up to her and tell her what was bothering him; but no, Henry wasn't very responsive. He seemed unusually distant with his mind occupied in another world, so she left him and went to the kitchen to give his order to the cook.

That afternoon there were only a few other people in the back room, and Marcy had to attend to their needs. Yet, whenever she had a moment, she glanced over to the far corner booth to see if Henry was any better, but there was no change. He continued to sit enveloped in a saturnine cloud of gloom.

When Henry's food was ready, Marcy brought it over to him and again she tried to talk, but he only responded with vague, monosyllabic words. Feeling a little frustrated, she left him to wait on her other customers.

Henry sat there, eating his chow, all the time wrapped in his personal atmosphere of darkness and despair. When he had finished eating, he pushed his plate away, but continued to sit nursing his beer, letting his troubled mind roam in melancholy mental pastures. For a time, he was able to make his mind a blank slate and think of almost nothing. Then he relaxed a little bit; but abruptly, without warning, those images of the assault on the bank and bloody battle that followed came to the forefront of his mind and once again his mind clouded over.

Those frightful images continued to pop up and plague him even through his second beer. During all this, Marcy had been watching him surreptitiously, stealing glances whenever she could. She saw the dark, troubled look on his face. She saw him kneading his hands. She had seen him looking lonely and depressed before, but never like this. She could tell by his manner that something was bothering him, that something must have happened to put him in this extreme depressed state but she couldn't imagine what it could be. She continued to glance over at him with increasing concern. As soon as she had a break she he went over to his booth.

"Whatsa matter Henry? Something bothering you? You seem kind of troubled today. More so then usual. You got some sort of problem? Anything you wanna talk about?"

She tried to say that in a sympathetic voice with a cheery, upbeat tone. She thought that maybe a jovial approach might shake him from his doldrums, but that didn't seem to work. Henry just looked up at her. She had come up so quietly and he had been so lost in thought that he never noticed her approach, but now she was standing before him. The sudden sound of her voice startled him and brought him out of his thought cocoon. He tried to say something.

"Well…not exactly…well sort of…I mean, it's not something…" He let his voice fade out. Marcy waited for him to continue but he said nothing.

"You still missing Augie?"

Henry nodded. "Yeah, but it's not that, it's…" Henry let his voice trail off again because he didn't know what more to say. He couldn't tell Marcy about the raid that he had witnessed in his mind's eye, because he knew that she wouldn't understand about his visions.

"What? If it's not Augie, then what's bothering you?"

"It's something that I...well it's kinda hard to explain. It's not something I can really talk about. I mean, I just don't know how to explain it."

If Henry thought that would make Marcy go away, he was wrong. She knew that something was troubling him. She cared about him and she was determined to find out what this was all about. She stood there by the booth for a couple of minutes waiting for him to continue, but he lapsed into silence. Marcy was not to be put off; she sat down and leaned across the table and fired a direct question at him.

"Did you have another vision, Henry? Is that what it is? Did you see something that bothered you?"

He looked back at her in complete surprise. *How did she know that he had visions?* He had never told her. Marcy saw the look of total astonishment on his face and knew at once the question that was circulating in his mind.

"Augie told me," she said.

Henry nodded slowly. Of course, Augie told her about his visions and at the same time, probably made her take a vow of silence. All this time she knew and she never let on that she knew. All this time, Marcy knew his secret and never even hinted that she knew that he had a mysterious ability to see into destiny. Augie told her to keep the confidence; and she did—until now.

"Do you want to tell me about it? Maybe it would help if you talked about it."

Henry nodded slowly but remained mute for a minute. He was still recovering from the shock of her revelation. Up till now, he thought that no one knew about his visions, but all this time Marcy had known. All this time she was aware of his secret but she never let on because Augie had told her not to say anything.

As Henry sat there and looked back at her, he thought that maybe, at last, unexpectedly, he had found a kindred spirit, someone he could confide and someone who would understand. Well, maybe she would and then again, maybe not, but he felt that he had to tell someone about his vision, and at that moment, she was the only one in the entire world who might possibly understand what he was going through. Anyway, it was worth a shot. With a measure of mixed relief and trepidation, he told Marcy of his vision of the attack on the Federal Reserve Bank in lower Manhattan.

Marcy listened to Henry's story without saying anything, but when he got to the part about the battle and filled in the gory details of bloody death and destruction that ensued, her eyes widened and her jaw dropped.

He told her the whole story of the dastardly attack, right down to the last scene. When at last he finished describing the full content of his vision, he took a swig of beer, sat back in the booth and looked at her for some sort of reaction. For a long moment she said nothing. This strange tale of a bizarre attack on the staid institution in the heart of financial district in Manhattan and the lurid battle scene with all its violence and carnage was still reverberating in her mind. She didn't know what to make of it. It was like she some sort of realistic video game that you know is pure fantasy but at the same time is so true-to-life that you can't quite believe it's not actually happening.

"Do you really think that all this is going to happen Henry? I mean, happen the way you described it?"

Henry nodded slowly. "Whenever I've had these visions in the past, they always came true. And it always happened just as I saw it. I have no reason to think that this one will be any different."

She nodded and was silent for a few minutes as she tried to think about the implications of everything that he had just told her. Finally, she looked into his face and asked, "Well, what are you going to do about it, Henry?"

He looked back at her with some surprise. "Do? What can I do about it? I can't go up against a bunch of terrorists!"

"Henry, you have got to tell someone about this. Go to the authorities, the police. You can warn them of what might happen."

Henry shook his head.

"Why not? What are you afraid of?"

"In the past whenever I told anyone about my visions, they always laughed at me and said I was a crackpot."

"Well maybe this time it will be different."

Henry shook his head again. "No, it'll probably be even worse. This is a story that's so fantastic that nobody will ever believe it."

"But Henry, you don't know that. I mean maybe the police will be different. After all this time you'll be talking to professional law enforcement people and this is a serious crime and they will have to take this seriously. After all, that's their job."

"I don't think so. I mean they'll probably think I'm some kind of a nutcase."

"But Henry, you don't really know that. And you won't know for sure unless you try."

"Maybe I don't know, but I just don't want to find out."

"Why not? What have you got to lose."

Henry was silent a moment while he thought about it. Then after a moment of reflection he said, "What have I got to lose? My self-respect. My sanity. Marcy, you don't know what it's like. I tell someone about what I've seen and then I get this look."

"What look?"

"They look back at me like I just dropped in from another planet. Like I'm some sort of mutant life form that doesn't belong here. Then after I'm gone, they tell other people about me, and soon I find that I've become some sort of weirdo to be avoided. It's like I'm a leper or something. And all because I just tried to help. Well, I've had enough of it. I'm through trying to help people. I just can't face those looks anymore. I can't face the ridicule."

Henry said that with a vehemence and conviction that stunned Marcy. She didn't know what to say. Yet, at the same time, she could see that in spite of his resolution he was still troubled and she felt a deep sympathy for him. She was silent for a few minutes before she spoke again.

"So, you're just going to sit there and do nothing."

He shrugged. "There's nothing I can do Marcy. I've come to accept that my visions come true no matter what I do. They're in the future. They're bound to happen and there's nothing anyone can do to change the future. So why even bother?"

"But in this vision, you saw people dying. A lot of people."

Henry nodded.

"If you don't try to stop this, then all that will really happen and all those people will die."

"It will probably happen no matter what I try to do."

"Yes, maybe that's true, but you really don't know that for sure. Maybe this time it will be different, and then again, maybe not. But you really won't know for sure unless you try. If you don't try and it happens and all those people die, then you'll have to live with the fact that you knew about it before hand and you did nothing to try and prevent it. You saw it coming and did nothing. Do you think that you'll be able to live with that?"

Henry was silent but Marcy could see that her words were having an effect on him. She continued.

"Okay Henry, maybe if you go to the cops, they'll laugh at you. And I know that will be tough to take, but which will be worse, having to face laughter or knowing that all those people died and you didn't do anything to even try and stop it?"

Marcy said all of that with passion and conviction, and her words and reasoning struck a chord deep within Henry's conscious. For a long minute he sat there, saying nothing but thinking about all that she had said. Maybe she was right, and maybe he should do something to try and stop the bloodbath that was soon to happen, but at the same he remembered that he had made a vow to keep his visions a secret. When he made that vow, he was determined to keep it no matter what. At that time, he was convinced that his resolve was unshakable; but now after hearing Marcy's words, he felt an inner pang of conscience gnawing at that buttress of determination. It was almost as if he heard a faint little voice deep within him telling him that he had to warn people about a disaster in the making.

So, Henry sat there wallowing in a moral dilemma. He didn't know what he should do, but he knew that time was running out; that vision could become a reality any day now. If he was going to do something, it would have to be soon.

He thanked Marcy for her support, then paid his check and got up and walked out of the room. Marcy sat there looking after him and as she watched him walk out, she sympathized with him. She imagined what he must be going through—the indecision, the uncertainty, the inner turmoil. She had tried her best to help him, but now and there was nothing more she could say or do. It was all up to him and she wondered what he was going to do.

Henry walked out of Gallagher's and when he was outside, on the sidewalk, he looked up at the sky. It was just beginning to get dark and there was a chill in the air. He buttoned up his coat then started back to his apartment, still undecided as to what he should do.

CHAPTER 26

Henry went home that night and he mulled over all that Marcy had said. It was certainly true that if he went to the police and told them his story they might laugh at him. That would be tough to face, but at the same time there was the alternative: if he did nothing and all those people died, then in a way it would be his fault. He knew if that happened it would weigh upon his conscience till the day he died. That would probably be more painful and gnawing than all the laughter in the world.

The more he thought about it, the more he realized that Marcy was right. He had to do something to prevent the bloody battle that he saw in his frightful vision no matter what personal consequences he might have to face. The next day he resolved to go to the police and tell them what he saw. This is what happened when he did.

Henry found a police station in lower Manhattan. He walked through the door and went up to the policeman behind the front desk. Henry told the officer that he had information concerning a bank robbery that was going to take place in the near future and that he wanted to discuss it with someone in authority. The police officer picked up a phone and talked to someone while Henry stood by waiting. Henry was told to take the stairs to the second floor where he would meet with a detective who would listen to Henry's story.

Henry climbed the stairs. When he got to the second floor a man in plain clothes was waiting for him. He introduced himself as detective Mike Longo. Longo led Henry to his desk and offered him a chair. The two men took up chairs facing each other and Longo began.

"Now Mr. Gainsvort, as I understand it, you have some sort of information concerning a bank robbery."

"Yes sir. The robbery hasn't happened yet but I'm pretty sure it will happen soon."

Longo nodded. "Do you know when?"

"No sir, not the exact day, and I can't really be precise as to when it the robbers will make the attempt, but I'm reasonably sure that it will probably occur sometime in the next couple of weeks."

"I see. Do you know what bank will be robbed?"

"Yes sir. It's the Federal Reserve Bank in downtown Manhattan."

At the mention of the Federal Reserve Bank, Longo sat up a little straighter. "That's a tough bank to knock over, Mr. Gainsvort. The walls are thick, there are bars on the windows and they have a crackerjack security force. It's like a fortress. Any bank robbers would be stopped before they ever got through the front door."

"The robbers—actually they're not robbers, they're terrorists—won't try to get through the door. They'll be going through the roof."

At this point Longo looked at Henry with a measure of skepticism and curiosity. This was a bold—even preposterous—suggestion that he was hearing, but there was something in Henry's voice, some vague hint of authority, that almost sounded as if he knew what he was talking about. Longo was intrigued.

"Mr. Gainsvort, suppose you tell me just how this robbery will happen."

Henry leaned forward and narrated the events of his vision. He told about the hang-gliders, and the use of explosives to blow a hole through the roof. He talked about the penetration into the chambers below. Moreover, Henry described the battle that followed—and for Longo this was the strange part, because Henry started talking about events and giving vivid details that no one could possibly know about. After all, how could someone describe the precise specifics of a battle that hadn't happened yet?

Longo listened to all of this without comment or question. He just sat there and absorbed it all, but at the same time, he wasn't sure what to make of this bizarre and strange tale because it sounded more like fiction than fact. As Henry was talking, Longo looked at his face and into his eyes. He wanted to see if this guy sitting opposite him was just making up this strange story, or if he was serious, or what.

After looking carefully at Henry, studying his face, searching his clear hazel eyes, Longo concluded that Henry really believed what he was saying—this was no put-on—still Longo couldn't understand how anyone could possibly know about such an audacious robbery down to the smallest details. Naturally he had to ask.

"How do you know all this, Mr. Gainsvort?"

And there it was, the question that Henry dreaded. The question that he had hoped that maybe he could duck. He only wanted to come to the police and warn them of an impending robbery without having to say anything about how he got his information. He just wanted to tell his story and alert the police so that they would be on guard. After that, he could leave, walk away and forget the whole incident. He wanted to avoid talking about his visions because he knew that if he did, the police would think him a weirdo. Now, however, Longo asked the big question and there was no way around it.

So reluctantly, in a quiet and subdued manner, Henry told how he had seen the whole incident in a vision while sitting in the park, eating his lunch across from the big bank. Henry tried hard to make his explanation sound creditable. He even told of some of his former visions and described how they came true; but as he was saying all of that he noticed a subtle change come over Longo's face. He saw the detective's hard face relax a little. He saw a twinkle light up in the man's eyes and he saw a slight upturn in the corners of Longo's mouth. When he saw all of that, Henry knew that he had lost credibility; the detective didn't believe anything he had said. Henry saw, in fact, that Longo was on the verge of laughing at him. At that moment, Henry knew that he had failed again.

Longo turned his head aside and coughed into his hand. This gesture was ostensibly done to clear his throat, but Henry could see that the detective used it as a ploy to stifle a laugh that was in his throat. That aside was a maneuver to break eye contact lest he lose his serious composure. After a momentary pause, he looked back at Henry. Longo had regained his serious expression. The slight vestige of the smile was gone, but the twinkle of merriment was still in the detective's eyes.

"Well Mr. Gainsvort, I want to thank you for coming forward with your warning. It's because of citizens like yourself that we in the police department are able to do our jobs. I can assure you, Mr. Gainsvort, that we're going to keep on top of this. We may even want to have helicopters hovering over the bank for the next couple of weeks. Again, I want to thank you for coming in with your information."

Now Longo tried to say this with seriousness and gravity, but even so, Henry noted that there was an underlying and very subtle tone of mockery in the detective's voice. Henry's instinct told him that Longo had mentally classified him as a crackpot and dismissed his warning as the product of an overactive imagination.

The two men stood up and shook hands, then Longo escorted Henry back to the stairs. Henry walked down the stairs and out of the police station then took the nearest subway back home.

Sitting by himself in the subway, as the train sped through the black underground tunnels, Henry looked down at his hands and reflected on the interview at the police station. He thought about all that he had said during the interview and of the subsequent reaction that he received, and he felt like a fool. He had come forward to report a serious, dastardly crime that was soon to happen and what did he get for his troubles? Mockery. True, it was subtle, silent mockery; but Henry knew that in the eyes and mind of detective Longo, he was the village idiot.

Henry was sure that the moment he walked out of the station house, Longo had started laughing at him. Probably his story circulated around the squad room and others were laughing as well. Well at least they had the courtesy to wait until he was gone before they laughed at him. However, that was a small consolation.

Yet in spite of his feelings of foolishness, Henry felt relieved. Before this morning he had been troubled and worried about his last vision. He saw death and carnage but he didn't know what he could do to prevent it. Well, finally he'd stepped forward, told his story and tried to warn the authorities of the impending tragedy. Now it was up to them. Maybe they would act but more than likely, they would just ignore his warning and do nothing. Well so be it. He had done his best, and there was nothing more he could do. As far as Henry Gainsvort was concerned, the matter was closed.

That's what Henry thought on the subway going back to Sunset Park, but unbeknownst to him, the matter was far from being closed. Soon the aftermath of his warning would come around to hit him, and this is what happened when it did.

Now Henry was right when he imagined that the men in the police station were laughing at him, because as soon as Henry was out of earshot, Longo dropped back into his chair and burst out laughing. The description of the daring raid on the most solid and impregnable bank in lower Manhattan was the strangest, most bizarre tale that Longo had ever heard. It was preposterous in the extreme and the detective could not help but laugh at the notion that a band of thugs would attempt to knock that bank over—and from hang gliders no less.

Curious, another detective sitting nearby, asked what was so funny. Longo told him about the weirdo who had just visited and of the absurd tale of the airborne attack on the Federal Reserve fortress-bank

The other man laughed also, then asked, "What are you going to do about it?"

Longo laughed. "I'll file it in compartment C." He nodded toward the wastepaper basket.

"Yeah, but since it's a federal bank, don't you think that you ought to let the feds in on the joke?"

Longo thought about it briefly then said, "You're right! Perhaps I should put in a call to the Bureau. They're a serious lot, but who knows, they might appreciate this story. Maybe it will loosen them up and give them all a good laugh."

Longo called the Manhattan office of the Federal Bureau of Investigation and talked to agent Lance Powers. He told Powers about the visit he had from Mr. Henry Gainsvort and how Gainsvort had just described an audacious plan to knock over the Federal Reserve Bank in lower Manhattan.

When he had finished, both men laughed. Powers hung up the phone then told some of his colleagues about the upcoming robbery and they too joined in on the laughter. In fact, everyone who heard about the hang-glider robbery laughed. After a while the laughter died down, but still, at odd moments during the rest of week whenever anyone chanced to think about the strange Mr. Gainsvort and his wacky yarn of an attempted knock-over of the invincible Federal Reserve Bank in lower Manhattan by a bunch of crazed terrorists riding hang gliders, the laughs erupted again.

But on the following Wednesday morning when lower Manhattan was humming as usual and all the many white-collar workers were going about their usual occupations, a strange thing happened. Five terrorists sailed hang-gliders from the tall buildings in lower Manhattan and landed on top of the Federal Reserve Bank. They used explosives to blow a hole in the roof and they forced their way inside. A vicious battle ensued. At that point, everyone stopped laughing.

The attack happened just as Henry had said it would. Fortunately, the assault had been thwarted and the terrorists were dead, but so were a lot of other individuals. The people of New York City, and indeed in the rest of the United States, suddenly realized that they were vulnerable to vicious strikes and aggression of hoodlums throughout the world. It was an unnerving thought and no one felt safe and secure anymore.

The battle was over, but not the talk. The news media covered the story and it appeared in all the papers and on every television news program. With the news reports came commentary, analysis, criticism, and finger-pointing.

How, everyone asked, *could terrorists launch such a bold and daring plan like that within the borders of the United States? Where was Homeland Security? What were the authorities doing while this plan was being hatched? Why didn't the police and FBI discover the plan and stop the terrorists before they got so far? Why was there no warning of this audacious attack?*

The press asked questions. The people wanted answers. Members of Congress started talking about an investigation. Everyone wanted to know why the American counter intelligence network had failed to detect the plot and what the law enforcement agencies were doing to safeguard the country. The law-enforcement authorities were embarrassed and chagrined by the attack. They scrambled to try to come up with explanations as to why they had been caught unawares. It was certain that heads would roll. A tide of anxiety swept through the law enforcement agencies as everyone rushed and jostled to cover their butts.

Back in the Manhattan offices of the Federal Bureau of Investigation, supervisor Brian Confrey held a special meeting with four of his agents in the Bureau conference room. In the room, assembled around a long table, were agents Lance Powers, Rick Buel, Dennis Fellows and Samantha Fingerman. The atmosphere in the room was quiet but heavy, and a little ominous because everyone present knew why they had been summoned: Confrey was already experiencing the heat from his superiors and from the press. Now he was holding the meeting to determine why his department had failed to anticipate the terrorist plot. The meeting was going to be a fault-finding expedition and each person was anxious to duck the pointing finger of blame.

Confrey got right to the point. "Well guys, I'm starting to get flak on this one. The boys in Washington want to know what we were doing here and why we didn't catch this thing before it happened. The press wants to know why our intelligence operation is so piss-poor. People are starting to accuse us of sleeping on the job."

"That's not fair," said Fellows, "we were doing our jobs."

"Then what went wrong? Why didn't we pick up on this sooner? How could something like this happen without us even getting a hint beforehand?"

There was a moment of silence; each person shifted uncomfortably in his seat and exchanged glances at his comrades. Silently each was trying to think up some sort of excuse, some sort of face-saving explanation. Fingerman finally spoke up. "It looks like the terrorists planned that whole operation out of town—maybe even out of the country. They probably waited to bring the operation to New York at the very last minute, so there wasn't time for word to spread as to what they were planning to do."

The others at the table nodded in agreement. This was as good an explanation as any, and just off the cuff it seemed plausible enough, and it provided a way to shift the blame, the focus, and the responsibility, to some other law enforcement agency outside of New York.

"Sure Brian," said Fellows, "we can't monitor terrorists beyond our area. We don't have the manpower and besides, that's not our job. If this group planned the operation in …well, say…Florida, then how could we be expected to know about it? These terrorists are getting smarter and they know not to stay in one place too long. I'll bet they waited until the very last minute before coming to New York just to keep us in the dark."

Thus, with each person adding bits and pieces of supposition to this last-minute-attack hypothesis, the group reached a consensus as to how to cover their butts by shifting the blame from their organization to some other, as yet unnamed, law enforcement agency outside the New York area. Thus, it seemed like they had found a suitable scapegoat and everyone relaxed a little.

It seemed like the group had come up with the ideal explanation, but then Rick Buel spoke up. "The only problem is that…well…in a way we did know about it. I mean there was that phone call from the NYPD. You know the one from Detective Longo about that strange guy who came in out of the blue and predicted the whole thing."

When Buel said that, Lance Powers shot him a dirty look. It was he, Powers, who took the call from NYPD telling them about the weirdo who foretold the attack on the Federal Reserve Bank; and it was he, Lance Powers, who had laughed off the whole thing as the zany talk of a crackpot psychic, possibly a publicity hound yearning for his place in the sun.

When the attack happened exactly as predicted, Powers thought back to that phone call and he remembered his casual response, but he hoped that no one else would. He feared that if word got out that it was he who dismissed the threat in such a careless manner, then he would be held responsible for not initiating a proper response. That would make him look incompetent and negligent and that would put an indelible blemish on his performance record.

Now Powers had been with the FBI for over ten years. And during that time, he had come to believe that he was the best agent in the New York office and probably in the entire bureau. He felt that he had an exemplary record with the bureau and he was sure that sooner or later everyone else would know it. What's more, Lance Powers was a handsome man with movie-star good looks. Powers was in fact, the supreme egotist believing that he had the right combination of brains, looks, and ability, and he was sure that he would someday be the shining star of the Bureau and in time he would eventually go right to the top in the organization.

But now that the attack had happened exactly as predicted, Powers realized that he was in an awkward position. A report of his cavalier response to the early warning could easily be misconstrued as dereliction in his duty and might torpedo his career. Powers had hoped that maybe he could keep this little tidbit of information hidden and thus sidestep the issue, but then Rick Buel had to open his big mouth and blab the whole story in the meeting. At that point, Powers wanted to reach across the table and strangle him.

"Yeah, we (Powers used the word, *we* here to make the call look like a group effort) did get a call from the NYPD saying some sort of crackpot came in with a crazy tale of an attack on the bank, but at the time it seemed too off the wall to be taken seriously. Even the NYPD thought the guy was a looney. So, we let it go."

"Except that it happened just as the guy said it would," said Buel

Damn it! Thought Powers to himself, *why couldn't Buel just keep his mouth shut?*

"So, we had a warning and just sat on our hands," said Confrey. "If the public ever finds out that we knew about this robbery before it happened and that we did nothing there'll be hell to pay."

"How could they find out about it? The only ones who know about it are us and the NYPD. They won't talk and neither will we, so we're safe."

Everyone was silent for a minute then Rick Buel spoke up again. "There's also this Gainsvort guy. He's the one who came in with the warning. He's still out there."

"Do you think he'll talk?" asked Confrey.

"I don't know, none of us has ever met him. We don't know what kind of character he is. There's always the chance that he might start telling people how he saw it all coming and tried to warn the police."

"So, what if he does," said Powers. "He's a crackpot. No one will believe him."

"Maybe, maybe not," said Confrey. "But can we really take that chance? The press is having a field day with this one and they're thirsty for blood. If word gets back to them about some guy who saw the whole thing and tried to warn us, then it's sure to wind up on the evening news. And we don't want that to happen."

"What can we do about it? We can't put a lid on the media."

"No, we can't do that; but maybe we can keep this Gainsvort guy under wraps until this whole thing blows over. Yes, we could do that. Suppose we invite Mr. Gainsvort to come visit us."

"Suppose he refuses?"

"We'll give him an invitation that he can't refuse. Lance suppose you and Rick drive over to Gainsvort's place and deliver that invitation personally."

Lance nodded, then he and Rick Buel got up and left the meeting. They picked up their coats then went down to the garage and got into a car. In a few minutes they were driving across the Brooklyn Bridge on the way to Sunset Park to pay Henry Gainsvort a visit.

CHAPTER 27

After the attack, Henry followed the news from the first flashes of the dastardly attack on the Federal Reserve Bank down to the follow-up reports about the investigations that were later undertaken to determine if the law enforcement officials had been doing their jobs or not. Henry read the various articles in the newspaper and watched the evening news. He assumed that his involvement in the whole tragic affair was over and forgotten, but he was wrong. Although the media and most of the law enforcement officials were unaware that Henry even existed, there were a few people who were very interested in one Henry Gainsvort and they were about to bring him back into the picture. This is the way it happened.

Two days after the attack, on a particularly cold morning, Henry was sitting alone in his apartment. He wasn't doing much of anything, just sitting there watching a humongous brown cockroach scurry across the far wall. As he sat there just looking at that solitary roach, the thought occurred to him that he had never really looked at any of those insects before—that is given them a hard, studied look. In the past, whenever one of those big, brown creatures appeared, his first reaction was to run over and try to swat the life out of it or else douse it with some noxious spray. But now that he thought about it, he asked himself, "Why this urge to kill? Why the need to destroy these creatures anyway? What had any roach ever done to him?"

Henry mused over this as he continued to sit there and watch the big insect. As he watched the large brown bug, he marveled at the way it moved. It didn't just run across the wall, but it ran for about a foot, then it stopped and stood immobile. It continued to hold its position for the longest time, its only movement being the sweep of its two long antennae. Those two long filaments swept around in broad arcs, like radar feelers, taking in the sensations and vibrations of the immediate vicinity. Then apparently satisfied that it had sampled everything the spot had to offer, the roach hurried along to another place and repeated the stop-and-sample procedure.

As Henry watched the bug, he wondered to himself what it must be like to be a roach. *What kind of existence do roaches have? Do they fall in love? When they mate do they have orgasms? Do female roaches ever nag the male roaches for being lazy? Are roaches ever lazy? Are all roaches the same, or are there some that are different? If one is different, then how do the others respond? Do they ostracize that one, or do they let it live with them and accept even with its faults and peculiarities as being one of their own?*

As Henry contemplated roach behavior. He concluded that roaches probably live in relative harmony with one another without dissent, injustice or discrimination. Theirs must be a totally egalitarian society. So maybe in the final analysis, cockroaches are the superior beings because they have lived on this earth without prejudice or bigotry since the time of the dinosaurs.

These were the thoughts that were going through Henry's mind when a knock on his door interrupted his solitude. Henry got up and opened the door, leaving the chain lock still engaged. Henry peered through the narrow opening and saw two men in overcoats standing in the hall before his door. One of the men spoke.

"Mr. Henry Gainsvort?"

"Yes."

The man held up his identification. "We're from the FBI and we'd like to ask you a couple of questions."

Henry immediately disengaged the chain lock and opened the door allowing Lance Powers and Rick Buel to step inside.

Once inside, Powers turned and faced Henry. "We've been given to understand, Mr. Gainsvort, that you went into a police station last week and told a police officer about the recent attack on the Federal Reserve Bank. This was before the incident occurred, but you were able to describe the whole incident in detail. You said that you had some sort of vision of the whole thing."

"Yes, that's right."

"We'd like to ask you some questions about that vision."

"All right," said Henry. "Do you want to sit down?"

"Not here. We think it might be better if you came to our office so we could sit down and talk over the whole thing in detail."

"Okay, I'll get my coat."

Henry went to his front bedroom and pulled out his coat from the closet. As he was putting his coat on, the thought occurred to Henry that maybe this interview might take some time. He called out to the agents, "Will I be coming back to my apartment this afternoon?"

Lance Powers called back, "This might take longer than that Mr. Gainsvort."

"Maybe later tonight then?"

"Maybe longer than that."

Suddenly Henry had the feeling that this was not going to be a quickie, friendly interview and that whatever was going to happen might be very serious indeed. Henry didn't know where they were going, but he suspected that he was going to be gone for a long time.

"Well, should I pack a bag with some of my things?"

"Don't worry about that Mr. Gainsvort. We'll provide you with everything you need."

As Henry walked from the bedroom back to where Powers and Buel were waiting for him, he passed by his bookcase and he was seized with the sudden impulse to stop and pick out a book. The volume he chose was *Ulysses* by James Joyce. Henry bought this book many, many years ago when he was in college. At that time, he had intended to acquaint himself with the great works of literature and *Ulysses* was going to be his starting point; but somehow, he never got around to reading it. It just seemed too long and too ponderous and he couldn't get up either the ambition or the time to tackle it, so it sat forever in his bookcase gathering dust.

On that particular morning there was something about his situation, some hint that he detected in the agents' tone, that suggested he was going to be away for a long while and that he would finally have the time for a long read. So, yielding to his impulse, he grabbed the book and tucked it under his arm.

The three men walked out of the apartment and into the hall. Henry turned to close and lock his door but before pulling it shut, he paused and looked back into the room. Some inner sense told him that maybe he would not be returning to his place for a long, long time—possibly not ever again—so he paused to take one last look. As he stood there looking back, he reminded himself that for the past five-and-a-half years this hovel had been his home, and he realized that in spite of the roaches and mice, that in spite of the gloom and dingy light, in spite of the hot summers and cold winters, he had grown attached to the place and now that he was going, he would actually miss it.

As he stood there in the doorway, just before he pulled the door shut, Henry looked across at the far wall. That big brown cockroach was still there clinging to the wall, and as Henry lingered to look at it one last time, he realized that the apartment would now belong to that ugly bug and all its brethren. Through all the times that Henry had waged his endless battle with the insects and the mice, it never occurred to him that he would lose that campaign; but now as he stood there in the doorway, it struck him that he was leaving his apartment and the field of battle to the vermin of Brooklyn.

Somewhere in the Bible it says that meek shall inherit the earth. Well, Henry didn't know about the earth, but at that moment, he knew that the meek were about to inherit his apartment. In spite of all his assaults and traps and sprays, the bugs and mice had outlasted him and now the place was theirs. With that final thought, he pulled the door shut and locked it. The three men went downstairs and outside to the sidewalk.

They passed by the window of the veterinarian's office. Inside the office, the receptionist, Janice Rule, was sitting behind the desk and she saw Henry walk by with two strangers. She watched as they walked across the street and got into a gray sedan parked at the curb. When the men got into the car and shut the doors, Janice noticed that the black lettering on the side of the door said, *Federal Bureau of Investigation.* And as the car pulled away, Janice wondered what kind of trouble Henry had gotten himself into.

The three men arrived at the Manhattan Bureau office about an hour later. Powers and Buel escorted Henry to the conference room where three others, two men and a woman, were sitting at the end of the table. Henry was offered a chair and Powers and Buel took up places with the other three. Henry sat down and faced the five people around the table.

Brian Confrey introduced himself and his colleagues then he thanked Henry for taking the time out of his busy schedule to come down for the interview. Henry thought to himself that there was a curious irony in Confrey's words; after all, his busy schedule consisted of nothing more than watching cockroaches walk across the walls in his apartment. Confrey also made it sound like Henry had come down to the Bureau office of his own volition, but actually, Henry felt that he had little choice in the matter.

He didn't say anything, however; but just nodded politely and waited for whatever was going to happen to begin. He figured that the sooner he got through whatever was coming, the better; so, he just sat there without a word and waited. He waited for what was coming next.

Confrey began the interview by saying that they knew of Henry's attempt to warn the NYPD of the upcoming bank robbery. According to the NYPD, as Confrey understood it, Henry claimed at the time that he had a vision of the entire attack before it happened. Confrey asked Henry if that was true and Henry nodded. Confrey then asked Henry to describe his vision and tell them exactly what he saw. Henry did so.

As Henry told of his vision, the others looked at him with unblinking attention. All regarded Henry with a mixture of curiosity, interest, and skepticism. They said nothing, but continued to stare with blank expressions on their faces as they listened to him talk about his amazing widow into the future. They listened with a kind of clinical detachment, showing no emotion or reaction, but holding their judgments and opinions until they had heard all he had to say.

Lance Powers, however, was different from the other agents. From all outward appearances he had the same dispassionate complexion as the others, but under his cool, poised shell, his emotions were churning. His composed, stoic exterior masked a growing, inner feeling of contempt for Henry Gainsvort. Almost from the moment that they met, Lance Powers formed an immediate dislike of Henry Gainsvort because he viewed Henry as an average, ordinary, mundane creature; and Lance Powers disliked people who were average and ordinary. He equated average and ordinary with being weak and gutless.

Powers had always admired people who were strong and forceful. He even had respect for the tough, aggressive, animal-criminals because he knew that when he captured and put them away, then he had accomplished something—he was the superior being. But he had no admiration or even respect for Henry Gainsvort, because he viewed Henry as being little more than a wart on the ass of the human race, a spineless toad in society.

Yet, at the same time, there was a curious paradox to Power's emotional state. Power's feelings of contempt were tinged with another base emotion. As he sat there listening to Henry talk of his vision, Powers was also secretly envious of Henry Gainsvort. He was envious because Henry possessed an ability that he, Lance Powers, did not have. Henry Gainsvort could see into the future—look into destiny—and Lance, all his aptitude and ability notwithstanding, could not do that. Powers envied that ability to see into tomorrow and he wished that he could do that. If he had that power then there was no telling how far he could go or how great he could be.

Instead, that gift was wasted on a worthless toad like Henry Gainsvort and Powers despised Henry for that. He saw Henry as a man who had a facility to do what no one else could, and yet he was doing nothing with it. As far as Lance Powers could see, Gainsvort was wasting his gifts and Powers hated people who lacked initiative and drive. He liked men of action, but he saw that Henry Gainsvort was anything but that. Still Powers continued to sit there, listening but saying nothing, because he was biding his time until the moment came when he could act decisively and squeeze the life out of Henry Gainsvort.

Henry continued to talk and tell the others how and when he first saw the attack on the Federal Reserve Bank. When he finished, the agents asked him questions. They asked him about his visions: "How often did he get them? How long had he been having them? What were some of the other things that he had seen?"

Then they asked him what else he had seen. They wanted to know if he could tell them anything about the terrorists. "Had he seen where the terrorists had planned their operation and did he have any idea who organized the whole thing?"

Moreover, they wanted to know if he had any visions since that one of the attack on the Federal Reserve Bank.

After over two hours of heavy cross examination, it seemed that the agents had explored every nook and cranny of Henry's conscious mind and learned all they could about his visions. For a few moments there was silence. Henry waited patiently for more questions, but there were none and Henry figured that at last it was all over and that maybe he could go home again.

Brian Confrey stood up and with a smile said, "I want to thank you for your input Mr. Gainsvort. This has been most enlightening."

"Can I leave now?" asked Henry.

Confrey shifted uncomfortably. "No, not just yet Mr. Gainsvort. We'd like you to stay with us for a little while. We want to look into your report and check out a few things."

"What things?"

"Just *things* and while we're doing our investigation we want to keep you close by."

"Am I under arrest?"

Confrey let out a low, artificial laugh. It was an obvious device to lighten the atmosphere and relax the situation, but it did nothing to alleviate Henry's concern.

"No, Mr. Gainsvort. You're not under arrest, but you're a witness, a witness to a serious and devastating attack on the United States. So, we're going to keep you here as part of our witness protection plan. It's purely a precautionary plan to insure your safety."

"How long will I have to stay here?"

"Well, that's hard to say right now because I'm not sure how long it will take for us to investigate; but it shouldn't be too long. Don't worry Mr. Gainsvort, we'll take good care of you. In the meantime, we'll make sure that you'll be perfectly safe when you do return to your home; and while you're here we'll try to see to your every need."

Henry wanted to protest. He wanted to say that he was a virtual non-entity and nobody—least of all the terrorists—knew anything about him. If they didn't even know that he existed then they couldn't possibly perceive of him as a threat. As long as he remained anonymous, then he was in no danger and he hardly needed protection.

That seemed obvious to him, but as he looked at the faces of the surrounding agents, he realized that they were all of the same mind-set. They were determined to keep him in custody and he knew that any protest on his part would be futile. Henry also suspected that they had another reason for wanting him to stay—although he couldn't imagine what it could be. But whatever their reasons, Henry felt as though he had no choice in the matter, because after all, he was only one man against the forces of the government, so he reluctantly submitted.

Rick Buel escorted Henry from the conference room to the elevator. They descended to a floor below ground level and they walked down a deserted hall to a small room that seemed far away from any human activity. Buel opened the door, turned on the light and motioned for Henry to enter. Henry found himself in the middle of a quiet, austere, nondescript four-by-six room. The few pieces of furniture were Spartan in the extreme, there was a simple cot, a small side table, a desk with a lamp, and a single chair, but no phone, television or even windows. Henry could see that he would have absolutely no contact with the outside world.

"Well Mr. Gainsvort, this is where you'll be staying for the next few days. I know this room isn't very big, but you should find it to be warm and clean. That door there is the bathroom."

"Is there a shower in there?"

"No, that's down the hall."

"Oh! How about meals? Will I have to eat in here?"

"No, when meal time comes around the guard will knock on your door to let you know that it's time to eat, then he'll escort you to the cafeteria upstairs."

"Guard?!"

"Well, he's not really a guard. Think of him more as your personal attendant. He'll be right outside just in case you need anything."

There was a moment of awkward silence while Henry tried to grasp the implications of all that was suddenly happening to him. Buel assumed that he had explained everything and he turned to the door. He just grasped door the knob when Henry called out, "Agent Buel."

Buel turned but still held onto the knob.

"Why do I have to stay here? I mean what's the real reason? Surely none of you can seriously believe that I am in any danger. After all, the terrorists who attacked the bank are all dead. And any others who might have planned the operation can't possibly know anything about me. So, where's the threat?"

Buel shifted uneasily from one foot to the other and he took a minute to frame his thoughts before answering. It was obvious to Henry that Buel had wanted to avoid any further conversation, and now that Henry was asking questions, he could see that Buel was plainly uneasy about having to answer them. To Henry it seemed as if Buel felt that he was about to tread out onto thin ice and was hesitant because he was afraid that he might say the wrong thing—whatever that might be.

"Well Mr. Gainsvort, there are other issues involved here."

"Such as?"

"Well, we want to check out your story and see if maybe there might be a greater involvement on your part."

Buel was being deliberately vague and Henry suspected that he was trying to hide something, but he had no idea what it could be.

"But I told you that I wasn't involved in any way. Surely if I was, then I wouldn't have tried to warn the police."

"Of course, what you say is true, but we're just going to run a few background checks to verify your story."

"Suppose I don't want to stay? After all, if I'm not under arrest and I'm not charged with anything then you can't keep me here if I don't want to stay."

Henry felt as if he had just played a trump card and won the hand, but then Buel pulled an ace from his sleeve.

"Well actually, we can keep you here Mr. Gainsvort. You see this was a deliberate act of terrorism here, and the Patriot Act says that we can detain anyone who might be involved in any sort of terrorism."

With that Henry knew that he was helpless. What could he do? He was just one puny being up against forces of immense power. He realized that he was helpless and there was nothing he could say or do to change the situation. Henry simply nodded, and Buel assuming that the matter was closed, turned and walked out, shutting the door behind him. That left Henry standing alone in the middle of the four-by-six room.

CHAPTER

Henry sat down on the edge of the cot and looked around him. There was really nothing to see; the walls were plain beige without pictures or even a calendar. There were no windows to look through to the world outside. The floor was of dull gray tiles without a rug. An olive drab, standard army issue blanket covered the cot. Curiously, there was an electric alarm clock on the small side table, and Henry wondered why it was there. It was like putting a time-keeping device in an environment where time had ceased to exist.

He looked to the other side of the room. There was an open door and Henry could see a small adjoining room, not much bigger than a closet; it had a toilet and a lavatory, basically it was just a half bath. And that was it.

As Henry looked about him he came to understand that this small space was now to be his entire world. The larger world that he had known all his life had, for all intents and purposes, ceased to exist. All he really knew at that point was that he was in a small room in an office building somewhere in New York City. Since he couldn't see or hear anything beyond that cell, he felt as if he could have been anyplace in the entire universe and he wouldn't know the difference because he had no way to see beyond those four opaque walls.

For a long time, he continued to sit on the edge of the cot remaining motionless except for his eyes. He let his eyes roam around the walls, the floor and the ceiling, taking in everything. As Henry looked about, scanning the various surfaces, he thought to himself that this room was really a metaphor for what his life had become: dull, uninspired, unimaginative, without color and without interest and without extension. It was as if the sum total of his entire existence amounted to nothing more than a mundane lifeless box.

Moreover, it seemed that somehow in the course of his existence he had inadvertently become an obstruction to society and now he had been pushed into an obscure pigeon hole in some featureless, monolithic building just to be put out of the way. So now here he was filed away like some scrap of paper, in some hidden cubbyhole, not to be retrieved unless needed.

Henry remembered that just before he left his apartment in Brooklyn, agent Powers said that the FBI would provide everything he needed while he was with them. Indeed, they had provided him with a place to sleep and a shower, and later he would get food and drink, but that apparently was all that would be provided. The one thing he would not get was companionship. As long as he was here he would have no one to look at, no one to talk to, and no one to listen to.

At that moment, sitting there all by himself, Henry wished that a cockroach or a little gray mouse would come scurrying by. Then at least he would be sharing his existence with another living creature, with some other life form to show that he wasn't alone in the world. But no, he was here by himself within the sterile, lifeless compound of these four walls where even the outside vermin could not—or would not—penetrate. As he thought about it, Henry realized the irony of his situation: ever since he moved into his crummy apartment in Sunset Park, he had waged a war to eradicate the roaches and mice around him, and now that they were finally out of his life, he missed them and longed for their reappearance.

On a whim, Henry got up and tried the door. It wasn't locked, but when he opened the door and looked out into the hall, he saw a man in uniform sitting on a chair reading a newspaper. This was to be his personal attendant, but the uniform made the man seem more like a guard. The man must have positioned himself shortly after Buel left.

Henry thought to himself that maybe that might not be so bad after all. At least with a guard stationed outside in the hall, there would be a living presence nearby and he wouldn't be totally alone. Henry decided that maybe he should try and make friends with the guard. He walked out of his room and approached the seated officer.

When he heard Henry approaching, the guard put down his paper and looked up. Henry tried to manage a cheery wave, a jovial smile, and a jolly *hello*. The stone-faced guard only offered a nod in reply. Henry then tried to start up a conversation, talking about the weather and politics and sports, but the guard only responded with vague head gestures and obscure grunts or monosyllabic words. It seemed that any attempt at conversation was futile. After a few minutes of trying to elicit some sort of intelligent response from the guard Henry walked away, unsure if the man even knew how to talk.

Just before going back into his room, Henry turned and asked the guard if maybe he could look at the newspaper when he was finished reading it. The guard said he wasn't allowed to give it up. Well, at least that was a human sentence, but it was small comfort to Henry who wanted more. Without sustained conversation and without being able to see the news, Henry felt as if his last links to civilization and humanity had just been severed.

Henry retreated back into his cell and sat down on his cot. There he was with no way out, and he was entirely at the mercy and whim of forces beyond his control. And as he sat there, it occurred to Henry that he was now just like one of those little gray mice that got stuck in the glue traps he had placed around his apartment. Here he was, trapped, stuck in the glue of bureaucratic rules and regulations. He was still alive and still breathing, but unable to move and totally impotent to change his circumstances. All that had to happen to him now was for the giant, cast-iron skillet to come crashing down and put an end to his existence. He didn't know it at that time, but that was soon to happen.

Henry spent the next days confined to his four by six world unaware of when the sun rose or set and completely isolated from the outside world. He tried to read *Ulysses,* but couldn't seem to get interested in it. He plowed through the paragraphs, reading and rereading the sentences, turning the pages, reading more words, not liking or disliking the narrative and never appreciating the imaginative brilliance of Joyce's prose. He continued to read anyhow, because it gave him something to do. The content of the book didn't matter because, at this point, nothing really mattered. The book simply provided a mechanism to occupy his mind and his attention. In that small room, it was the only thing he had to do.

There were times when he got a break and could actually leave his room. In the mornings a guard came and escorted him down the hall to the shower room. For meals a guard came and escorted him to the cafeteria. There he went through the line to get a tray of food, but he had to eat his meals by himself in a table off in a corner. There were usually a few other people in the cafeteria but he was never allowed to mingle with them or even speak to them. Henry didn't know why.

Why couldn't he just stop and chat with one of them for a few minutes? Where was the harm in that? What were they afraid of? He thought to himself that he would never know the answer to those questions.

By the end of the third day, Henry had lost the desire to chat with anyone. This happened when he was lying on his cot the previous evening, looking up at the ceiling. At that time, it occurred to him that even if he could stop and chat with someone he would have nothing to say. After all, he hadn't done anything of interest during the time that he came to this place. Moreover, it seemed to him that he hadn't done much of anything in his entire life; so, there was really nothing worth talking about even if he had the opportunity.

Besides, Henry had come to believe that his brain was starting to atrophy to the point where it no longer held thoughts or concepts that needed expression. Maybe that was it, or maybe he had just come to the point in his life when words didn't mean anything anymore. Maybe he had already said everything that there was for him to say, and now he had used up all his words and was incapable of further expression.

As he thought about that, it occurred to him that perhaps that was the plan behind this forced isolation. Maybe that's why they brought him here and were keeping him in solitary confinement. Maybe they were trying to make his brain shut down so it would cease to function. Maybe they didn't want him to talk because they were afraid of his visions and were now working to make sure he never had another one. Or if he did, then at least, he wouldn't have the ability to talk about them.

Yes, as Henry thought about that, it seemed like a likely explanation for his situation. As he lay there thinking about all those times in the past, when he told of his visions, he remembered the reactions of the people, he came to understand that deep down people aren't really prepared to look into the future and see what destiny holds.

They don't want to know what tomorrow holds, because they are afraid of what it might bring. Perhaps because they are afraid of the dark side of destiny and they fear the events that may lurk there.

Perhaps they fear him, average Henry Gainsvort, because they believe that whatever he sees must happen and cannot be changed. They would rather not know, then be confronted with a possible tragedy.

It's like booking passage on the *Titanic* then learning as the ship sails out of port that it will sink in the middle of the cold Atlantic, and there's not a thing you can do to prevent it. For you it would be a voyage of apprehension and fear, each minute filled with anxiety right up till the final hour. Better not to have that knowledge and enjoy the voyage while it lasts than live every moment dreading the inevitable.

In that single evening, lying on his cot, thinking about all sorts of possibilities, Henry came to believe that even the federal government with all its power and authority, was really afraid of him. True, he was only one little man, but he was a man who could see into the future and maybe that's what they were afraid of. And now they were taking steps to make sure he never talked to anyone and never again told about the events in the future. Well that's what Henry concluded in the privacy and loneliness of his room. He came to believe that because he could not see other reason for his confinement.

Those were the ramblings of Henry's mind on that one evening and on successive moments during the following days. Mental gymnastics had become his only activity because his life had settled into the most boring of routines with nothing to differentiate one hour from the next. On the fifth day of his captivity, something happened to give Henry a break, a little change in the endless monotony of his routine—and even a little hope. This is what happened.

Henry was lying on his cot when there was a knock on his door. He bid the person enter and the guard appeared. He told Henry to follow him but neglected to give the reason for this strange interruption. Henry saw it as a break in the boredom, so he got up and followed the guard down the hall to the elevator. He had no idea where they were going or why, but it was a chance to get out and move around.

They ascended to another floor. The guard led Henry down another blank hall and into vacant room that had nothing but a simple table and four chairs. Henry was instructed to sit down and wait, so he took up a seat and waited. For a few minutes there was nothing but then the door opened again, and Henry was surprised to see Marcy enter.

"Marcy!"

"Hello, Henry."

They took up seats and sat across the table from each other.

"Marcy, how did you find me? How did you know I was here?"

"It wasn't easy. At first, I didn't even know you were missing. But when you didn't come in to the restaurant for a while, I began to wonder about you and I asked around. No one seemed to know what had happened to you. So, I went to your apartment and knocked on your door but got no answer. The first time I did that I thought you were out. By the third day I began to get worried. After all, you never go anywhere so there was no reason why you should be away for so long."

Henry nodded, indicating that he was following her reasoning.

"Well, then I thought that maybe you were sick and couldn't get to the door. So I went into your apartment to look around, but I found it empty."

"How did you get into my place?"

"Augie once told me that you hid a spare key in a gap in the molding on the landing. I wasn't sure where it was, but I looked around until I found the crack and, sure enough, there was the key."

Henry nodded and at the same time marveled to himself how it seemed that—at one time or other—Augie seemed to have told everyone everything about everyone else in the neighborhood. "How did you find out that I was here?" he asked.

"Oh, that wasn't easy either. I started asking around the neighborhood to see if anyone had seen or heard anything about you, but no one seemed to know anything. Finally, I went in the veterinarian's office. You know in the place below your apartment?"

Henry nodded but didn't say anything.

"Well, the receptionist—Janice, I think her name was—told me that she saw you going out with these two men. They had a car waiting at the curb in front of the building. They put you in the back seat, got into the front and drove away. She saw that it was a gray vehicle with the words *Federal Bureau of Investigation* on the door."

"So, what did you do then?"

"Well, I called the Bureau but no one would help me. They said that they couldn't give out information about any investigation or about any of the detainees. Well, I didn't know what to do then. I was telling Freddie, the bartender at Gallagher's, about my problem when some guy sitting at the bar suggested I go to the ACLU."

"ACLU? What's that?"

"That's the American Civil Liberties Union. Anyway, I looked them up in the phone book and found their office. I went and talked to a lawyer there, a Mr. Berkowitz. He was very interested. He said that this could be that this was a violation of your civil rights and he said he'd look into it. Anyway, the next day he called me back to say that they located you here and he arranged for me to come visit you."

"That was good of you to care about me Marcy, and to go to the trouble of finding me. Thank you for coming."

"Henry! Henry, why are you here? What are they holding you for? What have you done?"

Henry shrugged. "I don't know. All I know is that these two guys came to my apartment and took me here. They brought me to a room and asked me a lot of questions about the attack on the Federal Reserve Bank and how it was that I knew all about it."

"Did you tell them about how you see things?"

Henry nodded. "Yeah, and they listened, but I'm not sure if they believed me or not. They're supposedly checking it out. In the meantime, they're gonna hold me here. They say it's for my protection, but they also hinted that they want to make sure that I'm not a threat to the nation. Other than that, they haven't told me much."

"Well, they can't just hold you for no reason. They have to charge you with something, some crime. That's the law."

"Maybe, but then again maybe not. They say that with the Patriot Act they can hold me if there is a possibility that I'm connected to a terrorist plot against the country."

"That's ridiculous! You weren't involved in that plot. In fact, you tried to warn them."

"Yeah, but now they're trying to figure out how I could know about the plot to bomb the Federal Reserve Bank before it happened. How I could know all about it in such detail unless I was somehow connected to the terrorists."

"That doesn't make sense. If you were a terrorist then why would you try to warn them in the first place?"

Henry shrugged. "I don't think that they gave that much thought. Anyway, they say that they want to do some more investigating so they get the whole picture. In the meantime, they're going to keep me here for my protection and until they're sure that I'm not a threat to national security."

"I can't believe how stupid they are. But don't you worry; Mr. Berkowitz at the ACLU is sure that we have a case against them. He says that we can get you out. It's just that it's gonna take some time."

"How much time?"

"He doesn't know yet, but he's working on it."

At that moment the guard poked his head in the door to say the visiting time was up. Marcy got up and started to leave then she turned back.

"Don't worry Henry, we'll get this sorted out. I'll try to visit you whenever I can."

"Thank you, Marcy. I appreciate all that you're trying to do."

When Henry said that he tried to force some sort of smile just to make it look like he believed that she really could do something to get him out of the place he was in, but deep down he had his doubts. He feared that he was a victim of the bureaucratic system and there was nobody who could do anything to save him. At that point, Henry had come to accept his fate as inevitable and he truly believed that he was never going to return to the real world again.

CHAPTER 29

For the next week, existence was pretty much the same for Henry. He continued to live within the confines of that strange establishment and he continued to go from day to day without contact or communication with the outside world. The only bright spot in his existence was Marcy. She came to visit him for a half-hour almost every day.

Those brief visits with Marcy were all Henry had to remind him that there was still a living world beyond the solid confines of the gray parameters of the building that he was living in. As long as Marcy continued to come and visit, Henry was able to sustain a faint belief that the civilized world that he remembered was still there. And Marcy's visits ignited a small spark of hope that someday he would return to that world.

For most of the time, however, Henry was desperately alone and far removed from any vestige of humanity. But all that was soon to change, and for Henry the change would be dramatic in the extreme. It happened like this.

Henry looked forward to Marcy's morning visits with anticipation; she said that she couldn't come every day so he never knew when she would show up, but when she did come, it was a source of joy for him. Her visits gave him hope. Even if the rest of the world had erased him from memory, he knew that at least she hadn't forgotten about him. One day she showed up and she was in a particularly happy mood.

Before she sat down, she blurted out, "Henry, I've got good news. I think we've found a way to get you out of here."

He looked back at her, unsure if he really heard her correctly.

"Really? How? Tell me about it."

"Well, Mr. Berkowitz called to say that he was going to file papers in court. He said that the ACLU was going before a judge to demand your release. He said that he was sure the FBI didn't have a case against you and the ACLU could get you out."

Henry was suddenly excited. It was as if the outside world had instantly come back into existence and now there might even be an outside chance for him to return to it.

"Oh Marcy, that is great news. If only it could happen."

"Henry, it will happen. I know it will because Mr. Berkowitz is a good lawyer and he said he can make it happen."

Henry was elated by this unexpected news and his mood changed from dour resignation to effervescence. He sat down and he commenced to chat with Marcy for the rest of their allotted time. Their conversation shifted from talking about his circumstances and the FBI and the ACLU to talking about what Marcy was doing, and what was happening at Gallagher's and around Sunset Park. With the prospect of freedom and a return to the real world, Henry wanted to know everything about what was going on outside. He wanted to know if the outside world was still the same as he remembered it. It was as if he could smell and taste that world and he wanted to devour as much of it as he could.

At the end of the visiting session, the guard came by to say that Marcy had to leave. They got up and walked to the door. He stood at the door and watched her walk down the long corridor. Halfway down, she turned back and said, "Don't worry Henry, Mr. Berkowitz at the ACLU says that he'll have you out of here in no time."

Now that was a simple enough statement, but at that time, in the open corridor, it was the wrong thing to say, because sitting in a nearby room, with the door barely cracked open, was Lance Powers.

Powers had been aware of Marcy's visits to Henry and from the first, he suspected that she might be trouble. So, whenever she came to see Henry, Powers managed to take up a position in an empty room adjacent to the one that Henry and Marcy were in. Most of the time he couldn't hear anything through the walls, but he persisted, hoping that at some point he might just catch a word or a phrase here or there that would give him some idea what she was up to. On that one day, he got lucky; she had turned in the corridor and revealed the part about the ACLU and he heard it.

Powers heard Marcy's words and he didn't like the sound of them. He had always regarded the ACLU as a nuisance at best and downright subversive at worst. To Powers the ACLU was a bunch of leftists who were more concerned with personal freedom and individual rights than about the security of the United States of America. Sure, he reasoned, personal freedom is good to have, but you can't have it if the country isn't safe; and he viewed the activities of the ACLU as undermining that very safety.

So, when he heard Marcy say that she was working with the ACLU, Powers realized that trouble was brewing. He knew that unless he did something, they would spring Henry Gainsvort and Powers didn't want that to happen. He didn't want Henry Gainsvort out where he could talk about his warning to the police about the attack on the Federal

Reserve. Not when the press was still sniffing around and Congress was forming a committee to investigate the Federal Reserve attack and the workings within the NYPD and Manhattan offices of the FBI. That could come back to him and Powers believed that his career was on the line, and that unless he took some sort of decisive action, his future could go right down the toilet.

But, he reasoned, his career was safe as long as Henry Gainsvort remained under lock and key and isolated from the curious press. Powers was convinced that as long as Gainsvort was in cold storage, then he was safe and secure and he was determined to hold onto Henry for as long as he could.

Now, however, he saw that this woman, Marcy, was about to interfere and her meddling might unravel all his carefully-laid plans. Powers knew that given time, the ACLU would find some way to work the levers of the law and get Henry Gainsvort released. Lance Powers didn't like the idea of losing his captive and he resolved to thwart the ACLU in any way that he could.

He weighed his options and it occurred to him that the courts couldn't free Gainsvort if they couldn't find him. If he could get the Bureau to transfer the prisoner out of New York City to some obscure holding area, then Gainsvort's ultimate release could be delayed with bureaucratic red tape. That delay would give Powers some time. In that time, maybe the heat from the aftermath of the terrorist attack would die down. Or maybe, the Bureau could come up with something substantial to make a charge against Gainsvort and hold him indefinitely.

It seemed to Powers that all he really needed was just to play for more time. With that thought in mind, Powers went up to Brian Confrey's office. Now Powers was a man of supreme self-confidence. He was sure that when he sat down and talked with Confrey he could easily convince him of the need to transfer Gainsvort. He figured that if he had a few minutes alone with Confrey he could affect his Machiavellian design. When he entered the office, he found to his consternation that Rick Buel was sitting chatting with Brian.

Buel's presence irked Powers. There was something about Buel that Powers didn't like. He had always viewed Buel as being too soft on criminals, a bleeding heart who was more concerned about the perpetrator's rights and about due process of law rather than about the more important issues of locking up the scum of society. Powers saw Buel as a worrywart who was always fussing over the technicalities of the law and upholding the fine points of the Constitution rather than zeroing in on the enemies of America.

When Powers appeared at the door, Confrey motioned him to enter and sit down. Powers did so.

"What's up?" asked Confrey.

"I just got wind of some disturbing news about our man Gainsvort. I think we should talk about it."

"Okay, go ahead."

Powers shot Buel a hard glance hoping that he would cringe and leave, but Buel remained undaunted by Powers' evil eye. Powers then looked back to Confrey. Now Lance Powers regarded his supervisor, Brian Confrey, as being experienced and competent, but relatively unimaginative. He also felt that Confrey was open to suggestion and therefore malleable. Powers was sure that he could persuade Confrey to accept his thinking if only he could sit alone with him, but with Buel sitting on the sidelines, possibly voicing objections, that might be more difficult. Still, he figured that if he tried hard enough he could pull it off.

"Well I just got wind that Gainsvort's girlfriend is working with the ACLU. They're going to go to court and file papers to get Gainsvort released."

Confrey shrugged. "Well, that's bad news but I don't think there's much we can do to stop them."

Powers was a little annoyed that Confrey lacked the imagination to see other possibilities in the situation. At the same time, he was smug in his self-assurance to demonstrate that he had a possible solution to the dilemma.

"Maybe we can't stop them in court, but I think we can do some maneuvering of our own."

"How?"

"We have a secret facility Upstate that we use as a holding tank for persons in our witness protection program. Suppose we transfer him to that place."

"What good will that do?" asked Buel.

Powers shot Buel another dirty look hoping to silence him and make him keep his meddling mouth shut; but Buel didn't seem to notice Powers' baleful glance.

"Well," said Powers, "then we could say that Gainsvort isn't here in Manhattan. We could say that he's in another facility but we're not sure exactly where until we check into our records. That would give us enough time to move him out of the state, away from the jurisdiction of the New York courts. That would keep Gainsvort on ice away from the ACLU and allow us to continue our investigation."

"But that would be tap dancing around the law," said Buel.

"Maybe a little, but we still wouldn't be doing anything illegal. I mean moving prisoners around to protect their safety is routine procedure. We do it all the time."

Powers was getting increasingly annoyed with Buel's interference, but at the same time he could see that Confrey was half-convinced by his argument, and he was sure that with a little nudging he could bring the supervisor over to his side.

"Look Brian," Powers continued, "right now the heat is on. The press and Congress are doing a witch hunt looking for scapegoats. If Gainsvort gets loose and talks, then it could put us in a bad light; but in a couple of weeks all this will blow over and no one will pay any attention to him, no matter what he says."

Confrey said nothing, but Powers could see that he was mulling the argument over, and all he needed was a little more convincing.

"Look Brian, this is just a temporary thing. It will give us some room to maneuver, some time to continue our investigation. If we don't find anything against Gainsvort, we can always let him go with no harm done. By then the heat will be off and no one will care much about what we did."

Brian Confrey leaned back in his chair to reflect on all that he had heard. Powers could see the wheels of cogitation churning in Confrey's head, and he was sure that he had won and that Confrey would give in—if only Buel would keep his mouth shut. Rick Buel did keep silent, and after a few moments, Confrey leaned forward and nodded.

"Okay Lance, set it up. When you've got it all arranged, let me know when you intend to move him."

Lance Powers nodded and smiled in satisfaction. Then he rose and walked out of Brian Confrey's office feeling particularly self-confident and especially proud of himself. He felt as if he had won the day, in spite of Rick Buel's meddling and opposition. He walked back to his office and started making plans to move his precious prisoner into obscurity.

By Monday afternoon, Powers had worked out the details of the transfer and made all the necessary arrangements. They would transfer Gainsvort to the Upstate facility on Thursday evening. No one would know about it except for the few agents involved. Once Henry was safely hidden away at the Upstate facility, it would take weeks for anybody to locate him. Even if somebody did manage to find out about him, then Powers knew that he could always make another move. Everything was in place, and Powers was satisfied; he knew that in few days Henry Gainsvort would be lost within the obscurity of the bureaucratic labyrinth.

To Lance Powers it seemed like the perfect plan, one that nobody would know about. Well, almost nobody. As it turned out, Henry found out about it. He found out because that very night he had another vision, and his vision revealed all about Powers' plan. It also showed Henry a scenario that even Powers could not possibly imagine. When Henry had that vision, he realized something else; he understood that this would be the last vision that he would ever have. It happened like this.

That very Monday evening after Powers had made all his plans and preparations Henry was in his room alone, lying on his bunk reading *Ulysses*. For a moment he lay the book down on his chest and let his head fall back and he stared up at the ceiling above.

That's when it came to him and he saw what was going to happen. He saw the three of them, Buel, Powers and himself leaving the room, walking down a corridor, taking the elevator to the subterranean garage. He saw the three of them get into the car and drive out of the garage through the streets and across the George Washington Bridge. He saw the ride up the Thruway and he saw them exit and turn off onto a secluded back road that went into the mountains.

He saw all of that, then he saw something more. He saw that they would never reach their destination. He saw their car hit a patch of ice on a mountain road and spin out of control, smash against a solid wall of natural rock then ricochet of the rock and land at the end of the road. They would sit trapped in a disabled car waiting for help. He saw a massive truck coming down the mountain, charging out of control. Then he saw the collision and it was all over. Everything went blank.

When Henry had that vision, he knew he was seeing the end of his life, and that end was only a few short days away. Yet in spite of the horrible disaster, and in spite of the nearness of the event, Henry remained calm. It seemed to him that what he had just seen was inevitable—after all his visions always came true—and he had no reason to assume that this one would be different. He accepted that. He accepted that this was the way his life would come to an end and that there was nothing anyone could say or do to change that. He also knew that fate was finally coming around to end his existence and then all the frustrations and uncertainties would be gone. So, he wasn't worried, he simply let his head drop back on the pillow and eventually he fell asleep.

CHAPTER 30

The next morning Marcy came to visit Henry again. The minute she entered the room she burst out, "Henry, I've got good news. Mr. Berkowitz said that he's going to bring a motion before the judge and have you released. He thinks that maybe he can get you out of here by Friday."

"Thanks Marcy, but you shouldn't have troubled. Actually, Friday may be too late."

Marcy looked concerned. "Why? Why is Friday too late? What's going to happen before then?"

"They're going to transfer me out of here. Somehow, I think they suspected that maybe someone would take legal action to get me released and they are moving to prevent that. They're going to hide me someplace so the courts can't get to me. This is going to happen on Thursday."

"How do you know this Henry? Did they tell you about their plans?"

Henry shook his head. "No. I saw it. I had another vision and I saw everything. I saw them taking me out of here and driving Upstate."

"Thursday you say? Well then, we'll have to get a move on and get you out of here before then. I'll call the ACLU when I get home and see what they can do."

Henry shook his head.

"You don't have to bother Marcy. It's never going to happen."

"What are you talking about Henry? What won't happen? Why won't it happen?"

"The court release. The trip Upstate. Neither will happen because I saw the whole thing, and I know what really will happen."

"You saw this in your vision?"

Henry nodded. "Yes, and I saw it all."

"What do you mean? What exactly did you see?"

"I saw three of us getting in a car and driving out of the city. I saw the car proceeding upstate on the highway. I saw us turning off and going along a back road into the mountains. Then I saw the car hit an icy spot on the road and spin out of control."

Marcy listened to all of this with mounting concern.

"You're going to have an accident?"

"Yes. Two in fact. The first one will just disable the car, but we won't be able to get out because the doors will be damaged. We'll just sit there for a long time on the side of the road. Right at the foot of an intersection. We'll be all alone in that car, just sitting there. Then, after a while, headlights will appear from above the intersection. The headlights will be those of a big truck. The truck will be coming down the mountain and it will be out of control without brakes. The driver will have no way to stop it and it will smash into us. That will be the end."

Marcy listened to all of that and was horror struck. Henry had just described his death. He paused for a minute during which, neither he nor Marcy said anything, then he continued.

"I realize Marcy, that I've had my last vision."

"Henry, we can't let this happen. We've got to try and prevent it."

Henry shook his head. "Marcy, I've learned that my visions always come true. There's nothing anyone can do to stop them."

"We've got to try Henry. We can't just give up. I'll call Mr. Berkowitz this afternoon, the minute I get home. I'll ask him to go to court before Thursday evening. We'll get you out of here Henry. We won't let this happen. I'll come back tomorrow with the good news."

Henry could see that Marcy was getting agitated because she was truly worried about his safety and well-being. She wanted to try and prevent his eventual end, but Henry knew that anything she—or anyone else—did would be futile. He had come to accept the inevitability of his visions; yet he did not say anything to discourage her. She was anxious and was trying so hard and he was touched by her concern for his welfare; he didn't have the heart to discourage her.

"Okay Marcy, you talk to Mr. Berkowitz and see what you both can do. In the meantime, there's something else that I want you to do for me."

"What?"

"You still have the key to my apartment?"

Marcy nodded.

"I want you to go into my bedroom, to the bureau beside the bed. Look in the top drawer, on the left-had side. You'll find my insurance policy there. When you come back tomorrow, I want you to bring it with you. I want to make you my beneficiary."

Marcy started to protest, but Henry continued.

"There's something else I want you to do. Try to see Mr. Berkowitz today if you can. If you do, ask him to draw up a simple will for me. I want it to say that I'll leave everything I have to you. Will you do that for me?"

"Henry, I don't want—"

"Marcy, please do this for me. It will mean a lot to me. I don't have anyone else and maybe it will be a small compensation for all the trouble that you are going to for me. Please!"

Marcy looked into Henry's face, into his two big hazel eyes and was captivated by the earnestness and sincerity they displayed and she was deeply moved.

"Okay Henry, I'll do as you ask, but we won't need those things because the ACLU will have you out of here in no time."

Henry nodded and Marcy started to say something else, but the guard appeared and said their time was up. Both Marcy and Henry rose and walked to the door and into the corridor.

Marcy started to go, but abruptly turned and said, "Don't worry Henry, we'll find a way to get you out of here before Thursday night. I'll call Mr. Berkowitz and get him right on it. It will happen, so don't you worry Henry."

Henry nodded, pretending that he really believed that she could do something to save him, but he was truly convinced that his fate was sealed and nothing could change that. He watched Marcy turn and walk down the corridor and exit through the door at the end.

When Marcy made that last-minute statement, she could not know that it was a tactical mistake because once again, Lance Powers was sitting in an adjacent room listening. He didn't hear anything of the conversation between Henry and Marcy while they were in the room, but when they were in the corridor, during the final minute of Marcy's visit, he heard her exclaim that they were going to get Henry out by Thursday. When he heard that, he knew that his carefully-made plans were on the verge of unraveling and he immediately went to work to prevent that.

Powers rushed back to his office and took up a place before his computer. He typed out an email to the Upstate facility saying that there was a sudden change in plans and they were going to bring their prisoner up one day earlier, on Wednesday evening. He sent the message then sat back and waited for a confirmation. As he sat there, he smiled with self-satisfaction because he realized that he was smart enough and clever enough to out-maneuver Gainsvort's little girl friend and the ACLU. Let them get their court order. By the time they got it, he would have Gainsvort far away from their meddling hands.

When the confirmation came through from the Upstate facility, Powers chuckled in delight. He wasn't sure how Gainsvort and the girl had found out about the transfer, but he suspected that there was a leak from someone inside the Bureau; Powers immediately thought of Rick Buel.

Well this time there wouldn't be any leaks because Powers resolved to keep this new change of schedule a secret so that no one could blab. This time he would keep this new transfer time to himself and not tell anybody else until the very last minute. That way there could be no leaks and no time for anyone to stop him. He chuckled again with fiendish delight as he realized how smart he was.

Yet for all his smug, self-satisfaction Powers could not possibly know that someone was about to find out about his devious machinations. That someone was Henry. Henry thought that his vision of the transfer and of the fatal accident would be the last vision that he would ever have, but he was wrong. He was about to have another vision and this one would be the most astounding and magnificent vision that he had ever had. It happened like this.

It was sometime in the evening and Henry was lying on the cot in his coffin-like room still trying to wade through *Ulysses,* but once again, he found it was tedious going. Finally, after an hour of total boredom, Henry let the book fall onto his chest and he leaned his head back against the pillow and shut his eyes. That's when it came upon him.

Another vision. It started like the previous one with a replay of the trip upstate. He saw the three of them leaving a day early. Once again, he saw the ride up the Thruway and the patch of ice on the deserted country road. He saw the accident. He saw himself sitting in the disabled vehicle with the agents. He saw the truck coming down the mountain and he saw the fatal collision.

Then came a totally new experience. Suddenly, Henry felt as if he were floating in space surrounded by a brilliant incandescent light. At the same time, it was as if the luminescence was radiating from a point deep within him. Then a grand and glorious feeling of euphoria—unlike any that he had ever known—filled his soul and penetrated into every nerve, fiber and cell of his body. All this came upon him so suddenly that at first, he had no idea what was happening to him, but he knew he was having another vision; only this vision was unlike any that came before.

With this all-encompassing brilliant, radiant splendor and euphoria, Henry knew that he was seeing into something more magnificent than anything that he had ever witnessed in his entire life. He perceived that he was tapping into a power giving him an inner clarity and a sense of contentment far sweeter than he had ever known. Henry believed that his soul had actually touched on a dimension beyond the universe and beyond life itself.

This vision with its magnificent light and glorious feeling, lasted for some time. When it eventually faded, Henry found himself returned to his former position in his solitary room, lying on his cot as before; only now he felt better than he could ever remember feeling and he knew within his heart and soul that all the questions that had plagued him for so long had finally been answered.

Feeling very good, with all his cares and concerns erased, Henry drifted off into a deep and sound sleep.

CHAPTER 31

It was early Wednesday morning when Henry awoke. He lay there in bed for at least fifteen minutes remaining motionless with his eyes open just looking around, scanning across the ceiling and going up and down along the walls.

There wasn't much to see because the room was dark. The only light came from the narrow gap under the door and from the illuminated dial on his bedside alarm clock. Those two vague sources provided enough light to give dim impressions of the blank walls and ceiling. As he looked at the clock, Henry saw that it was not yet five in the morning. So even if his room had a window, there wouldn't be much additional light because the sun wasn't up yet and it was still dark outside.

He looked at the clock face and he debated with himself whether he should get up or not. He wasn't sleepy, but at the same time he would have nothing to do if he did get up. So, he continued to lay in his bed enjoying the warmth beneath the covers and the quiet of the room. And as he lay there, it occurred to him that this was probably the last time he would ever wake up again and that this was the start of his last day on earth.

For most people that would be an unnerving thought, but Henry was not particularly perturbed because his vision of the previous night had prepared him for what was to come. It was that knowledge that fortified him for the future.

A full hour passed before Henry decided to roll out of bed and start the day. He put on his robe then went down the hall to the shower, shave, and brush his teeth. He returned to his room and dressed. Then, accompanied by his guard-attendant, he went upstairs to the cafeteria for breakfast.

Breakfast was simple, French toast, orange juice and coffee and it tasted like the stuff that food services typically provide for institutions. This morning Henry lingered over his meal and he took the time to savor each morsel of food and each sip of drink. It wasn't that the food was especially tasty, but Henry knew that this would be his last breakfast and he wanted to make every effort to try and enjoy it.

After breakfast, Henry returned to his room where he tried one more time to read through James Joyce, but again he found that he could not get interested in the story. He looked up from the page and let his thoughts drift off aimlessly. Before long, his mind started to replay the events of his past from the earliest recollections of his childhood right up to the present. The images and recollections were random—some in chronological order, many not—there were the events that he participated in and the people who had come and gone in and out of his life.

He remembered his mother and father, his classmates at school, some of his teachers, his college chums, Tiffany Blaine, the people he worked with after college and, of course, he remembered Augie. He saw pictures of himself growing up, going to school, eventually getting a job and the fun times he and Augie had at Gallagher's. For over an hour, he sat there in the chair, alone in his four-by-six room, as all those images flashed through his mind and he mentally relived a capsule edition of his life story.

As he was going through his cerebral scrapbook, his thoughts were interrupted by a knock on his door. The guard poked his head in and announced that Henry had a visitor. Henry nodded and got up then together they went upstairs to the sterile visiting room When Henry entered he found Marcy sitting at the table waiting for him.

The minute Henry entered the room, Marcy noticed something different about him, but it was a subtle difference—one that she couldn't immediately identify, yet it was there nevertheless. She watched him as he came into the room and walked around to sit opposite her. While he was doing this, she studied him and tried to pinpoint the change in his manner. Maybe, she thought, he had anticipated the news that she had come to deliver.

The minute he sat down, she blurted out, "Henry, I've got great news! I spoke to—"

Henry cut her off. "Marcy, did you bring the papers that I asked for?"

"Yes, I have them right here, but you won't need them. Not after you've heard my news."

"All right Marcy, but first let's get the paperwork out of the way, then you can tell me your news."

"Okay Henry," she said a she pulled the documents from her bag. "But I'm telling you that there's no need for them now.

"Well, let's just do this anyway just to keep our bases covered."

He took the documents, unfolded them and laid them out on the table before him. He proceeded to read through the papers and as he was doing this, engrossed in their content, Marcy looked at him. She studied his face and noted his features. She saw that there was definitely something different about him. After a minute of scrutiny, she decided that it was his expression. He didn't seem as sad or morose as he had been recently. He now appeared to calm and contented; in fact, he almost looked happy and she couldn't imagine what had happened to precipitate this change in his manner.

Henry looked up from his reading. "Marcy, I want to make you out as my beneficiary, but I don't know your last name. It's funny, but after all this time, and after all you've done for me, I suddenly realize that I don't know your last name."

"Greenplap," she said and she spelled it out for him.

"Greenplap. That's a pretty name."

"Greenplap! A pretty name! No, it's not! It's a terrible name; it sounds like a moist turd hitting the forest floor. I hate it. I'm hoping that someday I'll meet a guy with an ordinary name like Smith or Jones and I can marry him and change my name and get rid of Greenplap."

Henry looked at Marcy, surprised by the vehemence in her words. He wanted to say something, but he didn't want to risk offending by agreeing with her and at the same time he didn't want to get into an argument. So, he kept silent and returned to the documents before him. He filled in her name on the beneficiary line of the insurance policy then he turned his attention to the will. When it came to signing the will, they needed a witness. They called the guard in for that. When he left, Henry said, "Okay Marcy, now you can tell me your news.

Marcy leaned forward with anticipation.

"Yesterday, I talked with Mr. Berkowitz. He said that he's got an appointment to go before a judge tomorrow. He's pretty sure that he can prevent them from moving you, and he's confident that he can get a court order to get you released by the end of the week."

Henry shook his head. "Nice try Marcy. I appreciate your efforts, but by tomorrow it will be too late."

"Why Henry? What's happened?"

"Somehow they got wind of what you're trying to do and they've moved things up. They're going to move me out of here tonight."

"Tonight?"

Henry nodded and Marcy looked at him with alarm. She was stunned. She hadn't figured on this and for a long moment, she starred at him without saying anything. Henry also said nothing. He just sat there and looked back at her with a slight smile on his face.

Finally, Marcy broke the silence, speaking with as much determination as she could manage. "Well, we still have time. As soon as I leave, I'll call Mr. Berkowitz and ask him to see if he can get to a judge today. I'm sure that when I explain the situation, he will—'

Henry shook his head. "Don't bother Marcy. It won't do any good. The whole thing is going to happen just the way I saw it and there's nothing anyone can do that will change it.'

"We've got to try Henry. We can't just sit back and let this happen. We've got to do something to prevent it from—"

Henry raised his hand slightly and cut her off.

"Marcy, it doesn't matter anymore."

Marcy looked at Henry, uncertain what he was leading up to. "What do you mean it doesn't matter anymore? Why not? What's changed?"

"Marcy, last night I had another vision. Now, nothing matters anymore."

"Wait a minute. I thought you said that vision where you saw the ride Upstate and the accident was your last vision. You said that was the end for you."

"Yes, and that's what I thought at that time, but last night I had another vision and it the cleanest, brightest vision that I've ever had. It changed everything."

"How does it change everything? You mean there's not going to be an accident? You're not going to die?"

"No, all that is going to happen just as I said it would."

"Well, then what? I mean what has changed?"

"Marcy, in last night's vision, I saw what comes afterwards."

Marcy looked dubiously at Henry. She was still unsure what he was talking about.

"What do you mean *afterwards*? If you're going to die, then that's it, the end. How can there be anything afterwards? I mean when you're dead, it's all over and..."

Marcy's voice dropped off into silence. The uncertainty in her mind dissolved as she began to see what Henry was driving at. Henry saw the expression in her face change and he knew that she was beginning to understand. He nodded and his smile broadened.

"That's right Marcy. I saw beyond destiny, beyond death. I saw what happens on the other side."

"You saw life after death? That's impossible!"

Henry shook his head. "Before last night I would have thought so too, and I would have agreed with you. But then I had this vision, and I tell you Marcy that I saw the other side."

Marcy was highly skeptical. "What's it like? I mean what exactly did you see? Are there angels and white clouds and things like that?"

"Well, it's kind of hard to explain because I didn't see images or pictures, so I didn't see angels or clouds. In fact, I didn't see anything, but I felt things. It was all about feeling, not seeing. That's really what it is. It's a feeling that you get."

Henry could see the doubt and skepticism in Marcy's face. He knew that she was listening but not really grasping what he was talking about.

"I know that all this is hard to understand Marcy, and all I can say is that this vision was unlike any that I've ever had before. It was beautiful. When it happened, I was suddenly surrounded, engulfed, by this beautiful white light. I didn't know where it was coming from. I felt that it was around me, and at the same time I thought that it was coming from within me. I tell you it was amazing, unbelievable.

"But I think the most amazing thing was the feeling that I got. Suddenly I was overwhelmed with a feeling of goodness and well-being unlike any that I had ever experienced. It was at that moment that I knew in my heart and soul that I was experiencing the afterlife. I tell you Marcy that death is nothing to be afraid of, not when you know what comes after it."

Henry paused for a moment, but it was obvious that he had more to say, so Marcy sat there mute, waiting for him to continue, but she was getting concerned because during Henry's monologue she noticed that he was becoming increasing excited and animated.

Finally, Henry added, "Augie was there too."

"Augie? You saw Augie?"

Henry shook his head. "No, I told you that you don't see things there. You feel them and kinda sense them. And that's the way it was with Augie. I felt his presence and I knew that he was there and I knew that I was in touch with the genuine after life.

"I tell you Marcy that all my life, whenever I had one of my visions, I had to ask myself why. Why was it that I had these crazy visions when no one else had anything like them?"

"And now you know?"

"Yes."

"Why?"

"Because they gave me an insight, a presence into another world, but it wasn't just a little window. No, it was like a message that there is something beyond this world, this existence. All the visions I had before were a kind of preparation, a way of fine tuning my senses, my inner being, my spirit and soul for the greater glory that is to come.

"Last night I saw it...no, that's wrong because you don't really see anything. There's nothing to see. It's more like an essence, a presence that lies beyond the universe beyond destiny, beyond life itself, it's like..."

At this point, Henry paused because he could see in Marcy's expression, that she was trying hard to follow his words but he could tell that the meaning and significance in them wasn't registering in her mind.

"I'm sorry Marcy," Henry sighed, "I guess I'm not making much sense and all this probably sounds far-fetched and imaginative. That's because I'm trying to describe something that has no description. It would take someone special, someone like Jesus or Buddha to explain the glorious, spiritual world that is out there. And I'm not special. I'm just plain, average Henry Gainsvort and I don't have the ability to describe what I know is out there."

Marcy reached out and put her hand on Henry's hand. She managed a slight smile.

"You are special, Henry—to me. And I thank you for sharing your vision with me. It gives me hope that there is something after...well, just after."

At that moment the guard knocked on the door and said that visiting time was over and it was time for Marcy to leave. Marcy and Henry went into the hall. They parted at the door and Henry stood in place, watching Marcy walk down the corridor. Henry knew that he was seeing her for the last time.

As Marcy walked down the long corridor, she thought about all Henry had just said. She thought about his descriptions of bright lights and glorious feelings and she wondered if he really did see into eternity or if the many days of solitary confinement had made him delusional.

CHAPTER

It was a little after seven in the evening; Henry was lying on his cot waiting for the knock on the door that he knew would soon come. Sure enough, there was the sound that he had anticipated. Henry got up and went to the door. He opened it and there standing in the hall were agents Rick Buel and Lance Powers.

It was Powers who spoke first. "We're going to take a little trip. Better take your coat and your belongings."

Henry smirked at that; he didn't have any "belongings" except his coat and his book. He walked back and grabbed his jacket but left his book lying on the cot, then he returned to the door. Buel reached into the room to shut out the lights. He noticed that Henry's book was lying on the cot.

"You want to take your book with you?" he asked.

Henry shook his head. "No," he said, "I don't think that I'll need it."

"You should take it," said Powers, "You won't be coming back tonight. Maybe not tomorrow either. It will give you something to do. Something to pass the time."

Henry shook his head again. "No," he said, "I won't need it."

Powers looked hard at Henry. That seemed a curious thing to say, and Powers wondered what Henry Gainsvort was thinking. Did he think that his girlfriend would come to rescue him at the last moment? Or was there some other thought running through Gainsvort's mind that seemed to make him indifferent to what was happening?

Powers mulled that over as the trio walked to the end of the corridor and entered the elevator. Buel pushed the button. The door closed and the elevator started its descent to the garage level. Buel looked straight ahead not focusing on anything as he waited for the elevator to stop and for the doors to open.

Powers looked at Henry. Lance Powers never liked Henry Gainsvort and in the enclosed elevator, he stared at Henry with an intense glare assuming that the power of his evil eye could make Henry cringe and wither. It was not to be, however, because Henry returned Powers' venomous gaze with a benign, benevolent look that completely unnerved Powers. Yet Powers viewed this as a challenge and he was determined to outstare Henry; but at that moment the elevator doors opened and the visual contest ended.

The three men walked to a gray car parked on the other side of the garage. Buel opened the rear door for Henry. He closed the door after Henry settled himself then he climbed in the front seat on the passenger side. Powers assumed a position behind the steering wheel as the driver. Powers started the car and they moved from the garage to the street.

In less than an hour they were traveling on the Thruway north to their destination, an obscure hide-away where Henry Gainsvort would be isolated in a cloak of anonymity for an indefinite time.

About the same time that the gray FBI sedan was traveling north on the Thruway, Vinnie Pesecki was walking across the yard of The

Star Freight and Hauling Company about fifty miles from the Thruway. Vinnie was a short, squat fellow, only about five-foot six; but he was built like a human fire hydrant. He had a beer barrel of a gut that hung over his belt. His neck was so thick and massive that you really couldn't tell where it stopped and where his head began; it was as if the two were one column with ears, eyes and nose but no chin. His limbs were so massive that he couldn't bring his arms to his sides nor pull his ankles together. His thighs were so packed with meat that they got in the way when he walked and made his gait look a little like a hippopotamus ambling along the river bank.

Vinnie liked his foods rich with spices and garlic. Unfortunately, these foods didn't like Vinnie as much as he liked them, and their essences frequently made their way back up his esophagus in the form of audible belches and burps. This was an annoying and embarrassing display and he tried to correct it by chewing on antacid tablets. On some days Vinnie went through as many as six packages of antacid tablets.

Vinnie was a truck driver. He had been a truck driver all his life, ever since he was eighteen years old. He started by driving light trucks and delivering packages to the local towns. Gradually he worked his way up to the big rigs and by the time he was fifty he could brag that he had handled just about all makes, models and styles of truck that rolled along the highways of America.

After a number of years working for assorted companies around the country and a few stints as a freelancer, he was now working for The Star Freight and Hauling Company driving their rigs all around the state. He knew that he had an assignment for this Wednesday but didn't have the details yet. So that evening he walked across the yard into the dispatcher's office to find out exactly where he was going and what he was going to haul.

He mounted the steps to the office, and grabbed the door knob, but before turning it, he looked up at the evening sky and belched. The sun had just gone down and the last rays of daylight were fading. Vinnie sniffed the air; it was cold and damp. There was moisture in the air and it felt like rain. If it got cold enough, the rain could turn to snow and freeze on the road. That could make running difficult at best; but it might not be too bad if he was carrying a light load and if he was traveling along a straight, level road. Yeah, it might not be too bad if he got a lucky assignment. Trouble was, Vinnie never seemed to get lucky.

Vinnie entered the office. The dispatcher, Max Corso, was sitting behind the desk.

"You got a job for me tonight?" Vinnie asked with a loud belch.

"Yeah! You're taking number eighteen out. It's already loaded and waiting."

"What's it loaded with?"

"Radiators. Cast iron radiators. They came from a demolition site south of here."

"A truck full of radiators. That's gonna be one heavy load." He let out another belch.

"Where am I taking them to?"

"Griswald's Foundry."

"Griswald's Foundry!" He exclaimed with a belch. "That's on the other side of the mountain. I know that road. It's steep and winding, going up and going down. This is a hell of a run to be making at night with a heavy load."

"So, what? Come on Vinnie, you've handled worse jobs than this in your time."

"Yeah, but that don't make this one any easier. Are the guys at the foundry gonna unload the truck tonight?"

"Naw! They'll do it in the morning."

"Well why the hell can't I make the run first thing in the morning?" Another audible belch.

Max shook his head. "Sorry old man Griswald said he wanted it tonight. Said he'd feel better knowing his shipment is in his plant tonight"

"Well damn! How the hell am I gonna get home?"

"Mike McCormick, the manager at the foundry, will sign your papers then take you home."

"Does he know where I live?"

"Yeah, we already told him. He said it wouldn't be a problem. His home is in the next town over so he'll be glad to drop you off on his way."

"Greater love hath no man," said Vinnie sarcastically with another belch. "Is the tank all filled up?"

"No, it's not; you gotta take the rig over to the maintenance yard and get a fill up. Lenny's over there now waiting for you."

"Oh shit!" exclaimed Vinnie. "I gotta do the fill-up too? Can't you guys do anything?" Vinnie thought to himself that this was another sign of his bad luck.

"Max shrugged. "What can I tell you, Vinnie? Life is tough. Here are the keys to the truck and your manifest forms. Drive carefully and have a good night!"

"Yeah right," said Vinnie sarcastically with another belch—this one louder than the previous ones. "Have a good night. How am I gonna do that with a truck full or radiators going over the mountain when it may snow?"

Max only shrugged, and Vinnie walked out of the office with another belch and headed across the yard, cursing under his breath all the way to rig number eighteen. He had hoped that if he bitched enough about the job Max might postpone it until the next day when it was light; but no such luck. Vinnie just wasn't the lucky type.

So, Vinnie opened the door and climbed in the cab and took up a position behind the big steering wheel. He turned the ignition key and the big diesel engine turned over and started right up spewing a black cloud of exhaust from the vertical pipe alongside the cab.

At the moment the engine belched out the big black cloud from the exhaust pipe, Vinnie let out his own belch from his internal pipe. That's the way Vinnie Pesecki was, from the moment that he got into a truck and started the engine, it was as if he became one with the big machine. After all his years driving rigs across the country Vinnie had developed a sixth sense about trucks. When he was in the cab of a rig and the motor was churning, it was as if he became a symbiotic part of the entire vehicle, the engine, the chassis, the load bed and all the myriad components that make up the truck. And when the truck was rolling, his inner sense, his instinct, connected to every part of the truck and he knew just how it would behave and he knew just how to handle it. Driving a truck was like second nature to Vinnie; it was something he knew and felt as if by natural feeling.

Vinnie shoveled two antacid tablets in his mouth then put the truck in gear, let up on the brake, and eased down on the gas pedal. The truck started forward. Vinnie steered out of the yard through the gate and he stopped before going onto the road just to see if there was any traffic. When he stepped on the brake the rig came to a stop, but at the same time, Vinnie felt that there was something funny about the braking action. His sixth sense told him that there was something not-quite-right about the way the brakes worked. The trouble was that he couldn't put his finger on the trouble. He stepped on the brake and the truck stopped. *What was wrong with that?* Well nothing really; yet

Vinnie had the feeling that something wasn't as it should be, but there was nothing he could do about it.

He drove out onto the road and down to the maintenance yard where he pulled up to the gas pump. Gus Beck was waiting at the pump for him. Vinnie stopped the truck and turned off the engine then got out and walked around to Gus.

"Evening Vinnie. Got a night run I see."

"Yeah, just my luck to be taking a rig out on a crummy night like this," he said with yet another sonorous belch.

"Ain't too bad. Kinda cold, but at least it's dry."

"Yeah, but for how long? It feels damp and it think the weatherman said we're gonna get precipitation."

"It probably won't be much. Most likely it'll only rain."

"Not where I'm going."

"Where are you driving to?"

"I'm delivering to Griswald's Foundry," Vinnie said, blasting out another belch.

"On the other side of the mountain?"

Vinnie nodded. Gus was silent for a minute; he knew that it was cold enough in the mountains to turn falling rain to snow.

"Well maybe you'll get through it before the stuff starts to come down."

Vinnie shook his head. "Not bloody likely; not the way my luck runs. Besides that, I think the rig is gonna give me trouble."

"How so?"

"The brakes feel kinda funny."

"How so? The pedal feel spongy?"

"No, it's firm enough."

"What then? It goes too far to the floor?"

"No, it ain't that either."

"What then?"

"That's just it, I don't know," he belched out. "All I can say is that when I step on the brake, I get this funny feeling in my gut, that something ain't quite right. The trouble is, I can't say what's wrong; but I think there's something there. I just feel it. I hate it when I get feelings like that, 'cause I know something's gonna happen but I don't know what."

"Aw, you've just got jitters because he gotta make a late-night run. If this was in the afternoon then everything would be all right. Anyway, as long as the trouble is in your gut and not the brakes, then you got nothing to worry about."

Yeah, maybe that was it. Maybe he just had the jitters and was imagining things. Maybe so, thought Vinnie to himself, but that didn't ease the gnawing feeling in his gut.

Vinnie opened the door to the cab and mounted the step, but before climbing in behind the wheel he looked up at the sky. It was black without the glimmer of stars. The air felt cold and damp and Vinnie suspected that there was moisture up there in that dark, opaque sky. Well, if it was going to rain, then at least let it hold off until he got over the mountain. At least let him get that far, at least let him be that lucky; but when Vinnie climbed the cab and settled in behind the wheel, he knew that his was a forlorn wish because he never, ever, got lucky.

At about this time, the gray car with the Henry, Powers and Buel, turned off the Thruway and moved onto a back-country road. It was now completely dark—pitch black. The only illumination came from the headlights of the car, narrow cones of light that revealed the road ahead but not much else. It was as if the car were enshrouded in inky darkness except for the small circle of light cast on the narrow road that they were advancing into.

Buel noticed that Powers had an attitude of fierce determination and intensity and that temperament was evident in his driving. On the Thruway, Powers drove fast, barely staying within the speed limit, weaving around the other vehicles as if he were running an obstacle course. It was as if he were angry about something and was out to prove to the world that he was in charge. Buel tolerated this attitude while they were on the Thruway, but now that they were on a country back road wrapped in an opaque black shroud, he became increasingly nervous.

"Lance," he said, "don't you think that you ought to slow down a bit? It's black as tar outside and these back roads can be icy and unpredictable at this time of night."

Powers was annoyed by Buel's comment. He was already angry with himself because he felt that he had lost the staring match with that insignificant toad Gainsvort. Now, he had to put up with Buel's nervous-Nelly criticisms. Instead of slowing down, he pressed on the accelerator and went faster. Buel viewed this abrupt tactic with alarm. He felt that they were headed for disaster. He fears would soon be realized.

The gray car reached the mountain, raced up one side, came over the top, then started down the down the other side. The car picked up speed and it seemed to Buel that they were outpacing the range of the headlights. If any unexpected obstacle, ice or a deep pothole, appeared they would not have time to avoid it. Buel wanted to voice his concerns but he knew that if he did, Lance would only go faster out of pure spite. As the car accelerated down the steep mountain road, Buel was sure that they were headed for certain disaster. He was right!

When the car was about half-way down the mountain it ran across a patch of black ice and it started sliding laterally across the road. This unexpected hazard caught Lance Powers completely by surprise. His initial reaction was to hit the brakes. This was a mistake; the wheels locked and he lost control of the vehicle. It slid off the road and slammed with terrifying force and velocity against the dense rock wall bordering the road. The intensity of the collision was so fierce that the car ricocheted off the hard boulder, spun around and slide sideways down the road where it crashed into another rock wall and came to a complete stop.

At about the same time that the FBI vehicle with its three occupants collided with the hard-vertical rock at the bottom of the mountain, Vinnie Pesecki was starting to climb up the road on the other side of the mountain. So far all was going well, but Vinnie was still apprehensive because he knew that the most difficult, and potentially most troubling part of the drive was yet to come. But if he could get down the other side of the mountain without mishap, then all would be okay.

As Vinnie was slowly driving up the dark mountain road, his logical mind was telling him that everything was fine and that he had nothing to worry about. Vinnie's gut intuition, however, was giving him a different argument; it was telling him that calamity was in the making. In just a few minutes, Vinnie's gut would win that argument.

In the car at the base of the mountain, Powers was slowly coming around, trying to shake off the jarring, violent effects of the accident. Everything happened so fast that he didn't know what was happening even while it was happening. The collision stunned Powers but he didn't lose conscious.

Now that his brain was coming back on line and he was becoming responsive, he looked around to assess their situation. There was a solitary street light at the corner of the intersection and it cast a dim, yellow light that allowed Powers to see something of their surroundings and look in the interior of the car.

The car was at the end of the mountain road on an intersection and up against a solid rock wall. Powers tried to start the motor but when he turned the ignition key nothing happened. He tried to open his door, but it wouldn't budge because there was no clearance between the car door and the rock wall. He looked over to the passenger side and that's when he saw his partner, Rick Buel hunched over the dashboard.

"Rick," cried Powers. He pulled Buel back on the seat. "Damn it! He's unconscious. He must have hit his head on the dash. I wonder why in hell the airbags didn't activate? How about you Gainsvort? You okay?"

Henry was fine. He had foreseen what was coming and braced himself in the back seat so he could minimize the effects of the impending crash. He answered Powers query with a simple, "Yes."

Powers reached over past the unconscious Buel and tried to open the passenger door. It wouldn't budge. He was becoming increasingly frustrated and anxious.

"Damn!" he cursed, "It's jammed. Try your door Gainsvort. See if you can open it."

Henry casually reached over and tried the door handle. It didn't budge.

"No," he said, "it's locked. I can't open it."

"Well," said an angry and exasperated Powers, "try harder! Put your shoulder against it. See if you can force the door open."

Henry made a perfunctory lunge against the door but he only applied minimal effort—not even enough to crush a marshmallow. Henry's halfhearted attempt aggravated Powers and added to his mounting anger.

"Damn you, Gainsvort!" he howled, "Put your weight behind it. Force the door open,"

Henry didn't move. He just sat in the backseat calm and indifferent to Powers' fury. Powers was about to launch into a litany of profanity but hesitated when he saw Henry turn and look up the mountain road. Powers followed Henry's glaze; he saw a pair of headlights at the top of the road. He breathed a sigh of relief because he believed that the headlights signaled an oncoming car—a car that would stop and rescue them from their plight.

Powers optimism was misplaced, however, because the vehicle behind those headlights was Vinnie Pesecki's big rig and it was starting its descent down the mountain. The truck with its heavy load began rolling down the road, slowly at first then it picked up momentum. Vinnie knew that he had to hold the truck in check to control its acceleration, so he applied the brakes. That's when his worst nightmare was realized; the pedal didn't respond; the brakes weren't functioning.

The big truck gained speed and was moving faster. Vinnie knew that there was no way to stop the truck and no way to slow it down. He gripped the steering wheel and started to pray, "Our father who art in heaven...our father who art in heaven...our father who art in heaven..."

Over and over he repeated those words, hoping and praying that some omnipotent transcendent deity would hear him and save him from certain death.

In the disabled gray car at the base of the mountain, Lance Powers was watching the oncoming headlights with increasing concern. Something didn't seem right; those lights shouldn't be getting bigger so fast. He turned to look at Gainsvort. Henry was in the backseat looking at Powers not at the vehicle coming down the mountain.

The light in the interior was dim but there was enough illumination so Powers could see Henry's features. Henry's expression was placid, without expression. At first, this puzzled Powers. *Why was Gainsvort so calm and motionless?* Then suddenly, the light of recognition flashed in Powers' brain and he understood; Gainsvort must have had a vision and he knew what was coming. Gainsvort had a vision of imminent death. That's why he was oblivious to Powers' intimidation and that's why he didn't take his book with him.

Powers turned to the oncoming headlights. He saw that they were getting larger and brighter and coming closer. He was gripped with the icy realization that destiny was closing in on him. Instantly, his egregious hubris faded and his unbridled self-confidence and his colossal arrogance crumbled.

He turned to Henry in a pathetic gesture and said, "Henry, please—"

He never finished that sentence because the car, the truck with the heavy load of cast iron all came together in one deafening crescendo, and in less than a minute it was all over.

Just before the fatal crash, when Powers looked up with ever-growing alarm at the once distant headlights that were coming closer, closer. Vinnie Pesecki was coming down the mountain road praying and trying desperately to tame his out-of-control vehicle. He saw that he was fast approaching a solid rock wall at the bottom of the mountain and he knew that he was facing certain death. Then he saw something else; he saw a gray car parked at the end of the road directly in the path of collision.

Vinnie's instinct told him that he had to do everything, anything he could to avoid hitting that car. When he reached the intersection of the two roads, he pulled hard on the steering wheel. The truck swerved and spun to the right narrowly missing the gray car; but the wheels of the over-loaded trailer were on black ice and it whipped around and smashed into the disabled gray vehicle with a deafening crash that reverberated off the solid rock walls around the road.

When the violent, explosive noise faded and the turbulent earthshaking vibrations settled into tranquility, Vinnie Pesecki was able to shake off the effects of the collision and feel out his situation. At first, he was sure that he had died and gone to another world, but as he looked about, he sensed that he was in the same world that he had always known. He was still a little numb and he assumed that some of his bones were broken and his body was physically damaged. He rotated his head from side to side and moved his arms about. Everything seemed to be in working order with no pain or blood.

He opened the door of the cab. Cautiously he moved his legs to the running board, stepped out of the cab and lowered himself to the ground. He advanced slowly and deliberately for fear that one of his limbs, damaged by the collision, would collapse under him. But nothing malfunctioned—his entire body had survived the crash with no ill effects. He swallowed hard and realized that he wasn't belching anymore. Somehow the pace and excitement of the mad, frenzied run down the mountain road must have reset his internal metabolism.

He raised his eyes to the sky and said, "Thank you God. Thank you for hearing my prayers and keeping me alive and safe." Vinnie realized that for the first time in memory he got lucky.

Then he turned and looked at the trailer and saw to his anguish that it had swung around, smashed a parked car and crushed it to half its width. Vinnie tried to peer inside the vehicle, but couldn't see anything because the flattened metal had crushed the windows and closed all gaps. He hoped that the car was vacant; if it wasn't, then anyone inside would now be crushed beyond recognition.

Vinnie couldn't know it, but inside the car were the remains of Henry Gainsvort, Lance Powers and Rick Buel. The trailer with its tonnage of heavy cast iron had crushed the three men into oblivion. In one fleeting moment their luck had run out.

CHAPTER 33

Henry's will designated Marcy as his next of kin and she applied herself to the grim task of seeing that his remains and memory were properly preserved. Marcy managed to have Henry's remains transferred to the Sanderson Funeral Parlor in Sunset Park, and she arranged for a three-day wake.

The wake was a quiet little affair with a few people dropping in from time to time. Marcy sat in the front row and whenever anyone came in and walked up to the casket to say a prayer or pay their respects, she got up to greet them and maybe have chat about their remembrances of Henry. There weren't many visitors—not like at Augie's wake when it seemed like half of Brooklyn showed up. No, this was a quiet little affair with only a handful of the regulars from Gallagher's dropping in from time to time.

So, for most of the day, Marcy just sat there with her hands on her lap and passed the time in aimless thought. Sometimes she looked at the shiny brown casket resting on the pedestal between the torchieres in the front of the room. It was a closed casket—it had to be, Marcy supposed. After all, Henry had been smashed in an automobile wreck so his body wouldn't be very nice to look at now.

But what was in the casket? Marcy wondered, *A bag of pulp? A two-dimensional figure like a cardboard cutout?* She was curious but she understood that she would never know the answer to those questions and it was probably just as well that she didn't. Better to remember Henry as he was, a warm and good-natured guy who had the odd ability to see what was coming tomorrow than to see him as a piece of mashed-up human flesh.

On the last afternoon of the wake, Marcy was sitting there in the first row, all alone with her thoughts, reflecting on the many times when Henry and Augie came into Gallagher's, when she heard someone enter the room. Marcy didn't hear footsteps or talking or even breathing; what she heard was the sound of metal chains jingling. She turned and was surprised to see an attractive, well-dressed woman with shining strawberry-blonde hair coming down the aisle toward the coffin. The jingling metal chains were the sound of the woman's many bracelets rattling on her wrists as she walked down the aisle.

Marcy had no idea who this stranger was. She had never seen her before and indeed never seen anyone quite like her except in fashion magazines or in the movies. She was quite beautiful with sparkling hair, a stunning figure and a lovely face. Marcy looked at that face and saw that there was something hard and serious about it. It seemed as if the woman was so self-assured as to be cold and indifferent to the world around her.

The stranger walked up and stood in the aisle between the first row of chairs about eight feet from the coffin. Marcy waited for a few minutes to see what the woman would do—if she would approach the coffin and maybe kneel for a prayer; but the woman did nothing. She stood there motionless. Marcy got up and stood beside her.

"Hello," she said, "I'm Marcy Greenplap."

The woman turned and looked at Marcy. "Tiffany Blaine," she replied.

There was a moment of silence between the two women while Tiffany stood there staring at the coffin. Finally, Marcy spoke up.

"Did you know Henry very well?"

Tiffany shrugged. "Not really. We went to the same college together. We sat in the same art history class."

"How did you find out that he had died?"

"I read about it in the paper. In the obituaries. I was sitting in my father's office waiting for him call it quits for the day. Well, while I was sitting there, just waiting, I started to look through the papers. My father gets all the city papers because he's in real estate and he likes to check on all the news in the boroughs, just to see what's happening. My father is Judson Blaine, a big man in the city. You've probably heard of him."

"No, I'm sorry but I don't think I've ever heard the name."

"What? You are from Sticksville if you've never heard of Judson Blaine. His name is on some of the biggest buildings in town. Well maybe not around here, because this area is a bit of a dump, but in other places. Well anyway, when I was reading the paper I saw the notice about Henry Gainsvort I just decided to come out and see for myself."

"That was nice of you."

"Yeah, well I just wanted to see something for myself."

"What was that?"

"When we were in college together, a rumor went around that Henry could see into the future. At first, I actually thought that maybe it might be true, but then I found out that he really couldn't do that. Still, I had my doubts. Anyway, when I saw the notice about him in the obituaries, I decided to come out and see for myself, and now I know for sure."

"Know what?"

"That he couldn't really see into the future."

"Why do you say that?"

"Well, it stands to reason that if he could see into the future, then he would have seen his own death coming and he would have avoided it. Isn't that right?"

"Not necessarily."

"Sure, it does. I mean, after all, if a person sees that death is coming then he's gonna get out of the way. That's human nature. But Henry's dead, so he probably didn't see it coming. In fact, I don't think Henry ever saw anything coming."

Marcy said nothing. She wanted to defend Henry and tell what she knew about him, but at the same time she didn't want to get into an argument with this strange woman, clad in silk and satin with all those jingly-jangly bracelets. Marcy had no idea who this woman was or why she showed up, but it was obvious that she was opinionated and wasn't about to listen to reason. So, Marcy just stood there beside Tiffany without saying anything; the two women just standing and looking at the coffin before them.

After a few minutes of silence Tiffany asked, "How do you know he's in there?"

"I beg your pardon?" asked Marcy.

"How do you know Henry is in that coffin? I mean the lid is closed and you can't see anything, so how do you know if he is even in there?"

Marcy was a little taken aback by this strange question and she didn't quite know how to answer it.

"Well," she said, "the funeral director told me that they put his remains in the casket."

"And you believed him?"

"Yes, of course. Why would he lie about something like that?"

"Oh, I don't know. I read somewhere recently about how some funeral parlors were selling parts of bodies to laboratories for medical research. I mean maybe that could have happened here."

Marcy thought to herself that this was certainly a macabre and grisly concept to introduce at a solemn occasion like this, and she wondered how this strange woman could even entertain such a thought in her fluff brain let alone talk about it.

"Oh, I don't think that they would do such a thing here."

"Oh no? Well you can't really be sure, can you? I mean not unless you were down in the embalming room with them. Right?" Tiffany paused for a minute as she continued to look at the closed casket. "Oh well, I don't suppose it matters much where he is. I mean the point is that he's dead. So, who really cares where his remains are?"

The was another long moment of silence while the two women stood there, side by side, just looking at the coffin. Tiffany finally broke the silence. "What's that thing on top of the coffin?"

"It's a statue."

"I can see that, but what's it doing there? I mean, it looks like a statue of a race horse and rider. That seems like a strange thing to put on top of somebody's coffin."

"It belonged to Henry. Actually, it belonged to Henry's friend Augie. When Augie passed away he left to Henry. It meant a lot to both of them. I just figured that maybe…well…maybe it might be nice there…kind of like a symbol of remembrance…I mean it seemed appropriate at the time."

Tiffany shrugged. "Well if you say so, but it still seems strange to me."

There was another long moment of silence as the two women stood there contemplating the coffin.

Tiffany finally broke the silence. "Well I've seen all I can. Gotta run. Toodleoo!"

Tiffany turned and was about to leave, when Marcy said, "Don't you want to say a prayer before you go?"

"Why would I want to do that?"

"Well," stammered Marcy, "I guess so you could talk to God."

"What would I have to say to God? I mean, after all, he's up there and I'm down here. I should think that if anybody would want to talk to God it would be Henry. I mean, after all, the two are together now, right? Unless Henry's in the other place, then it's probably too late for him to talk to God. You know what I mean? Oh well, I've got to run to my jeweler's. Bye!"

And with that Tiffany Blaine turned and walked out, leaving Marcy standing there to look and wonder just who that strange woman was. When Tiffany exited, Marcy continued to sit there in the funeral home alone and in silence for about an hour. Then the funeral director came in and told Marcy that it was time to go to the cemetery. Marcy nodded and got up and took the statue from atop the coffin. Then she waited while six men in black suits wheeled the coffin out of the building to a hearse waiting outside.

Marcy got into the black limo behind the hearse. She and the driver were the only ones in the limo. The hearse started to move out with the limo following. The two vehicles drove to Greenwood Cemetery and moved along the winding paved road to the mausoleum. It was the same mausoleum where Augie Martello was resting.

Marcy had arranged for a priest to come and say a prayer and maybe a few words. He was standing in the mausoleum when they arrived. The priest said a few words, but she and a nearby cemetery worker were the only ones to hear them.

What followed was much the same as Augie's interment; the worker operated a hydraulic jack and raised the coffin into a niche about five rows up. Once the coffin was in the niche, the worker sealed the compartment with caulking compound and positioned a cover panel over the opening. He bolted it in place. There was a brass plate on the cover with Henry's name and the dates of his existence on earth but nothing else. There was no indication of who he was or of his strange prophetic ability to peer into destiny. There was nothing to tell people of the trials and tribulations that Henry experienced when he tried to tell people of his uncanny visions of the future. Henry Gainsvort was now just a memory, sealed away in his final resting place.

Marcy Greenplap stood before Henry's compartment and said a silent prayer. Then she left the mausoleum and walked along a winding path that led to the cemetery entrance. As she ambled along the path she glanced at the many tombstones that marked the grave sites on either side of the winding path and she remembered Henry's last vision, his vision of eternity. She recalled Henry's vivid description of the feelings and sensations that he experienced and she wondered if Henry had really seen such a dimension or it was a figment of his imagination conjured up by the many hours of confinement in that desolate and sterile chamber in the bowels of some monolithic federal building.

When she was a little girl her parents and Sunday school teachers told her about heaven and hell that came in an afterlife. As a child she accepted these images without question, but when she grew to maturity she asked herself if there were such places *out there* or if they were just notions fabricated by adults to make children behave and lead a moral life. Later she dismissed the issue as an imponderable conundrum without a solution. But Henry's last vision revived that internal debate long buried in the labyrinths of her mind, and now she and wondered about what comes next again.

Marcy came to the Gothic Revival Towers at the main entrance of Greenwood Cemetery. She remembered that Henry told her that over a hundred parakeets were supposed to nest there. As Marcy looked up and searched the towers for signs of the birds she was overcome and captivated with a strange and wonderful feeling. It was as if a magnificent sensation of peace, tranquility and contentment surged through her entire body. Her mind seemed illuminated by a brilliant and wondrous light and she felt that she was suddenly overwhelmed by an all-encompassing spiritual presence.

She knew in an instant that this mystical, transcendent spirit was Henry Gainsvort. He had returned from eternity to transfuse her body and soul with the essence of eternal peace. In that moment Marcy knew that Henry's last vision was a genuine glimpse into the glory of the afterlife. She looked up at the vast sky above and she knew that somewhere in the dimension beyond our known world, Henry had found peace, tranquility and happiness.

That thought gave her a sense of wellbeing, comfort and peace of mind. Marcy turned and walked through the big gates of the cemetery to the street. She felt good. She felt very good.

The End

www.ingramcontent.com/pod-product-compliance
Lightning Source LLC
LaVergne TN
LVHW042244070526
838201LV00088B/10